THREE TIMES REMOVED

M. K. Jones

Maze Investigations – The Genealogy Detectives
Book 1

This is a work of fiction. Names, characters, places, and
incidents either are the product of the author's imagination or
are used fictitiously. Any resemblance to actual persons,
living or dead, events, or locales is entirely coincidental.
Where real historical persons are featured, they appear
only as the author imagined them to be.

Third paperback edition February 2022

Book design by Alison Morgan AliCat Design

ISBN NUMBER 978-1-80227-420-2

Prologue
12 May 1883

Alice feels the needles of rain stab her eyes. But she doesn't blink. She is fixed on the casket as it judders and jerks into the pit.

Above her head a dense, grey fog, is sucking itself towards the earth. Water has already run down her neck into the back of her new coat. Underfoot is a freezing swamp, the water soaking up into her boots, turning her feet to ice. She is shaking, and has been unable to stop shaking for four days now. But still she does not blink.

The coffin disappears from view. Each black-clad bowler-hatted man, heels dug in, carefully manoeuvres his rope from hand to hand. The ropes, glistening in the rain, give out sodden squeaks that sound like tiny screams. She hears it hit the bottom with a squelch and a sigh.

Essy is gone now. Her best friend. Her only friend. Dead in her place. Guilt and terror well up inside. But Alice dare not let them out.

Her hand, gripped by her mother's, is shaking badly. Her mother squeezes a warning and Alice remembers her words of the previous evening. *The attendance of a child will be shameful. We will allow it, although we know we will be considered disgraceful and disreputable in certain quarters. You will not bear your grief in public.*

Alice understands. She glances round. Dada stands next to Mama. Then Essy's mother, barely able to stand, supported by her husband. Then the holy scandal-lovers, expressions arched, lips pursed.

And finally, staring straight back at her, It. Has no-one else noticed that It doesn't get wetted by the rain? Just like when It held Essy's head under water? Then It put its head right in to check that she was dead and came back up dry? As Alice had watched, horrified, from behind the trees, It scooped out a lump of grey and red from the hole It had made in Essy's skull, tilted its head back, and poured the mass into its mouth. Alice shudders at the memory.

The service is over. It is still staring at her. Alice has looked away but she knows. She feels the ice. *I am coming for you. Soon.* She feels the words. It moves forwards to her parents. Speaks words of condolence. Mama smiles and nods. But not warmly. She doesn't like It. Nor does Dada.

Rumours are spreading about Alice. The other children watch her all the time. She can hear their questions.

"Did Alice Jones really arrive too late? How did Essy get that big hole in the back of her head if she fell into The Pond face first?"

The policeman believed her story. Didn't he? The rain eases, but not the cold.

Alice feels a soft tingle on the back of her coat, between her shoulder blades, as if someone is gently scratching her with a very small fingernail. She turns her head to look behind her, across the path. Who is it, staring at her, waving gently? She waves gently back. A girl shimmers into view, inching closer. Alice gasps in surprise. It's herself. Her own face staring back at her. Is she becoming mad? Will they put her in the asylum? The mirror image smiles and wiggles her fingers again. Away in the background she can make out a shadow Mama, who seems to be hacking at a gravestone back across the path. Alice tentatively waves back. But a cold agitation turns her around again. It can see this mirror Alice too. Her fingers turn from a wave to a warning, flashing backwards and forwards. The girl sees. She can see It, too. She nods and moves away. Disappears into the mist.

Mama moves away to speak to the minister. Freed from her grip, Alice walks forwards to stand on the edge of the open grave. As she stares down at Essy, clasping her hands as if to pray. But instead she whispers softly, distressed. "I miss you, Essy. I'm so scared all of the time now. I want to tell Mama and Dada who did this to you but they won't believe me. Did you send that strange girl? Am I gone mad? I don't know what to do. What shall I do, Essy?"

Mama returns and pulls her back by the arm. She wants to get away from the holy scandalmongers. Hidden in the mist, the other girl can still see. She watches them for a moment, then turns back to shadow Mama.

Chapter 1
May 2015

Maggie Gilbert loved a good cemetery.

She felt a rush of excitement as she turned off the road and through the black wrought iron gates, thrilled to find there might actually be a cemetery to search, after weeks of mounting frustration.

The information had come in a chance encounter at the Council Tax office, chatting to the clerk.

"Family history? Me too, I love it! I've managed to find ten generations. Mind you, some of them turned out to be a bit unsavoury. Where did yours live?"

"I don't really know," Maggie had replied. "I've tracked back to 1841 on the census records, but I can't find out any real detail on where they lived or what they did. How did you find out about the unsavoury bits?"

"Oh, mainly through their professions and where they lived. And where they died. A couple of mine died in the workhouse. Have you checked the municipal cemetery?"

"There's a cemetery?"

The hedges that separated the cemetery from the main road into the town centre had grown high, so drivers speeding by on the highway would never know it was there.

The clerk had told her that when it was opened as a new municipal facility in 1883 it had been a well-known landmark, but had filled up its allotted space by the 1960s.

The tarmacked car parking area had six spaces, all empty. The car park was bordered by the warden's abandoned cottage, a whitewashed chapel, and a low stone wall. Beyond the chapel lay an acre of headstones sloping down towards a drab 1960s council estate. Maggie shivered as she got out of the car and pulled her scarf up around her neck to her short brown hair.

It was cold for May, at the end of what had been a disappointingly late spring. There weren't many blossoms, or early summer flowers. Although it was mid-morning, the lingering mist from the previous night's frost floated low across the graves, the sky a silver-grey through which a pale sun fleetingly appeared. Even for a graveyard it was quiet. Maggie shivered again and headed for the chapel to search for clues.

Maggie Gilbert, family history detective! she thought wryly as she prepared to hunt down the past. *Woman on a mission – unemployed woman who ought to be out looking for a job.*

She could see that the chapel was boarded up and the smaller windows high up were broken by stone-shaped holes. She peered hopefully through a gap in the boarding but the chapel had been stripped bare, not even the altar remained. On the front porch at the top of the arch, 1883 was carved into the stone.

Dead end, she thought, liking her pun.

She could see that many of the graves were sinking and overgrown. More than half of the ornate headstones in this top area leaned precariously, as if they might keel over at any moment. Some were laid flat. A footpath dissected the rows of graves, connecting the housing estate with the main road and the budget supermarket across the road from the entrance. Apart from a pedestrian in the distance pushing a shopping trolley she was alone.

The grass was overgrown, weeds roamed freely across the ground and the atmosphere spoke to Maggie of forgetfulness and neglect.

She followed the path around the outside of the chapel and began to look at the headstones to get her bearings. The first burials had been closest to the chapel and dated from 1883. They stood in the shade of a tree close to the back of the chapel and were all children's. That made her plan simple. She'd start close and work her way along the rows out towards the far wall. Her main problem was going to be discipline – to make herself concentrate on who she was looking for and not get distracted. Maggie knew she might be looking for more than one grave, but hoped she would find everyone she was searching for in one plot.

She couldn't remember when this love of graveyards had started. Whenever her parents had taken her and her sister to visit an old church, she had made a beeline for the cemetery and had spent her time studying the graves. She liked to play a game of "find the person longest dead" and conjure up a picture of them.

Setting off slowly across the uneven ground, she reflected grimly on how her originally tepid interest in her family history had deepened strangely and quickly into obsession, taking up time that should have been spent on more practical things, like finding work to shore up her rapidly dwindling bank balance.

It had begun shortly after moving into her new house, on a rainy afternoon, idling away time, waiting for the children to come home from school. Dozing in her favourite armchair in front of her beautiful view, a random idea had come into her head, like a dream that couldn't quite be recalled, with images of her father, who had been dead for over twenty years and the people who were his family. But she had barely met any of them and wouldn't recognise them if they passed on the street, so how did she know that was who they were? Suddenly, and inexplicably, she needed to know.

In the weeks that followed she searched library archives and genealogy files. At first it had been easy, working back through her parents' birth certificates, then census records. She had got back to her great-grandfather, John Jones, in 1851, when he had been eight years old and living with his grandparents and younger sister, Mary Anne. But despite many hours of research and investigation she was stuck and couldn't discover what had happened to his parents.

She had first come across her great-grandmother, Ruth Jones, in 1871. They had married in September that year when John was twenty-eight and Ruth eighteen, but it had taken some time to find them in the April 1871 census. She found John first, working on the municipal railway and living with some family members who she thought were probably his grandmother and a maiden aunt – who herself had a ten-year-old son with, according to his birth certificate, no recorded father.

He'd have taken some explaining away at chapel, Maggie had thought wryly. She vaguely remembered her father's family from occasional gatherings, as a serious, unsmiling, strongly religious horde.

It was some time before she found Ruth in the period before her marriage, but eventually she discovered her at seventeen years old – working on a farm as a servant with her parents, William and Ruth, a blacksmith and serving woman. Maggie imagined that they had met at chapel, for where else would a railway worker meet a farm servant? When that census was taken that year they were probably courting. They had been married at the Ebeneezer Baptist Chapel and William, the first of their five children, was

4

born in 1875. She had been able to trace her family from there to the present day, but she couldn't get any further back.

Her sister had no interest in family at all. "Who cares, Mag?" Fiona's response to Maggie's story about her research had been a shrug. "Dad never did. They don't even acknowledge us, so why waste your time?"

Why indeed? Maggie asked herself. Why had she become *so* interested in finding out about her father's family? Why was she particularly drawn to the image of her great-grandmother Ruth? She couldn't explain it.

But as soon as she began searching they had become real to her, as she found out their names, and where they had lived, and what they had done, Maggie found that she had become obsessed with – what? She didn't know, but it was like an itch. There was something about it that bothered as well as enthralled her, and she had to find its source. She kept digging because she had to know.

Maybe it was her emerging detective skills that kept her searching through websites and archive files long past the time she knew she should be somewhere else. And there was the fantastic feeling of excitement when her perseverance paid off and she found a piece of information that added more to the picture she was building from the fragments of the past.

Her children, family and friends had been amused, then amazed, at how she kept at it. They had looked at her strangely, without understanding, when she explained that something in the past, born out of a memory in a dream, was crying out to be understood. When she tired of the sarcastic remarks she said it was just a hobby. But it was much more than that. As time went on, Maggie felt that she was being directed. And that scared as well as excited her. She had told no-one that she was going to search a cemetery today for people she felt she knew who had been dead more than a hundred years. Well, almost no-one.

She continued to walk up and down the rows of graves, picking her way gingerly over the wet grass and taking care to avoid stepping on the dead. But she became distracted by the names, dates and details she found. She was unable to stop herself from reading the information carved into stone. Most of the graves had traditional Welsh names: Jones, Williams, Morgan, Evans. The detail fascinated her. So many loving wives and beloved husbands, so many stories. She read about the children, too, close to the chapel. Elijah Williams aged four and his brother David. Died on the same day in 1885, grief stricken parents. Esme Ellis, aged twelve, died tragically May 4, 1883, greatly missed by her loving family. Poor little thing. What tragedy? William Lewis, eighteen months, taken suddenly. By what, or whom?

After a dozen rows she checked her watch. *Damn! Lunch time. Come on, concentrate. Just look for the names,* she chided herself.

She hurried, giving each gravestone a quick once over. This was just a first visit anyway. It would be a miracle if she found what she was searching for first time. A couple more rows then she'd have to leave it.

Rushing along a final row she stumbled a few times over the uneven ground and, as she stepped over a fallen headstone, she caught her foot and tripped on some creepers that had run across the ground from a particularly ornate grave. Now on her hands and knees she glanced at the stone in front of her and – this was it! A beautiful but overgrown pale stone, tall and pointed with elegant, smooth, rounded dark green marble columns at each side. The wording, elaborately carved, was reasonably clear, although overgrown by moss and ivy.

John Jones, beloved husband of Ruth.
Died 4 May 1909 at…

Damn! She tried to remove the ivy covering the next line but it clung tenaciously. At the bottom she could just make out, *…and Ruth, devoted wife. Died 21 November 1936. Together with God.*

Maggie leapt up, elated at having succeeded, and desperate to clean the stone further to find the full details. Then she realised that she was going to be late. "I'll be back," she said to the headstone, then felt foolish that she had spoken out loud. She ran back on the path and around the chapel to her car.

Chapter 2
12 May 1909

The day began fine, unseasonably warm for early May. By midday it was too hot. Inside the packed chapel the mourners sweated their way through the service. But any man who tried to surreptitiously ease his high, starched collar was frowned on by stiff, silk-clad women. They would not be permitted to show themselves up by any such lack of respect. Fidgeting children were stilled with a sharp poke.

In the hush at the end of the hymn, Minister Robinson rose. He nodded compassionately at the family in front of him. He had liked and respected John Jones, the man now in the coffin.

Two years earlier, at sixty-four and physically drained, John had retired from his farm and left his eldest son, William, to carry on the family business. Although not a man of great physical stature, his firmness in his beliefs, together with a fine mind and upstanding values, had given him the aura of a powerful, righteous man, which had made him a respected local figure. But from the sudden onset of sickness, he had spiralled down to a sucked-out shell and his slow, excruciatingly painful death had been a terrible thing to witness, as Minister Robinson had done, day in, day out, for the final four months. Every day, Richard Robinson had walked the half mile from the chapel along the canal bank to the splendid retirement house that John had built for Ruth and his family.

A beam of sunlight entered the high window behind him and illuminated the coffin. The memory of John's last words fleeted through the minister's mind as he looked down at Ruth. "Help them to live here without me. They never thought… they would have to", rasped out of a throat with few words left in it. 'Keep them safe, Richard. Help…' a pause, another huge effort, and a weak smile '…help Ruth… to accept'. He knew that John wasn't talking about his own death. As he had done many times before, he thought bitterly to himself, *If only I had been here then. There must have been something I could have done. Perhaps it could have been different.* But he knew this was no more than his own vanity.

Snapping back to the present, he nodded again at the rows of solemn faces and the congregation rose in unison. Outside in the sunshine, the crowds and the carriages were waiting. The chapel elders lined the path from the chapel door to the road as the coffin passed through.

The chapel stood on the bank of the canal and had been built about twenty-five years previously. Today the opposite bank was lined with blossoming trees down towards where the dark water dropped steeply to the Two Locks. Minister Robinson led Ruth to the first family carriage and William and Sara and their three children climbed in after her. Her other children, Walter in his army uniform, Maud with her husband James and their children and the youngest, Evan, followed in a second carriage. Only George, now in South Africa, had not been able to attend.

As the horses jolted the carriage away, Ruth glanced briefly from behind her veil at the faces at the side of the lane. The number of people at the chapel had surprised her. So many friends. Others she didn't know so well, but she felt grateful for their presence. She frowned as she passed a family that had stationed themselves a little way from the chapel wall. Bessie Morris smiled sympathetically as the carriage passed, but Ruth saw the smile disappear as soon as Bessie thought she could no longer be seen.

9

They knew something, but they kept it to themselves, Ruth thought, remembering the trouble that Bessie Morris had caused when they had first come to the farm, with her jealousy and suspicions and rumours. *I'll know soon what it was.* She followed Bessie's gaze as she turned to acknowledge a family in the crowd. And she frowned again as she glimpsed a face she recognised that ought to be familiar. She couldn't remember why but felt firmly that this was someone who should not have been there. She felt butterflies in her stomach. But nothing came to her, so she shook the thought away. She turned back and fixed her gaze on the coffin in the hearse in front of her, where the man she had met and loved instantly as a girl of seventeen was now being carried away.

Forty-two years they had been married. A fine family of children, all grown except one, but today was not the day. Too late, the thought brought a stab of dread that hadn't abated despite the passing of so many years. *At least this time we have a funeral.* Ruth tried to push the unwelcome thought from her mind but, as always, couldn't banish it completely. She had promised to obey him and had succeeded in everything, except that one thing. She had come to hate him for a time, unable to understand how such a good man could act so harshly and, to her belief, so lacking in the love he had promised her at their marriage. She shook the disloyal thought away again as quickly as it had arrived, but knew she would bring it back later, now that she had time to do so.

The journey to the graveyard was short. The carriages slowed at the high iron gates before passing through, the only noise the muffled clopping of the plumed horses' bandaged feet.

The farm workers waited for the procession to arrive. They stood with their families, uncomfortable in black in the heat, but silent and respectful. John Jones had been a good employer in a time when farm work was hard to find. Since the new century had turned, many men had left for the pits and ironworks further up the valley, or to the newly emerging industries around the docks in Newport. Those remaining, and their families, counted themselves lucky – very lucky. A good man gone was a great worry, but the farmer's son would offer continuity. Their work would be secure, their homes guaranteed. John Jones' family had supported the board school that gave education to their children, provided help during their sickness, and given them Sunday off to attend chapel and take a little time for themselves. They knew their luck and thanked God for it. They would do nothing to threaten their livelihood with this family, so they bowed their heads respectfully to Ruth and her family as the cortège passed them.

The carriages halted just inside the cemetery entrance. Ruth had been thinking again about that first meeting – she a servant girl, he a railway guard with such a beautiful tenor voice that had made her look up during the service to see who sang so wonderfully… She took a sharp intake of breath as she realised they had stopped.

As her son William handed her down from the carriage and she walked across the grass to the graveside, there was hushed silence. The earlier breath of wind had died completely. Ruth could hear only the rustling of the soft silk of her dress. She kept her gaze to the ground as she stepped across the rough grass, picking her way slowly and, in spite of the intense heat of the sun, found that she was shivering.

As she crossed the path that separated the two sides of the cemetery she glanced up and saw the waiting grave for the first time. She felt cold and a shiver of fear from the knot in her stomach passed up to her face. It came upon her so suddenly she glanced back to see if something had happened behind her to make her feel like this, but there was nothing that shouldn't have been there. She paused for a moment, slowing her steps, trying to settle herself.

It wasn't as if she didn't know what was coming, that her John would be put into the ground today, their final, permanent separation. She had to face it, so she looked up towards the grave again. It seemed to her that it was darker than the rest of the graveyard. She paused again and took a deep breath. Ruth was not a woman given to hysteria. She had always been a sensible wife and mother, pragmatic and solid. Her mind must be overwrought, the result of her grief.

"William!" she called, but he had fallen back to walk with the minister. "Maud, what is that?" Her daughter, who had been a few paces behind, came quickly.

"What do you mean, Mother?"

"At the grave? Is someone there already?"

"There's nothing there, Mother." Maud looked back at her mother, concern showing on her own, pale face. "What did you think was there?" She saw her mother shaking. "Are you well, Mother? Are you too hot?"

"Rather, I feel cold. What is that?" She gestured towards the grave.

William had caught up and heard the question. "Where, Mother? I can't see…" His voice trailed off as he saw the frown on his mother's face. *'It has been too much for her,'* he thought. Then, out loud, "I'll walk with you. Richard is coming too."

Seeing the procession ahead had halted, Minister Robinson made his way to the front of the group to find out the cause of the delay, leaving the coffin with the undertaker's men.

"Are you well, Ruth?"

"I am well, Richard. I thought I saw…" But as she looked at their faces, she knew that they could not see what she had seen. Of course not. It was just imagination resulting from an overwrought mind. She took a deep breath and continued, this time calmer, "I am well, truly. Please continue."

She shook her head and walked on, flanked by her son and the minister, to the graveside, her head down again. The rest of the family moved closer, as friends and acquaintances held back to give them room and privacy, and to allow the coffin to pass through to its final resting place.

Richard Robinson began to speak, reciting as the undertaker's men lifted the coffin and lowered it into the ground. Ruth did not take her eyes off the casket until it slowly passed down and out of view, and kept her head bowed in the silence that followed the final words. Those assembled waited, watching Ruth to see what she would do. She sighed. And, at last, as her three sons and daughter began to move nervously forward, she lifted her veil and raised her eyes to give them a sign of her love and acceptance, to tell them she was ready to move on.

But what she saw pinned her to the spot. Unable to breathe, her mouth open but unable to speak, she saw clearly standing at the end of the grave, not these grown-up children, but another child, the missing child, little Alice as she had been so many years before on the day she disappeared. Her face, her smile, the same child, exactly as she remembered! All the old pain and heartache returned in that moment filling her with agonising joy.

Then a voice, right next to her, from someone she had not known was there but so close as to seem to speak within her ear, murmured, "Say hello to Ruth, Alice."

"Hello, Ruth," said the child, looking up from the grave. Ruth stretched out, whispered to her child, "Alice! Alice!" and stumbled forwards with both arms held out to enfold her little girl, but found herself clutching mist. There was no-one there.

Chapter 3
May 2015

As Maggie turned into the school grounds, she could see the thin, upright figure of her daughter, waiting indignantly. She sighed. She was only five minutes late, but this was an exact child. Maggie pulled up, opened the door, and spoke.

"Sorry, but I have a really good reason!"

The look of disgust said everything and Maggie fought to keep her face serious.

"You'll never guess what! I found the graveyard! I thought they might have been buried close to their farm and chapel. Well, I was right. I found them!"

Silence.

"Aren't you impressed? Just a little bit?" More silence. But she knew that curiosity would win out, so she said nothing.

"So, do I get to see them, then?" her daughter asked grudgingly.

"Of course," Maggie smiled. "They're your ancestors, too. Let's get to the dentist. Then we'll go home for lunch. I need to get some secateurs and my camera, too. It looks like no-one's been near the grave for years, it's so overgrown. We'll go and clean it up a bit, then we'll pick up Jack."

* * *

Maggie's house was in a cul-de-sac, set back from the main road. The last in the row, it was on the edge of what was once a small hamlet on the eighteenth-century canal on the outskirts of the town.

Maggie drove out of the town and headed uphill towards the mountain, turning off at the last road before the urban landscape surrendered itself to farms and fields down towards Newport and the coast beyond.

Although they had been at the house for five months, every time Maggie approached it she couldn't help smiling.

The decision to buy had been impulsive. She had already found a modern 1960s terraced box on the edge of the town and registered the children at the local primary and comprehensive schools. She wasn't excited about it, but she hadn't intended to get excited about a home again. It would do well enough. Her sister and family were nearby, too, and were going to help them to get settled. On her final visit before signing the contract, Maggie had been driving around trying to get re-acquainted with the town that she had left over twenty-five years before. She tried to recall where her grandmother had lived and any locations that might spark other childhood memories, when she realised that she was lost. Knowing she was getting closer to the older houses, she turned off the main road into a lane to try to get her bearings. And there was the house, bearing a tattered "For Sale" notice.

It was a large, run-down, Victorian, grey stone building standing at the end of a row of more modern houses, out of place, but, to Maggie, exceptionally beautiful. The state of the window casings and the greenery growing out of the chimneys told a story of neglect. But something about it reached out to her and drew her in, tugging on her heartstrings in a way she knew was dangerous, but couldn't resist.

She called the estate agent to enquire and he agreed to come out to show it to her immediately. Maggie sensed from his eagerness she was the first person in a long time to show any interest.

From the moment she entered the porch with its black-and-white chequered floor Maggie felt at home. She knew instinctively which room was which. The estate agent expressed surprise when she told him she had never been in the house before.

Brian, being a decent agent, had pointed out the problems – the disgusting carpets, the rotten window frames, the kitchen that hadn't been updated since 1946, the decrepit roof, and the all-pervading stench of neglect and decay throughout. Maggie was realistic enough to acknowledge these problems. But she saw original fireplaces, and solid oak floors through the holes in the carpets. From the huge bay window at the back of the main living room, she saw a magnificent view straight across the enclosed garden sloping down to the canal and on to the hills rising up to the mountain. To the left, along the valley, the gentle green patchwork slopes traced down to the outskirts of the city.

She could imagine that the original owner must have looked out on just that view, through a window designed to capture the expanse and fullness of it. And that he too had loved what he saw.

After showing her the jungle of a garden, Brian took her to the front of the house where they stood and looked at the entrance. The name was carved on a plaque at the side of the front door: Garthwood House 1907. Maggie was lost in a multitude of ideas of what she could do to the house to bring it up to a habitable state when she realised that he was speaking to her.

"… local landowner, and in its day, it was one of the old village's finest family homes."

"Sorry, Brian, what was that?" Maggie turned her attention back to him.

"Oh, nothing. Just some local history. So, what do you think, Mrs Gilbert? I can find a builder to help you get an idea of what the costs of repair will be. It's basically a sound building, but you'll want to know, and how much time…"

"I want to buy it," Maggie interrupted. "How much are they asking?"

He took a deep breath and gave her the figure. "Of course—" he began but got no further into his suggestion that the current owners might be open to negotiation.

"Too much. Unrealistic. I'll offer them fifty thousand less, to cover the repairs. Subject to survey, of course. Tell them it's cash – if they're prepared to move quickly. No chain. Will there be any problem?"

She hoped she sounded calm and business-like. She had put her hands in her pockets so he wouldn't see that she was digging her fingernails into her palms with excitement. The gleam in his eyes told her the answer. "I don't think that will be a problem," he replied quickly. "I'll call the owners as soon as I get back to the office."

"Tell them I want to start work at the beginning of December and move in by Christmas."

Brian's face showed a fleeting exasperation with this wildly unrealistic demand, but he didn't want to spoil the moment. He had been trying to sell this house for five years. Four times he had come close but each time something had inexplicably gone wrong. He had started to wonder. "That's only six weeks away," he said cautiously.

"In by Christmas," Maggie replied firmly. "That's my offer."

He called her half an hour later to confirm her offer had been accepted and the house would be hers in six weeks. The survey then confirmed that it was a sound building, and the purchase went through easily.

She was thrilled but, inevitably, her family had been horrified – that she had bought such a "ruin", as her sister, Fiona, called it, "without proper advice from anyone apart from a surveyor and on such a ridiculous whim, when you had a nice little modern house ready and waiting!"

Maggie knew that Fiona was peeved that her opinion had not been sought. When she had first walked into the house with Maggie she had stood open-mouthed. Maggie fleetingly hoped it was admiration.

"There's no central heating. And the windows are falling out! The kitchen looks like it's been there since World War Two. The whole place stinks! What were you thinking? And it's way too expensive. This time you've really gone crazy!" Fiona had bellowed. Then she'd sighed, "After all you've been through, Mag. Why couldn't you just stick with the easy option, just this once?" But Fiona knew Maggie well enough to know her sister just couldn't take the safe, easy option. Ever.

At nine o'clock on the tenth of December Maggie received the keys from Brian and she and the children walked into their new home. They had already been in town for ten days, staying in cramped conditions with Fiona and her family, their vanload of possessions in the care of the moving company while the final exchange of contracts took place. At their first sight of the empty house with its damp and rot and peeling wallpaper the children had been appalled and threatened to walk out at once. It had taken some work on Maggie's part to convince them that within a week of owning it they wouldn't recognise it.

She had made good use of her time in the six weeks it had taken for the sale to complete, lining up builders, carpenters, plumbers and all of the craftsmen she needed to bring the house back to the state of grandeur she firmly believed it deserved.

On the first day, the house became a building site. But ten days later, the day Maggie had decided they would move in, the interior was unrecognisable, and about ready to be lived in.

Jack, who at fourteen wasn't keen on having to do anything that seemed like real work, had remained sceptical, but his sister immediately understood Maggie's fascination with this strange old house.

"I hate to say it, Mum, but you're right. It's talking to me, too. It likes us."

Maggie looked at her daughter with amused interest. "How do you know, Alice?"

"Mmm, not sure. I just do. Have we been here before, when I was small?"

"No," said Maggie, her interest sharpened. "Why do you think that?"

"I knew where all the rooms were."

"That's funny, so did I."

Jack agreed to work on his bedroom, persuaded by Maggie's generous bribe of complete choice of décor, and he stripped the wallpaper and repaired the cracks in the plaster. Maggie and Fiona scrubbed up the living and dining rooms, and the small room that would become the study. They did their best with the kitchen and the bathroom that, after Christmas, was to be completely gutted and replaced. They removed carpets, sanded floors and scrubbed tiles.

The roofers spent a week replacing the grey slate tiles and cleared the moss, ivy, and birds' nests from around the chimneys, which were then swept, ready for the fires to be lit. The builders quickly completed the installation of central heating, much to Fiona's relief, as they were going to spend their first family Christmas together in a long time.

On Christmas Day, they sat around the log fire blazing in the grate, with furniture and possessions in place. Fiona had agreed, grudgingly, and with surprise, that perhaps Maggie wasn't quite so mad, after all, even if she was lucky as hell. Maggie had expressed her own amazement that everything had gone without a hitch. She'd thought on more than one occasion that the bubble must surely burst. But it was as if the house wanted her to take up residence as soon as possible.

The builders had also opened up the staircase to the loft. During one of her frequent visits to check on the progress of the work, the foreman pointed out to Maggie that some previous occupants had left a couple of dirty trunks in the huge attic space. As she wanted eventually to convert it into a room for the children, she decided to sort it out after Christmas, but in the meantime she took advantage of the storage space. Access to the attic was through a staircase behind a door on the first-floor gallery. The stairs were narrow and twisted round sharply but the attic at the top was surprisingly spacious and would make a great space for the children.

Having heaved boxes up the stairs and deposited them as close to the door as possible, Maggie could just make out the old trunks under the eaves. The musty attic had not been used for many years.

* * *

Searching through kitchen drawers and cupboards Maggie remembered that she had put the secateurs in the attic with the Christmas decorations. Searching through the Christmas boxes she saw the old trunks again and reminded herself that she should make some time soon to get back up there with a torch and open them up.

Maggie and Alice were soon in the car again and on their way to the cemetery, where Maggie located the grave and waved in triumph to her daughter.

"Here they are, your great-great-grandparents. Stand next to the headstone and I'll photograph you. Say hello."

"I can't just say, 'Hello, great-great-grandparents.' That's stupid. What are their names?"

"They were called John and Ruth. That a coincidence, isn't it? Me choosing Ruth as your second name?"

"Which one shall I speak to first?" asked Alice.

"I think your great-great-grandmother, Ruth." Maggie lifted her camera. "Say hello to Ruth, Alice."

"Hello, Ruth," said Alice, smiling.

Chapter 4

As Alice spoke, and Maggie clicked the button on top of the camera, she felt movement near her feet. The camera focus blurred so she couldn't see clearly. She shifted her balance slightly, to clarify the picture. But instead her foot caught on something and as she lurched forwards, the camera fell and bounced on the grass.

Her daughter looked at her, concerned. "What's wrong, Mummy? Why did you shout at me?"

"I didn't shout," Maggie replied, picking herself up. "I might have sworn, but just a bit, under my breath."

"No, you called me. You said my name. You said, 'Alice! Alice!' I thought something was wrong, but I couldn't see you properly when the flash went off."

"I didn't shout at you, Alice."

"Yes, you did!"

Maggie picked up the camera. The flash was switched off. Her daughter was still blinking and shielding her face with her arms, as if to ward something off. Maggie quickly looked round, but there was no-one else in the cemetery.

"I'm just going to clear up this grave and see what the rest of the words are. Can you see how much it's overgrown? It won't take long. Do you want to help me, Al?"

"No, thanks. I'm going to take a walk over there." She pointed towards the back of the chapel. "See what's going on." Maggie guessed she was going to play the graveyard game.

"OK," she called back, "but keep me in sight. Don't wander off any further."

Alice pulled her usual face of huffy boredom at her mother's warning as she picked her way to the footpath and crossed over towards the chapel. Maggie turned back to the gravestone, and began to snip at the creepers and ivy with the secateurs. In a moment she would be able to read more of the story. She knew from her research that it was customary at that time to record the place of death on the gravestone if it was of consequence. Perhaps she would add another piece to the puzzle. She knew from the 1901 census the family had lived on their farm, which had been a sizeable property. Now, it was a small courtyard of expensive houses. John Jones must have been a successful man, beginning life as a railway worker but ending up a farmer, a farm owner too, not just a tenant. But she had no idea what had happened to them beyond that.

With a sharp wrench the last piece of ivy pulled away. She rubbed the stone hard with a cloth until she could make out the words. What she saw left her speechless. She almost stopped breathing with the shock: John Jones died 4 May 1909 at Garthwood House. Maggie had bought her great-grandfather's house! The very house in which, according to his gravestone, he had died. But it had only been built two years before that, so John must have been the landowner Brian the estate agent had been talking about. This was incredible!

She tried to focus – but where to begin? She couldn't think of anything, her mind was blank. Then she realised that Alice was standing next to her.

"Are you OK, Mum?" Her voice was troubled, "You've gone white."

"Look at the stone," Maggie whispered.

Alice read the headstone. She looked puzzled, but not upset. "Is that our Garthwood House?"

"Yes, I think it is."

Alice scrutinised the headstone, taking in the details, then looked up at Maggie and asked, "Are you sad, or happy?"

"What?" Maggie shook her head, trying to concentrate. "Are you sad that he died there, or happy we got the house back?"

"Got it back? I hadn't thought of it like that. Yes, I suppose we have got it back." She smiled at her daughter. "That's a good way to think of it."

She was just starting to feel a bit more relaxed, thinking of it as an amazing coincidence, when Alice spoke again.

"Can I tell the girl over there to cheer her up?"

"What girl, Alice?"

"Over there," she gestured towards the chapel, "where I went to see. She's very unhappy because her friend died. She's scared too."

Maggie glanced across the graveyard. "There's no-one else here, Alice."

"Oh, they've gone. I was watching her, from the path. Bit odd, though. She looked like she'd been standing in rain, but it hasn't rained today, has it? She was watching her friend's funeral. And her family. But they didn't see me. I think the other one could see me too, the one she was scared of."

There was no funeral taking place in the cemetery. Maggie didn't know how to respond, but felt instinctively that she should not disbelieve her daughter.

"How do you know the girl saw you, Alice?"

"She waved to me, sort of, just with her fingers. The other one saw her do it and looked round at me. She smiled but it wasn't a nice smile."

"Then what happened?"

"I came back when I saw you staring at the stone. I think the burial was finished so they must have gone home. They were walking away."

"What do you mean by 'the other one', Alice?"

Alice thought for a moment, biting at her bottom lip. "You know when you know that someone doesn't like you by the way they smile? That's all, really. It made me feel like I should back off, so I did."

"Had you seen these people before?"

"No, of course not. Can we go now?"

There didn't seem to be any point in probing further, so Maggie agreed it was time to go. She gathered up her things and as they walked she looked towards where Alice said she'd seen the funeral. There was nothing, no sign of the recent presence of people, no footsteps in the grass, and certainly no recently dug grave. Maggie recalled from her earlier visit that no burials had taken place in that part since the cemetery was opened. Maggie distracted Alice with trivial chat until they reached the car. They got in and put on their seat belts and Maggie started the engine, then exclaimed, "Damn, I've left my camera! Stay here."

She turned off the engine, jumped out, and started to run before Alice could follow. But instead of going back to the family grave she headed for the patch of ground behind the chapel and under the tree. She had passed these graves earlier when she was searching. There was only one girl's grave.

26

Esme had been buried about a hundred and thirty years ago. Maggie wondered what the date of the funeral was. That would be in the church records. But what tragedy? If it had been a really big tragedy it might have been recorded in the local newspaper. That would be in the library archive. Checking that her camera was still safely in her pocket, Maggie went back to the car.

* * *

Jack had a homework project, so Maggie worked with him on the computer that evening, then tested Alice on her spelling sheets. She kept what had happened at the cemetery in the back of her mind. It was only after the children were in their rooms reading and watching TV that Maggie allowed herself to think about it. She poured herself a glass of wine and sat in her favourite place – the big picture window at the back of the living room that looked out across the hills to the mountain and down the valley.

The light was fading. The trees on top of the first small round hill grew steadily darker and spread shadows down towards the canal, where the motionless water had darkened to look like black syrup. The few farmhouses in the distance shone lights against the deep blue, almost purple, sky.

As she drank her wine, Maggie pieced together everything that she had found out, trying to reassure herself with a logical explanation, especially Alice's story.

Maggie liked to take everything at face value. She had bought this house on a whim (not for the first time), spending almost all her savings (also not for the first time). She was relying on good

27

luck or chance to survive the crisis that would inevitably come from this folly. Last time she had taken a chance like that she had lost virtually everything, retrieving just enough to sell up, buy a small house and exist carefully for a couple of years. She'd devoted her time to nursing her family's psychological wounds. Buying Garthwood House had put paid to that. And now she was caught up in a conundrum, which would take up time that she hadn't got if she was to find a job. She resigned herself to the knowledge that she was going to pursue this mystery regardless. It was too bizarre to ignore. Her sister would despair when she heard.

As she sat there, relaxing in her lovely, friendly, comfortable home, instinct told her that this time it *was* different. She knew that she had a real connection to her house, to the man who had built it, and to the family who had lived in it. This had shocked her, but it didn't disturb her. It just whetted her curiosity to find out more.

Alice's earlier behaviour did disturb her, though. Maggie knew there hadn't been anyone else at the graveyard. Was it just a child's imagination? If it wasn't, then what had happened? What *had* Alice seen? Maggie was convinced that Alice believed she'd seen something.

Maggie took a gulp of wine and a long-suppressed fear welled up, and with it an old anxiety that death was not the end of a straight line. And there was something else, some nagging feeling that she thought she recognised but couldn't put a name to. She had felt it a few times since her investigations had begun and she didn't like it. It felt unsafe.

Apart from seeing her sister, family commitments were something that she had avoided. But now she was hooked… no, obsessed. Perhaps she was meant to be? No point struggling for a clear picture. There wasn't one yet. Maybe she could get some help. There were already a few things to do at the library and the archives, and they had experienced people there. She thought of the attic, and determined that tomorrow she would search those trunks under the eaves. Might they yield information about the house's history?

She could put off looking for work for just a little longer, say a week, maybe two. Maggie smiled guiltily to herself, acknowledging that this was a poor excuse. At least this time it was an excuse with a purpose. She could last out financially for a month or two more, just.

She had been so caught up in her thoughts that she hadn't noticed it was almost dark outside. All she could see now was the outline of the long mountain ridge against the last fading westerly light. This window seemed to have been designed especially for quiet contemplation of the view, with its changing colours throughout the day, and season by season. This view must hardly have changed in the century or so since the house had been built. No roads or traffic, just the countryside as it always had been. She knew from the old maps she had researched that the farmhouses she could see today were the same ones that were there a hundred years before. She was amazed that no new buildings encroached upon the mountain, or up from the town to spoil the view. It was a rare and precious thing these days, to have so much land untouched. The thought made her smile as she stood up and leaned forwards to draw the curtains.

As she caught her reflection in the window, gazing out into the distance again, something stopped her. Staring more keenly at herself, she thought it was raining, because raindrops seemed to be running down her face. But it wasn't raining. It was her reflection that was crying.

Chapter 5
May 1883

After breakfast, Ruth settled herself at the round table in the small parlour that looked out over the front of the farmhouse, to do her accounts. John raised his eyebrows seeing her there. She usually performed this task in the evening in the drawing room when they were together, and always on a Friday, never on a Wednesday. He said nothing, understanding why she was really there.

The table stood in front of the long window that looked out over the fenced-off garden of lawn, flowers, and a small vegetable plot. And the bench that John had put there for Ruth to sit on to enjoy the sunshine that favoured this aspect. It was Ruth's favourite spot. The back of the farmhouse was given over to machinery storage sheds around a cobbled courtyard and dwellings for the animals.

For the past hour, whilst she worked, Ruth watched Alice. She was sitting on the bench stroking the orphaned lambs that John had reluctantly allowed her to feed, and that gambolled around her feet. But mainly Alice gazed into the distance at nothing at all. From time to time the girl's lips moved and she shook her head, and it seemed to Ruth that her daughter was caught up in an internal argument with herself.

Perhaps that was the same indistinct muttering that Ruth had heard coming from Alice's room during the past two nights. Ruth knew that the child was sleeping poorly, and this morning Alice had dark circles under her eyes. She argued against going to bed, wept and begged to stay longer with her parents. John had been angry, and Ruth supported him, but this was out of character for Alice. She longed to comfort Alice, to find out what was troubling her, but John felt it was best to let her be and grieve for her friend. So, Ruth didn't speak of her concern to her daughter and tried to remain cheerful. But she watched her carefully and, one time, when Alice thought she wasn't looking, Ruth saw a look of such despair in Alice's eyes that she feared that Alice was retreating ever deeper into her grief.

How different from the scene a few weeks earlier. She had embarrassed Mrs Ellis when, watching the girls from the same spot, she'd remarked, "They're so alike they could be sisters." She'd seen Gwen Ellis blush, but went on, "It's their dark hair and green eyes and those heart-shaped faces. Very different characters, though."

Gwen had nodded. "Your Alice is much stronger than my Essy, even though she's two years younger. Essy is small for her age. She loves your Alice."

Essy came to the farm every day after school. Ruth had no objection to the farmer's daughter playing with the servant's child. She'd watched in delight as Alice showed gentle Essy how to milk cows and feed pigs, and how to chase chickens when they thought adults weren't watching. They'd walk to and from school together and had time to play before Mrs Ellis finished her work.

At Easter, the first talk of change came. Essy would soon reach her thirteenth birthday, which meant leaving school to work to contribute to the family income. Ruth knew that Essy dreamed of working on the farm. She was frightened of having to work at one of the factories, especially the local ironworks whose distant roar reached them at night. Essy was not physically strong and children had to be tough to survive factory work.

Ruth recalled a conversation between small girls planning to be friends for life. Settled comfortably after school in the cowshed above the unoccupied pigsty, Alice shared her secret plans with Essy. They were drawn from the exploits of famous people in *The Star of Gwent* and *The Merlin*.

"Wherever did you get the paper, Alice? Your Dada doesn't approve." Essy's worried whisper carried into the courtyard to where Ruth was preparing feed for the livestock.

"I get them in the village and from school. Someone threw this one away. It's a week out of date, but that doesn't matter. Just a moment." She put her head out of the barn opening and quickly looked round, but didn't see Ruth directly below. Ruth knew that Alice was checking for her father.

Alice began to read out the story of a polar bear that had escaped from the circus and entered a house in Newport, killing a chicken and destroying the crockery, taking on a new voice for each character in turn.

"How big do you think it was, Alice? It must have been very fierce!"

"Oh, at least twenty feet, I'd say."

Ruth stifled a spurt of laughter at the terrified squeak from Essy. But Alice began to plan how she would get to see a live bear, one day. Then she began to read about the forthcoming excursions across the Bristol Channel by the steamer, the PS *Waverley*. "Here, Essy, look at the illustration. Isn't the funnel wonderful, and the huge paddle wheel. We shall stand on the deck in the sunshine, and gaze down the Bristol Channel!"

"Perhaps we shall see as far as Devonshire!"

"Devonshire! I should think so, and more!"

"Where else, Alice?"

"If we go far enough out in the Channel, we might see the coast of France."

They squealed and laughed and continued to talk about their plans. Ruth heard the swishing sound of her daughter dancing around in the hay.

* * *

Alice sat hunched on the bench, her legs waving backwards and forwards aimlessly above the ground, one arm feeling out for the lambs, but her eyes staying fixed on a spot in the distance. When she couldn't find the lamb she glanced up, and saw her mother watching her from the parlour. Again, Ruth thought she saw a look of longing. She was desperate to reach out, but held back, willing Alice to come to her. The look was so piercing that Ruth half stood but, remembering John's wishes, she sat. She waved to Alice and returned to her accounts. When she glanced up again, Alice was gone.

After ten minutes, when there was no sign of the girl, and Ruth realised that her pen hadn't touched the paper, she sighed, gave up and walked from the parlour to the front door. She stood in the porch, her hand shielding her eyes against the bright sunlight, and looked round the garden.

There was no sign of Alice, but to her left the gate at the side of the house that led to the back of the farm was open. Ruth quickly moved to close it, to stop the lambs escaping, which would have angered John. Alice had only been allowed to keep the lambs because she'd begged her father so desperately and pleaded that she and Essy would take good care of them.

Ruth looked quickly around the yard, but there was no sign of Alice. She gave an exasperated huff and walked back to the front of the house, stopping to tie up some spring boughs close to the front door, before returning to her work. Had she waited a moment, she would have heard the sound of sobbing coming from one of the pigsties. Unknowing, she continued to work with her papers until it was time to supervise the farm workers' lunchtime meal.

Chapter 6

After that night's supper, Ruth sat in the main parlour on the sofa in front of the fireplace, having seen the younger children to bed. She had listened to Alice read her Bible and then quietly closed the book as John came in and sat in his armchair next to them. He and Ruth had agreed earlier what should be done next. Now it was time to tell Alice.

"Alice, your mother and I have talked over what is best and have decided," he began firmly, glancing at Ruth for support, "that it is time for you to return to school." He held his hand up to stop what he expected to be her inevitable protest, but none came. Instead, Alice dropped her gaze and stared at her stockinged feet.

John was puzzled, as Alice had begged, and they had agreed, that she should have a few days following the funeral to herself. He continued, "I know that it will be hard to start your lessons again without Esme but you must take the first step."

Still no response. He took a deep breath then said more loudly, "Have you heard what I said, Alice?"

"Yes, Dada."

"So you will return to school tomorrow morning. Is there anything you wish to say to us?"

"No, Dada."

"Good girl. Now kiss your Mama and go to your room. She will come to you to hear your prayers."

He glanced across at Ruth and saw her look of concern but frowned and turned away impatiently. They had decided. There was no reason for further discussion.

Alice rose, leaned across to her mother and raised her head to kiss the proffered cheek. As she did so, Ruth again thought she caught a flash of misery and appeal, but Alice quickly lowered her head.

They heard her soft footsteps cross the hall, run up the first flight of stairs, then on to the landing upstairs, and down the passage to her room. As soon as Ruth was sure Alice was out of earshot, she spoke.

"John, I'm so worried about her. Now before you say anything, I know what you're thinking!" She held up a hand but softened its harsh gesture with a smile. "You think she's best left alone to her grieving and return to her schooling, but there's something more to this, I know there is!"

John was about to protest, but the alarm in Ruth's voice made him hesitate.

"Well, we had decided, but perhaps you should speak to her, Ruth. I didn't think it right, but if you are so worried, perhaps we should try to find what's troubling her, and I must agree that I can see that something is troubling her, more than I would have expected. Two days ago she was begging not to go back to school. Perhaps we have overindulged her!" He ran a hand through his thinning dark hair.

"I think we must," Ruth suppressed her relief. "I'll go now."

At the top of the stairs, Ruth could hear Alice beginning her prayers. She stopped for a moment in front of her door, then hesitated again as she caught a few words of what Alice was saying in a voice of strong supplication, "I don't want to be hurt like Essy..." Ruth's sharp intake of breath at these words was loud enough to attract Alice's attention. She glanced round, saw her mother, and stood up quickly.

"I'm finished, Mama," she said quickly, jumping up onto her bed.

"Good child. Would you like to speak with me?"

She wanted to let the girl know that she had overheard and to encourage her to explain her last words. Alice usually liked to talk to her mother about the goings on at the farm and within the farm community. But tonight she replied, "No, thank you, Mama. But I want to ask you a question."

"Of course," said Ruth, thinking that if this was about Essy, it was her opportunity to probe.

"Did I have a twin sister, Mama? Did she die?"

The question shocked Ruth into momentary silence.

"No, Alice. You had no twin... sister *or* brother. What has caused you to ask such a strange question?"

There was silence; the candles on the tallboy flickered, casting shadows around the room. Ruth saw Alice's hands squeezing and releasing the sheet underneath the bedcover. A breeze from the open window caught Ruth's hair and blew a loose strand into her eyes. She brushed it away slowly, so as not to disturb Alice's attention, which remained fixed on her mother, unspeaking, frowning.

"Alice, what has made you think you had a twin sister?"

"Are you quite sure, Mama?"

"Of course. Now, what is the reason for this peculiar question?" she demanded.

"I saw... someone who looked..." She paused, concentrating all her efforts on finding the right words, never taking her fierce stare from her mother's face.

"How did she look, Alice?"

"She was *me*, Mama."

Ruth breathed in slowly, bemused at the simplicity of a statement she could not comprehend. She breathed deeply and quietly and asked patiently, "What do you mean, Alice, she was you? I don't understand."

"She had my face. My eyes, my nose and my... look." Ruth knew the intense glare that had caused Alice to be told off so many times before for staring, when she was, in fact, concentrating hard. The new schoolteacher had condemned it many times, despite Ruth having explained that Alice was a good student and not the impudent, rude child she had been accused of being.

"When did you see this person, Alice?"

"At Essy's burying, Mama. She was there, the other me."

"Ah, I see." Ruth thought that she might know what she was dealing with.

"We have not spoken of Essy, my dear. We – your Dada and I – thought it best to allow you to grieve for your friend in your own way. Perhaps we should have spoken. This has obviously upset you more that I realised." She got no further. A look of fear and hopelessness such as Ruth had never seen crossed Alice's face and she was so shocked by the power of it that she stopped speaking. She felt torn between her husband and child, between duty and love. She knew what she had to do.

"Alice, you will become reconciled. Time will heal." Again, she was stopped in her tracks, this time by the low moan of pain.

"Mama, please, you don't understand what I saw..."

38

"Stop this now. Essy is gone. You miss her, but you will recover. That's enough. We will not speak of it again."

"No, Mama!" Alice now spoke in shaking sobs, which dropped to a pleading whisper as tears ran down her face. "Please, help me. Don't let... hurt me... others too... hurt the other... the other Alice. Please, don't let it!" She grabbed at her mother's arm. Ruth pulled away.

"Enough, Alice! You are overwrought. Tomorrow you will go back to school and we will say prayers for Essy's family. That they may bear their loss. Now sleep. We shall speak again tomorrow, when you're calm."

She smiled, but the look of defeat in her daughter's eyes made her falter. But what could a child of ten know about such emotions? She could see Alice shaking under the bed covers, still staring pleadingly. For a moment she hesitated, as she sensed that something odd had touched her. It was pulling at her, unwillingly, like an animal straining on a leash, back towards the bed. She felt agitated and disturbed. As the line pulled her, all of Ruth's instincts screamed that something was dreadfully wrong. This must have shown on her face, for Alice's wide eyes responded to the change in Ruth's expression, with an instant of hope.

"No, Alice," she said, speaking more to herself than to her daughter, "that's enough for this evening. Tomorrow..."

She crossed to the tallboy and blew out the candles. Alice didn't speak. Ruth turned at the doorway. Alice's stare had not left her mother.

"Goodnight, Alice. God bless you, daughter."

There was no reply.

Ruth sighed and left the room, returning to John in the parlour, deciding to tell him nothing of the conversation, not yet. She was puzzled and troubled at Alice's hysterical behaviour, but knew that John would have no time for such peculiar moods.

That night she lay awake for hours, thinking over the events of the past ten days and wondering what Alice had been trying to say to her. Perhaps it was more than grief. Perhaps she should have listened, not dismissed her so easily. Such a strange question! Had there really been someone at the graveyard, a real person, not the result of Alice's imagination? She herself had not seen anyone bearing Alice's description. Despite the fact that John wouldn't like it, she resolved to speak to Alice again after school.

The following morning Alice dressed herself, took up her slate, and left for school, accompanied by her brother, William. She said little to either parent before she left and did not turn back at the top of the lane to wave to her mother as usual. Ruth sighed and turned her attention to Thursday baking.

Three hours after Alice should have returned home, and after the farm workers had searched the village and all the surrounding fields with a frantic John, Ruth knew that she had made a terrible mistake.

Chapter 7
May 2015

For the third day in a row Maggie signed herself in at the entrance desk at Pontypool County Hall and made her way across the plush vault-like lobby through the glass turnstile to the lifts. She descended to the basement that housed the county archives. Stepping out of the lift, she found a striking difference in atmosphere. After the opulence of the entrance, the basement was stark, white, and bare, with three long, empty corridors, punctuated by unmarked closed doors. Her footsteps echoed on the concrete floor as she made her way along the furthest corridor towards the windowless archives room. There were few people in the research room, and the ambiance was the usual calm hush.

She smiled at the archivist as she signed in. "Hello. Me again!"

Noleen, the usually dour archivist, smiled back. "I've found something that might help you. It's the right area, anyway."

They had got to know each other a little. When she first arrived Maggie had little idea where to start. Despite her habitual unwelcoming demeanour, Noleen had proved to be helpful, listening to Maggie's story and suggesting various documents that might help in her search for information on John Jones and his elusive parentage.

Maggie was thrilled when she was handed a pile of church registers from the parishes around the area in which John had been born and where he would have grown up. Each was a leather-bound volume, around two feet high and held together with frayed black ribbon. She was amazed at the excitement she felt in being allowed to handle these historical documents. Before opening them she reverently brushed her fingers over the hard leather covers, imagining the hands that had first touched them, the clerks and scribes of the parish, a cut above the common herd, and relatively affluent because they could both read and write.

The first volume she opened was of the parish of Llanmartin, covering the births in that area from 1820 to 1890. Each event had been carefully entered in a beautiful copperplate hand, registering the names of the parents and the child, and the date of baptism. In some cases, the names of godparents were also recorded. The paper on which the names were inscribed was a kind of parchment, Maggie guessed, heavy and rough, the colour faded to grey, but still with thick black ink, legible after nearly two hundred years.

She went painstakingly through the lists of names, checking each Jones, but not finding John. One of the most surprising discoveries was the number of births recorded as "base" or even "bastard". Her notion of the nineteenth century had been of an era of great propriety and strict morality. Evidently, this was not the full story, particularly among the lower classes, as many of the people in the register seemed to be agricultural labourers, jobbing tradesmen, or servants.

Noleen handed Maggie another set of registers. "Here's what I told you about, the Anglican registry, but I don't know if you'll find anything, if the parents were Baptists. Have you tried Newport library yet?"

"What would they have there that I can't get here?" she asked as Noleen placed the three-foot-high stack on the table in front of her.

"You could try another angle, perhaps. They have the local papers on microfiche, and other documents. It's worth a go, if nothing turns up here." She hesitated.

"Maggie, it's possible that your great-grandfather's birth was never registered, you know. They were all supposed to be, from 1837 onwards, but in the early years some of the country people just didn't bother. If the child was born at the family home, and if this was their first child, then they might just not have realised the importance of registering. Remember, these were uneducated people."

"But they recorded themselves on the 1841 census," Maggie countered. "So they must have known that registration was important before he was born. And I still can't work out from the census if he was John and Eliza's son or grandson. The 1851 record says "son", but later, when he's a working man and head of his own household, Eliza seems to be recorded on the 1871 census as "grandmother", which would make him her grandson, not her son." She put her elbows on the table. "I just can't figure it out."

"It would have depended on who was present in the house to give the information to the census recorder. Let me see your records again."

Maggie showed her the documents she had collected. It was easy to see how Maggie's confusion had come about. John appeared on the 1851 census as "son", aged eight, in the household of John and Eliza Jones. Also present in the house was Mary Anne Jones, "granddaughter", aged six. But whose daughter would that have made her? The only other adult was sixteen-year-old daughter, Anne. So John's date of birth would have been around 1843. But as Eliza's age on the 1851 census was given as fifty-seven, that meant she would have had young John when she was fifty years old. Maggie couldn't see how this was possible. Old John would have been fifty-five when this child was born. Maggie knew from the 1841 census that they had had a daughter Elizabeth living with them at that time, aged fourteen. And she had found evidence of another son, William, who would have been around seventeen in 1841. At first she thought that he might have been the father of young John, but study of the dates brought home that this, too, could not be possible. Receipt of John's marriage certificate showed that he recorded his father as being named John Jones with the profession of farmer (deceased) in 1871 when he married Ruth. But her census research told her that that Old John was an "Agricultural Labourer", not a "Farmer", and was illiterate. Farmers in the 1840s were usually educated and literate.

So, she searched for a birth in the general register. But the name of John Jones came up with forty-seven responses covering 1844 to 1846. With the General Registry Office charging almost ten pounds a certificate, it was proving to be prohibitively expensive to find out which was her John, and without a mother's name she already had three "possibles' and was still checking 1845 births. Very frustrating!

"I see what you mean," Noleen said when she had gone through Maggie's records. "It's just possible that he was born to elderly parents, but I would think it more likely that he was staying with his grandparents when the census was taken, which would mean that his parents either lived elsewhere or were already dead. You could check the death records, but without the mother's name it's going to be hard to track him down. Still, where there's a will," she smiled at Maggie and turned back to her desk.

Maggie smiled back, but it was forced. Noleen's comment had brought back to mind her discussion with her sister Fiona the previous evening.

She had been thinking about whether to confide in her sister, but had held back because she was uncertain how Fiona would react. Her best friend, Janice, would have listened to her without judgement, but Maggie held no such expectation of her sister. In the event, Fiona had called round unannounced that morning to check how Maggie and the kids were doing. Or at least that was what she maintained. Maggie had expected that the cross examination would start as soon as Fiona got her cup of tea in hand and seated herself at the kitchen table.

"So, how's the job hunting going?" she had launched straight at her sister as soon as Maggie broke off from her computer and sat down at the table.

"Nice table, by the way. Bit big for the kitchen, though."

"Thanks," Maggie had acknowledged, pleased with this small possibility of diversion. "I found it in that disgusting old shed at the bottom of the garden, when Graeme knocked it down last weekend. It's come up well, hasn't it?"

"Don't change the subject."

"I didn't. You asked about the table. It's very old, by the way, at least a hundred years. I stripped it down and varnished it back up. Goes well with my old kitchen chairs, doesn't it?"

"Now you're changing the subject."

"Yes, I am. But really, Fee, it isn't any of your business." She saw her sister's eyebrows rise as her mouth opened, and cut in quickly to head off the protest.

"Before you get wound up, think for a minute. I came back on the understanding that I'd be allowed to lead my own life. I know you mean well, but I know what I'm doing."

"Oh, really?" The response had been as sarcastic as Maggie expected. She knew that her sister meant well, but as far as Maggie

45

was concerned, Fiona suffered from the family "disease" of aiming low and taking no risks.

Fiona had married Graeme at the age of nineteen, had raised three children and had never known the stress of having to lose anything because of financial problems, or any other reason. Fiona had never had what Maggie called a job. She lived for her family, was a school governor, chair of the PTA, and was a stalwart of the local church. None of which Maggie aspired to. Maggie had looked at Fee, who now stood up with her tea mug and began to march around the kitchen table. There was no similarity between them. Fiona, tall, dark, and elegant, was always beautifully groomed and superbly dressed. Maggie preferred what Alice and Jack called the "lived-in" look when she wasn't working. They often joked that she was a prime candidate for a TV makeover show, which could never be said for Fiona. Fiona was practical and no-nonsense. She believed in what she could see and understand.

"So, what are you going to do?" Fiona had asked again, more vehemently. There had been enough real concern in the question to stop Maggie from getting angry.

"I'm going to do something this weekend, I promise." Maggie had refused to discuss the matter any further. The interaction had also made her decide against sharing with her sister her growing concern about the effect her research was having on herself and Alice. And as for what she had found earlier in the day when she had printed the photograph of the grave. She didn't know who she was going to confide in about that, but she was going to have to speak to someone soon, because it was all becoming too much to keep to herself, and Janice wasn't due back from the US for another two months.

Maggie decided she might as well give the library a try. It was still early, so she could put in a few hours before she had to pick up the children from school. Noleen called goodbye as Maggie left and shouted out something to her. Maggie returned the wave and tried to make out what Noleen was saying. It sounded like, "Beware the gorgon!"

Chapter 8

Twenty minutes later Maggie stood at the entrance to the ugly library building on the main square of Newport, a three-storey concrete block, much in keeping with the architecture of central Newport.

From the outside it didn't seem promising, but Maggie resolutely pushed open the glass doors and made her way to the reception desk, then to the second floor. As the steel doors opened, the reference room was directly in front of her; it was surprisingly impressive. Bright and light with ceiling-to-floor windows on two sides and row upon row of books, filing cabinets and long tables with computers and microfiche readers interspersed by new individual desks. Beyond the entrance to the right was an old wooden desk with a notice that read "Family History". The desk was unstaffed.

"Great," thought Maggie. "So, what next?" While she looked around uncertainly, she was approached by a tall woman in a black twinset, wearing black "librarian" glasses, and a badge that gave her name as Eileen. She asked, "How may I help you?" but with no conviction that she meant it.

"I'm doing family history research. Are you the person I should speak to?"

"No." The response was terse. "The local society has a desk here, but the person looking after it today has gone out."

"Do you know how long they'll be?" Maggie asked. "I have to be home for the school run. Is there anything you could help me with in the meantime?" She gave the librarian her most winning smile.

"More than my job's worth to interfere with them."

She shrugged her head towards the battered desk, but, seeing the disappointed look on Maggie's face, she relented a little. "I could show you how the microfiche readers work and where the records are. That will get you started." She glared defiantly at the empty desk. "That shouldn't cause a problem." Looking back, she raised her eyebrows in expectation of Maggie asking the obvious question.

Maggie didn't miss the expression or the strong emphasis on the "shouldn't" but decided not to pursue it, although she sensed from Eileen's expression that she would have been only too pleased to go into detail if Maggie had shown any inclination to listen.

"I'll leave a note on the desk to say where I am."

Maggie followed Eileen across the room to the table of microfiche readers on the back row of desks. A moment' instruction was enough for Maggie to pick up the basics of reading records, but a few minutes more elucidated that the births, marriages and deaths records were the same as those at County Hall.

"I've already been through those at the county archive. Is there anything else I can look at? The archivist said that you have all of the local newspapers going back to the 1870s?"

"Earlier than that," replied the librarian triumphantly. "Our staff have indexed the articles so you can look by subject and name, as well as by year."

"Wow, impressive." This was encouraging enough for Eileen to launch enthusiastically into an explanation of how to work through the indexing system, but all the time, she checked furtively over her shoulder at the still empty Family History desk.

Maggie decided to start looking around 1875. She had worked out that this would have been around the time that John and Ruth moved into their first farm. She didn't expect for a moment that it would have given rise to comment in the local newspapers, but it was at least somewhere to start.

Over the next half hour, she read through ten years' newspaper headlines, fascinated by many of them and determined that as soon as she had time she would come back to read them in more depth. She discovered the opening of the first Royal Porttown Hospital, paid for by public subscription and with the support and patronage of Sir Charles Knyghton, Earl of Monmouth, local Lord of the Manor.

Maggie had a particular interest in anything to do with the earl. His ancestral home, Knyghton House, one of the finest in the area, and possibly the whole of Wales, had been given to the Church when the family could no longer afford the upkeep and death duties and then turned into a boarding and day school for girls, which Maggie and Fiona had attended.

She learned that the incumbent earl in 1875 had been a respected local benefactor. But there was no mention of John Jones, farmer, of the community of Garth Hill. Then her eye was caught by a name she recognised, in a paper dated 1 June, 1883.

The heading was *Tragic Death of A Local Child*, and told of the accidental drowning of a schoolgirl, aged twelve, Esme Ellis. The article described the place of death as a local lake popular with children, known as The Pond, and gave a dire warning to parents to forbid their children to stray there unsupervised.

Maggie was immediately drawn to the story. She knew right away that this was one of the children whose graves she had seen a week ago, when she searched the cemetery for John and Ruth. It was the grave where Alice said she saw a funeral taking place, and close enough to the name that Alice had cried out in her nightmares almost nightly since that day. She had been shouting the name "Ezzy". Alice remembered nothing each morning. Indeed, she'd seemed calm and serene.

Maggie read through the information carefully, and nearly shouted out in excitement, limiting herself instead to a high-pitched squeak, when she found the first piece of information that gave her a clue about her family. Esme Ellis's father was a worker on the estate of local farmer, Mr John Jones, a well-known and respected resident of Garth Hill. So, there it was: the first piece of evidence of events in the life of John Jones's family. The first connection.

The squeak had not gone unnoticed by Eileen at the librarian's desk, and she walked across to see what was happening. She listened with interest, then read through the article herself. She suggested how Maggie might cross-reference the report with other articles about the tragedy, and about John Jones, and suddenly stopped in mid-sentence. The expression on her face dropped as her ears picked up the main doors' opening, followed by a cessation of noise from the other users.

Maggie picked up a strange noise coming from somewhere at the front of the reference room, behind the filing cabinets. It was a methodical clicking that moved along behind the furthest row of cabinets, then turned and moved down the next row, getting louder as it reached the row closest to Maggie and Eileen. Maggie saw the librarian's face tense the closer the clicking came to them. She watched, intrigued, waiting to discover the cause of the approaching noise and reason for Eileen's discomfort.

From behind the closest filing cabinet came marching at great speed a short woman, barely five-feet tall, sporting purple, six-inch stiletto shoes that brought her almost to Maggie's height. She possessed an hour-glass figure exaggerated with a huge bust, a tiny waist, well-rounded hips, and a thrusting walk that ensured that anyone would get out of her way as quickly as they could. Maggie was fascinated by the woman's face and hairstyle. Her jet-black hair was piled high on top of a small head in a coiffure and dressed with jewelled clips. She had a long, beaky nose, slightly protruding teeth, and high cheekbones. As she walked she led with her chin, which was in line with her bust. She was smartly dressed in a two-piece black designer suit, and immaculately made up. Maggie guessed her age to be around sixty.

She marched straight at Maggie and the librarian and stopped with a stamp of her feet in front of them. Her small, dark, and piercing eyes stared straight at Eileen, but she said nothing, just held up Maggie's note. Maggie waited to see who would give in first.

"This lady wishes to speak to you, Mrs… Trevear," muttered the librarian, turning to walk away, her shoulders hunched, defeated.

The woman smiled thinly at Eileen's back. She signalled with a sideways nod of her head for Maggie to go to the Family History desk. She walked round it and sat at the opposite side. Maggie left her microfiche and followed over to the desk as indicated, fascinated and amused, and a little awed. Here was Noleen's "gorgon".

"Well, what do you want?" There was neither preamble, nor introduction, just a cold stare.

"I'm trying to trace my family history and I need some help," Maggie began, but got no further.

"Well, obviously. Why else would you be here? Get on with it, then."

Maggie was thrown, not sure what she was supposed to say next. "I'm not really sure where to start."

"Try the beginning." The tone was bored sarcasm.

Maggie surveyed the woman for a moment. She was annoyed by her aggressive rudeness, and was half-inclined to leave. But something stopped her. She was not put off by oddity, and this little woman was certainly odd. She was not easily rebuffed, either. Then Maggie Gilbert made one of the most important decisions of her life. She decided to stay and tell her story.

Chapter 9
May 1909

Three days after John's funeral Ruth arose before dawn. Despite no longer having to worry about being there for whatever John needed, it was too soon to break the habit of being at the heart of the morning hustle and bustle. She turned up the lamps in the hall, then went to the kitchen to make a pot of tea. When it was brewed, she poured it out into her favourite Queen Victoria jubilee china cup, then walked to the drawing room.

She left the curtains closed at the front but opened up the back of the room. The maid would arrive soon to light the fires and prepare breakfast. Maud and her children would wake at any moment, but for now the room was cold and empty, and silent, apart from the ticking of the grandfather clock in the hallway.

Ruth pulled her old shawl, in which she had wrapped herself every morning for innumerable years, tightly around her shoulders and sat in the rocking chair facing the garden at the back of the house, waiting for dawn to unfold before her.

The shawl had been a gift from John, to mark the first anniversary of their earliest smallholding. How proud she had been to receive this token of their growing prosperity. In those days, despite being so much more financially comfortable, they were still not accustomed to the luxury of buying a spontaneous gift.

He had used a journey to market in Cardiff to buy it for her, and had taken great care to buy the best he could find. It was beautifully woven and fringed in red, green and gold, made of the best Welsh wool.

At first, Ruth refused to wear it except on special occasions. She felt a little scandalised by what might be viewed by others as a sinful waste, knowing how some people thought at chapel. John had laughed at her.

"When did my proud girl become so worried about what the old ones will say?"

She had been angry with him. "You expect me to flaunt luxury in their faces?" With that, she had flung the gift back at him. "You know what they'll be saying behind our backs!"

She smiled now, remembering his contrite expression and how far she had allowed him to go in his apology before she'd stopped him. Then she'd smiled and promised to wear it every Sunday and on her birthday.

Now her shawl was threadbare, the colours hardly recognisable, and it barely kept her warm. But the love that had bought it sustained her always, particularly recently. As she clutched it around her shoulders, she bowed her head, closed her eyes, and tried to remember the comfort of John's embrace. But no comfort came. She stopped and looked up through window. He was gone. No point reminiscing. She had to carry on without him, and this didn't help.

The first light from the east lit up the top of the mountain and was beginning to spread down towards the house. A jangle and thump told her the front door was being opened. Cerys, their maid, had arrived. Soon the daily flurry would begin, but Ruth still had a little time to herself. She shivered slightly. Although it was May, icy dew covered the lawn and the fields.

Ruth caught sight of herself in the window and sat forwards, to examine her reflection. *I'm an old woman*, she thought in surprise, noting the strands of grey in her dark brown hair and the lines on her face. The strain of the last six months, from John's sudden illness to his death, had narrowed and pinched her face. She'd tried to hide it from him as much as possible, show him a calm, smiling façade, and speak quietly and with as much dignity as she could manage. She hoped he hadn't noticed how tired, how grey she became as his illness intensified. In the latter stages, his pain became so excruciating that most of the time he had been insensate from the laudanum. *Just as well*, Ruth thought grimly.

The cancer had attacked from the inside, growing out of his intestines in a monstrous carbuncle. Eventually, barely able to eat or drink, he shrank to a shell of a man, hardly recognisable as human. His hair fell out and the pain twisted his face into a grotesque caricature of an animal begging to be put out of its misery.

As she watched this relentless decline, Ruth fought to keep in the forefront of her mind the splendid figure he had been when they met. Not tall, and with a strength of character that marked him out. She had admired his full head of dark brown hair, his beautiful moustache, the way his chin was always raised. His demeanour gave him the look of a confident, self-assured man. Some thought him high-minded and aloof, but Ruth had discovered a quiet sense of humour and shyness.

She also came to know that when John made up his mind about something he was unmoveable, truly believing in his own sense of what was right and just. Ruth never blamed John for his implacability, even when it caused him to take the wrong course of action, with disastrous results. She believed, now, that he had come to regret his refusal to change his mind, although he never said so.

She was several years younger than John and little more than a girl when she married him at eighteen. Now, she was a

56

fifty-five-year-old widow. John left her well provided-for, but she realised that if she had the constitution of her maternal family, she, too, would live into her eighties. That frightened her. The thought of thirty years without him was unbearable. Ruth knew herself to be a strong woman, in body as well as spirit. After a farming life and six children she was still sturdy. But the strain of John's illness had so worn her down that she had lost a great deal of weight. Lately, she found herself struggling to walk far before shortness of breath forced her to rest. She had to regain her strength quickly, particularly now that she had something to do. Something that she could not have done when John was alive.

The clock in the hall chimed seven. She could hear movement above. Evan, Ruth and John's youngest son, would be up and preparing for school. An industrious scholar, he was determined to make up what he had missed recently. He wanted to be a schoolmaster and needed to take his matriculation exam in a few weeks' time.

James called out to Maud, and their children. They would soon be here, expecting to see her at her place in the kitchen with Cerys, darting around, directing the preparation of breakfast. With a firmness of purpose that she struggled to feel, Ruth breathed deeply, planted her feet on the floor and stood.

Chapter 10

Two hours later, the house was silent. Breakfast had been muted, the shock of John's death still causing them all to speak in hushed voices. During prayers, as well as remembering John, Ruth added another name. "We remember Alice and pray that she is well."

This was a sudden decision. Ruth saw the looks of surprise dart between Maud and James, and the puzzled look on Evan's face. The children knew that their grandpa was gone and that they must be quiet to respect the adult grief. They didn't ask who Alice was. Nana Ruth didn't offer any explanation, and the expressions on their parents' faces told them that this was not a time for being inquisitive.

James left first for his law office, kissing Maud and quickly whispering something to her. Maud herself departed shortly after to take the children to school then going onto a chapel meeting, followed finally by Evan, who still wasn't speaking much.

As the youngest child, born fifteen years after his closest sibling, Evan had to fight hard for his parents' attention, and soon stopped trying. A naturally quiet boy, he rarely confided in them. John had worried about him, but Ruth recognised that the boy had inherited his father's implacably decisive nature.

Evan decided to become a teacher and only a catastrophe of immense proportions would prevent him achieving his ambition.

One more year at school and he could attend Cardiff College, the first of his family to do so. Ruth was so proud of his achievements. Her father, William, and John's father, Old John, had both been unable to read or write. Ruth herself had not had the benefit of schooling but had been taught by John after they married.

By the time the clock chimed nine, Cerys had finished washing the breakfast dishes and could be heard upstairs singing to herself as she made beds and tidied the children's toys. Ruth returned to the sitting room, back to her favourite position at the window.

The sun was now high above the back of the house lighting the crest of the mountain. It was a particularly clear day, the air cold and clean, which meant that Ruth could see the mountain in detail. She could make out the paths that ran from the base of the medieval mound at one end of the mountain range. Others ran in and out of the copses, whose trees were turning a fresh shade of green. Her eyes followed the dark brown lines into and out of the trees, winding across and up to the far end of the ridge where no trees grew, until they disappeared into what she knew was a narrow gulley away to the right. In the centre of the fold was the mountain pond. There Esme Ellis had drowned.

It had been so long since Ruth had thought about Essy's death, and deliberately so. John had been relentless, as always, his voice rising in what sounded like anger, but Ruth suspected was fear. "We will not discuss it, now or ever, wife. We must accept that Esme's death was an accident and that Alice has gone. There is nothing to be gained from constantly looking backwards. It troubles the other children. I forbid it!"

Eventually, Ruth put all questions from her mind. At John's insistence, she tried to find peace and forget – accept that her daughter had died and that they would never know what had happened. But every year something brought Alice's memory back to her.

Ruth never forgot Alice's birthday or special events. Like the day she would have finished at the board school and moved to the senior school. Or her and John's summer outing on the *Waverley*, the trip Alice had been so excited to make across the Channel. That had been Alice's twelfth birthday. Ruth had enjoyed the day, but neither spoke of the shadow that sat on the deck between them. Secretly, Ruth had never accepted that nothing more should be done to find Alice. As time went by she forgot more often, but never completely. John never spoke of his lost daughter. It was the one subject in their lives that was a barrier between them. The younger children were told that they had a sister who died. None of them pursued the subject. Most families they knew had lost at least one child, through accident, sickness, or other tragedy. It seemed normal.

Now, John was gone and Ruth could think about Alice again. She expected to feel some disloyalty, some guilt, planning this so soon after her husband's death. She was surprised to find that she felt no such emotion.

Sitting quietly in her chair in the calm peace of her home, Ruth accepted that the incident at the funeral had come from her exhausted grief. She had been thinking a lot about Alice during John's last days and the incident at the graveside confirmed to her how much she always hoped that Alice would return. But Alice would be thirty-six years old now, a mature woman. Not the child that Ruth had seen.

"I do not believe in ghosts and spirits. These are ungodly thoughts," she told herself sternly. But something in the deepest, most secret part of her mind wouldn't let it go. Perhaps, this was Alice's spirit returning to be with her dada?

"No!" She spoke out loud, emphatically, much to the surprise of Cerys who had just come down the stairs and dropped the dusters she was carrying.

"Should I not have come down, Mrs Jones?" the girl asked with a sob in her voice, as she crawled around on her hands and knees at the bottom of the stairs gathering up the pile of dusters into her apron.

"I'm so sorry, Cerys," replied Ruth, hurrying out to her. "I was just thinking aloud, not shouting at you." She saw the tears. "No need to upset yourself." She patted the girl gently on the back and gave her a handkerchief. "Come, now. Nothing harmed or broken. Take the dusters back to the pantry. We'll put the kettle on the hob and make ourselves a pot of tea."

Nodding and smiling, the girl blew her nose and trotted into the kitchen.

So, like her sister, Ruth thought, *as far as I can remember. And just as quick to tears.*

Five minutes later they sat in the kitchen, at ease, facing each other across the table. The table was too big for this new kitchen, but Ruth found that she couldn't bear to part with it when they'd left the farm. Alice had sat there, once.

"Cerys, how is your mama going along?"

"Much the same, thank you, Mrs Jones. She doesn't know any of us no more. But she talks a lot about the past, before I was born." Cerys paused for a moment, her head down, peering at the bottom of her cup. Without looking up she continued, "She keeps calling me Esme."

Ruth could see that the girl looked worried.

"You look a lot like her, Cerys," Ruth smiled at the girl. "And your characters are much the same."

"I… I didn't know her, of course, me being born so long after she died. What was she like, Mrs Jones? Dada would never speak about her. He got angry if anyone mentioned her name. But lately Mama has said some funny things, so I wondered, you know… what was she like, our Esme?"

"What kind of funny things, Cerys?"

The girl looked embarrassed. "Just odd things, Mrs Jones. She keeps saying that she wasn't there."

"Who wasn't there?" Ruth's legs trembled, hearing this again after so long. She wouldn't miss her chance this time.

"I don't know, ma'am. That's what she says. She calls out, 'Essy, Esme Ellis, are you there?' and then says, 'She wasn't there'. But I don't think she was talking about our Esme."

"What makes you think so?"

"There's a funny tone to the 'she', disapproving. Different to when she calls out for Esme. Then she sounds a bit frightened. And she talks about other people, and school, Mrs Jones. Names she says. Mr and Mrs Pugh, Miss Probert, Mrs Morris, Elsie Morris. Then she says again, '*She* wasn't there'. It seems to upset her." Cerys paused, turned her head away and sipped her tea, still glancing nervously at Ruth out of the corner of her eye. "She said something to me yesterday, too. Can I tell you?"

"Of course." Ruth was riveted. After so much time, just hearing the names brought it all back. And she had a feeling that she was about to learn something important.

Cerys drew in a deep breath. "She grabbed my arm and said to me that I mustn't tell anyone, because all of her children would be taken away. I couldn't understand why she was saying that, because I'm the only one left at home."

This was not what Ruth had expected and she fell silent. Cerys was staring at her, eyes wide, expecting some reaction, worried that she had told when she wasn't supposed to, but clearly needing some reassurance.

"I think, Cerys," Ruth replied, choosing her words carefully, "that your mother thought she was back at the time of Esme's death and this might have been something that someone said to her. Did she seem to think that she was talking to you, or to someone else?"

"I couldn't tell, ma'am. She wanders so much in her mind these days. What do you think?"

Ruth didn't want to disturb the girl any further, but wanted to know more. "It was a bad time for all of us, Cerys. I had a living child before William, you know, a girl, called Alice." It was clear from Cerys's widening eyes that she hadn't known. "We don't talk about her because she didn't die. She disappeared."

Cerys's mouth turned to an "ooh" then opened to ask something, but Ruth pushed on.

"Your mama was made very ill by Esme's death, and then by my Alice disappearing. Your dada had to look after all the children and keep working. I know he found it difficult and sometimes he had to leave the children alone when he was at work. So, someone may have said something cruel to your mama. You wouldn't expect such things when someone has lost a child, but at such times you find out what a cruel place this world can be."

Ruth found herself thinking back to the reactions she and John were subjected to when Alice disappeared. "There are good people, of course, kind and generous and helpful, like so many at our chapel. But there are also those who get pleasure from hurting. I wouldn't be surprised if your mama found this. I remember it, as did my husband."

She could see that the girl was hanging on every word. "Don't worry yourself about it, Cerys. As you say, your mama wanders in her mind. Would you like me to come and see her?"

Cerys's small, heart-shaped face lit up in a great wide smile in which Ruth at once recognised Essy. And it reminded her of something that she had forgotten for many years.

"That would be lovely, Mrs Jones, if you are ready to go out, that is."

Ruth nodded. "I think I may leave the house to visit your mother without anyone feeling too scandalised."

"Aunty Bella is there all day till I get back. I'll let her know you're coming." Cerys made to get up from the table, but saw that Ruth was about to speak again and paused, half standing.

"Cerys, would you like to see what Esme looked like?" The girl looked surprised, and puzzled. "I would, Mrs Jones, but how can that be?"

"Because I have a photograph. I haven't looked at it myself for many years. I have it locked away. I'll visit your mama tomorrow, after you return home and I'll bring the photograph with me."

"Lovely, Mrs Jones." Cerys beamed. "Shall I get on, now? I still have to finish sweeping the bedrooms."

"Yes, thank you, Cerys. Let me know when you have finished."

The girl stood, rinsed her cup and saucer in the sink, and left them on the draining board. Then she skipped out of the kitchen and went upstairs, humming to herself.

Ruth sat motionless at the kitchen table. She was taken aback by the forwardness of her own proposals. She shouldn't be going out, even to visit a dying woman, for at least a month. And then there was the shock of remembering the photograph.

She had put the photograph in the trunk with Alice's things, at John's insistence, never to be looked at. She had looked at it, secretly, many times before they moved from their old farm, but it gave her so much pain. As the months, then years, went by, she decided to put it away for good. Now she realised that it was at least ten years since she'd last seen it. As much as she retained an image of Alice as she was when she disappeared, getting the photograph out again was not going to be easy.

But she had promised Cerys and was now bound to find it. She would have to do it today, before everyone came home, so she could regain control over herself before they realised that anything had happened. She allowed Cerys to finish her work early, sending her off after lunch with a promise to return home with her the next day. With a smile the girl waved goodbye, the other hand clutching at her black hat, which the wind was trying to whip off her head. Ruth waited until Cerys was out of sight, then closed and locked the door. She had about two hours before the children and Evan came home.

Chapter 11

When she had composed herself, Ruth took the key from behind the kitchen door and walked upstairs. There was no light in the attic so she took a small candle. The entrance to the attic was always kept locked, to deter the children from exploring where they might hurt themselves. At least, that had always been their excuse. In truth, she was afraid that someone would go up and find the trunks.

The door had not been opened since shortly after they had moved into the house, and the large iron key was stiff in the lock. With a few forced turns it clicked. Ruth opened the door and began to make her way up the stairs. She rounded the bend at the top and faced the second door, to the attic itself. With a shaking hand, she turned the knob. The attic door swung open.

Stuffy, musty air attacked her nostrils. At first she could see nothing, so stood for a minute to accustom herself to the faint light given out by the flickering candle. Across the attic she could just make out the shape of the trunks.

She knew that the floor was firm and there was nothing to trip over. But even so she walked across the floor tentatively as her legs were now trembling so badly that she had to force one foot out in front of the other.

It seemed to take an age to walk the few yards of the attic to the far end, her goal becoming clearer with each step. By the time she stood in front of them her breath came in sobs and shakes. Emotion at what she was about to see engulfed her, and she sank to her knees in front of the larger trunk , placing the candle carefully on the floor. She knew she would have to open it quickly and look through its contents. If she didn't act now she would be lost, and be forced to make an excuse to Cerys. With shaking hands, she snapped the lock and flung back the lid.

"Oh, my dearest child!" The words burst from her in a flood of emotion, escaping like a vent of steam.

The first thing she saw was Alice's school dress and pinafore, the clothes they had found in the pigsty where Alice must have waited and changed after school, before setting off. Ruth was transported back and the old pain stung like a hot needle as she remembered how she had heard a noise and gone outside, but done nothing. If only she had called out, Alice might have come out of her hiding place and run to her.

"We could have dealt with anything, Alice," she wailed quietly in the darkness, "however bad it was."

But she had done nothing and was now left with only a set of neatly folded clothes, locked in a trunk for a quarter of a century. She began to sob but caught herself and wiped the tears from her cheeks.

Ruth knew that the photograph was here. The other trunk contained keepsakes that had been precious to Alice and a copy of the newspaper in which Alice had seen the advertisement for the *Waverley*. She remembered now that she had put the photograph in the bottom of the larger trunk. She rummaged through the clothes, finding stockings, dresses, boots, and hats, each one with its own memory. She dug further in and searched frantically with her fingertips, until at last she found the edge of a piece of stiff paper. She pulled it out and stared at it in the gloom.

Even after over twenty-five years, with almost no light, her eyes instantly found Alice, second row up, third from the left, in her school clothes, hair combed neatly, staring solemnly into the camera. She gently ran her fingers over her face. Unchanged in her memory, small and beautiful, her first and most beloved daughter. Just as she had seen her three days before at John's graveside. And there, sitting next to her, with her small, heart-shaped face and dark hair tied back off her forehead, was Esme Ellis.

"Side by side, as always," she whispered.

She couldn't make out any other details. Making sure that the clothes were all neatly folded again, she closed the trunk, put the photograph in her pocket, blew out her candle and made her way back downstairs.

She placed the key on its hook behind the kitchen door as she heard children chattering as they walked up the path to the front door. Composing herself quickly, Ruth put a smile on her face and pushed Alice to the back of her mind, as the children told her news of their day.

Chapter 12

After supper, Ruth read Bible passages to the children until bedtime, then Maud took them upstairs. James went out to a chapel meeting. Evan was in the kitchen, studying for his forthcoming examinations.

"Say goodnight to Nana Ruth," Maud instructed them as they stood in the doorway of the living room, where Ruth sat, as ever, in her chair.

She smiled at the children and beckoned them for a kiss each before they ran up the stairs to their rooms. She pulled her shawl, which she realised she had not taken off since the early morning, tighter around her shoulders. Now she was alone and unlikely to be disturbed for at least an hour. The light was fading, the hills turning a deep green. A barge, pulled by a strong white carthorse, slid silently past the house at the bottom of the garden. Ruth watched as the bargeman led the horse along the canal path, expertly navigating it under the bridge and out of view on its journey to Newport. There was no sound now except for the hollow ticking of the clock in the hall. Ruth reached into her pocket, fighting her own sobbing breath as she stared at the photograph.

How stern and serious the children looked. Alice and Essy had been such happy, boisterous children that it had been difficult for them to pose for the length of time that it had taken the photographer to set up his camera equipment and instruct the children in how to comport themselves. It had been such a special occasion, organised by Richard Robinson before he temporarily left the district. Unprecedented, in fact. The photograph was to be displayed in the school entrance, and copies were to be developed for parents who were willing to pay.

Several parents, including Ruth, had gone along to help keep order. The first two rows of children were seated, being mostly the infants and junior girls. The older boys stood in two rows behind.

The photograph was taken in front of the school door. It was a cold winter day and a few of the smaller infants cried because of the cold, so were allowed to keep their coats on. William was one of them. Ruth smiled softly at his scowling face in the front row, his cold hands shoved deep into his pockets.

Next to William was Bessie Morris's younger daughter, Sara, holding a pendant hanging from her neck. Where was the elder daughter? Ruth searched the rows of faces and found Elsie Morris, at the far end of the row above Alice and Essy. The photograph had worn after so many years in storage and Elsie's face was almost obliterated. But she was still distinguishable by her long wavy hair tied with a ribbon and the caped coat that she was so proud of and had refused to take off for the photograph. She examined each of the children's faces, trying to remember names. But her eyes flicked back every few seconds to Alice and Essy. She hoped that Mrs Ellis would be alert enough to recognise Essy in the photograph tomorrow.

Glancing one more time before she put the photograph away, her attention was attracted by a figure standing at the end of the back row, barely taller than the children. Ruth looked hard at the face of the school teacher, Miss Eira Probert. At that moment something clicked into place, something that caused Ruth to speak out loud in amazement.

70

"It cannot be!"

She glanced up, but there was no response to her exclamation, so she returned to Eira Probert. The face and form were exactly as she remembered: short and wide, round shouldered, lightish hair pinned back tightly and held in a bun at the back of her head, almond-shaped eyes, open wide in that unnerving, unblinking stare, the small, thin-lipped mouth, and almost no chin.

Exactly as Ruth remembered from twenty-six years ago, and exactly as she had looked when Ruth had glimpsed her in the crowd at John's funeral just three days earlier. Watching. But how could that be? Miss Probert must have been in her mid-forties back then, so she should be around seventy years old now. But the face at the funeral was that of a forty-year-old.

Ruth stared at the picture before her, remembering the lizard-like eyes that once had been so close to hers.

She was always watching us, she thought suddenly. *I couldn't see it then, but whenever we were within her view, she watched us.*

Ruth stood up hurriedly and put the photograph into the drawer of the dresser. She felt a tremor of fear. On the same day, she saw Alice just as she had looked when she disappeared, and the schoolteacher, also unchanged. Was this also the result of her imagination? But she hadn't thought about Eira Probert for many years. Why would she have imagined *her* face at the funeral, of all people?

Overwhelmed, Ruth knew that she couldn't keep it to herself. She would go to visit John's grave the following day where she might reflect quietly and talk to him. She could expect few other allies. But there were two people she trusted who would at least listen to her. Richard Robinson, of course. She would see him tomorrow. And her sister, Mary Anne, who had been such a great support when Alice had disappeared. Mary Anne had moved back to the family in Carmarthen, and Ruth decided to write to her immediately.

Mary Anne had been a great favourite of Alice. That brought her back to Alice and in her mind she saw the events of that last morning, when Alice had gone to school without looking back, never to return. The memory was too much, and, her emotions released, Ruth wept. Looking out of the window she caught her reflection, but was startled to see that the face staring back at her, with a puzzled expression, was not crying.

Chapter 13
May 2015

"Well, are you going to say anything, or just sit there staring at me?" the woman demanded of Maggie.

"I'm going to do both," replied Maggie, smiling at the woman, "but I do require that you listen and not interrupt until I'm ready for you to speak."

The woman's eyebrows shot up into her elaborate coiffure. She was evidently not used to this level of impertinence. Her carmine-rouged mouth opened, then pursed and she was on the point of making a cutting remark, thought twice and simply barked, "OK."

It didn't take Maggie long to explain what she knew of the history of John Jones and outline her problem, keeping it precise and factual.

"Let me see your chart. You do have a chart?"

"Not quite," she replied. "I've drawn something up myself. I've put in everything that I think could be useful. I'm afraid it's a bit crowded, but here it is." She fumbled around in her bag, found her file, and took out a scruffy page. The woman reached across to take the paper, and frowned. Maggie waited.

"Get a program," the woman said suddenly and without even looking up from the paper.

"Pardon me?"

"A program, a family tree maker. There are lots on the market. You can pick one up anywhere. Makes it a lot easier to read what's going on here."

She continued to stare at the sheet of paper, the little woman's lips moving silently as she traced her way through the chart, her head moving from side to side as she asked herself silent questions. Then her head shot up to look at Maggie, a knowing look, accompanied by a wide smile.

"Missing child – maybe more than one." Her forefinger stabbed at a spot on the page.

Maggie leaned forwards to look at the spot under the finger and felt a surge of excitement and anxiety. The missing child was on John and Ruth's line, right at the beginning. This made perfect, if worrying, sense.

"What made you realise that?"

"These two here were married in 1871, yes?" Maggie nodded. "This first child, William, was born in 1875. Not possible, you must see that." Maggie shook her head, her expression still puzzled. The woman looked exasperated. She sighed and rolled her eyes in a way that told Maggie that this level of ignorance was not unusual to her.

"If you think they were prudish about sex, think again. I could tell you some stories that would make your eyes pop. So, 1871, just married, no contraception. Nine, maybe ten months, maximum one year – baby!"

Looking at the chart and the other dates, the gap jumped out at Maggie, so much so that she was amazed that she hadn't seen it herself.

"Probably died early." She returned to the chart.

"I don't think so," Maggie said quietly. The woman looked up.

"Something is happening." It wasn't a question, even a hint. It was a statement of absolute fact.

"Yes. I'm not sure what, but there have been some strange… conversations with… with a member of my family. This must all sound very silly."

"No. It happens. Sometimes, not often."

"What?" Maggie found that she was tugging at the strands of hair that hung at her neck, so she let go and placed her arms on the table. "What happens? Please, I need to know."

She was relieved to see the woman's expression changing. She was no longer bored, cynical, or angry. Her eyes had softened and widened slightly with genuine interest, although her expression remained grim as she looked across the table. It seemed to Maggie that she was trying to make up her mind about something. Then she slowly reached out across the table, her hand outstretched. Maggie took her hand obediently.

"My name is Zelah Trevear. Would you care to join me for coffee?"

Minutes later they were seated in the café at the entrance to the library, each with a latte. Zelah also had a cream slice that she began to eat as soon as she sat down. Maggie noticed that some of the occupants of the café left when Zelah arrived.

"Your name, Trevear, is it Cornish?"

"Yes." The reply invited no hint of encouragement to continue, but Maggie went on anyway.

"I thought I recognised it. There's a place called Trevear in southern Cornwall. I love the place. I take my children there every year." She smiled at Zelah, who just looked back at her.

"Hate it. Never go there." She continued to devour her cake. Zelah settled herself in the chair, then picked up her cup, which she cradled with both hands and jutted her chin forwards at Maggie. "So, where shall we start?"

"OK. I've given you the bare historical facts that were all straightforward. Now for the stuff between the lines."

She started by giving Zelah a summary of her own history of how she had come to buy the house, which she felt was relevant to what was coming next. She was about to continue the story when Zelah, who had begun shuffling in her chair, interrupted abruptly. "What's your life history got to do with it?"

Stung, Maggie decided to let her have it right back. "I asked that you listen. You agreed. Let me finish!"

"Sorry," muttered Zelah. "I'm not very patient."

Maggie went on to explain how she had searched for the grave, and found the children, and then found John and Ruth's grave, and discovered that she had bought her own great-grandfather's house. This time there was no interruption. Then she told Zelah about Alice's belief that she had seen a funeral and seemed to make a connection with a girl at the funeral, but that Maggie had not seen anything there. She could see that Zelah's gaze was becoming more intense. She occasionally nodded and grunted as she acknowledged each new piece of information. Maggie spoke about her daughter's disturbed dreams of the past week, calling out what sounded like a name. "I thought it was Izzie, but now I think it might be Ezzy or Essy."

"Why?"

"Because this morning I discovered that a girl called Esme Ellis accidentally drowned in May 1883. I saw Esme's grave when I was searching and it's exactly where Alice said she saw the funeral. And today I also found out that Esme's father was working as a farm labourer for my great-grandfather John when Esme's accident happened. I think Ezzy may be short for Esme."

Maggie paused. Zelah was completely still. "I'm sorry," Maggie said tentatively, "am I being foolish to be concerned?"

"Depends on the part you've left out, doesn't it?"

Maggie opened her mouth, hesitated, then asked, "What do you mean?"

Zelah sat upright in her chair, bristling. "You seem like a decent woman. You want… no, you need my help. I'm not fazed by what you've told me, not at all, but if you don't want me to walk away now, tell me the rest. And don't fumble around. I accept everything you say, so you don't need to apologise. There's nothing foolish or crazy about any of this. It's serious, and feasible. So, you need to tell me everything, even the things you don't think are relevant; the things that may seem trivial, probably aren't at all."

Maggie smiled with relief at being taken seriously, but now she wasn't sure what to say next. If she felt that it was all crazy what did this say about the woman opposite her who believed every word without question? Was she crazy too? *Absolutely!*, she thought, and grinned.

"What are you smiling at?"

"You!"

Zelah laughed out loud. It was a great bellow of laughter that caused the woman serving at the counter to look over at them.

"Fair enough. You aren't put off by me?"

"No. Not yet."

She was surprised to see that the woman's small face briefly screwed up, and Maggie thought that she detected wistfulness in the sharp features. It didn't last long.

"Most people don't like me. They think I'm rude."

"You are. But that's your choice. Are you always so combative?"

"I say what I think. I don't stop to consider the reaction. Never learned how not to do it like that. Too late to change now."

Maggie didn't agree, but kept that to herself.

"You said 'it happens' earlier. Now I've told you everything, please tell me what you meant."

Zelah replied slowly, "I believe in… a theory."

"Does it fit what I've described?"

"Yes, I think so." She hesitated for a moment. "I think that our physical inheritance from our ancestors doesn't just stop at hair and eye colour, and temperament. I believe that we can inherit memories."

"What, you mean genetically?"

"Yes." There was a short pause. "Scoff all you like!"

"I'm not scoffing. But I've never heard anyone propose that before. Is there any science behind it?"

"There is some research. It's difficult to prove because the people we get these memories from are usually dead. Sometimes it lies dormant for generations. I think your daughter may have genetically inherited memories that were dormant until she came to live here. You may need to talk to her a little more. Find out what *exactly* she's dreaming."

"I'm not sure about that," Maggie replied. "She isn't unhappy and doesn't seem to remember, so I'm reluctant to push it. I'm going to have to think about all of this."

"Of course. But, in the meantime, if it'll be all right with you, I'll look for your missing baby. I'll see what I can find out."

"That would be amazing. Thank you." Maggie checked the clock on the wall above the food counter and was surprised to see that they had been talking for almost an hour. "Damn, I'm going to be late collecting Alice. So, what happens next, Ms Trevear?"

"What happens next is that you call me Zelah. Can you get back here this Thursday morning?"

Maggie thought quickly. She was supposed to meet Fiona but she could put her off. "Yes. Elevenish?"

"Best meet in here, not the library. Too many nosy parkers there. Do you have anything else we can get our teeth into? Any papers left to you, any documents?"

"Nothing, I'm afraid." Maggie decided this was not the time to talk about the photograph. That could wait.

"Shame. Can't be helped, I suppose. What about relatives? Anyone else in the family you can speak to?"

"No. It's just me and my sister, who knows nothing about the family and isn't interested anyway. My dad never bothered with his family, so I don't know them. I expect there are some of them around, but with a name like Jones, I could be related to half the country!"

"No help at all," said Zelah with a straight face, so Maggie couldn't tell if she was angry or joking. "What about your house, in the purchase documents?"

"Not that I remember, although I didn't really look."

But something about the house *was* nagging at Maggie. "Just a minute. There is something. There are some old trunks. I think they are up in the attic. It's a long shot that they'd have been there since John and Ruth's time, but I'll take a look this evening."

"Excellent." Zelah jumped up and gave her hand to Maggie. "That's a plan, then. I'll see you here on Thursday. Here's my card. There's my telephone number, in case anything happens in the meantime that you want to talk about." She turned and marched across the café and out through the doors, the clicking of her heels fading into the distance.

Chapter 14
May 1883

As the first sign of morning crept over the mountain, Ruth slid down into her high-backed parlour chair. Her legs were shaking. She had paced around the house throughout the night, stopping at intervals to open the front door and listen for any sound coming from the farmyard. Once, just after midnight, she'd thought she had heard a noise and had run out into the yard. But after a few agitated minutes of intense listening, all she could discern had been the shuffling and grunting of the livestock. She'd retreated inside to resume her pacing.

John and the farm men had searched the surrounding farmland until the early hours of the morning. When the full moon disappeared behind heavy rainclouds and their flares were extinguished by the downpour, John accepted his helpers' advice that there was nothing further he could do, save resting and starting again at first light. Before collapsing into bed he made Ruth promise to wake him early. She had already made some breakfast for him and put food and drink into packages for the men to take with them the following day.

But now she crept quietly up to the top of the staircase, into their bedroom, and softly called his name. He woke instantly, glanced up at her and then desperately out of the window. Without a word he got out of bed and began to dress. After Ruth checked that the children were still asleep, she went down to the kitchen where the first of the farm hands had arrived. To her surprise, Mrs Ellis was there, putting the kettle onto the hob to make tea for the men.

"Thank you, Gwen. There was no need for you to return so soon. And you, too, Arthur. You must both be exhausted."

Mr Ellis nodded his head curtly and turned to help his wife, who responded for them both.

"We would like to do whatever we can to help, Mrs Jones." She added, "Alice and our Esme were such friends. I would like to be here, doing something. I have been unwell, but now my mother and our Gwenny are looking after the little ones."

Ruth smiled at her, realising how hard it must have been to walk back into this house for the first time without her daughter. She put her hand on Gwen Ellis's arm and, for a few seconds, the two women stood with their heads bowed.

John walked into the kitchen and began to speak with Arthur Ellis about where they should look, as three more farm hands arrived at the back door. Ruth invited them in and Gwen Ellis poured tea. Several more men appeared, whom John had evidently not been expecting.

"We've come from Rhiwbina Farm, Mr Jones," one of them explained, twisting his cap in his hands. "We heard about your search and Mr Morgan said to come and see what we could do to help you, like."

"Tell Mr Morgan that we're grateful indeed. We shall need your help." The group hushed as one, as he turned to face them.

"Today we are going to search up the valley and down towards the port. We fear..." He hesitated and looked at Ruth, choosing his words carefully in the presence of the Ellises. "Our daughter has been deeply upset recently following the death of her friend Esme.

We fear she is in a most unhappy state of mind and has run away. We cannot understand why this is, or where she would go, but if she was outside in last night's rain, she will be soaked through, hungry, and cold."

"I've spoken to our local police constable and he's bringing help up from the port. I have informed him that today we will organise our own search of the local land, which he approves as we know this area better than the constabulary. I shall take one group to search in the direction of the port. Arthur Ellis will take the other and work up the valley towards the disused mine shafts." He paused, licked his dry lips, and swallowed anxiously.

"If it becomes necessary to search around the active shafts, the police constable will make arrangements with the owners. I have a photograph of my daughter here. Please look at it." He placed the photograph on the table, pointing to Alice, and had each man look at her face. "My wife has made up parcels of food for us. Please make the best use of daylight. We'll meet back here again at the end of the day, unless of course there is any news to report before then."

As he finished speaking, Ruth stepped forwards and handed out the packets of bread and honey, cheese, and oat biscuits. The men began to speak in low voices amongst themselves until Arthur Ellis called them together and announced that his group would leave immediately. Arthur nodded grimly to his wife, , and led half of the men out of the kitchen.

Ruth brought John his scarf and coat, and a package. As he put his coat on she spoke to him in a low voice. "You'll need this for Alice." John glanced into the package and saw Alice's winter coat. He squeezed Ruth's hand for a second, and was gone with the second search party.

In the silence of the empty kitchen Ruth and Gwen gathered up the crockery, washed it, and returned it to the dresser. Then Ruth poured a cup for each of them and they sat down at the table.

"You look tired, Mrs Jones. If you would like to go and rest, I can stay here and look after the children."

"I'm sure you'd prefer to be with your own children, Gwen."

"Not yet, Mrs Jones. I would prefer to be out of my house, doing something. They keep asking for Esme."

Ruth heard the tremble and put her hand over Gwen's as the words came out in a rush. "I've tried to explain to them that she's gone to heaven, but they don't understand. And Arthur just shouts at them. Gwenny understands of course, but she won't even say Essy's name. I know we must try to bear, Mrs Jones, but some days..." Her voice trailed off into a barely-stifled sob.

"Has Mr Pugh been to see you, Gwen? Perhaps he can be of some comfort?" Ruth wasn't hopeful that Minister Pugh would be much interested in bringing comfort to one of the poorest families in his ministry, but she was still unprepared for Gwen's response.

"No, he's been nowhere near us... and I don't want him in my house, anyway!"

"Gwen? Not one visit from him? Surely he has sent you something?"

"Nothing, Mrs Jones. I think ..." she broke off and stared defiantly at Ruth, "I do not think that he is a nice man."

Ruth had never heard meek Gwen Ellis speak ill of a living soul. Gwen must have known that John and Ruth didn't have the best of relationships with the minister, or with the schoolteacher, or indeed the deacons. The accusations and arguments had become public knowledge and had caused Ruth much embarrassment and pain but she had spoken of her feelings to none save John.

They had decided to keep their own counsel, being newcomers in the eyes of most of the congregation, and remained unsure of who they could count as friends to trust. She was shocked to hear Gwen's opinion, but uncertain of what to say next. She was saved from having to think by a child's cry from upstairs.

"Walter is awake, which means that William and Maud will follow soon. I had better go up to them. I shall need to explain something to the boys about their sister." She left Gwen sitting alone at the kitchen table.

Half an hour later the three children were out of bed, washed and dressed and sent down to the kitchen for their breakfast. When Ruth got back there, Gwen had tidied up and was preparing vegetables at the sink, her head down. She didn't look up when Ruth came into the kitchen to feed the children.

During breakfast Ruth explained as carefully as she could to William and Walter that Alice had run away, and that their father was out looking for her. She also told William that he would not have to go to school, which pleased him. Walter, at five, was too young to understand that there was anything wrong. Two-year-old Maud listened attentively then continued eating her breakfast.

"Alice was crying before school," William said, smiling in satisfaction through a mouthful of bread, but the smile faded rapidly on seeing the horrified expression on his mother's face. He hurried on, "Sara Morris said something nasty about her. Is that why she has run away?"

"Sara Morris?" Any mention of the Morris family caused Ruth concern. "What did Sara Morris say to Alice, William? Don't be afraid to tell me. I shan't be angry." But William shook his head.

"Why won't you tell me? It might be important to help us to find Alice." She saw him glance up at Mrs Ellis's back, then he shook his head again. Ruth got the message.

"Let's take the children upstairs to play with their toys," she said quietly and led him out of the kitchen. When they reached the boys' bedroom she put Walter in charge of Maud on the floor with their wooden train. She turned to William, who was now sitting on his bed, picking at the edge of his eiderdown.

"You know you need not be afraid, William. Tell me what happened. I'm worried about Alice. We must find her soon and I know you will want to help your sister." Her voice was gentle but firm and William knew that he wasn't going to get away with anything but the truth.

"Well," he said, twisting the knot of bedding around his fingers, "some of the children have been saying things this week, since Essy died, things about Alice and…" He paused. Ruth could see that his hands were shaking despite his firm grip, so she prised them away, took his hands in hers, and smoothed his palms as she spoke to him.

"Always tell the truth, William. It may be uncomfortable, but it can never truly hurt you."

William gazed up at her with piercing blue eyes. "Alice didn't think so. She thought that if she told the truth she would get into trouble."

"Tell me what Alice said, William."

"It was yesterday morning, when we were walking to school, Mammy. She was being really slow, and she told me not to speak because she was thinking. I asked her what she was thinking about and she said that she was thinking about something that she saw, but couldn't tell anyone. I asked her why she couldn't tell anyone and she said that if she told what she saw, no-one would believe her and she would get into trouble. So, I told her what you always say about if you tell the truth it can't hurt you and she said, 'Not this time, William'. She was crying a bit and I asked her why. But she said not to ask her any more, because she was still thinking."

William hadn't taken his eyes off his mother's face and he stared at her in silent deliberation. Ruth let go of his hands and put her arm around him. As she listened to her son, Ruth had been thinking back over the past week and about Alice's behaviour. She was beginning to see a pattern, from the disturbed dreams to the strange conversation about having a twin. She was starting to comprehend that there was more to Alice's knowledge of Essy Ellis's death than Alice had told anyone.

"And what did Sara Morris say that upset Alice?"

"It was in the yard at playtime, Mammy. Sara was with her sister Elsie – I don't like Elsie, she's mean and cruel and she's been horrid to Alice ever since we came here. She tries to get her on her own and say bad things – and so do some of the other big girls. And Miss was there too."

"And what did they say?" Ruth guided him gently.

"They was talking loud and Sara Morris said that they wondered how Essy got the big hole in the back of her head if she fell forwards into the water. They was wondering if Alice had really got there too late."

"And what did your teacher say to them, William?"

"I think she said that wickedness was its own enemy, or something like that. I didn't really understand. Then she sent the girls away, but she was looking over at me and Alice and she knew that Alice had heard."

"Is that everything?"

"Well, Mr Pugh arrived then and he was speaking to Miss Probert and they were both looking at me and Alice. Alice was trying to play with me and take no notice, but she knew that they were talking about her. Her fingers were shaky. Then Mrs Morris arrived too, because she takes the girls for sewing. And she talked to them and then they were all looking at Alice and me. Did I do something wrong, Mammy?"

"No, William," Ruth said emphatically. "And nor did Alice, I am quite sure," she added, "apart from not being able to tell me or her father what was troubling her so much. That makes me sad. But don't you worry about it any longer. I must go out for a little while, so I want you to make sure that Walter and Maud play quietly. Mrs Ellis is in the kitchen and she will take care of you."

"Will you be a long time, Mammy?"

"No." She smiled at him. "Just an hour or so."

Her calmness reassured William. He got down from the bed onto the floor and joined in playing with the wooden train set with his brother and sister. Ruth took a deep breath, walked out of the bedroom and back down to the kitchen.

"Gwen, I have to go out to make some enquiries for myself. If you would stay here with the children, I would be most grateful to you. They are playing quietly upstairs and shouldn't trouble you. I am going to the school," she added, "to speak to Miss Probert."

Gwen looked up from the sink. Her stare was intent and she opened her mouth to speak. Ruth paused for whatever Gwen was about to say, but Gwen seemed to think better of it, closed her mouth and nodded. As Gwen turned back to the sink, Ruth said quickly, "You know that you can trust me, Gwen, if there is something, anything, that you want to say to me…" Gwen paused and looked directly at Ruth, pursing her lips then biting them. "Be careful, Mrs Jones."

"Of what? My Alice is missing. I need to know whatever there is to know, so we can get her back!" She spoke sharply, raising her hands in enquiry.

Gwen flushed and turned her attention back to the parsnips. Ruth saw tears starting in her eyes and knew that she had been too abrupt. She walked up to Gwen and put an arm around her shoulder. "Forgive me, Gwen. You are kindly helping me out when your own family is grieving, and I should not have spoken so."

"That's all right, Mrs Jones. I know how worried you are. But you should be careful what you say to them at school. They do not have your best interests at heart. And…" She broke off, her expression reddening and uncertain, frowning indecisively about what to say next.

"Gwen, it may be that you and I should talk soon, but for now I must go to the school. Thank you for your concern, but please don't be worried for me." She smiled reassuringly. "I shan't be disturbed by any… unkindness I may encounter."

Chapter 15
May 2015

Maggie had to run down the stairs and across the square back to the car park. Luckily the traffic hadn't begun to build up, so she was only five minutes late. But Alice was waiting at the gate in her hand-on-hip, bored-of-waiting pose.

"You're late – again."

"What do you mean, 'again'? I'm never late." Maggie quipped, ignoring the arched eyebrow and pout. "Get in quickly. Jack's waiting, too."

She had expected to tell Alice about her meeting with Zelah and what transpired, but as she drove home and the children chatted together, she found that she was reluctant to mention anything that might bring about a discussion of Alice's dreams. She decided to get home and through the usual routine of homework, dinner, , then relax and think through what she had learned during the day. She wondered whether she could avoid the subject of dreams altogether.

She wasn't able to follow up with her research that evening, as Jack needed help with a piece of history homework. He wasn't a great researcher or writer, so after a half an hour of sparring with him and batting back reasons why he just had to do one more thing before he got started, Maggie gave up any hope of going into the attic to bring down the trunks and instead concentrated on helping

Jack to write an appraisal of British military leadership during the Great War. She quickly became absorbed in the subject.

Maggie had accepted the straightforward, textbook opinion of history but, reading through Jack's notes, found that the reality was more complicated.

Much like my own situation, she thought gloomily, as she tried to explain to Jack how to structure arguments for the opposing opinions. Jack was supremely uninterested and secretly hoped that Maggie would do most of the work for him. As usual, she did.

She had planned to go into the attic the following morning, as soon as the children had been delivered to school. But during a disturbed night's sleep she had thought a great deal about the consequences of continuing with this search. At around four in the morning she had concluded that she should stop, resume her normal life, go back to work, and accept that the story was a mystery that would have to wait. After that she slept.

Daylight inevitably brought doubt about that decision too. Back home after the school run, she made herself a cup of tea and wandered around the garden to try to clear her mind of the confusion.

The morning was warm, the frosts of earlier in the month having subsided with fine weather predicted. The dew had dried and at last there was a smell of flowers in the air. Maggie was no gardener, but she had managed to bring the wasteland at the rear of the house back to a semblance of the lawn and flower beds that it must once have been. She had plans for a bigger transformation during the summer and autumn, but that was also behind schedule because of her family history research.

As she walked around the rose beds and wandered down to the bottom of the garden where the canal ran, she sat on the bench she had put there, and thought through her discussions with Zelah Trevear.

This woman was prepared to take her seriously and would be supportive and helpful, albeit in her own distinctive way. Maggie had taken a liking to Zelah so it would be good to have someone she could trust to work with. But could she carry on, knowing that those trunks were up in the attic but not looking at what was in them?

No, she thought, *I have to know. Now*. With that she jumped up from the bench and made her way back to the house, to collect the key, and go up to the attic.

This time the key turned easily in the lock. She had left a torch at the top of the stairs, which she clicked on. Deciding it was now or never, Maggie picked out a route across the dusty floorboards, and made her way to the cases. They were heavy-looking, old-fashioned trunks. And she had seen something similar before. Her mother had kept an almost identical trunk in a cupboard in which she kept old sheets and blankets, relics of the past that she didn't want to throw away. That trunk had been constructed from brown leather, solidly made, with big brass buckles, as were these. The trunks were matching, but different sizes, one large the other much smaller. She couldn't remember, but she thought the trunk in her mother's possession had belonged to her grandfather George, and was inherited by her father when George died. George had been John and Ruth's son. She thought Fiona might still have it. She could check later. It could well be the third of a set of three.

Carefully she dragged each trunk across the floor. They were heavy, and swayed alarmingly as she moved them. She pushed and half-carried them down the winding stairs, along the landing and into her bedroom. Whatever the contents of the smaller trunk were, they had rattled as Maggie had moved it and she was worried that she might have damaged something.

Maggie sat staring at the big brass buckles holding each shut. Now she had reached daylight she could see that the trunks were identical to her mother's blanket store. It was now just a matter of which to open first.

Both were filthy with dust and the buckles looked rusty. After a few minutes of pulling and straining, the first buckle gave way, followed more easily by a snap of the second, which caused the lid to fling back with the momentum of her struggles. A great wave of dust rose straight into Maggie's face that sent her groping backwards for a handful of tissues from the bedside table. Once her sneezing and coughing had died down, she saw that the large trunk held clothes, neatly folded and packed. She wanted to dive in, but common sense told her that these garments had been packed a long time ago, and there was a chance that they might disintegrate.

She remembered from some TV programme that, when examining historical artefacts, it was important to note the order in which they had been assembled. She scrabbled around inside the bedside cabinet until she found a notebook and pen, which she placed next to the trunk. Maggie gingerly put a couple of fingers on two corners of the first garment and gently shook it from side to side. More dust came out, but the fabric seemed in reasonable condition. Maggie unfolded it, to find that she was holding a child's dress made of grey, serge-like material. The design of the dress was plain, a high neck, buttoned at the back, with long sleeves.

As she picked it up, Maggie saw that another garment was wrapped with it, which she could now see was a white pinafore. Putting the two together, it was clear that this was a uniform. She wrote a quick description of each, carefully placed the two garments on the bed on the other side of the trunk. She unpacked two more dresses of a simple design, underwear of white cotton, stockings, two nightdresses, a coat, buttoned shoes, and a pair of stout brown boots that looked hardly worn. Taking care, she wrote a brief description of each item before laying out the garments on her bed. Her certainty increased that this was the wardrobe of a young girl of around nine or ten – her own Alice's age, and of a similar build.

Maggie didn't know enough about fashion history to guess the era in which the clothes would have been worn. Her best estimate was around the turn of the previous century. She would have to consult Zelah, who would no doubt turn out to be an expert in this, too.

Finally, at the bottom of the trunk, was a shawl. It was old and worn, the colours long since faded, but it didn't look as if it had belonged to a child. It had been wrapped tightly and Maggie thought that she could feel something more solid than wool at the centre. As the last fold opened, it revealed a largish, rectangular piece of card with a few words of miniscule, copperplate writing on it. She couldn't make out what the writing was, so she turned it over, and found that she was holding an old photograph. It had a name and date written in the same script: *Garth Hill School, January 1883*. This was a big clue and potentially dated the clothes. The photograph was black-and-white and partly faded. But it was still possible to make out details of the faces of the thirty or so children seated and standing in four rows in front of the dark wooden door of a whitewashed building. She surmised that the building was Garth Hill School. She noted how solemn they looked.

She recognised the uniform from the trunk on the girls in the photograph. As she scanned the picture she saw that the uniformity extended beyond the clothes. They all sported a similar pudding-bowl haircut; some of the boys wore a long jacket buttoned to the neck on which they wore at the breast pocket a dangling watch chain. Many of the jackets looked shabby, with straining buttons, which she guessed was the result of the wearer being well down the line of family members to inherit the school coat.

Then she began to examine the photo in detail, row by row, face by face. She was searching each face for any sign of a family feature that might help her to identify a child as a relative. At the second row from the bottom, third from the left, she stopped, mouth open, staring at two small girls' faces. She pondered what to do next, then stood up, went downstairs to the hall, picked up the phone, and dialled Zelah Trevear's number.

Chapter 16
May 1883

Ruth walked slowly down the lane, as there was still an hour to the start of the school day and she didn't want to linger around the schoolhouse for too long awaiting the arrival of the teacher. As she walked, she thought over the conversation with Gwen Ellis. Gwen was the meekest person Ruth had ever met, so she had been shocked by such an outspoken display of dislike of the minister. Ruth could understand the dislike. It had been an effort to keep her own face expressionless each week as she and John endured Pugh's sarcasm and spite so obviously aimed at them during his sermons. They had had many fruitless discussions, trying to understand what had caused this animosity towards them.

* * *

When they had arrived at the farm, less than a year previously, and introduced themselves to the local community they had been welcomed, albeit primarily as objects of curiosity. There had been questions about their past, where they had come from, and why they had chosen to move to the Two Locks area of Garth Hill.

The local shopkeepers and traders were, on the whole, friendly and as soon as their curiosity was sated they maintained a good relationship with the family. Whenever Ruth visited the shops and businesses surrounding the green next to the chapel, conversation settled down quickly to the daily matters of mutual interest. Garth Hill was a small but thriving community, and there was much to discuss. John and Ruth made it clear that they had no interest in local gossip or scandal. However, being the owner of the largest and most productive farm in the community, it wasn't long before John was sought after for his opinion on local matters.

By Christmas 1882, Ruth felt that they had become a part of the everyday life of the community. Then, quite suddenly, the minister, Richard Robinson, with whom they had developed a friendly relationship, was called away to his dying mother. His place was taken by Robert Pugh, a short, dark, stubby, middle-aged Englishman, from Herefordshire.

Pugh drew them into his circle, asked their advice, and told them how much he valued their friendship. It soon became clear that he only welcomed people who agreed with his point of view. If either of them ventured to offer an alternative opinion, Pugh became resentful and rude.

He was a man with a barely-concealed disdain for the Welsh. "The Welsh must learn", he would pronounce, "that immoral behaviour is not acceptable in decent communities".

Also, part of Pugh's close circle were the Morrises, Charles and Bessie. Outwardly, Charles Morris took his role as senior pastor seriously, but Ruth found that he always deferred to his wife.

Bessie Morris welcomed Ruth's confidences, shared her own, particularly about fellow chapel members, which were frequently no more than gossip, and made plain her disdain towards the poorer members of the parish. One conversation had goaded Ruth into a sharper retort than was wise.

"I'm surprised you allow your daughter to mix with the servant child, Mrs Jones. I would not allow mine to do so. Alice should not be so friendly with Esme Ellis."

Ruth let Bessie know that she had no such qualms. "Indeed, Mrs Jones. No offence intended, I'm sure. I was only trying to advise." But Bessie Morris's tone told Ruth that a great deal of offence had been taken. The resulting coolness between them became icier and for a while they avoided conversation. For Ruth, this would have been a satisfactory outcome. But for Bessie Morris, who brooked no argument on any matter, ascendency over Ruth became an obsession, as did finding out all she could about the Joneses.

John and Ruth were shocked at the start of the New Year of 1883 to learn that Bessie had gone back to their old farm, and then to the colliery where John had worked as a traffic manager, and even to where he had worked for the rail board. Disgusted as she was, Ruth began to fear that Bessie might dig far enough to find out what John wanted most desperately that no-one should know.

As she walked, she thought again what Bessie had insinuated in their most recent confrontation in January when much had been said that should have been regretted, but was not.

John had been dignified, as always, but angry. The anger had not been caused by Bessie Morris's spiteful insinuations about him, but by the support she received from the school teacher, who had added a direct assault upon their children, and upon Alice in particular.

He could tolerate Bessie's suggestions that he was not what he seemed, but when Miss Eira Probert hinted that Alice got her wicked nature from her father's family, that was too much for him. When he questioned Eira Probert's own background, her sudden

97

appearance at the school, and her suitability to teach, Ruth became apprehensive about what was developing.

Eira's insinuations had been vocally supported by Minister Pugh, the Morrises, and the other chapel elders. But when she claimed that she had been invited to Garth Hill with the support of Robert Pugh, Ruth saw Pugh's head twitch, and a furrow appear between his eyebrows, his eyes flickering questioningly at the teacher. Nonetheless, he had leapt to her defence, exclaiming so loudly as to silence everyone else gathered in the meeting room behind the chapel that Eira Probert was an excellent woman and had his total support. He had worked himself up to a fury, declaring that all the others were untrustworthy, and working against him.

John waited a moment in the stunned hush that followed, then smiled slightly and said, with a sideways nod to Bessie Morris, whose fat cheeks rouged as she stared defiantly at him, "I understand you, sir. But I am not satisfied. For I have daily witness of distressed children who were before happily involved with their studies. So, despite your excellent endorsement, I will make my own enquiries." flushed

Since that day, the Jones family and the aforementioned group had, by undeclared but mutual consent, rarely spoken to each other, maintaining a frigid public civility.

Ruth knew that Bessie Morris continued to make enquiries, going so far as to speak to a cousin of Ruth's at a chapel meeting in Cardiff to ask about John's family background. When they discovered this covert activity, John was angry, but Ruth assured him that the cousin had said nothing, didn't know anything more than any other member of Ruth's family, and had, after all, been loyal enough to inform Ruth at the first opportunity. With that they had to be content. John intended to write to the school board. However, the insidious attacks on Alice's and her friend Esme's characters and morals continued from Eira Probert.

If Essy hadn't died, Ruth knew that John would have taken further action, despite possible exposure and further detriment to himself. He cared not that requests for his opinion in the community had declined in the weeks before Essy died. He made this indifference clear to Pugh and Charles Morris, whom he was sure were behind it. What John didn't know, and which Ruth had found out from a conversation with the wife of the postmaster, who had heard it from the manager of the iron foundry, was that the coolness was due to questions about John's heritage. *Bessie had done her work well*, Ruth thought ruefully.

* * *

Deep in thought, her eyes fixed on the uneven ground, Ruth was jerked out of her musings by the strong scent of lilac that filled the air around her. She looked up and found that the whitewashed schoolhouse building was already in view. There were no children around. She had covered the ground too quickly and was early.

She saw, too, that she was about to reach a fork in the lane, where a smaller, rougher path led up the mountain, one of several that wound their way past cottages and smallholdings to the summit of the ridge, and to The Pond, where Esme Ellis had drowned.

Ruth had never been there, but Alice had described it as a favourite place of the children, because wild lovehearts grew among the trees just back from the water. Alice and Essy had arranged to meet at The Pond after school that terrible day to pick the flowers.

Now she realised that she had never questioned this aspect of Alice's story. Why had Alice been late meeting Esme? And, from what Ruth knew of The Pond, this path came out along the side of the water, but Alice had spoken about coming from behind when she had found Essy.

I must see this for myself, she thought and turned to head up the mountain.

The route was longer and steeper than Ruth had expected. After she passed some cottages and a few farm buildings, the hedgerows disappeared and the land opened up. The track itself became much rougher with both large stones and potholes, so that she had to concentrate on where she stepped, but when she looked up she could see that she was already quite high. Here there was no respite from the sharp wind that buffeted the heather and gorse that went to the top of the mountain ridge. Ruth pulled her shawl further around her shoulders and walked on resolutely.

She followed the twists and turns of the track into the gulley of the mountain that couldn't be seen from the valley below. There was only the sound of the wind among the plants and the intermittent bleats of sheep that scrambled to find secure footing among the gorse bushes. The wind caught loose strands of her hair and blew them into her eyes so that she had to pause to tuck them back before she continued. As the path straightened and rose up a short incline she got her first glimpse of The Pond, sheltered from the wind by the bowl formed in the mountainside.

What a lonely place to die, she thought, sadly.

The path was flatter and wider now, and much easier to walk along as she approached the water's edge. The Pond itself was roughly oval, around fifty feet long, and twenty feet wide, shallow around the edges, and deep in the centre. Grass and mud ran seamlessly to the water's edge except for two or three wooden walkways that jutted out into deeper water. A group of trees nestled against the mountainside close to where the path came in. At the valley side of the water was a large rock, which Ruth knew was where Essy had fallen in. She walked up to it and could see the bottom, about three or four feet below. She supposed that Essy had been standing or crouching down on the rock when she had slipped, hit her head and fallen in. But what had the girl been doing here? Alice had said that she and Essy had come to The Pond to pick the lovehearts, and they were in a small copse of trees which was about thirty feet away from the water.

Alice said that she had come up the path behind Essy, found her in the water and pulled her out, then had run back to get help. There had been no mention of flowers so Essy must have waited for Alice by the water's edge. But Essy had always been naturally nervous, so Ruth was surprised that she would have ventured over the water by herself. And how could Alice have been behind Essy if she wasn't in the trees? Something wasn't right, but she couldn't work out what it was.

She stood up and looked around. She took in the deep blue of the fading lovehearts that carpeted the grass among the trees. The colour drew her around the water and she walked slowly towards the trees, with a vague feeling of concern, suddenly imagining that the trees could be sheltering more than lovehearts.

Stop! This is foolish imagination, she told herself.

She walked past two prominent trees that stood like sentinels. Their trunks were almost touching from their bases to waist height, then separated, forming a Y-shape as they rose. Ruth stooped within the little wood to pick a few of the pretty flowers, but remembered that she had to go to the school and stopped. She turned and noticed that from this angle the twin trunks formed both a barrier and a perfect view of the rock at the edge of the water.

She walked again to the edge of the lake where she stood for a moment in sad contemplation of the fun that Alice and Essy must have had so many times here.

Chapter 17

The whitewashed school sat just off the main lane into the village and close to the central green. Around the green were the shops and post office that made up the village of Garth Hill. The school served both the village and the outlying farms, plus the growing number of ironworkers' children from the cottages that were spreading out from Newport. The children were all taught together in one classroom, with the small children at the front and the big ones assisting and sitting in a row of higher desks at the back.

Ruth walked up to the entrance door. It was locked. She peered through the glass circle in the top half of the solid wooden door for a sign of the teacher moving inside, when a voice close behind her ear made her turn quickly in surprise.

"May I be of assistance?"

Ruth looked into the blank face of the schoolteacher, Eira Probert. Eira Probert's small-eyed, expressionless stare bore into Ruth, who instinctively retreated a pace, pressing her uncomfortably against the handle of the door. She felt cornered. To add to her discomfort Eira stepped closer so that their faces were just inches from each other and Ruth could feel the other woman's warm breath on her cheek.

Eira had always looked pallid, and close up Ruth saw that her skin was pale and sweaty, like uncooked dough. For a moment Ruth thought that the skin was swirling. Her light brown, tightly bunned hair, seemed to be plastered to her scalp with something akin to animal fat. She gave off the aroma of a rotting carcass. Ruth felt sick.

"No wonder the children dislike her!" she thought. Then aloud: "I have come to speak to you about Alice and William, Miss Probert, and would be grateful if you would allow me five minutes of your time." She smiled weakly at the teacher.

There was no response in Eira's expression, but she retreated enough to allow Ruth to move away from the door. Eira produced a large iron key from her pocket, turned it in the lock, and they entered the school with Ruth taking the lead. Ruth was unable to hear Eira's footsteps and when she reached her desk and turned around, Eira was standing just a few inches in front of her.

Eira Probert's hands were clutched in front of her with her fingers pointing up to make a bony spire. She stared, unblinking, expressionless, waiting. Interpreting both her stare and the proximity as an attempt at intimidation, Ruth determinedly kept her feet still, despite a feeling of crawling flesh and a strong desire to step backwards. She returned the stare for **a** moment before she spoke.

"I think you know that my daughter is missing, Miss Probert."

Eira's head inclined, but she remained silent. Ruth detected a thinning of her lips into the ghost of a smile.

"I think you know something."

Eira hesitated, her mouth open and her eyes widened in surprise at the directness. Ruth pressed on.

"I understand you encouraged unkindness towards Alice yesterday when she returned to school. I would like to understand why."

She saw twitches in Eira's face as she blinked and shuffled backwards. Ruth, to her own surprise, moved a step towards

Eira, straightening her back and clutching her shawl closer to her chest.

"Well, Miss Probert? You spoke of 'sin being its own enemy' or some such. I believe this was in response to words spoken too loudly by Miss Elsie Morris."

Ruth held her ground and stared at Eira. The teacher looked down at the ground, then slowly up at Ruth. As her head came up the look of sheer malice in her face was unmistakeable and made Ruth's heart pound so loudly she felt sure that Eira could hear it. If the woman had looked at a child like this… But she had no intention of letting her know how nervous she was.

Ruth could see sweat appearing on Eira's forehead as her lips curled into a snarl. With a sudden sweep she raised her arm above her head. Ruth stepped back in alarm, convinced a blow was coming, when the door behind them opened, and the minister, Robert Pugh, walked in. Both women turned to see him framed in the doorway, staring in confusion. Eira Probert slowly lowered her arm, smiled at the minister, and turned a newly-composed face towards Ruth as if they had been engaged in nothing more than polite discussion.

"I cannot recall overhearing Miss Morris say something unkind about your daughter, or indeed any other child. I do not recall any such comment. Perhaps you should check the source of your information."

Pugh's face contorted into an angry frown. He marched to stand beside Eira, and folded his arms.

"Is there a problem, Mrs Jones?"

"Why yes, Mr Pugh. I believe there is." Ruth kept her gaze fixed on Eira. "Alice ran away after school yesterday and I have information that some hurtful words were spoken by Miss Elsie

Morris and," she paused to look directly at him, "by your own Miss Probert. I am here to ask her about this and if there was anything further that might have upset Alice so much that she ran off."

Pugh shuffled and moved his head from side to side. He usually responded to anything less than flattery with belligerent abrasiveness but this time he seemed to be thinking first.

"You have proof of what you say, Mrs Jones?"

"Yes, Mr Pugh. My son William overheard it all. He was witness to her distress."

Pugh's face reddened. "You are accusing Miss Probert on the word of a five-year-old boy?"

"Yes, Mr Pugh. And William is eight years old." Ruth spoke firmly. She was still looking at Pugh but at the edge of her vision she could see Eira's eyes flicking between the two of them, like an excited lizard.

Pugh jutted out his neck in Ruth's direction. "How dare you accuse Miss Probert on the word of a mere child! How dare you malign the Morris family!" He was so close to her now that each breath smacked into her face and she could see blood vessels colouring his cheeks. Ruth's legs were shaking at the viciousness, but she struggled to maintain an outer calm. She saw Eira smile and turned back to her.

"Miss Probert will tell you that I have made no accusation. I have reported to her what I have been told and have simply asked for an explanation." She turned back to Pugh. "I would remind you, Minister, that my child has been missing all night, and that my husband and members of your own congregation are even now searching, and that my concern is great. I expected more compassion from you, of all people."

If she had expected a softer response, it was not forthcoming. Ruth knew that he liked sycophancy from his supporters. He was about to lose control of his fragile temper. But before he could launch into a diatribe, the schoolteacher placed a firm hand on his arm.

"You must not let yourself be troubled so, Mr Pugh. I will answer Mrs Jones's questions. If there was any unkindness in the words spoken I was unaware. And I am sure that Miss Elsie Morris meant no offence. But there are many questions being asked. Perhaps you should consider how to respond?"

"I am not aware of any questions, Miss Probert. If they are indeed being asked, then it is done behind my back. However, I do know that Alice was troubled by something she had seen and probably didn't understand, and which has given her a serious fright. I'm sorry that she didn't confide in her parents, but I assure you that she will do so as soon as we find her. There are indeed questions to be answered."

"What are you implying?" Pugh's face contorted.

"I make no implications, Mr Pugh, merely ask questions, which seems to be what is happening around and behind me, if Miss Probert is correct. There is little reason to continue this conversation. I am going home to pray, and to await Alice's return. Then we'll find out what secret she was protecting. Miss Probert, William will not be attending school today."

Pugh made no move to let Ruth by, but gentle pressure on his arm from Eira made him reconsider. He looked at the schoolteacher, as if for permission. She nodded and he stood aside, but Eira remained in Ruth's path.

"Alice told you nothing, Mrs Jones, that would explain her sudden departure?" Ruth thought she sounded relieved. She shook her head and left.

Ruth entered the playground as the first of the children arrived for school and began to play sticks and stones on the grass. She walked rapidly past them, ignoring the curious glances. Once out of the schoolyard she walked along the length of the whitewashed boundary wall until she reached a secluded corner. She checked that no-one could see her, bent down, and sobbed until she was physically sick.

Chapter 18
May 1883

Although Alice knew that she'd been in the pigsty for many hours since nightfall, she wasn't sure of the actual time or whether or not it was safe to come out.

She had been lying with her head on the back of her favourite sow, whose piglets were snuggled up under them both. The sow's hypnotic breathing had sent Alice to sleep a few times and this last time, when she awoke with a start, it had taken a moment to realise where she was, and why.

Despite her determination to get away and shift the dangerous eye off her family, she was again overwhelmed with reluctance to leave. She considered the risk in telling her mother everything. She dug her nails into her arm to remind herself of why she was taking such a desperate measure. To give herself the courage to go on she thought about how she'd been so violently cornered earlier that morning at school. She saw herself, pressed against a wall, that face inches from hers. She remembered her nausea at the wet, putrid breath.

"You came back then, you stupid girl. Now you're going to jail for the murder of your friend. Not what I intended, but good enough. You won't like it there. Your family is going to suffer such agonies. And don't think about telling them, because no-one will believe you, I'm making sure of that."

Reflected in the centre of the pupils Alice saw her own face in wide-eyed terror. The smell was overwhelming, worse than anything on the farm.

"You're alone, just you and me in the whole of the world." She glimpsed a flash of red in the black pupils.

There was a pause, as her tormentor raised its chin, closed its eyes, and drew a deep breath in an ecstasy of satisfaction.

"Why do you hate me so?" Alice whispered.

"Hate is what I am, witless girl. Just hate. Your hate."

"Who are you really?"

"I am made this way and will remain so, thanks to your family."

"I don't understand."

"Of course you don't. I make you afraid, then you hate me. That's when I destroy you all, each time."

Then, as if nothing had happened, her tormentor walked away, leaving Alice shaking.

At that moment she had decided to run, believing that the only way to make her family safe was to go away and hide. She must sacrifice herself. That would help make up for Essy's death as well. As she sank down in the corner, she didn't know where to go, but wherever it was, it had to be now. As soon as she was able to sneak out of school, she ran home, crept past her mother and Gwen Ellis, and went to her room.

She found a scarf into which she bundled a dress and some stockings, a handkerchief and ten shillings that she had been saving for two years. Going through her drawers to decide what would be best to take, she found the newspaper article for the *Waverley* that told her that the boat would depart on Sunday morning. That was it. She could take a passage across the Channel to Weston-super-Mare and hide there. She had been hazy about what to do after that, but certain that something would occur to her. Perhaps it would be safe to come home.

After a few minutes of packing and listening to the distant talk between her mother and Mrs Ellis, she crept back downstairs, and ran to hide in the pigsty until dark. Before falling asleep with the pigs, Alice had tried to work out how she would get to Newport, and from there get on the steamer. She decided that it was best to follow the canal, as that ended up at the port. She had two days to think about it.

Now, gazing out into the pitch-black night, she was filled with doubt, with fear of the dark, and of what might be lying in wait for her. Whatever it was, it couldn't be worse than what was in store if she stayed.

"I have to go. I must go," she repeated to herself, chanting it in her head like a Sunday school prayer.

She crept out of the pigsty and carefully closed the gate, but the oversized latch slipped through her fingers. In the dead of night the sound was like a giant, clanging bell and Alice froze. Sure enough, a door opened at the front of the farm and she ducked down behind the wall. She held her breath as she heard footsteps move around the side of the house to the gate at the entrance to the courtyard. The steps stopped. Someone was listening. The steps were light and Alice thought immediately of her mother. If it was her mother and she called her name Alice knew that she would have jumped up and rushed into her arms, whatever the consequences. After a moment, the steps moved away and the front door closed. A tear fell from her eye. She wiped it away.

Clutching her bundle under her arm, Alice ran out of the farmyard and down the lane to the chapel beside the canal. She crossed the footbridge, and walked on the canal path, the beginning of her journey to the port.

Chapter 19

At first, the walk was easier than Alice had expected. The moon lit up the path and allowed her to pick her way over the stones and potholes without stumbling too much. But increasingly the moon disappeared behind clouds and a wind whipped up that made her shiver. After about an hour, she felt weary and cold. Looking for somewhere to rest she saw a gap in the hedge next to the path, with a small ditch in front of it. She squeezed in.

Not a moment too soon! Just as she settled down, voices carried on the wind towards her from the direction of the port. She made herself as small and inconspicuous as possible as the voices became louder. Trembling with fear, she pushed her head into her chest, praying that they wouldn't stumble across her. She had heard her parents discuss their outrage at the increase in drunkenness and violence in the area. Recently an inebriated man had fallen into the canal and drowned. If the people coming towards her were drunk, perhaps they would throw her into the canal, for sport!

When the voices were almost level with her, Alice could make out snatches of the conversation through the wind.

"I think… something wasn't right about it."

"Aye. Pugh said…"

"Man's a fool!"

"Ran away, though, but my girl says… Not fair, it wasn't."

Alice held her breath as the men passed and their voices faded away. She climbed cautiously out of the hedge. She had recognised the voice of Arthur Ellis, Essy's father, and he had called Mr Pugh a fool! The "runaway" must be her. They were already out searching. That must be Dada's doing. He might even have been one of the group. The sudden realisation of the pain she must already be causing her parents brought tears to her eyes. Perhaps her parents were strong enough to fight the terror, after all? No. She couldn't risk it. If they failed, her whole family would be broken, even the babies. She turned back in the direction of Newport and trudged on again on her journey.

The moon disappeared behind a bank of heavy clouds and a fine drizzle came down. At first it wasn't too bad, and she was able to keep walking. But the lack of moonlight made the darkness profound. She had reached a particularly uneven part of the path where she feared there was a risk of losing her footing and falling into the canal. She needed to stop to take shelter for a while, so she crossed the path to look over the hedge, knowing that there were houses and farms along the route where the bargemen would buy provisions.

Standing on tiptoe, and shaking the rain out of her eyes, Alice made out a light in a building not too far away. Perhaps it would offer some shelter in one of the outhouses, or in a barn? But as the thought crossed her mind, dogs barked loudly. She shook her head. Her father's dogs would have done the same, protecting the farm from intruders or strangers passing by. Another light appeared from within the building in response to the dogs.

"No shelter there," she thought dejectedly, returning to the path.

Rain was now falling steadily and the wind drove it into her face. Feeling cold, miserable and homesick, she found a gap in the hedge where she could squeeze in. She wound her shawl around her head to protect it from the stinging rain, and tried to sleep.

When she awoke the rain had ceased but the sky was grey. For a moment she struggled to remember where she was, while wetness penetrated to her body. Standing quickly, she found that the ditch she had crawled into had filled with water and had soaked her to the skin. Feelings of heat, cold, and clamminess brought her to her knees, and a sore throat made her cough and feel dizzy. When she felt steadier, she stood and looked around, checking for others on the path, but there was no-one. Now she could see over the hedge and along the path, she saw that there were no other buildings ahead, which meant nowhere to buy food.

The soreness in her throat burned so she risked a drink of water from the murky canal. The taste wasn't brackish, so she cupped her hands into the water and drank a few more mouthfuls. Then she smoothed the creases and mud from her dress as best she could.

Fortunately, she had pushed her bundle of clothes and small possessions well into the hedge and all had escaped the rain. Her spare dress wasn't too badly creased, so it would still be possible to be presentable when she bought her ticket for the steamer. She set off down the path.

The sun didn't come out that morning and the cold seeped into Alice's feet and hands as the heat intensified in her head. The walk was hard now, particularly on an empty stomach, and became a slow trudge. She needed to find something to eat.

When the sun finally appeared, Alice spotted some men in the field on the other side of the canal, workers who had stopped for a break. There was a bridge in the distance and they seemed to be laughing and joking with each other as they ate, so she decided to risk crossing over to ask if they had anything they could share with her. As she approached she saw that the men had seen her coming. The closest stood up as she approached.

"What do you want, beggar brat?" He turned and laughed at his friends.

"I'm not a beggar, sir. But I am looking for some food and wondered, please, if you might have something to spare?"

"Spare? For a beggar? Get out of here before we run you out!" He raised his hand and before she understood what he was doing, a sharp object struck her on the side of her head. The pain was terrible and she fell to her knees, crying and clutching her left eye, feeling blood. She looked up and put a hand out, but this just made them laugh again, and she could see them looking around for more rocks. She stumbled to her feet and ran, back across the bridge, stopping only to pick up her belongings before she bolted down the path, dizzy, bleeding and sick.

Glancing back, Alice could see that they were not following her, but pointing and laughing. Once she was out of sight she stopped as her lungs were aching for breath. She fell onto a patch of grass at the side of the canal, paralysed with shock. Putting her hand up gingerly to her head again, she felt blood streaming down her face. Now the tears came. With her free hand she rummaged in her parcel until she found her handkerchief. After holding it to her head for several minutes she checked and found that the bleeding had slowed, but touching the spot made her cry out with pain. Probing gently she felt a gash that stretched from her ear to her forehead, about two inches long and quite deep. Carefully, she dipped her handkerchief into the canal and washed away the blood but the wound started bleeding again, so she pressed the handkerchief into her head. Lying on the ground, filthy and bloody, Alice wept for her mother.

Chapter 20
May 1883

When there was nothing left in her stomach but foul-tasting bile, Ruth pulled herself to her feet. Her breathing came in panting gasps and she could feel a black lump in her chest that she feared was going to crush her. With great effort to control her gasping breath, her sobs subsided and she began the walk home. She walked without thinking, still in shock and not yet able to consider what had happened at the school. The sickness had left her with a dry mouth and her legs were shaking, so much so that she had to pause several times to regain her balance and her composure. She had to try to control her emotions before she saw Gwen and her children.

In ten minutes she was at the entrance to the farm, calmer but in need of something to take the bitter taste away. Her throat was so dry that she knew she would have difficulty speaking. She walked to the back of the farm and stopped at the well where she pumped a handful of water and swallowed it quickly.

In the kitchen, Gwen was at the sink. "Oh, Mrs Jones. I was beginning to wonder. Maud is asleep and…" She glanced around at Ruth as she spoke and was so shocked at what she saw that she rushed over to the door and led Ruth to the nearest chair.

"Whatever has happened, Mrs Jones? You are grey! Has someone hurt you?" She wrinkled up her nose as she saw the vomit on Ruth's shawl. "Let me get you something to clean that. Do you need a drink?"

"Just a little salt to clean my shawl, thank you, Gwen. And a cup of tea, if you would be so kind."

Ruth squeezed and opened her fingers and rubbed her hands together as she sat, while Gwen put the kettle onto the rack on top of the fire. As they waited for the kettle neither spoke. The silence was broken when William and Walter flung open the back door and hurtled into the kitchen.

"We saw you in the lane, Mammy! Do you have Alice? Are you staying home now?"

"Your Dada is still looking for Alice, William, but I am staying home until he returns with her." She smiled at the boys and Walter, satisfied with her explanation and smile, ran off towards the stairs, calling to William to come with him. But William remained, hovering uncertainly next to the range, watching his mother.

"Go with your brother, William. And please play quietly, so as not to wake Maud."

"Yes, Mammy." He moved towards the door into the small parlour, and turned back to look at her.

"Is Alice all right, Mammy? Dada *will* bring her home, won't he?"

"We must pray that he will find her, William." She wanted to give him the reassurance that he craved, but she couldn't. "Now go to your brother and sister."

She waited in silence, listening to his footsteps drag slowly up the stairs, where he stopped at the top for a moment, before walking to the nursery.

The kettle had begun to bubble and hiss. Gwen prepared tea for Ruth.

"Please take one for yourself, Gwen. We'll sit for a moment before I check the dairy."

"I did it earlier. Jane finished the milking. I've put your pot into the larder, and Mr Davies collected the rest half an hour ago. Jane has started on the butter, but she wants to talk to you about the cheese."

Ruth rested a hand on Gwen's arm. "I'll speak to her as soon as we've had a cup of tea. Then I must help Ifor move the sheep. John wants them in the top field. William and Walter can come to help. Could you…"

"Of course, I'll mind Maud."

"Then you must go home, Gwen."

Gwen responded firmly. "No, Mrs Jones. Gwenny and my mother can manage quite well. I'll wait until Arthur returns. Now, here's your tea. I have the salted cloth, so if you take off your shawl, I can work on it."

Ruth took her cup from Gwen's hands, placed it on the table in front of her, then unwrapped her shawl and handed it to Gwen. Gwen sat and rubbed vigorously at the stains, occasionally glancing at Ruth, as if waiting for a conversation to begin.

"I did indeed meet with unpleasantness, Gwen," Ruth began, "as you expected. It was shocking, but perhaps not unanticipated." Gwen was about to remonstrate, but Ruth held up her hand.

"Later I shall speak to my husband about the response I received at the school. But I would ask you not to speak of this in the village. I know that you don't gossip," she smiled at Gwen, "or ever speak of our family affairs no matter how hard others pry, and I thank you and Arthur most gratefully for that."

"I would never do so, Mrs Jones. But…" Gwen stopped and bit her lip, but shook her head, and returned to the shawl.

"If you mean people press you, I know that," Ruth cut in. "It will be hard in the coming days, too."

"No," Gwen interjected. "It's just … I don't understand…"

"Would you like to explain, Gwen?" Ruth probed gently, mindful of Gwen's circumstances. Gwen thought for a moment as she battled with her thoughts.

"I would like to think on it a little further, Mrs Jones, if you don't mind. Perhaps later. Or anyway, it is just that…" she paused, then spoke again in a whisper, so quietly that Ruth thought that Gwen had not realised she had said them aloud.

"She wasn't there."

A loud knock on the back door made both women jump. The top half opened and Jane, the dairymaid, appeared, looking anxiously at Ruth.

"I'm coming now, Jane. Gwen told me that you want to start the cheese." She stood up, saw that Gwen had lowered her head down to apply herself to the shawl.

"If the children want me, please send them to the dairy." Gwen nodded without looking up.

Chapter 21

For the next hour Ruth and Jane worked on the new vat. Jane had only worked in the old way and was frightened of the machine that released near-boiling water into the outer jacket to warm up and separate the milk. Ruth had been uncertain at first, but had made it her job to teach Jane how to work with the machines, and now they were both becoming adept. After Jane was comfortable to be left alone, and they had turned the cheeses on the shelf in the drying room, Ruth called the boys and took them up to the sheep.

She watched in amusement as William and Walter chased after stray sheep and generally impeded both Ifor and the dogs.

Ifor was a shepherd, like his father, and John trusted him completely. He had lost his wife in the winter and now lived with his daughter, Gladys. Ruth had been shocked that, at eighty-five, he still worked to supplement the family income, but she soon realised that Ifor would only stop farming when he died. He was tolerant of the children, so Ruth encouraged them to spend time with him, learning as much as they could. Walter viewed it all as a game, but William took his role seriously.

"I saw the men leaving at dawn. Do you have any news yet?" Ifor said.

Ruth shook her head. "Not yet, Ifor. It's too soon. Arthur Ellis is due to return with his men this afternoon, to finish off the farm tasks. He may have some news."

"She's a good girl, Mrs Jones. She always speaks politely, like, and she's kind. She'd have been upset enough about that little friend of hers. People that know her know she's a good girl."

Ruth swallowed back tears. "Thank you, Ifor. I'm sure the men will find her soon. It's comforting to know that we have friends."

"Maybe Mr Robinson will return soon. He will be of help to you and the Ellises."

Ruth looked at Ifor, who was watching William and the dogs manoeuvre the ewes and their lambs into the top field.

"I'd better go and help Walter," he grinned. "That ewe'll run him all over the field. Some sheep aren't as daft as they look."

Ruth stayed where she was. Mr Pugh's behaviour was observed more critically than he knew, she thought. She also suspected it would not make any difference to how he behaved even if he did know, as he set little store by the opinions of people he considered to be unworthy. His treatment of Gwen Ellis confirmed that.

Walter came running back towards her, breathless, red-faced and beaming. "Did you see me, Mammy? Did you? I nearly got that one!"

He stopped abruptly in front of her, uncertain about the scowl on Ruth's face caused by Pugh. She smiled at him. "Very good work, Walter. We must tell your Dada how helpful you've been today. Look, here comes William."

"I shall tell Alice how clever I was, when she comes home with Dada, too!"

William glanced at his mother, saw her biting her lip, and took his brother's hand. "Come, Walter, let's go back to the farm and you can tell me all about it."

Ruth brushed the older boy's head and William smiled comfortingly at her. She waved to Ifor, then followed the boys back

121

to the farm. As she approached, she could hear men's voices and she thought she recognised Arthur Ellis. She picked up her pace and ran down the last short incline, bursting into the yard just as men disappeared through the back door and into the kitchen.

Out of breath, she opened the door and rushed in after them to find Arthur standing next to Gwen at the range, where Gwen was hovering over a steaming cauldron. They both looked up as Ruth entered and the room fell silent. She knew immediately that they had not found Alice. The men turned their heads to the floor, or avoided her gaze. Arthur walked towards her, his cap held in both hands, to tell her their news.

"I'm so sorry, Mrs Jones. We found no sign, not even a sighting."

"How far did you search, Arthur?"

"We went right to the top and across, past Upper Cwm, over to Cwmynyscoy, and down to the iron works. We decided that it wouldn't have been possible for her to get any further than that since yesterday afternoon."

"Of course," Ruth replied, holding her stomach to try to quell the sensation there. "And the mineshafts?"

"Owners have had them all checked. Nothing there, ma'am."

"Well, at least that's a relief. Thank you, Arthur. We must wait for Mr Jones to return."

Ruth saw William, who had been standing in the doorway holding Walter's shoulders, drop his chin to his chest. He turned Walter around and they disappeared.

Gwen stood next to Ruth. "I've prepared something to eat and drink for the men, Mrs Jones. Then Arthur can direct them back to their work until Mr Jones returns."

For a moment she didn't respond, but stood staring into the space in the doorway where the boys had been.

"Mrs Jones, would you prefer something else?"

"What? I'm sorry." Ruth shook her head to clear the image of mineshafts and the fruitless search. "What did you say, Gwen?"

"The men are going to eat now, then they'll return to work until Mr Jones is back."

"Yes, thank you, Gwen, Arthur. I'm sorry. I think I must sit for a little while." Ruth looked shaken.

Gwen took Ruth gently by the arm, steering her into the parlour to sit her down. As they walked she could feel the trembling throughout Ruth's body.

The kitchen had been silent as they passed through but, as she sat, Ruth heard the hum of voices next door. Gwen hovered behind her. "Please look after the men, Gwen. I just need a few moments to myself."

From the kitchen she heard the sound of Arthur ushering the men out of the back door and giving them instructions. After a few minutes of silent contemplation Ruth felt better. She stood up and went back into the kitchen.

For the next two hours Ruth and Gwen worked silently, preparing food and finishing the ironing on the kitchen table. At half past five Arthur returned to let them know that all of the tasks were done and that the men were going home. Ruth tried to persuade Gwen to return with him, but she was adamant that she would wait until John returned. Ruth protested, but Arthur interjected.

"I can manage the children well enough, Mrs Jones, and Gwen's mother is there with our Gwenny." With that, he turned and left. His footsteps echoed across the yard then stopped at the gate. After a brief pause and a low mumble of voices, the sound changed to the louder march of more footsteps returning to the farmhouse. Ruth's head snapped up to look out of the window. "It's John!"

Chapter 22
May 2015

After speaking to Zelah, Maggie spent a couple of hours wandering around the house and garden, mulling over their discussion and arguing backwards and forwards with herself about what to do next. Zelah's opinion had been clear, but Maggie still couldn't make up her mind.

"Get it out in the open," Zelah had recommended, with well-argued reasons. But she was still reluctant to involve Alice more. She wasn't afraid of showing the photo or the clothes, it was what she suspected about what else Alice might see, what Maggie couldn't control, that might lead to further danger. "Further danger? Do I really believe this could be dangerous?" Maggie thought.

She had to acknowledge it. Instinct told her that every new piece of information that she uncovered was revealing not just family history but potential danger to Alice. She hadn't been explicit about this with Zelah but something in her own hesitancy about her explanation of the photograph, told Maggie that her anxiety was increasing.

Zelah had advised her to meet with her at the library the next day, as she had also found out some interesting information. Maggie had been so wrapped up in her own thoughts that she had forgotten to ask what it was and had put the phone down before she realised that she hadn't given Zelah the chance to tell her any more.

She spent so long thinking about what to do that she found herself late for the school pick up. Grabbing her keys, she ran out of the door, forgetting to pack the clothes back into the trunk. Traffic was on her side again and she was only a few minutes late. Jack had walked to the front gate of Alice's school. Maggie could see them arguing. She screeched to a halt on the pavement in front of the gate. As they climbed in she asked, "What were you arguing about? You know I hate you two arguing."

Jack's tone was indignant. "Actually, we weren't, for once. I was giving Alice some advice."

He was about to go on, but Maggie caught a glimpse in her rear-view mirror of the face that Alice was pulling at him, that said *shut up!*" Maggie had no intention of leaving it there. "Advice about what? Anything I can help with?"

"No!" Alice replied, rather too quickly. Maggie couldn't carry on the conversation, as a car was now approaching them from school drive and she needed to get out of the way. As soon as they started moving she asked again, "So, can I help?"

Alice was silent and Maggie caught further glimpses of hand gestures and facial expressions that told her that this, for the moment, was just between them.

"OK, if you don't want to tell me. But don't let it turn into a big problem, OK?"

"OK," they said in unison.

She sighed, knowing that this was as much as she was going to get. Despite being close to her daughter, Maggie knew that Alice kept a lot to herself, particularly things that she didn't know how to deal with. Maggie understood that Alice wanted to resolve her own issues, but she was just ten. No matter how hard she tried, Maggie had never been able to convince Alice that adult experience could actually provide a helpful perspective.

It had been like this since David died. Jack seemed to cope well enough after the initial shock. He understood that he had to get on with his life and despite occasional moments of anger that his father was gone, he managed well enough. Alice reacted differently. From the time that Maggie had broken the news to them that their father had died in an accident on the motorway, Alice never talked about her father's death. She carried on as if nothing had changed. Nothing Maggie could say persuaded Alice to speak about her feelings. She remained the same matter-of-fact, straightforward little girl, but increasingly kept her secrets to herself. Maggie had made appointments with psychologists and counsellors but Alice refused to speak to them.

When Maggie had to tell her children that they also had to move out of their home and find a new school, she felt as if she was bringing their world to an end. Jack was upset and cried at the prospect of losing his friends. But he accepted that his mother could no longer pay the mortgage and that there was no choice – sell up or be bankrupted and thrown out. Put like that, he saw that there was no point in arguing, so he said goodbye to his friends and packed his belongings.

Alice had said nothing. She had come to the town as a small child and knew nowhere else. She also shared her mother's love of their home. She loved her room and loved inviting her friends to play there with her. Maggie operated an "open house" policy, and they became known for their hospitality. Friends and neighbours admired both the house, and the home that Maggie had made of it. She'd tell anyone who asked that she had found her perfect place to live, for her family, and that she had the perfect job, and the best friends. Losing it all was more traumatic than losing her crooked, corrupt, bankrupt husband. But she never told anyone that.

Thinking about Alice and Jack's experiences occupied her journey, so much so that she found that they were at their front door. The children jumped out of the car and bolted into the house, throwing their bags and coats in a heap on the floor and rushing up to their respective rooms. Maggie walked into the hall after them and picked up their things, shouting simultaneously, when she remembered that she hadn't packed up the trunk, and knew at the same time that it was too late.

"Mum, what's all this stuff on your bed?"

With a feeling of resignation, Maggie trudged up the stairs and into her room, where Alice had jumped onto the bed and was kneeling in front of the trunk, gazing around in fascination at the clothes spread before her.

"Do you remember those old trunks that we could see at the far end of the attic?"

Alice nodded.

"I decided to get them down, to see what was in them. It's mainly clothes, a child's clothes. You can take a look, but be careful. They're very old. I've laid them out in the order that they came out."

"Can you explain it all to me?" Alice frowned, not taking her eyes off the bed.

Maggie went through the clothing explaining that they had been carefully packed by someone a long time ago and probably all at the same time.

"That's a strange thing to do, isn't it?" Alice asked. "Why strange?"

"Well, when my stuff gets too small or whatever, or I get fed up and don't want to wear something any more, well, you put it in charity bags, but a bit at a time, not all at once. This is all at once, isn't it? So there must have been a reason for someone to do that."

"Yes, that's right," Maggie replied, "that's what I thought when I saw them. I think they're over a hundred years old, and this," holding up the grey serge dress and white pinafore, "is a school uniform."

"Can I hold them?" Alice asked, gingerly prodding the dress.

"Yes, but very carefully, please." Maggie handed Alice each garment. Alice turned them around in her hands, then held them up to herself.

"They're about the right size for me." She examined the back of the neck openings.

"Did they have name tags in those days, Mum? Is there some way we can find out what her name was?"

This was the moment Maggie knew was coming and she was still unsure about the right thing to do. She replied, "I have a clue, I think. I found this," she held up the photo, "wrapped inside a shawl at the bottom. Be careful!" Alice had snatched the photo out of Maggie's hand and was peering closely at it. Maggie held her breath. Alice peered at the photo and Maggie could see that she was scanning the faces with great concentration.

"Ha! I knew it!" Alice looked up at her mother with a triumphant grin, pointing to the photograph.

"So, how does it feel?" Maggie asked tentatively. "I *knew* it was her."

"What do you mean... her?" The face she had seen and that had caused her to phone Zelah in confusion and worry was Alice's face.

Different hair and clothes, but undeniably Alice's features, not just similar, exactly the same. So who did Alice think she was looking at?

"It's the girl at the funeral. You know, the one in the graveyard last week. I told you, she waved to me. Why is she in this picture?"

Maggie felt a knot grip tightly in her stomach. "Alice, it's your face. Can't you see yourself there?"

"Of course, Mum. Didn't I tell you that she looked just like me. She was very sad. Who is she?" Alice didn't sound at all troubled, just curious.

"What makes you think that's the same girl?" Maggie asked, trying to keep her voice casual.

"I knew when I saw the coat and boots," Alice replied. "That coat there and those boots," she pointed to where they sat on the bed. "She was wearing them that day. I told you, she was really wet."

Maggie didn't know what to say.

"Mum, do you think something happened to her? Is that why her clothes were packed away? Perhaps her mother packed them."

"Maybe. I don't know." Maggie was struggling to think what to do next. This was what she had feared. Something a long-time hidden was trying to get out. Through Alice.

"There's something else about this photo." Alice was looking at the other faces. "I thought I recognised someone else." She peered again. "Her, maybe?" She seemed to be identifying an older girl standing in front of the teacher.

"Perhaps she looks like someone you know at school?" Maggie ventured.

"Hmm. Not sure. Can we keep the photo out, so we can look again later? What about that other one? What's in there?"

"Yes, of course," Maggie replied, relieved at the change of subject. "I haven't had a chance to open the second one yet. It's got something rattly inside. Let's leave it all now and get your homework done. We can come back later. I'll have to pack it all away before I go to bed, so we can open the second one then."

Alice put the photograph on the bedside table and they went downstairs together.

Alice seemed to put the contents of the trunk out of her mind for the next couple of hours, as she did her homework and chatted with friends on her computer. But around eight o'clock she appeared in the kitchen as Maggie finished emptying the dishwasher.

"Can we open the other one now? Please say yes, Mum! I've been telling Jade and Cerys. They think it's really cool! Can they come over tomorrow after school and have a look?"

Maggie felt relieved. Whatever happened in the graveyard, and whether Zelah's belief about inherited memory was feasible, finding the clothes and photo had only sparked a natural level of curiosity in Alice.

"Yes, of course. Tell them that they can come home after school for tea, if that's OK with their parents."

"Cool! Thanks, Mum. I'll go and tell them now and then we'll open the other trunk, OK?" She skipped out of the kitchen.

Maggie went up to her room to wait. She decided that Jack should have the chance to see what they had found too, so she called him. He had joined in the speculation over dinner about the owner of the clothes and what the other trunk might contain, but Maggie thought that whichever game of magical fantasy he was playing out on his computer would be too gripping to leave for a couple of musty old trunks from the attic. But she was wrong. He signed off right away and joined her. While they waited for Alice to arrive, Jack looked through the clothes.

"What do you think, Mum?"

"About what? I don't know whose they are, if that's what you mean, and I don't know who the girl is in the photo. Do you think it looks like Alice?"

"Spitting image," said Jack, looking at the photo again. "If you didn't know it was ancient you'd say it was her. I think it must be related, don't you?"

"Yes, I just don't know how," said Maggie quietly.

"Keep checking it out, Mum. If you're doing it for good reason, you won't hurt Alice. I'm keeping an eye on her too."

Maggie smiled fondly at him. Despite his frequent bouts of aggressive teenage angst and his fourteen-year-old assumption that he had already worked out everything that was worth knowing, Maggie knew that he cared deeply about her and his little sister, and that she could rely on him to protect Alice. It was comforting to know that Alice turned to Jack for advice when she didn't want to speak to her mother and that Jack never turned her away.

Alice arrived in a rush and threw herself onto the bed. "OK, guys, let's open her up!"

Jack dragged the small trunk onto the bed and began to work on the buckles. They were rusted together and difficult to move, but leverage with a chisel soon resulted in both buckles springing back. He threw the top back and they peered inside.

There were no clothes in this smaller trunk, in fact it had little inside. The contents appeared at first glance to be toys and knick-knacks. Maggie had warned the children while Jack was battling with the buckles that she wanted to record everything as it came out, so they took out the items one by one, Jack and Alice taking turns to pick something out and describe it to Maggie, taking notes.

They found only half a dozen things in the trunk: a rag doll, a couple of embroidered handkerchiefs, a small glass cockerel wrapped in an old newspaper article about an escaped bear, a cushion with a motif that said, "Praise the Lord" and a newspaper cutting, that was about the anticipated steamship crossing from Newport to the seaside resort of Weston-super-Mare across the Bristol Channel on the following Sunday.

"If these belonged to the girl, she didn't have very much, did she?" Alice remarked as they took the newspaper out of the small trunk, which then sat empty on the bed.

"I guess that Christmases are much better now than they used to be," Maggie replied with a grin. She was always generous at Christmas, joking with Alice and Jack that she single-handedly kept the toy and electronics departments of several large stores in business.

Jack had picked up the trunk to examine it in more detail. "What do you think it was?" he asked.

"Well, it looks to me like a luggage set, so perhaps it belonged to someone who needed to go on a long journey," she replied as he looked at the buckles.

"Look!" Jack exclaimed, "I think these might be initials. What do you think?" He was scratching at a small area of leather between the two buckles that was encrusted with grime. Maggie and Alice moved their heads in to look more closely and could see that where he had scratched what seemed to be the letter "T" had appeared in an elaborate script.

"Can I take it to my room and work on it some more?" Jack asked. "I'll try the other one, too. It's just as dirty, so it might have some letters in the same place."

"Of course," Maggie replied. "Do it carefully. It looks like the initials may have been painted on, so be sure you don't scratch the paint off along with the dirt. Alice, will you help him?"

The children took both trunks into Jack's room, then went to find dusters and wet cloths to begin the clean-up.

Maggie moved the clothes and the other possessions from her bed onto the settee under the window. As she picked up the article wrapped in the newspaper, she noticed that the top of the page was similar to the one that she had seen previously at the library, from the local newspaper of 1883, *The Merlin*. If she took it with her tomorrow, she might be able to find the original report, and date this article. Perhaps she could do the same with the information for the ship crossing? She was excited at the prospect of some real detective work. She carefully unwrapped the newspaper and put it with the article into a plastic pouch which she put in her briefcase ready to go to the library.

A little while later she went to check on how the children were doing with the cleaning. They had uncovered what looked like "J" but it was very faded. Both trunks, however, had cleaned up well and were made of hard, brown leather.

"We can carry on tomorrow," Maggie said as she sent them both off to bed.

Once they were both settled, weariness overtook Maggie. She didn't even feel like looking at the photo again, so she put it into another pouch in her briefcase, went to her room, and fell quickly asleep. But her sleep didn't last long.

Chapter 23
May 1883

Ruth jumped to her feet and put a hand to her mouth. She glared expectantly at the back door for what seemed like an age, before John entered. He was alone. He stood in the doorway, returned her gaze and shook his head. Ruth slumped dejectedly back into her chair.

The men who had been with John crowded the doorway behind him and he moved towards Ruth, to let them in. Gwen began at once to fuss over them, taking their packs and chiding them to remove their boots.

"We walked about halfway to Newport," he said quietly, sitting next to her, taking her hand. "There was no sign. But," he squeezed her fingers, "we did find a group of men working in a field who said that a dangerous-looking vagrant child approached them and asked for bread and water, but they chased her off. I think from the description that it might have been Alice."

"How did they describe her?" Ruth looked intently at him. "Tell me!"

"They said that she was unkempt, and wet. Her hair was wild and straggling around her face."

"Oh dear Lord! What can have happened to make her do this?"

"Whatever it is, we shall discover it as soon as we find her, and she shall tell us why she has given us such worry over her," John replied, his face grim, supporting her by her arm. "Tomorrow we'll all search towards Newport, for I believe that's the direction in which she is going."

Ruth nodded. They sat silently together, as Gwen gave the men bread, cheese, and cups of tea.

"What time would you like us back tomorrow, Mr Jones?" asked one.

"As soon as you can get here, let's say around seven o'clock?" John stood and faced the half-dozen men. "I thank you all for your time and effort today. I believe we must continue our search towards Newport tomorrow." He turned to the three men from Rhiwbina Farm, who stood near the back door.

"If Mr Morgan is able to release you, we'll be in the vicinity of Bassaleg around eight and I'll call there for you."

The men nodded to John, then to Ruth, then took their boots and left the kitchen. John's farm hands followed.

"I'll be leaving now, Mrs Jones, if that's all right?" Gwen Ellis untied her apron and took her shawl off the hook next to the kitchen door. "I'll be back in the morning with Arthur, around six."

Ruth smiled gratefully, unable to speak. John walked her to the back gate.

"Mrs Ellis, I cannot begin to tell you how grateful we are for your support…" he began.

"It's no more than you've done for me and Arthur, Mr Jones. Mrs Jones is taking this hard, despite her trying to seem well. She was sick this morning. I don't want to tell tales but…" she hesitated before lowering her voice, "…but she went to the school this morning and was not well received."

John raised his eyebrows, but didn't say anything. Instead, he shook Gwen's hand, causing her to blush and look down at the ground, then turned and walked back into the farmhouse.

John spoke to William and Walter to explain that he had not yet found Alice and that he expected them to behave well for their mother in the coming days. He congratulated them on their help with Ifor and the sheep.

"I nearly got the sheep, Dada!" Walter exclaimed.

"You will catch her next time, Walter. William, I heard from Ifor how well you managed the dogs. I am very proud."

William blushed. "Thank you, Dada. Will you find Alice tomorrow?"

"We must pray that we do, William. Your mother told me how Alice spoke to you yesterday and what you have been able to tell her. It has been most helpful."

"She wanted you to know that she is not wicked, Dada."

"Of course not! Was that a worry for her, William?"

"Yes, Dada. I think she was upset that some people were saying so."

"Who was saying so?" John asked, although he guessed at the answer.

"I'm not sure who she meant, exactly, Dada. She didn't say."

"Thank you for telling me, William. Alice will explain it all when she returns to us. Now, wash yourself ready for supper."

"Yes, Dada."

There was nothing to do now but wait for the night to pass. Following supper and evening prayers with the boys, and after Ruth had seen them to bed, she lit the lamps in the sitting room where they sat down together and each gave an account of their day.

John was shocked to hear of the hostile reception Ruth had received at the schoolhouse, and equally worried that she had been made unwell.

"I don't know how long we'll be searching, not long I hope, but I think that I should fetch your mother to be with us to help with the children and the farm. You're going to need some time to devote to Alice once she's home again."

"Yes, that's an excellent thought, John!"

She wanted time to spend with Alice and, although Gwen was a great help, she would be needed for the day-to-day running of the farm. The children were very fond of their grandmother, Ruthie Evans, who not only minded them well but whom Ruth trusted completely.

After the children were asleep, Ruth paced, unsure if she would sleep with so many thoughts flashing in and out of her head: pictures of Alice and the events of the past ten days. But exhaustion overtook her and she was asleep before midnight. She slept heavily, so much so that John had almost dressed and left the bedroom before she awoke the following morning. He was tiptoeing out of the bedroom when Ruth called him, befuddled by sleep.

"John! What's happened? Is there news? What time is it?" She sat up and put her feet out of the bed.

"It is a little after six and Arthur Ellis has just arrived, my dear. The other men will be here shortly and I'll leave with them. Please, rest a little more."

"Just a few minutes and I'll join you." She shook her head, searching around the room for her shawl. John walked around the bed and lit Ruth's lamp, then he took up his own and went down to the kitchen.

By the time Ruth had dressed and reached the kitchen, ten men were waiting there, ready to leave. Gwen was clearing cups and plates into the sink. As the men filed out of the back door, John spoke to Ruth.

"We're going to take the carts down to Bassaleg and ask at any farms and houses we missed yesterday. Once we've collected the men from Rhiwbina we'll cover all of the remaining farms and perhaps reach the outskirts of Newport. I'll send word if I'm able." He saw her look of pleading. "I promise! I'll send someone back to give you news." He left, leaving Ruth and Gwen alone again.

John and Ruth had decided that William should not attend school again. It would just have been for a half day, it being Saturday, but they felt that he should wait until Alice was back, so as not to face the other children alone. So, Ruth was surprised to find him in the hallway dressed for school.

"William? I believe Dada told you that you don't have to attend school today?"

"Yes, I know, Mama. But I want to go. If anything is being said about Alice I want to be there to tell them that she is a good girl and hasn't done anything wrong." Ruth was moved to tears. "That's very brave of you William, but those who know Alice won't say bad things. And we shouldn't listen to the others."

"Please, let me go, Mammy. Dada said I should help you however I can and I think this will help."

She was reluctant, but he seemed resolved. It was going to be another long day. Nevertheless, she was worried about exposing him to the spite of Eira and the Morris children.

"I won't be upset by them, Mammy," he said, sensing the cause of her concern. He put his arm around her neck. "I will not be tempted to fight, or to say anything bad back to them."

"Very well, William. But I'll walk with you."

Chapter 24

By the time they left the farm the sun had come up and the day promised to be hot, which would be better for Alice if she was still out in the open.

As they reached the school there were already small groups of children waiting in the playground and as they passed, each group fell silent or whispered among themselves. William held his head up but clasped his mother's arm tightly.

The two Morris girls were waiting near the door with their mother and a few other mothers that Ruth knew. She prepared herself for the inevitable greetings, which began with an exchange of nods. Elsie Morris smirked at William, when she thought that Ruth couldn't see.

Ruth walked with William up to the door, which had just opened to reveal Eira Probert standing on the step. Ruth gave no-one a chance to speak.

"Miss Probert, William wishes to return to school this morning. I trust you will welcome him back?" She spoke gently, but the arching of her eyebrows belied the civility of her words.

"I trust he will be able to concentrate on his studies, Mrs Jones."

"I believe so, Miss Probert. But under the circumstances, a little kindness would be most welcome if William occasionally allows his attention to drift. I'm sure he will be easily called back."

The teacher nodded briefly and stood aside to allow the children to enter. Once they were all inside, the door was firmly shut, leaving Ruth and the mothers standing outside. Ruth immediately turned to leave, but was brought back by a call from Bessie Morris.

"No news yet of your daughter, Mrs Jones?" Ruth turned to see Bessie Morris at the centre of a small group of women. Her expression was sympathetic, but the faces of the other women were like leering cats.

"Not yet, Mrs Morris. Thank you for your concern. Perhaps your husband will be joining the search later? Or indeed any of your husbands?" These were the wives of the elders of the chapel, who, Ruth knew, would be influenced by whatever Robert Pugh was advising. The other women looked discomforted, but Bessie Morris smiled back.

"My husband has important business this morning."

Ruth said nothing. She simply stared until the smile faded from Bessie Morris's mouth and she drew herself up. If Bessie was looking for an argument, she was to be disappointed. Ruth turned and walked out of the playground, leaving Bessie staring silently after her. The hum of voices followed her. As soon as she judged that she was out of sight, she ran back to the farm.

At midday, Bessie wasn't waiting, much to Ruth's relief. She took William's hand and they walked home. "No, Mammy, no-one said anything horrible. Sara Morris pulled a few faces at me, but the other children were kind. They asked if Alice was home. I said no, but…" He looked at Ruth hopefully, but she shook her head.

"It's too early yet, William. Dada said he would send word early afternoon."

"Can I do any work this afternoon, Mammy?"

"Yes, William, some of our friends have sent their men to help us out and there's a great deal to do, so I'm sure they'll welcome your assistance."

As they reached the front of the farm a man in police uniform appeared, walking towards them. Ruth froze.

"That's not our local constable," said William.

"I know. Ruth walked quickly up to the policeman and stopped in front of him.

"I'm Mrs Jones. Do you have any news for me?"

"No, ma'am. May we return to your home?"

"Of course." Ruth led the way to the door into the kitchen, where Gwen was working. The constable motioned them to sit down.

"Your husband's search has not found your daughter, ma'am, and he has asked for additional help from the constabulary. Our officers are going to make enquiries in Newport. I have come to ask you some questions about recent events, anything you can tell us that might assist our search."

Ruth took him to the sitting room.

Following Ruth's discussion with the constable, he had wanted to question William who, although nervous, did his best to answer the questions put to him about what Alice had said, going to school. Ruth thought that she had managed to keep the tensions at school and chapel out of her responses, and was alarmed when the constable said that he would be going to interview the schoolteacher. She reluctantly told him about the confrontation the previous morning.

"So, Mrs Jones, relations are not good between your daughter and some of her schoolmates? Might this have caused her to run away, in your opinion?"

"I think not," Ruth replied. "She never spoke about their treatment of her before, but she was very frightened about something or someone."

"Very well, thank you for your time. I'll let you know if we receive news."

She showed him out, indicating the way to the school and chapel. Feeling unable to continue her work, she sat in the parlour and waited for John to return.

In the hours that followed, the first seeds of doubt crept insidiously into her head and heart. She tried to push them away and make herself believe that Alice would be found alive and well. But she was only distracted when the sound of voices in the kitchen told her that John had returned. By then the sun had gone down and the sky was turning pink. She walked quickly to the kitchen where John was talking to Arthur Ellis.

"The constable has been here, has he not, my dear?" John asked.

She nodded.

"Then you know that there is no news. The constabulary believes that Alice is heading towards Newport, so they are going to commence a search there at first light." He stopped. "Ruth?" He moved towards her and took her trembling hands in his. "We will find her. You must keep strong!"

She nodded, turning to Gwen to discuss arrangements for the next day. John watched her with a grim expression. He had seen the doubt, and she knew he had seen it.

Chapter 25
May 1883

No-one passed by as the afternoon progressed, so Alice didn't have to hide. She closed her eyes now and then, but couldn't sleep for fear of tumbling into the water. The pain in her head had increased, although the bleeding had stopped under the pressure of the handkerchief. This was so soaked in blood that Alice considered throwing it away, but as she had nothing else for her wound and it had been a present from her mother, she tried instead to rinse it out in the canal and press it to her forehead to cool down the fire that burned there.

The cool cloth helped and she decided to try walking again. When she stood up she swayed so much that she was afraid that she wasn't going to be able to carry on, but her vision settled enough to allow her to start the walk towards Newport. She stopped several times to drink from the canal. On one occasion she saw a small fish at the edge and tried to catch it, but it slipped easily through her fingers.

As day faded into evening, the effort of walking, and the pain in her head, became too much. She had to find a ditch for the night, praying that it wouldn't rain again. Her prayers were not answered.

By dawn, Alice knew that she was sick. Her vision was so blurred that she could barely focus, even if she concentrated. The wound on her head felt puffy and the area of sensitivity had spread out, reaching her cheek and her eye. Her feet were sore and swollen.

Around mid-morning, after making little progress, she spotted activity in the distance. Pressing herself as close into the hedge as she could, she crept cautiously around the bend until the hum of voices became audible. She had reached a lock where a bargeman was struggling to coax his reluctant horse along the narrow path to steer the barge in through the lock gates. The man swore and cursed at the horse, using words that Alice had never heard before, but sounding sufficiently violent and intemperate as to have surely shocked her parents. The lock-keeper stood at the nearer gate with his back to her, offering advice to the bargeman.

"A bit more, that's it. He's nearly in. Hold his head! Hold it! No. Yes! That's it!" As the stern passed into the lock the lock-keeper turned the paddles that closed both giant gates. Alice had always loved watching the passing of a barge through a lock and this was a much larger lock than the one just by the chapel. She moved from the hedge to the centre of the path.

When the gates were shut the keeper strolled to the front gates and opened the paddles. She could hear the roaring of the rushing water as the barge sank slowly out of sight. What caught Alice's attention was that the bargeman had taken a hunk of bread and cheese from his pocket, eating it with one hand while he steadied the stumbling horse with the other.

After a few mouthfuls, the horse suddenly reared its head and the man dropped the food. As it fell to the ground the horse's restless hooves stamped on it and the bargeman, cursing the horse, kicked the whole lot into the hedge.

It was all Alice could do to contain herself. It seemed an age until the horse pulled the barge out of the lock and she prayed

145

that no rat got to the food first. Rocking with anxiety, she waited as the men spoke.

"Be there by tonight, then."

"'Spect so. Bit of rain to come, though," replied the bargeman, glancing at the sky.

"Aye. Got to get back up by Thursday. Regards to Fred. He'll be through before evening. Tell him I said I hope his missus is better. Now come on, you great bugger! Pull!" With a final curse he urged the horse forwards. The lock-keeper went back into his cottage. As soon as she heard the door slam Alice ran past the lock to the hedge. The food was still there, dirty but otherwise untouched. She quickly wrapped it into her bundle, checked that the lock-keeper hadn't come out, and ran onto the path.

When she could no longer see the lock and was sure that no-one else was coming, she stopped, sat down against the hedge and took out the food. Once she had picked out as much of the dirt as she could, Alice stuffed the food into her mouth and thought about what she had just overheard. She was close to Newport now and would be able to see it by nightfall. She also needed to keep moving, as another barge was coming.

Tomorrow she would buy her ticket for the paddle steamer and escape to Weston-super-Mare, which gave her momentum to get up. She had become stiff and cold sitting by the hedge, although her headache had eased a little. The food was gone. Time to move on quickly, as it looked like rain again.

She met no-one all afternoon. She'd glance back from time to time, to make sure she was keeping ahead of the next barge. The trees crowding overhead cast shadows on the dark water, but there was no wind to disturb the dull black surface. The only sounds were the twittering of birds in the trees and hedgerows, and the occasional bleating of sheep. The sky had been mostly clear since her lunchtime encounter with the bargeman and the lock-keeper, but now a sharp breeze cooled her face and the inevitable clouds arrived overhead. It was time to find shelter.

Ahead there seemed to be a gap in the hedge into a field. Approaching cautiously Alice saw what looked like a shepherd's shelter. With her heart beating she pushed through and peered into it. It was empty and looked disused. Probably a winter shelter, she thought. Ifor had something similar. There was some old straw, dirty but not smelly. She put her bundle of clothes down and returned to the canal for one more drink, before settling in for the evening.

She fell asleep immediately and awoke suddenly, instantly alert. But there was nothing. Peering out of the shelter she saw the lights of Newport. At last, she was close. Although the pain in her head had returned and now burned fiercely, Alice lay down and slept.

Chapter 26

The bleating of sheep woke her early the next morning. It had rained in the night and haze was rising from the grass. The sun was just visible and it was going to be a reasonable day. Alice jumped up, ready for the next part of her journey, but the sudden movement caused a ripping pain through her head and she stumbled, putting her hand up to her wound. She felt a swelling, agony to the slightest touch, and her right eye was completely closed. Her legs were shaking and she feared that she wouldn't be able to stand. By holding on firmly to the door jamb she managed to pull herself to her feet. With a deep breath, she wrapped up her bundle and spread out her dress. It was dry and relatively clean, but creased. She changed and smoothed it out as best she could. The shawl was dirty and damp, but she needed the scant protection it could give her against the early morning cold. Wrapping up her remaining possessions and putting the newspaper page and her coins into her pocket, she returned to the canal for a drink and tidied her hair as best she could.

About an hour later she reached a fork in the canal path. This was unexpected. As she stood puzzling, the sound of voices made her dive for cover. There wasn't time to look and her dress snagged on the briars, but she thought she was well enough hidden. The sound of hooves, footsteps, and the movement of water came closer, then stopped. "This is where I'll be leaving you, then."

"And thank you for the company, sir. It's good to 'av talk. Damned 'orse don't have much to say for 'imself!" Two men laughed.

"You be enjoying your day, sir. Sounds like a rare treat."

"Indeed. The steamer is said to be an amazing sight. My friends and I have been looking forward to it. Right. I'm for the shortcut over the hill. I must hurry now, only an hour to boarding. Good day to you, bargee. An easy journey back to Blaenavon, I hope!"

"Indeed, sir. Perhaps one day I may see that Weston-super-Mare as well."

Alice had to move fast. Scrambling out of the hedge, her hand caught in the rent in her clean dress, but that didn't matter compared to the opportunity to follow the man who knew the shortcut to the port and the steamship! It was hard work keeping up with him as he left the canal path and followed a lane that ran steeply uphill. Already exhausted and dizzy Alice stumbled several times as they made their way up the hill. Once or twice the man looked back over his shoulder, puzzled by some noise behind him, but each time he carried on, impelled by his need to reach the port.

At the top of the hill, Alice saw that she had no further need of him. She stopped to catch her breath and marvel at the sight before her.

The Bristol Channel filled the view, the hilly contours of Somerset shimmering pale white in the weak morning sun on the opposite side. She had never imagined so much water! On the near side she could see where the river fed in, and following loops of the river upstream, there was the port, great ships nudging the banks on either side, and finally, Newport itself, a bridge at its centre spanning the river next to an ancient castle. There, in the sunshine, tied up next to the bridge, the *Waverley* sat sedately, the occasional puff of smoke belching out of its tall black funnel.

Breathing more evenly, clutching her bundle to her chest and her handkerchief to her head, Alice walked quickly down the path. She soon lost sight of the bridge and the ship, but at the bottom of the hill the footpath reached Bridge Road. She had only to follow it. As she walked she gave some thought to what she would say to the ticket seller, if questioned about her journey. She decided that she was going to see her sick grandparent, who had sent her the fare. That would do. Questions then crept in about what she was going to do when she got there. Where would she sleep? What was she going to do about her wound? She banished them, unresolved. When she reached Weston-super-Mare, she could not be found and her family would be safe and everything else would resolve itself. Somehow.

As she neared Newport there were more people and Alice noticed that a few looked and nodded in her direction, their faces puckering with distaste. It must be her eye. She smoothed her dress again as she walked and tried to hide the tear. She tidied her hair as best she could but a hand touched to the top of her head told her that her hair was stiff and sticky. She probably didn't look right. Well, there was nothing she could do about that. She could fix it when she got to England.

Bridge Street widened into a two-lane road, big enough to allow carts and horses easy passage. More people were walking here, and no-one was taking notice of her. She could hear the blasting of a ship's horn close by. Another bend in the road and there it was!

She took in the dockside scene. The ticket vendor was in a tall, striped wooden box with a picture of the steamer fixed to its pointed crown. People had already boarded and were strolling around the decks. There were children on board, hanging over the side to watch the great paddle wheel, guarded by frowning parents.

There were stalls around the dockside, doing a brisk trade in cakes and lemonade, small knick-knacks, and food of all kinds. Evidently, people took picnics with them when they crossed the Channel. Alice knew that she would have some money left over when she had bought her ticket. After two days without proper food the smells tempted her to buy something first, but she controlled herself, took a deep breath and headed for the ticket stall.

"Any more, now? Any more of you fine ladies and gents? Come and marvel at this wonderful experience – a great paddle ship, the most modern of its kind – and the wonderful town of Weston-super-Mare, never before available to visit for just a day. See its pier, its great sands, the exotic pavilion. Come on, ladies and gents, you can't fail to enjoy yourselves!"

A crowd had gathered on the quayside to get a good vantage point to see the ship as it departed. Some of them shouted back to the ticket seller.

"What if it sinks, mate? Not much of an experience, then?"

The crowd laughed and the ticket seller wagged his finger. "Safest vessel on the seas, my guarantee. Now, come on, ladies and gents, last chance now! It's high tide and the ship must leave. Only ten shillings, there and back."

Alice had edged her way to the ticket stall when a man and woman stepped out from the back of the crowd in front of her. The crowd cheered them as they bartered with the ticket seller for a reduction. Alice, standing behind them, her fare in her hand, swayed from side to side, worrying that she wouldn't have time to buy her ticket and some food. And she was finding it difficult to remain on her feet. At last the couple moved away. She stood in front of the ticket seller and held up her coins.

"I wish to buy a return ticket to Weston-super-Mare, if you please, sir."

"What did you say, girl?" The ticket seller glared at her, shouting.

Anxiously, she repeated her request, but as she did so, she knew that the words weren't coming out, just a guttural growl from the back of her throat. Her eyes widened in desperation as she tried to make the man understand her and with a huge effort she growled, "A ticket, sir."

"What, you want a ticket! Filthy little vagabond, you want to get on my nice clean boat!" He was shouting as much for the entertainment of the crowd as for her. The closest people on the quayside heard and turned to watch. Tears stung her good eye. "Please, sir!" she begged. "I must get to Weston-super-Mare. My family!"

She knew her words were garbled noise. The man reached out a hand as if to take her money but instead pushed her in the chest and she fell backwards, dropping her bundle and her money. It clattered in the gutter as the crowd laughed uproariously and several ragged children ran forwards to grab at it. She scrambled around with them, but was no match for their experienced gutter-cunning. Her precious coins were gone. She had no ticket.

The ticket vendor closed his window and was making his way to the boat, where sailors had begun to cast off. A great vent of steam rose from the funnel and the hooter gave three long blasts. The crowd lost interest in Alice and surged to the edge of the quay. In a flurry of shouted orders and warnings, the paddle began to turn and, as Alice watched in despair, the steamer inched away from the quay.

Chapter 27

The steamer was leaving without her. This was not how it was supposed to be. Desperation launched her to her feet. If she ran quickly, maybe she could jump across the small gap onto the entrance to the boat, which the sailors had not yet secured. She was about to try when she stopped dead in her tracks. It was the smell, the reek of rotting flesh that she had smelled at school. That meant only one thing. Her tormentor was here, had known where she was going, and had followed her here.

The boat was now six feet away from the quay. She could never jump that distance. She had failed. The pain in her head seared and she swayed, but knew that she had to hide at once and pray that she hadn't been seen. Although the smell was vile, there was no immediate sign of its source.

There were a number of stalls at the back of the quayside against the wall of the bridge, some of which had curtains covering their lower half. The proprietor of one of these had moved to another stall to speak to his neighbour and she seized the chance to dive under the cover. Just in time, as the stallholder's feet appeared. Alice sat hugging her knees, and what was left of her possessions. The stench became unbearable, until she thought she was going to be sick, then a second pair of feet appeared at the front of the stall.

"Can I help you?"

"I am looking for information, of a missing child. A girl, around ten years old. Have you seen a runaway in these parts?" The voice was muffled.

"No, I have not." A pause, another step back and a retching cough. "Are you ill? There's something dripping from your muffler. And…" he hesitated. Alice held her breath.

"Pardon me. I…have a condition that troubles me. I will not bother you further. Thank you for your time." The feet disappeared. As the footsteps moved away, another pair of feet took their place.

"What's the matter, Jack? You're green, you look like you're about to retch! Shall I fetch you some water?"

Alice heard the stallholder take several long, deep breaths until his friend returned, and the sound of deep gulps. The stallholder blew out a long breath. "Dear God, did you smell that?"

"What? Smell what? That person who spoke to you? Bit of odour never hurt anyone. You're getting very particular." The friend laughed, until he was cut off abruptly by the stallholder.

"Odour? That wasn't any odour from a human being! It wasn't just the smell, either, I think the face was coming away! My God! I think it was a leper!"

Alice heard a sharp gasp from the second stallholder. She had never heard of a leper, but the reaction of the men told her that it was a bad thing.

"Fetch the police! They shouldn't be wandering around the streets, harming decent folk!"

"What do you mean, 'they'?"

"That one over there mentioned a missing girl, so there must be more than one. Look, over by the castle. There's a couple of Specials. Call them over." The second stallholder moved round to

154

stand beside his friend. "No, let's go and speak to them. They won't hear us from here."

"Ay, you're right." The feet ran off. Alice peered out around the edge of the curtain. Other stallholders' attention was drawn by the men running to the constables, so they didn't see her. She saw the pair reach the constables and point over to the far side of the bridge where her tormentor must have been seen last. Then they pointed back to the stall and she pulled her head in.

Guessing that they would return any minute, she grabbed her bundle and crawled out of the other side, stood up, checked around, then walked away from the quayside. Without consciously thinking about it, Alice knew where she was going: home. There was something wrong with her tormentor, something that people would be able to see and now they would believe her. Her mother's face, smiling and welcoming, rose in front of her and she smiled back. Now she just had to find the track that led to the canal path. Despite her hunger, weakness, and pain, she was sure she could get home.

"There, over there, that's her! She's the one trying to get onto the boat!"

The shouts came from behind her and as she turned she saw a crowd standing next to the stall where she had hidden, together with the two constables, pointing at her.

She ran, stumbling along the street leading into the town. She arrived at a street where well-dressed people were strolling, and hid in the doorway of a closed shop, to catch her breath. What seemed like seconds later, the whistle-blowing constables ran down the street, parting the crowd before them.

She left the doorway and ran back the way she had come, but hesitated at the quayside. There was another, rougher path that seemed to follow the bend of the river. There was no other choice, so she took off down the river path, with the river on her left. No-one seemed to be following. Desperate to get away, Alice ran and ran until her legs gave way and she fell into the long grass at the side of the path.

She knew that this was the wrong direction, taking her away from the road home. But as she lay there, shrill whistles in the town told her that they hadn't given up. As soon as she could breathe again, she got up and ran further down the path until she reached flat, open countryside, where the ground was marshy, with a tang of sea in the air. The path was less defined, and springy underfoot, which made running easier. After a while she couldn't hear any whistles at all.

The sunshine of the morning disappeared and a fine drizzle fell. It felt safe enough to stop, so she sat in the long grass at the side of the path, to think about what to do next. Her thirst and the dryness in her throat made her choke. There was no source of water, save the dirty brown river, but the need to drink took her across the path to the bank that dropped steeply to the water's edge a couple of feet below. A strong current stirred up the whirring, gurgling water. Just a couple of footsteps caused her to slide dangerously close to the water's edge and she had to grab onto grass and nettles to stop herself falling in. The stinging of the nettles made her fingers tingle and burn so, planting her feet as firmly as she could, Alice leaned forwards and balanced over the swirling water. Reaching out, she dipped her free hand into the water. The cold eased the tingling immediately and she left her fingers in the running water. Deciding to risk a mouthful, she cupped her hand and brought water up to drink. The taste was more vile than she imagined. Mud, salt and dirt. She spat it out, coughing and retching. The sudden movement caused her feet to slip and they sank into the mud. One foot came out at once, but the other wouldn't budge despite heaving and tugging. The more she panicked, the further she sank. She was up to her ankle in mud. Leaning over, she pulled the laces looser, releasing her foot, but not the boot, which disappeared.

Alice scrambled back up the bank, across the path to where she had left her bundle and lay down, sobbing. Her hand throbbed from the nettle stings and her bootless foot was soaking wet.

No-one had come along the path. The mountain, at the base of which the canal ran, was further away than before. To get home, she had to get back in that direction, but she couldn't risk going back to the town. This path seemed to be taking her to the sea, so the only option was to leave it and walk across country, towards the mountain. She didn't know what type of terrain she might be facing but at least it was in the right direction.

She thought about her mother and father, her brothers, and her baby sister. They would all be at chapel today. "I'm coming home, Mammy," she whispered, then started to walk across the fields.

After what seemed like hours, the mountain didn't seem to be getting any closer. She passed a few people as she walked through the fields. Some had looked curiously, some had nodded, and one shouted a "Hello, girl. Are you alright, there?" Whatever their reaction, Alice kept her head down and walked on.

The drizzle turned to rain, heavy black clouds appeared over the mountain and the wind increased. Still Alice kept walking, sodden, miserable, shivering uncontrollably, barely able to see, but always keeping her face towards the mountain ridge. Darkness came early, brought on by the black clouds that filled the sky. Alice was now so exhausted that she had to find some shelter, but there was nothing that she could see, no building or hedge, that would give her respite from the rain. Then the thunder and lightning started.

Chapter 28

Alice had always been frightened by thunder, hearing so many stories of animals and people struck down when they were caught in the open. She remembered what her father had instilled into her: If you are ever caught outside in a storm, find a tree to shelter underneath. The bolt cannot pass through the branches to the ground.

She spotted the shadows of what could be a clump of trees away to her left and she ran in that direction. As she approached, she saw that they were on the far side of a substantial wall, but it wasn't too high and she was able to climb it. On the other side, the trees were still a little distance away. It was pitch black between lightning flashes, the rain hammering onto her body, the thunder rumbling everywhere in the sky.

She waited for a flash of lightning to show her where the trees were again. As soon as she saw, she ran flat out, blinded by the rain and her closed eye, with her heart hammering. Her unshod foot caught on something solid and she catapulted through the air, disorientated and screaming, before she landed in water.

Her body sank quickly as she flailed around, trying to find something to catch onto. Panicking and terrified that she was going to drown, she held her breath as she thrashed. Then her hands felt mud, firm enough to allow her to push up away from, and her head surfaced. Scrambling, her feet down, she found that she was only thigh deep and a flash of lightning showed that she wasn't too far from a low wall, which must have been what she had tripped over. The flash also revealed the outline of a building, where a light suddenly appeared in a window. Not caring what they might think, she pulled herself out of the water and staggered towards the light.

As soon as her feet hit solid ground, an agonising pain shot through her ankle, but she kept moving. Underfoot was grass. Dragging herself on, Alice realised that she had nothing in her hands but her handkerchief. She had lost her bundle. Everything was gone. Sobbing and crying, she half-limped, half-crawled to the building.

It was a huge place with what looked like hundreds of windows, but she couldn't see a way in. There was an archway at the end of the wall which led to a cobbled courtyard and, at last, a door. Pulling herself into the doorway, Alice summoned all of her remaining strength and gave one great shout for help. No-one came. Her world shrank to a pinpoint of blackness as she lost consciousness.

At half past five the following morning, as the cocks were beginning to crow and the first wash of grey lightened the sky, the door opened.

Chapter 29

May 1883

After supper and before retiring John and Ruth discussed what they should do on the following day. John had already told the men that he would be going to chapel with Ruth and the children in the morning, then would make his way down to Newport in the afternoon, to meet with the constables. He hadn't consulted her on this decision, frustrating Ruth and causing her to initiate a discussion on how they would proceed. "When I return from Newport, where I expect to find Alice, I will go immediately to ask your mother to return with me. It will be too late to return in the evening, so I shall stay overnight and she and I will walk back here first thing Monday morning."

She frowned at him.

"It's the best plan," he said, looking at the journal on his lap, his way of letting her know that the conversation was over. She left the room and went upstairs to bed. It was several hours later when she heard him walk quietly up the stairs and into the bedroom.

"Ruth, are you awake?" he whispered softly. She didn't move or respond.

As they approached the chapel on Sunday morning, the tension that had grown in the night was occupying Ruth's thoughts and the journey was mostly silent. As they walked past the school and the chapel came into view, they were surprised to see a small group of people waiting outside. As they drew nearer, it became clear that the crowd was waiting for them. Some moved towards them, patting them sympathetically, shaking their hands, and offering help with the search for Alice. Not everyone, however. As she returned the good wishes, Ruth saw Robert Pugh, the Morris family, and a few of the other deacons standing apart, their expressions conveying irritation towards her and John.

Pugh, unable to contain himself, signalled to the crowd that they should enter the chapel. The assembly filed in, John and Ruth taking their customary places and when all were seated the service began. Robert Pugh mentioned the sad demise of Esme Ellis and asked for prayers for her family. But he said nothing of Alice Jones, nor did he request any help from the congregation in finding her.

Outside in the patchy sunshine, Ruth found John surrounded by a group of men discussing how the afternoon's search should continue. As soon as he saw her, John excused himself and joined her. William, hovering anxiously next to his mother, spoke to his father as he approached.

"Dada, I have been thinking, instead of going to Sunday school today, perhaps I could come with you to look for Alice?" His gaze, intense and hopeful, moved John to a smile, but he shook his head.

"Thank you, William, but no. I need you to stay with your mother. I am going to lead the men down towards Newport, but then, when I have found Alice and sent her home, I'm going over the mountain to fetch Granny Ruth. I shan't be back until tomorrow morning, so you must be the man of the house." He put a hand on his son's head and stroked it gently. "You are becoming quite a young man, William."

"Thank you, Dada. I'll stay, if that's what you want me to do."

Ruth opened her mouth to protest that there wasn't much that an eight-year-old boy could do at the farm and that William was showing signs of real distress that might be relieved by being with his father and doing something helpful, but John went on. "William will spend his time well at Sunday school. I do not like these things to be neglected." He smiled at her. "Come, Ruth. I must go now. The men are waiting. I will see you again tomorrow morning. The constables will find Alice at the port this afternoon."

"If you say so, John." He waited for more, but when there was nothing he turned and walked back to the group of waiting men.

She led the children away, carrying Maud on one arm, the other hand holding Walter's, with William following a few paces behind.

They ate their lunch in silence in the dining room, after which William took Walter in hand and set off for the chapel and Sunday school, leaving Ruth with Maud. She usually reserved Sunday afternoon for needlework or reading her Bible, with John at her side. But today, she couldn't settle. As soon as Maud fell asleep, Ruth went to Alice's room.

It was neat and tidy because Alice was a neat and tidy girl. She went through the drawers in the tallboy, checking yet again what was missing, although she knew. Alice had taken a dress and the few shillings that she had saved, plus one of her clean handkerchiefs with her embroidered initials – her Christmas gift from Ruth. "My lovely, foolish little girl, even running away from home you took a handkerchief."

Alice's few remaining possessions were in one drawer. The fact that she had left them behind gave Ruth hope that Alice intended to return. But, like the first time she'd looked, and every time since,

Ruth knew that something else was missing, something important to Alice. She sat on the bed, trying to recall conversations between herself and Alice, and between Alice and Essy, but nothing came back to suggest what it might be. She stood and walked downstairs. As she reached the bottom step she heard footsteps at the front of the house. It was five o'clock. She had been sitting in Alice's room for over two hours. The boys should have been home over half an hour before. Panic seized her – wild, mad panic.

She flung open the front door, dashed through the porch and found Arthur Ellis with William and Walter, crouched down on the flagstones in front of the door, peering at a small object on the ground.

"Where have you been? Why are you late?" she screamed. The boys and Arthur jumped to their feet. The boys were frightened into silence by her wide-eyed terror, but Arthur replied. "When they returned, I believe they were unable to rouse you, Mrs Jones, so they found me in the yard. We have been looking at this caterpillar." He pointed down to the small wriggling insect on the ground at their feet.

"What do you mean? How dare you suggest that they couldn't rouse me. I was not sleeping."

"They didn't say that you were sleeping, Mrs Jones, but that you didn't respond to them." Arthur spoke gently, averting his eyes and clutching his cap in his hands in front of his chest.

"Thank you, Arthur. Come inside, boys." The boys walked uncertainly past her, into the parlour, glancing up at Ruth, who kept her eyes fixed on Arthur Ellis.

"What news do you have for me, Arthur?"

"No news of Alice, Mrs Jones. A search is being carried out around the port by the constables and they'll report back to

Mr Jones tomorrow. He has walked over the mountain to fetch Mrs Evans."

Ruth showed no emotion at his news, but dismissed him with a nod and the expectation of seeing him the following morning. As she walked into the parlour both boys jumped to their feet.

"We didn't mean to upset you, Mammy!" William began.

Ruth held up her hand.

"No need to apologise, William. You must have been concerned when I didn't speak to you." She smiled at them. "I was deep in thought about your sister." She put a hand to her stomach to quieten the fluttering sensation that had returned. "Granny Ruth is coming to visit tomorrow. Dada has gone to bring her. She will help look after you whilst Dada and I continue to search for Alice. I know how much you both love Granny Ruth." Smiles lit up their faces and Walter clapped his hands. "They'll arrive in the morning. Now, let's continue our Sunday, as we always do."

Chapter 30

By eight o'clock on Monday morning Ruth and Gwen had already boiled up two washing coppers and were starting on the third when John walked in with Ruth's mother. John often teased Ruth that in physical appearance no-one could ever have guessed that they were mother and daughter, and that Ruth had a way to go to match her mother for toughness and resilience.

Ruthie Evans, at fifty-five, was deceptively short, pale and frail in appearance. She was a quick-witted woman, who had birthed nine healthy children. She now took one look at her eldest daughter, gave her a short, questioning frown followed by a perfunctory hug, and said, "You need to rest. Give me that dolly." She took the washing stick out of Ruth's hand and turned to John. "Take her to the kitchen. I'll speak to Mrs Ellis, then I'll join you."

John's momentary annoyance was balanced by acknowledgement that Granny Ruth put the welfare of her children above all else, and that there was no point in arguing. He took his wife by the arm into the kitchen. They sat at the kitchen table in silence. John looked at Ruth, who stared at the table. In the background, they could hear Walter, complaining to baby Maud that she would tear the arm off Alice's rag doll if she pulled any harder.

John stood up. "I must go, Ruth. The postmaster offered yesterday to take me to Newport in his trap. I'm already late. I must meet the inspector to find out what they have discovered."

166

Ruth still didn't look up from the table. "It rained again last night. A great storm."

"Yes. We heard it. Mrs Evans is concerned that Alice will have taken a chill, so she has made up some goose fat preparation to use on the journey home."

John hovered impatiently, unable to make up his mind whether to leave or to wait for Ruth to speak.

"I must go, Ruth." He hesitated. Still no response. His voice rose with his growing impatience. "I am better doing something!"

She closed her eyes for a moment, then looked up at him. "Of course, you must go. I'm afraid, John—"

He cut across her so harshly that she moved back in shock.

"Don't speak of it! Everything is being done that can be done. We *will* find her. Then we'll know what's behind this disgraceful behaviour."

Ruth's mouth dropped open, but no words came out. Her worries had been increasing, and she had assumed that he felt the same. She felt no resentment towards her daughter, being now quite certain that what had occurred had been so terrible that Alice had run away out of fear. She felt guilty that Alice had not spoken to her. That John could feel anger towards Alice horrified her. Her expression altered as these thoughts darted through her head. John knew her well enough to read the feelings that his outburst had brought out.

"I know you're concerned for her welfare. I share that concern. But I cannot condone her running away from us." His tone was half anger, half plea.

"So, what's making you more angry, John? Alice running away, or Alice running from you and me? Does this undermine your discipline or hurt your pride?"

Her words hurt him. She knew that and she had meant them to. He waited for her to explain, or to retract. When she did neither he left. She sat unmoving until she heard the clip-clopping of the horse's hooves as the trap passed along the lane, without stopping. As the trap faded, Ruth's mother walked into the kitchen.

"Gwen says that's the final copper for today, so she's going to start on the rinsing. Now, talk to me, girl." She sat down in a chair on the opposite side of the table to Ruth, arms folded, leaning forwards.

"He's angry with Alice. I can't believe it, Mam."

"He's just frightened. Men are different. They don't like to show their fear. He may be a little harsh on her when she comes back, but it won't last. He loves her."

"What if she doesn't come back?"

The older woman sat back in her chair. "How long have you been thinking like this?"

"I sat in her room yesterday. It's so empty. What if she's dead?" Ruth whispered, her head bowed.

"What if she is?" Ruthie Evans spoke the words slowly, each one emphasised. Her daughter's head snapped up in astonishment.

"Then, what if she isn't?" her mother continued immediately. "What is the point of thinking like this? You have three other children, and something else to tell me?"

Ruth smiled. "You don't miss anything, do you?"

"Gwen told me what happened yesterday. It's going to affect you badly again, if yesterday was anything to go by. You must take care of your health. Alice will need you to be strong. Does John know?"

"No, I haven't told him yet and he hasn't noticed. I'll tell him later. I wouldn't like him to find out from anyone but me." She frowned at her mother.

"Not a word from me, I promise. But make sure you tell him tonight. I think he will insist that you speak with a medical man."

Ruth shrugged but before she could reply, Gwen came into the kitchen and the conversation turned to who would do what for the remainder of the day.

Throughout the day Ruth went about her tasks, not speaking unless it was about household management, knowing that her mother was watching her every move.

William, who had again attended school, was delighted to be met at the gate by both his grandmother and Walter. He chatted animatedly to her as they walked back to the farm, then took Walter out into the fields to find Ifor.

In the evening, when the children were in bed, Ruth listened keenly for the sound of the trap returning, but by the time they lit the lamps and sat in the parlour, John had still not come back. After a further couple of hours of uneasy pacing downstairs, there came the sound of footsteps at the back door. The look on John's face told her everything. He was accompanied by their local police constable, who asked Ruth and her mother to sit at the table. "We spent the day in Newport, Mrs Jones, and we have discovered some information." For a moment her heart rose, but he was still unsmiling.

"There was a child, the stall men and the boat owners at the port believed it to be a vagabond child, who was trying to get onto the paddle ship that sails across the Bristol Channel to Weston-super-Mare. Mr Jones tells me that this was an interest of Alice's?"

"Of course!" Ruth jumped up out of her chair. "That's what was missing from her room. The newspaper article of crossings for the *Waverley*. She's trying to get across the Channel. We can find out the times of the crossings!" A wave of dizziness hit her and she sat down heavily, grabbing at the edge of the table.

"Ruth!" John's voice was tinged with panic as he rushed to catch her as she was about to fall off her chair.

"Take her upstairs. Talk to her." Her mother spoke quietly to John, trying to convey a meaning in her voice that he heard but didn't understand. John led Ruth up to their bedroom.

In the kitchen, Ruthie Evans turned to the startled constable. "My daughter has not been sleeping well. A glass of beer whilst we wait for Mr Jones to return?" She nodded to Gwen, but he intervened with a smile.

"Thank you, ma'am, but no. It's discouraged nowadays. Besides, I don't think there will be any in this house."

Ruthie returned a reserved smile. "No, you're quite right, of course. A cup of tea, then?"

"Excellent, ma'am, thank you."

She walked behind him and moved the kettle from the hob. For ten awkward minutes they sipped their cups in between stilted conversation, until John came back. He gave a knowing nod to his mother-in-law and resumed his place at the table.

"I have told my wife what we know and what is our plan." He turned from the constable to Ruthie. "We are going to wait here while the constabulary search Weston-super-Mare to see if a child got off the boat there yesterday afternoon, or was seen moving around the dockside. They have already been telegraphed. As soon as there's a reply we'll be informed. In the meantime, we must go on with our lives here."

"Are you intending to go to England too, John?"

"Only if there is something to search for." He ran a hand through his hair, unconsciously pulling hard at it. "I must think about the farm. It can't run itself."

"How long before we hear something?" Ruthie asked the constable.

"We should get a reply by tomorrow morning, ma'am. If there's been a sighting, then Mr Jones can go there to meet the constabulary and search himself."

"And if not?"

"Then we have run out of information, ma'am. It might be time to bring in the detectives. But…" he paused with a frown, "… but we should wait to find out the news from Weston-super-Mare first." With that, he stood quickly.

"I'll be going now, Mr Jones. I'll be at the station house. If there's any news, I'll be sure to call round immediately."

John saw him to the door. As soon as he returned Ruthie spoke. "He has something on his mind. Did he tell you, John?"

"He has speculations, but that's all they are. Now, let's stop discussing this, please. I need to see Ifor at his cottage before it gets too dark." He went to put on his coat, but she put a hand on his arm.

"You spoke to Ruth?"

"Yes. She thinks it will be in November. I've asked her to see the local physician to tell him about the previous times." Ruthie nodded and went upstairs to her daughter. Ruth was sitting on the side of her bed, staring through the open window into the garden. Her mother sat down beside her, taking her hand with a gentle squeeze.

"We just have to wait, girl. Just wait. I'm here. The children will be fine with me. Just wait… and hope." Ruth's head sank onto her chest.

Tuesday was quiet and uneventful. Granny Ruth took William to school, supervised the laundry and the dairy, and managed the

171

tasks for Gwen. A few visitors and well-wishers called, enquiring after progress and looking for an opportunity for gossip. John had left early for the fields, leaving a message with Gwen to inform him via Arthur as soon as any word came from the constabulary. Ruth tried to work with Walter on his letters and numbers, and to occupy Maud, but she found that she had little concentration and twitched at every sound at the front and back of the farm.

John didn't return as usual at lunchtime, but sent word via Ifor he would remain in the fields until supper. He returned at seven o'clock as the light was fading and the full moon emerging in the late spring sky.

The family sat down to supper. No-one spoke; even baby Maud seemed to pick up on the atmosphere and she played quietly with her spoon while the boys sat staring at their plates. They had just finished their meal when a loud knock at the front door caused them all to jump. John went slowly to the front porch. Ruth remained seated, gripping the edge of the table as she heard the voice of the constable ask if he could have a word in private. Then she heard their footsteps fading into the parlour. She waited uncertainly, looking from her mother to the boys to the open doorway.

"He'll be back presently, just wait!"

The parlour door opened and John ran into the kitchen. One look at his ashen face told her it was bad news. He gripped her shoulders so tightly that she was unable to move. "The constabulary in Weston-super-Mare has contacted ours. The body of a child has been found in the sea. They want me to go immediately." Staring into his face, a blackness began to fall across her vision, a howl was the last thing to fade.

Chapter 31

"Ruth, Ruth! Can you hear me? Are you listening to me?" A rough hand shook her shoulder, irritating her enough to cause her to open her eyes and frown at whoever was shouting. Ruth saw her mother looking grimly back at her. She clutched at her mother's hand.

"Where is John? What's happening? How long have I been here? I must go with him!" She tried to jump up from the bed, but the weakness in her legs and her mother's firm hand held her down. She felt an emptiness in her stomach like hunger.

"What do you remember?" her mother asked.

"The news, of course. The child in the water. What else is there to remember? Did I become faint?" She glanced around. "Did John bring me here? I remember someone crying." She angrily shook her mother's hand off her shoulder. "Where is he? I must go with him."

"John has been gone two days." The statement took a moment to sink in.

"Have I been senseless for two days? It can't be"

"We haven't been sure if you were conscious or not. Sometimes your eyes have been open, sometimes closed. Nothing has roused you, not even the children crying for you." Ruth could hear the criticism. "The doctor is to call soon and if you hadn't yet spoken, he was going to arrange for you to be taken to the hospital."

"But you would not have let him?"

"What choice would I have had?" Now the tone was bitter and angry. Ruth closed her eyes and tried to summon calmness. Arguing with her mother wouldn't help.

"Please, Mam, just tell me what's happened," she implored in as serene a voice as she could muster.

"Well, you did faint, at first. John carried you upstairs and waited for some time. But after a couple of hours, he sent for the doctor. The doctor said it was probably shock, but on hearing of your condition and past troubles, he said that you must rest quietly. John decided to set out at once. He put together a case of clothes and ran to the postmaster for the trap and they left the house at around nine."

She saw Ruth was about to interrupt, and held up her hand. "Let me finish what I know. I heard later from the postmaster that John put up overnight in Newport, in order to take the early coach to Gloucester where he expected to stay the night, then today has travelled on to Weston-super-Mare by train. He will arrive there this evening and has an arrangement to meet with the local police inspector. He will check… the… child… first thing tomorrow. As soon as there's news, it will be telegraphed to us."

Ruth sat on the bed, staring at her mother, squeezing her shaking hands, with the realisation that there was nothing that she could do for John, and that there was nothing to be gained from asking further questions.

"What time is it, Mam?"

It's just after two in the afternoon. I'll go and——" She was cut short by a knocking at the front door.

"That'll be the doctor. Stay there." Ruthie commanded. "I'll bring him to you. Then you should speak to William and Walter, who are desperate to hear your voice."

174

The doctor was relieved that Ruth had regained her senses, but put it down to her prolonged loss of consciousness and begged that she should do nothing to exert herself in the coming months, if she wanted both herself and the child to survive. Ruth's response caused him to leave the house shaking his head with hopeless exasperation.

"Call me if anything happens, Mrs Evans. Which I expect will be the case before too long." He gave her a knowing look, shook his head again, and left without waiting for a reply.

As soon as he had departed, Ruth dressed and went to Walter and Maud, who were playing in the boys' room. They squealed at seeing her. Walter asked if she was better now and as soon as she had reassured him, they returned to their playthings and she went on down to the kitchen. Gwen was delighted to see her. Having heard that she was on her feet again, she had prepared tea and bread and butter. The sight of food increased her hunger pangs and she sat at the kitchen table. In response to her questioning, Gwen informed her of the local news.

"A great many people have been asking about you, Mrs Jones. In the village, there's concern about the news from England. The deacons are meeting tonight to pray for your family."

"Not all of them, I assume, Gwen."

"No, Mrs Jones, not all of them. But most."

"That's considerate. But my mother tells me that we shall receive a telegraph message tomorrow morning. So now I must wait."

With that she left for the yard. Gwen went to follow but Ruthie moved into her path.

"Let her go, Gwen. She needs to fill her time. In an hour she can walk with me to meet William. She has to prepare herself for whatever news is to come."

At four, Ruth and her mother walked to the school. As they crossed the green she could see the enquiring stares from villagers, but she walked with her head high. They stopped and waited at the schoolhouse in silence.

William was the first child to appear. "Hello, Mammy!" His smile turned into an enquiring frown.

"No, my darling, no news." She held out her hand and stroked his cheek. "Nanny Ruth tells me that you've been a wonderful help to her."

"I've tried my best, Mammy."

"And it was good enough, William. Good enough." She took his hand and they walked back to the farm.

"Sara Drew said that she missed Alice. That was nice, wasn't it?"

"Indeed. Has anyone else spoken to you of Alice?"

"Not really, Mammy. Miss Probert kept looking at me, but she didn't say anything. Mrs Morris asked if you were well. I said no."

Ruth and her mother exchanged glances. "Did Mrs Morris offer you sympathy?"

"No."

"Well, we have enough to think about for now. We shall hear from Dada tomorrow morning. We must all wait and pray."

"Can we pray when we get home, Mammy?" As he looked at her he could see her anguish.

"Of course, William."

The next twelve hours were the hardest that Ruth had ever known. In the evening the family ate in silence and Ruth didn't insist on William reading his Bible or going to bed at his usual hour. The younger children were put to bed by Granny Ruth while Ruth and William waited in the parlour, as the sun set and the light faded. Ruthie joined them with her sewing, saying little. When they had to accept that there wasn't going to be any news, they all went to bed.

They woke early, breakfasted and had been waiting in the parlour for a couple of hours when the knock finally came, just before nine o'clock. Ruth couldn't stand. She took William's hand as her mother went to answer the door to show in the constable. He didn't waste any time.

"It wasn't Alice, Mrs Jones."

Chapter 32

Ruth's chin dropped to her chest and it rolled slowly from side to side. She could hear William breathing heavily.

"Ruth!" It was her mother in the doorway, fearing another fainting episode.

"Nothing to be concerned about, Mam. William, fetch me a cup of water. So, Constable, what now?"

"Mr Jones said that he will set out for home this morning. He'll need one night on the road, so he should be home tomorrow evening. We will talk again then." He shuffled and looked at the door. "I'll take my leave of you then. Ladies."

"Thank you, Constable." Ruthie moved towards the door ahead of him, but he hesitated and turned back to Ruth.

"Just one thing, Mrs Jones. Our detective in Newport reports that just before Mr Jones was there last Sunday, there was another woman at the dock looking for a missing child. A girl, your Alice's age. Do you know who she could be?"

"No, indeed. Every day it was our men, and men from the village that searched, not the womenfolk. There were some farm hands from Rhiwbina, but I didn't hear of a woman joining them. Why would someone be looking as well without telling us?"

"It's probably just coincidence. The woman caused a stir. There was some thought that she had," he coughed in embarrassment, "an illness."

"What do you mean, constable? What illness?" It was Ruthie who asked sharply.

"There was some concern that she might have been…" his voice was a whisper, "a leper, ma'am. Well, good day to you both."

As the constable left, William returned and handed Ruth a cup of water. She signalled for him to sit beside her. From the hall she could hear the murmur of voices for a minute before her mother closed the door and returned.

"Thank God," she said as she came into the parlour. "As soon as John is home he will know what to do next."

"We'll keep searching, of course! What else is there to do? She cannot be far. She's waiting for us to find her. We can't let her down." Ruth's voice had risen and William glanced anxiously from Mammy to Granny.

"Of course, we won't let her down," Ruthie replied. "Now, William, go and see if Walter and Maud are behaving." He obediently left the room. "Now, what are you thinking, girl? This is good news. John will be home tomorrow evening. I know you've been worrying yourself that he might not find her. But keep faith."

Ruth smiled weakly at her mother. "I will never lose faith, Mam. Yes, my worry increases daily. And now I think that I need to know, whatever the outcome."

Ruthie nodded. "John will be tired and in need of a good meal when he gets home tomorrow evening. You need to rest and look after the children. William can go to school this afternoon and tomorrow morning. John will want that. Gwen and I will take care of the kitchen and dairy." She stood up, satisfied with her arrangements and went to the kitchen, leaving Ruth alone.

She felt helpless. After an initial refusal to accept what her mother suggested, she realised that there was nothing further she could do. She spent the rest of Friday and Saturday as normally as she could manage, but her head full of plans and fears.

* * *

John arrived home just before midnight on Saturday. Ruth welcomed him in, took his coat and travelling bag and put them in the hallway then led him to the kitchen for supper. Ruthie was waiting there. She greeted John then quietly excused herself. As he ate, Ruth waited for him to speak, but he said nothing, head down concentrating on his food.

"John, what have you to tell me?" she began after five minutes of silence. He didn't reply.

"John—" But she got no further.

"Please, Ruth, not tonight. We can speak tomorrow." He stood abruptly and left, leaving her astonished and bewildered. Having heard footsteps on the stairs, Ruthie, who had been waiting in the parlour, joined her daughter.

"Well?"

"Nothing! He will say nothing. He is tired and wants to wait until tomorrow."

"It has been a difficult few days for him, girl. Think about it."

"And how has it been for me, Mam?" she shouted. "Am I to be left in ignorance, not worth speaking to?"

"You are upset, I understand. But what could he tell you? Do you want to hear about the other child? He has travelled so far to look at a dead child, not knowing if it was his, then travelled again. What is there to tell?"

"I want to talk about what we do next."

"Yes, but not today. John will have plans. He'll tell you tomorrow." Ruth said angrily, "So he'll make plans. But what of mine?"

"Leave it to your husband. Men know best."

Ruth stormed out and up to her bedroom. John was already asleep.

The following morning, they dressed, and left for chapel in silence. News had spread about the body in Weston-super-Mare and, as they approached, friends and villagers pressed around John for news, leaving Ruth on the outside with the children, so she couldn't hear what was said. Conversation ceased when Robert Pugh opened the chapel door.

Ruth thought that Pugh must say something this time, but again he ignored their plight. However, he had news that shocked the entire congregation.

"It is with regret that I inform you that I shall be leaving Garth Hill with immediate effect. I shall be taking up a ministry in Herefordshire. In England." His supercilious smile caused shuffling in seats, but what he told them next brought a smile to many faces.

"Mr Robinson will be returning this week. He will resume his position as your minister here in Garth Hill." His smile faded as he saw the general reaction. He was going to speak again, but thought better of it.

At the end of the service small groups gathered outside the chapel, quietly discussing the news. It was clear that the return of Richard Robinson was being greeted with relief by most. But a small group of elders stood around Charles Morris, shaking their heads. Eira Probert and Bessie Morris also stood apart. Ruth couldn't help nodding a gracious smile in their direction.

She was anxious to get home so that she and John could speak. So, she took the children and whispered to him that they would go ahead and wait for him. He nodded curtly.

Back at the farm, Ruth fed the children, then sent them back to Sunday school, and she and her mother waited for John. Two

181

hours passed, the children came back from the chapel, but John had still not returned.

"Where's Dada?" asked Walter.

"I believe he has been held up at chapel. I expect he's talking to the men there."

"No, he isn't," William replied. "As we walked there after lunch I saw him heading to the fields. I think he was going to speak to Ifor."

During the evening, Ruthie attended to their reading and prayers as Ruth paced the house and waited for John's return. Her ankles and feet were swelling, making walking painful, so she sat instead in the parlour, staring into space. When the children went to bed, she briefly visited them then returned to her chair.

At midnight, she heard footsteps cross the yard, and someone enter the back door. She waited in the parlour. After a moment John looked in, surprised to see her there. The hostility between them was tangible.

"Did you not think I would want to speak to you, John? Why have you kept me waiting so long?"

"I had a great deal to think about."

"I, too."

"I have made a decision, my dear."

"I, too."

His puzzled expression told her that this was not what he expected from her. He sat in his armchair facing her.

"Well, Ruth. The past few days have been difficult. Yes," he held up a hand "for you, too. There is still so much that we don't know. Did Alice manage to cross the Channel? For there is no sign of her this side. Did she ever reach Newport in the first place? We have come to a dead end and there is no obvious place to look."

"Then we must re-double our efforts and look everywhere!"

"No, Ruth. I believe now that Alice intended to hide herself away so completely that we could not find her. Therefore," he paused, "I have spoken to the constabulary and have told them that we will cease searching for her. We will wait until she decides to come back to us."

Ruth stared at him, eyes wide. "I cannot believe that you still think this is wilful, John! She's ten years old and every instinct I have tells me that she is terrified of someone not far from us, because of something she knows about Esme Ellis's death." She paused to take a breath. "I know my daughter, despite what she's done. She is relying on me... us... to find her. I know she never intended to be away for this long. We *must* keep looking!" She began to cry and rose to pace around the room, but the pain in her feet stopped her. "And if you won't do it, I will." She had never shouted at him before and he seemed profoundly shocked.

"You're barely able to walk. What are you thinking?"

Nor had she ever disagreed so vocally with him. He had expected her to be upset about his decision, but it never occurred to him that she would refuse to accept it.

"You will remain here and look after our children and the farm. And the coming child. You know how ill you've been before. Have you forgotten little John?" He was shouting now, towering over her.

"How dare you suggest that I don't remember. But I never knew him. He was ahead of his time and already dead. Alice was my first child. I cannot let her suffer alone. How can you ask me to do so?"

"I've asked the constabulary to employ the services of a detective. He will search and report back to us. In the meantime,

183

I believe we should resume our lives and do what we can for our family."

"No!" she screamed at him.

"I will not tolerate this insulting behaviour from you, Ruth. I have decided. No more discussion. Please go to bed. You are not looking well and you must think about your health."

He marched out of the room and up the stairs. Ruth couldn't bring herself to join him. She didn't think that she could climb the stairs anyway, so she lay down on the sofa and thought about what he had said for hours, deciding that she would speak to him one more time in the morning. The idea of abandoning Alice was terrifying. And unthinkable.

Chapter 33

John rose early but Ruth was ahead of him and as soon as he entered the kitchen he stopped dead at the sight of her sitting at the table waiting for him.

"If you're hoping to change my mind, you will not."

She stood and walked towards him. "How can you be so uncaring, so cruel? She's no more than a baby and out there at the mercy of everything bad in this world."

"If she has had an accident, or worse, it would have become apparent by now. So, we must assume that she's hiding. And, therefore, she will eventually return. Now, I must look to the farm."

He made as if to leave, but she put an arm out.

"I will never give up. And I will never forgive you, John!" In his anger and frustration, he pushed her arm aside, which caught her off balance and she stumbled against the chair.

"Ruth, please, I'm so…" but before he could finish she recovered and ran ahead out of the kitchen and into the yard. John followed, but there was no sign of her. After several minutes of searching the barns and outhouses, he went back into the farmhouse and called for Ruthie.

"I'll go to look for her. She can't have gone far," Ruthie offered, but John shook his head.

"No, Mrs Evans. It should be me. Which direction do you think she might have taken?"

"Towards the village, possibly? She can't get very far because her feet are bad."

"She's going to do herself harm. Please look to the children and get William to school. I'll find Ruth." He picked up his coat and headed for Garth Hill.

An hour later he came rushing back, hands tearing through his hair. "I can't find her anywhere. Where in God's name can she be?"

"Ask in the cottages on the lane. Someone must have seen her!"

He left the farm and ran from cottage to cottage. At the sixth cottage, a woman said that she had been out collecting wood and had seen a woman heading up the path in the direction of the end of the mountain range where the medieval mound was. John couldn't believe that Ruth would attempt this, but when he asked, the description was of Ruth. So, desperately, he headed up towards the summit of the mountain.

Ruth had already reached the open tranche of marshy land at the top of the mountain ridge. She could no longer feel pain in her legs and feet, nor notice that her breathing was becoming shallower and more difficult. Without her shawl, in the biting and raw wind, she was shivering violently. But this, too, she ignored. She had been driven by panic and distress, not sure where she was going but knowing that she needed a vantage point. The mountain top was the highest point around.

She reached the base of the mound and struggled up the stony steps, grasping at the boulders at each side, barely able to catch her breath when she reached the top. At last, in the perfectly clear day, she faced what she feared.

Over the Bristol Channel, she could see the distant hills of Exmoor in Devon and to the east, the sweep of Weston-super-Mare, up the Channel to where the estuary narrowed at Gloucester. Below her was the expanse of the Welsh coast, Newport directly beneath, bending round to Cardiff, and behind her, the peaks of the Brecon Beacons.

It was a huge vista, where thousands of people were living and working. How could she possibly find one little lost girl? As she turned round and round, taking in the enormity of it, the realisation hit her, like a punch in the stomach, that it was impossible. She sank to her knees, looking up at the sky, now the colour of the lovehearts that Alice and Esme had gone to pick. She wept and howled until she had no more breath. She lay on her back looking up at the uninterrupted sapphire-blue sky, until her eyes slowly closed.

Chapter 34
May 2015

Still feeling weary, Maggie drove into the car park in the centre of Newport and ran across the grey concrete square to the library. Having spent too long checking emails, she was now running late, and the steady rain meant slow traffic adding to her frustration. By the time she reached the café she was out of breath and anxious.

The café was doing a brisk trade. Conversation buzzed in the queue, from which Maggie gathered that there was an exhibition of paintings by a well-known artist in the museum on the floor above. She took the last empty table in front of the full-length front window and stared out at the town square below, sipping her coffee and rehearsing what she planned to say to Zelah.

Ten minutes later, Zelah appeared, at great speed, from the direction of the reference library. Today, she was dressed all in blackcurrant, with opal pins holding her hair in place, and stilettoed purple shoes. As usual, she ignored the stares of the diners and charged straight for Maggie.

"Sorry, I was so close to getting all of this…" she waved a batch of papers in her hand, "that I thought you wouldn't mind waiting. I told you yesterday that I'd found something significant, well, there's more!" She was about to launch into her findings, when Maggie stopped her.

"That's great, Zelah. But I need to tell you something first."

Zelah stopped and frowned.

"It's about my daughter," Maggie explained.

"Ah. What is it?"

"I told you that the photo, this photo," Maggie handed it to Zelah, "is not just like her, it *is* her face. Well, I showed it to her, and she told me that this was the girl in the cemetery at the funeral that wasn't there. Remember? Esme Ellis's funeral." Maggie drew in a deep breath. "I don't know where this is going and I don't like it. Alice told me that she recognised the coat and boots that I found in the trunk, because the girl at the funeral was wearing them. She also thinks she recognised another girl. What the hell is going on here, Zelah? I've been awake half the night and I'm actually scared. This isn't just a piece of family history research any more, it's my daughter's well-being!"

Maggie had become flushed and her voice had risen loud enough to attract the attention of diners, several of whom were whispering to each other.

Zelah shrugged. "OK, you're upset, I can see that. What do you want me to say? You came to me and told me you wanted to find out about this mystery in your family. If you don't want to carry on, say so. I'll understand."

Maggie's mind raced. Did she want to carry on or not?

Zelah stood up. This was the moment to decide.

"Zelah," Maggie began, "I want you to tell me more about this theory about inherited memory. With as much detail as you've got. And tell me what you've found."

Zelah sat down.

"I don't have much more to tell you," she began. You can find information on the internet, but basically, the theory is that memory is inherited genetically, the same way as physical characteristics, so it's part of you, not learned. You inherit memories in the same way that you inherit green eyes or red hair. I don't know how or why. Like any memory, if you don't need it, you won't recall it. Most of us never need these memories, so they stay dormant unless some event brings them to our consciousness. In your case, coming back here seems to have triggered something for you and your daughter. There's usually a reason for it coming back. So I say, find out why. Same for your daughter. If there's any danger, well, she has you to look out for her. And me." She paused for a moment. "So… can I get on with what I've spent hours tracking down for you?"

"Yes, there is something else. Did my Alice really see Esme Ellis's funeral?"

Zelah took a moment to think. "I don't know, but I don't think so. She was looking at a memory. And yes, I know that sounds odd! And I could be wrong. Because it's understandable that you're connected to your great-grandmother's memories, but I can't work out Alice's connection." She paused and screwed up her face with the effort of choosing her words carefully.

"It seems to me that you and your daughter have inherited strong memories from your great-grandmother Ruth, but in following up your research you came on that day to a particular place and time where a significant part of those memories was playing out. What was the date you saw this in the graveyard?"

Maggie thought back. "It was the twelfth of May, about midday the first time. I remember because I was late picking Alice up for the dentist. We went back around two."

"We can check the cemetery records, but I think we'll find that both your great-grandfather and Esme Ellis were buried on the same day in May in their respective death years. I wouldn't be surprised if the funerals took place at midday."

"Are you saying it was no coincidence that I went to the cemetery on exactly the same day?"

"Difficult to say," Zelah replied. "When you first told me your story you said that you felt compelled to follow this research up but you had no idea why the compulsion was so strong. Now you know."

"I can accept that," Maggie replied. "But it still doesn't explain why Alice thought that people in the memory could see her. How could my Alice be a memory for them?"

They looked at each other, and Maggie continued. "How do I explain this to Alice?" Maggie looked perplexed. Zelah was silent. "When I was in the graveyard I took a couple of photos of the gravestone. Then I dropped the camera. When I printed them out, I found this." She handed a photograph to Zelah. It showed the bottom of the grave and some grass, and a woman's arm clothed in black silk with the hand in a black glove, reaching towards the camera. Behind the arm were wispy black shapes.

"I presume that's not your arm?"

"No. There was no-one else there. But it does mean something. In the past, I've had a dream, like a still picture, of a coffin and a group of people walking across grass. I don't get it often and I always wake up before it ends."

"Then this," Zelah pointed at the picture, "is a ghost, and before you start to argue with me, let me explain." Maggie's surprise levels had been so significantly raised, she felt she had to hear more.

"People generally believe ghosts are spirits of the dead who, for some mad reason, don't want to be dead. Well, that's rubbish! Ghosts are fractions of memory. Something within our mind is

191

projecting out, so we think we can see it. I think that's what Alice saw at the cemetery, but in her case it was incredibly strong and detailed. It may also explain why she thought the girl could see her. I don't know, I'll have to think about that, do some research. In your case, you've just projected your old dream. It may be more than a dream. Maybe it's an image of the memory of your great-grandfather's funeral. If you were in the same place, on the same day, and at the same time that it actually took place, the projection was strong enough to appear on the photograph."

Maggie chose her words carefully. The first thoughts that had come to mind as Zelah spoke were, "embarrassing" and "crazy". She settled for, "Wow! That's quite difficult to come to terms with."

"Hmm. Very diplomatic. What you really think is that I'm crazy. Well, I told you, it's a theory. Got a better one?"

Maggie smiled. "You know I haven't. But you've got to accept that this is a lot of strange information in a short space of time. I want to think it through before I can give you my opinion. That's how I like to do things."

"Works for me," Zelah replied. "Let's move on. Back to these." She pointed to the papers lying on the table. "I can tell you that what I've found fits with what you're telling me, and convinces me that there's a much bigger story here. Now, I told you that there was probably a missing child? I was right! It's a girl, born in 1873, in May. I've also checked every death of a child of the same name up to and including 1911. I can't find any record of a death. Now, let's say she just wasn't at home when the enumerator called. Where would she have been? Other family, grandparents, maybe?" Zelah wasn't asking questions that needed answers. "Not that I can find yet, but I'll keep looking. I've checked every family that you traced – you did a good job, by the way. Following the diverging lines of parents, just enough to give me access to where they all were at each ten-year interval. There wasn't any child of that name in Monmouthshire, either with family or working as a servant by 1891, or 1901. She just… disappeared. So the next step is to find out what happened to her."

Maggie spotted a pause in which to ask a question. "What was the girl's name?"

"You know full well, Maggie. Alice. To give her full name, Alice Ruth Jones. Exactly the same as your daughter."

Maggie exhaled slowly and shrugged her shoulders. "How do we find out what happened to her?"

"First, show me everything you've got with you from the trunk. Now that we know her name, let's see if there's anything we've already got that makes sense."

Maggie brought out the school photo and the newspaper article with the crossing schedule and placed them on the table. Before they could begin to examine them, the café door opened and footsteps approached their table. Maggie looked up at a dark-haired, rotund, middle-aged man in a grey suit and sober tie hovering behind Zelah. She smiled at him questioningly.

"Zelah, sorry to interrupt, but we need you upstairs for a couple of minutes."

"Not now!" Zelah snapped, not looking up.

"It's OK, Zelah, if you need to go," said Maggie.

"Later." Zelah retorted.

"The Mayor, Zelah… you agreed!" The man was hovering from foot to foot like a child delivering bad news to a teacher.

"Go, Zelah. You can't keep a mayor waiting!"

Zelah snorted and stood up quickly. She nodded to the man, who in turn nodded gratefully to Maggie as he and Zelah left.

Maggie took the opportunity to get herself another cup of coffee. She could tell that the woman behind the counter had watched the exchange and departure with interest. Maggie couldn't resist asking, "You know Zelah quite well around here?"

The woman rolled her eyes, then looked warily at Maggie. "It's OK." Maggie smiled reassuringly at her. "I don't bite. Who was that man?" she asked.

"That was Sir Roger Williams, the patron of the museum." Maggie was astounded. "Perhaps she didn't know—"

The woman cut her off. "Yes, she did know who he was when she brushed him off. I've never heard her speak nicely to anyone in all the time I've been here," looking at Maggie for sympathy.

"Perhaps because no-one speaks nicely to her. I find her friendly and helpful." Maggie knew this wasn't strictly true but determined to speak up for Zelah. In truth, she was amazed that Zelah hadn't been banned from the building.

"Not that they'll do anything about her," the woman went on grumpily. "Can't, can they?"

Maggie wanted to ask why not, but didn't want to let on that she didn't know that much about Zelah.

"Have you been up there, yet?" the woman asked, referring to the art exhibition on the floor above, which explained the greater than usual number of people milling around.

"No," she replied. But perhaps I will while I'm waiting. Will you keep an eye on the things on our table please?" The woman nodded and went back to stacking tea cups.

Chapter 35

Grabbing her bag, Maggie left the café and, seeing posters advertising the exhibition followed the signs upstairs. The exhibition was on the top floor of the library, in a gallery next to the museum. Maggie walked in to find a crowd of people admiring the display of fifteen paintings. In front of one of them, the mayor of Newport stood in a group being photographed, with Sir Roger Williams next to him. Standing on his other side, with a tightly fixed smile, was Zelah.

Maggie recognised the artist's name: Martin Fitzgerald. She had seen an article in the local newspaper and knew that he was gaining an international reputation. The article said that he had died a few years earlier, that his family infrequently showed his paintings, and they rarely put any up for sale. When two had been sold, the auction had attracted much interest. Both paintings had been sold overseas, and each for a six-figure sum.

Maggie walked around looking at the paintings: scenes of the countryside and coast of south Wales and the west coast of Ireland. She found them delightful, bright, and vibrant. Although many were painted in autumn and winter, it seemed to Maggie that Fitzgerald had captured a tremendous love of the countryside, so that even the fierce, devastatingly destructive winter storm on one huge frame gave her a feeling of exhilaration. She could understand why he had such an excellent reputation. What a shame there would be no more.

While admiring the storm painting, Maggie was distracted by a waving arm trying to attract her attention. Zelah was gesturing discreetly towards the exit to go back to the café. Maggie left, followed by Zelah a moment later. Maggie hoped for an explanation of what had been going on upstairs with the museum patron and the mayor but, instead, Zelah carried on the conversation where they had left off. She silently and intensely examined Maggie's items on the table intensely.

"This clipping doesn't have a date on it. But we can probably check it in the archives. The steamer information is from 1883. Someone was intending to take a trip. Doesn't look like there are any more leads from these. Shame. I'm going back into the reference room after this, so I'll take a look at *The Merlin* archives, to see what I can find."

"Thanks," Maggie replied.

"I also had a thought about trying to find out more about your family, but it means going public. How would you feel? Some people don't like the idea of sharing family details in the open. Might find some dirty linen."

"It would depend on what you mean by 'going public.'"

"Post on family history forums, for a start. Someone else may be looking for a connection and put the story on the website. Lots do that."

"Sounds good. Anything else?"

"No, unless you want me to explain what was going on upstairs?"

"Only if you want to tell me, Zelah. If you don't, that's fine." She was curious, but she didn't want to satisfy her curiosity if it made Zelah uncomfortable.

"I introduced myself to you as Zelah Trevear. It's my maiden name and I prefer to use it." She looked up for the first time in their conversation. "You and I get on, I think?"

"Yes, I think we do."

"And you said that you liked me. Well, I'm not an easy person to get on with, never have been. But you don't seem to mind that."

Maggie sat back in her chair. "I don't look for faults in people, Zelah, if that's what you mean. I give people the benefit of the doubt. I'm an easy person to get on with, unless someone really pisses me off. But it takes a lot to do that. But past your obvious rudeness I see a kind and interesting person. You've helped me so much, and got me further in a couple of days than I would have managed in weeks. You didn't have to help, so I appreciate it. I would like to know why you chose to help me when you're so off with other people, but it's up to you to tell me, if you want to."

"Big speech," Zelah replied, smiling. "I believe you see in history what I see, a connection to the past, to real people. I don't just see a name or a title. It's more than just certificates and gravestones. I see real, thinking, acting, loving, hating, arguing people. Sometimes I feel like I *know* them, and I think you're the same."

Maggie smiled and sat forwards.

"Yes, that's just how I've felt since I started this. For me, there's a deep sense of knowing. I've always had a good imagination, but I lost the sense of enjoyment it gave me. Until now. I feel like I have a real sense of purpose again." Maggie paused. "Anyway, you were explaining to me about your maiden name?"

"We agree then. So, you are probably the only person in the building who doesn't know my married name is Fitzgerald. Martin

Fitzgerald was my husband. I use my maiden name because I don't want to trade on his celebrity. When people know they suck up to me and I hate it."

"From what I saw, your husband was a wonderful artist."

"Martin was a wonderful man. His talent was natural, too. He just… had a gift."

"Well, he got to use his gift. You must be proud."

"I'd like to talk to you about him. But not today. Now," she went on briskly, back to her usual manner, "are you going to post the story?"

"Yes, later today, or over the weekend." Maggie remembered she had agreed that Alice could bring her friends round after school to look at the clothes.

"My sister's coming later. She's got a bee in her bonnet about something, so she'll be around to check on me. I'll risk asking her again if Mum or Dad left any more papers. When shall we meet next?"

"How about early next week? I'm going to be busy with this exhibition over the weekend. If either of us find anything interesting in the meantime, we can call." Zelah paused. "And, Maggie, if you're worried about anything your daughter says, please let me know. I really would like to help."

"Thank you, Zelah. I'll call you after the weekend. Good luck with the exhibition. Take the newspaper clippings."

Chapter 36
May 1883

Mrs Moira Davies checked her appearance for the final time in the mirror in her sitting room, sighed deeply at what she saw, shrugged her shoulders, and prepared to leave the house. In the seventeen years that she had worked at Knyghton House, from her time as a serving maid to her rise to housekeeper, her appearance before the other servants had never been anything less than perfect.

Her above-average height and strong build had prevented her from being bullied as a junior and when her talent and dedication gained her the role of housekeeper, at the age of forty, a wordless stare from such an imposing height could quell even the cheekiest parlour maid.

The reflection of Moira that stared back today was lanky and gaunt. Black circles under her eyes and yellow skin evidenced the desperate circumstances of the last few months. Throughout the series of deaths, first of her parents, then her husband, she had struggled to keep herself well dressed, tidy, and stern, despite the lack of sleep and the grief. But the death of her sister, almost her last remaining relative, just two weeks earlier, had finally torn a ragged gash in her façade.

She had seen the servants stare and look quickly away, whispering to each other as the black circles expanded down her colourless cheeks. Uncharacteristically, she didn't chide and chivvy them or order them to return to work. Often she found herself in some part of the house with no idea how she had arrived there, crying quietly to herself.

There was only one person who came close to being a confidante, to whom she had eventually related the tragedy of her sister. The butler, Mr Mervyn Hughes, had been greatly concerned when they retired to her sitting room after dining in the servants' hall the previous evening. It was then she told him her plan.

"Mrs Davies, I can't believe you are serious in this intent! Her Ladyship will not be pleased if you just depart without notice. It's clear that you haven't been sleeping well. Your behaviour has been, shall we say, erratic."

He paused to cough behind his hand with embarrassment.

Their relationship, although cordial, was strictly professional. She sat up stiffly in her armchair as he spoke, equally embarrassed. They had worked together for ten years and had only occasionally spoken of personal matters. He had been sympathetic when her husband died and later, her parents, but had asked no questions.

"I am aware, Mr Hughes. I have not been unnoticing of the servants' behaviour. But I hope I have continued to do my job to His Lordship and Her Ladyship's satisfaction."

"There's been no criticism from His Lordship and Her Ladyship. But they have asked questions and I've taken leave to tell them of your most recent loss. They are, of course, sympathetic," he smiled at her, to convey his own sympathy, "but they will expect that if you need time to visit Weston-super-Mare you will give some notice, at least."

"I can only apologise, to them and to you, Mr Hughes. But I must go. I cannot rest whilst my niece is missing. It was disturbing enough to hear that she'd been moved to the poorhouse after my sister's death, but to find that she has run away…" she glanced at the letter that lay open on the table next to her chair, "makes me fearful for her safety. I must go immediately to find out what happened to her. The poorhouse!"

Her face conveyed the misery she had felt since the news of her niece's fate had reached her in stages during the week. It had culminated in the letter from the poorhouse that had arrived earlier that evening. Now she felt nothing but determination to find the girl, as much as anything for her own salvation.

"Perhaps she didn't receive my letter. I told her that I would come as soon as I could. Or perhaps she didn't believe me. There has been little contact between Margaret and me since our parents died, or even before. I didn't even ask about her child." She gazed into the fire, talking more to herself.

"Twelve years old and quite a simple girl, they said. Not much... intelligence. But where could she go? Back to their lodgings, perhaps. It all happened so quickly. She must have been so frightened. Perhaps no-one has explained anything to her! Perhaps she can't read. I never thought of that!" She jerked her head back to the butler. "Of course! She couldn't read my letter. But she must have known it was from me because there is no-one else who would write to her!"

Hughes watched her, pursing his lips, uncertain if he should agree with her or say what he really thought.

"You may well be right, Mrs Davies. A frightened child may indeed take irrational action. But—" He got no further before her train of thought interrupted him.

"Irrational? Yes! What could she have done? Perhaps she has taken my letter to find someone to read it to her? I shall begin at my sister's lodgings. Someone there may have seen the child." She nodded, then stood.

"Goodnight then, Mrs Davies. I shall inform His Lordship that you'll be taking some days leave of absence. Shall I discuss the arrangements for your absence with Miss Eskwith?"

"I shall speak to her before I leave. Thank you, Mr Hughes."

"At what time will you depart?"

"Shortly before six. I have asked Morgan to have the carriage ready to take me to Newport station. I believe I can take a train from there to Gloucester where I shall stay overnight before travelling on tomorrow. I shall keep you informed of my progress."

He nodded, left the sitting room, and made his way to the butler's pantry where the under butler was awaiting final instructions on locking up for the night. He had decided not to speak to the earl and countess until the following morning. The earl would be mildly annoyed but would sanction the action as long as everything in the house was unaffected. Mrs Davies was too excellent a housekeeper to lose.

Moira pulled her curtains against the thunderstorm and prepared for another sleepless, guilt-filled night, conjecturing and worrying about the fate of her niece. She felt responsible for the girl's disappearance. She would find her and look after her. She had failed to save any of the others. But not this time. Not with this last one.

The following morning, after speaking to Miss Eskwith about the arrangements for the following week she put on her coat, pinned her hat in place and made her way to the servants' entrance door at the back of the house. Most of the servants who lived out arrived at around six o'clock. She guessed that some might be there already. Pulling back the bolts on the great wooden door, she opened the door to find not servants, but a small, muddy girl lying senseless on the doorstep.

Chapter 37

It took a moment of open-mouthed incredulity before her brain began to work again. Looking around the cobbled yard, and seeing that no-one else was yet about, she bent and picked up the child. She carried her to her own sitting room, laid her in a chair, then ran across the corridor to the servants' hall, where she shouted at an under butler to find Mr Hughes immediately and ask him to come to her sitting room.

When Hughes arrived, somewhat out of breath and startled, he found her kneeling over the body of a half-dressed girl, with a pile of wet filthy clothes on the floor.

"Mrs Davies! What is this?"

"On the doorstep," she muttered, pulling at shoes and stockings, "unconscious and can't be woken." She patted the girl's hands and cheeks again, and as her hand touched her right cheek, the girl moaned.

"Look at this wound, Mr Hughes. It's festering and stinking. Why is her face so black? Please organise one of the maids to fetch some clean hot water, cloths and some arnica. It must be cleaned at once."

He went next door to the kitchen where he found the senior seamstress lingering in the kitchen for a cup of tea with the pantry maids. All were waiting to hear the reason for the commotion from the housekeeper's room.

"Mrs Fitzgerald, please fetch hot water, cloths and arnica, at once."

"Yes, sir," the woman responded. "Shall I fetch Nurse?"

"What?" He was distracted, both by concern for Mrs Davies and by Honora Fitzgerald's strong Irish accent. "Nurse, sir. In the nursery?"

"Oh, yes. Good idea. Fetch first what Mrs Davies has asked for, then get Nurse down."

The woman left the kitchen, watched by the pantry maids who had been whispering to each other. The butler rounded on them. "Carry on with your work. No fuss, please. Mrs Davies is dealing with the situation. Return to your work now!" The firmness of his words sent them scuttling. A bell rang in the corridor.

"His Lordship's valet," Hughes said to the cook who had just appeared in the kitchen. "He'll be wanting the tea tray. Get on with it."

When Hughes put his head around the door of Moira's sitting room half an hour later, Honora Fitzgerald had delivered the water and cloths, and Nurse was in attendance, gently examining the head wound. The child was moaning, her eyes still closed. He called softly to Mrs Davies for news.

"Not good, Mr Hughes. Nurse is very concerned. The wound is festering and the child is shivering from cold, although her skin is hot. There is a severe fever."

At that moment the girl cried out and opened her eye. Seeing the people gathered around her, she tried to stand, but fell murmuring.

"What is she saying, Nurse?" Mrs Davies demanded, going back to stand next to the chair.

"A name, I think, Mrs Davies. I asked her who she is. She cried and shook her head. The she said 'Mama' and 'Esme' and 'sorry', I think."

Moira put her hands to her mouth and shrieked, so loudly that the butler ran into the room to catch her, fearing from her white face and swaying body that she might be about to faint. But her face looked joyful.

"Esme. She said Esme. Are you sure, Nurse?" She took the startled nurse by the arm. "Are you certain she said Esme?"

"Yes, Mrs Davies. That's how it sounded." She shook Moira Davies's gripping hand off her arm. "This child is very sick indeed and may not survive. The doctor should be summoned."

Hughes stood beside Moira Davies and whispered so that the others could not hear. "Do you know who this child is, Mrs Davies?"

"This is my niece, Esme Peach," she whispered back. "She has come to find me."

Chapter 38

Despite opening her one good eye, Alice became more deeply unconscious as the hours passed, unaware that she had been carried into the small bedroom next to Mrs Davies's sitting room, undressed and put into the bed, and her head wound cleaned and dressed. She continued to moan and attempted to turn her body from time to time, but spoke no further.

The doctor, who had been summoned from Newport, arrived in the early evening. Having spent a half hour with the girl, he finally turned to an anxious Moira, who was hovering in the doorway.

"I can give you no good account of her condition, Mrs Davies. It's a serious fever, which may be the result of a contagion, or may be simply from becoming very cold. I believe it to be pneumonia. The lungs are weak. This child had not, I think, drunk well enough for many days before she arrived here."

"But you can save her, Doctor?" She pleaded with him, in a voice filled with passion that he had never heard before from this normally aloof woman.

"I'm sorry, Mrs Davies. I make no promises. She is going to need careful nursing. The wound on her forehead has become septic and may be affecting her brain. The blackness is the path of infection. If it spreads further, then it may be fatal. It must be kept clean and covered and place this on it." He handed her a pot of black ointment and, seeing her forlorn face, put a hand on her arm. "Time, and good nursing, will tell. I shall call again tomorrow morning. In the meantime, try to get her to take some broth, whatever you can get into her."

Moira nodded and turned to the girl, but not before she saw him pause in the doorway, look at Hughes and shake his head.

"You will not die," she whispered in Alice's ear. She took her hand and buried her face in the pillow next to her head. "You will not die."

As the servants arrived the following morning the sudden appearance of Mrs Davies's niece, and Mrs Davies own state of mind, were the only topics of discussion in the kitchen. Cook and Nurse had spent much of the day helping Mrs Davies, but they could see the girl's condition was deteriorating, as her face swelled with infection and her breathing became more and more laboured. Rumours of imminent death had run through the house throughout the day, even reaching Her Ladyship's personal maid.

At seven o'clock, after dinner, the countess appeared without warning in the kitchen, throwing the thirteen-year-old kitchen maid into a nervous skitter.

"You, maid, what is your name?"

"Mary Evans, Your Ladyship." The girl bobbed an off-balance curtsy.

"Don't shake, girl. I'm not going to eat you. Where is Cook?"

"I think… I'm not sure," she quailed and her lip quivered under the countess's frown, but Her Ladyship was not an unkind woman.

"Just tell me," she spoke in a softer voice.

"She has gone to see if she can be of help to Mrs Davies, Your Ladyship," the girl stuttered, her head bowed.

"Thank you, Mary Evans. Please return to whatever you were doing. Don't sniff, girl. I can't abide it."

"No, Your Ladyship. Sorry, Your Ladyship." She had never seen her employer in her three months at the big house, and had never expected to speak directly to her. In a state of great excitement, she leaned around the kitchen entrance, watching the elegant swishing silk bustle disappear down the servants' corridor and around the corner into Moira's sitting room.

Moira was sitting in the armchair facing the fire with her eyes closed, but was not asleep. The swish of silk alerted her to a presence and as soon as she saw the countess, she stood up, swaying slightly.

"Please, Mrs Davies, sit down. You look exhausted."

"Your Ladyship, I… I… yes, I am very tired, but I wasn't sleeping, just resting. Mrs Collins is sitting with my niece."

"I heard the story from Jane. How is the girl?"

"Not well, ma'am. Not well. She has a pneumonic fever and a badly infected wound on her head. The doctor has given us some medicine but there is no relief as yet. And she seems to have a damaged ankle."

"May I see her?"

"Of course." She walked to the door of the small bedroom and spoke back over her shoulder. "There's no risk from the infection, Your Ladyship."

As they reached the doorway Moira stood aside and the countess was able to look in. The cook, Mrs Collins, sat in a high-backed chair at the bedside, mopping the brow of the girl, who lay motionless. The swelling had spread across her forehead and down her cheek, the skin stretched and black, making the face look grotesque. Cook looked up and the countess could see from her expression just how serious the situation was.

"No improvement, then?"

"I'm afraid not, Your Ladyship." Mrs Collins glanced across at Moira. "In fact, I think the badness is spreading. I think the doctor should be called again."

The countess saw that Moira had put her hands behind her back to hold onto the door jamb.

"I shall ask Jane to telephone to the exchange to bring the doctor immediately." She waved away the thanks from Moira. "And, Mrs Davies, would you come with me back to your sitting room, please."

Moira nodded and followed. The countess indicated for her to sit and she sat also, which would have amazed Moira if she had thought about it, for the countess had rarely visited her sitting room, let alone sat with her.

"It seems that the doctor's remedy is having no effect?"

"It's getting worse, ma'am."

"I see. This child is your only family now, Mrs Davies?"

"Yes, ma'am. I have no-one left but her." Tears came to her eyes and she made no attempt to wipe them. "Speak to Mrs Fitzgerald. At once."

"Ma'am?" This was most unexpected. What was the point of speaking to the Irish seamstress? The countess saw her puzzled expression.

"I have spoken many times with Mrs Fitzgerald, about her past and what she knows. Her mother was a herbalist and, well… a woman of certain abilities in Ireland, as was her mother and her grandmother before. They passed on… special knowledge to

Mrs Fitzgerald. She knows a great deal about the relief of many conditions, probably more than the doctor." She paused, and leaned forwards towards Moira. "She may be able to help you, if the doctor has nothing further to offer." With that, she stood up, nodded briskly at Moira, and left the room.

Moira sat, quite stunned, as what she had just heard sank in. She had rarely spoken with the seamstress on any matter, other than those that directly affected her work. The woman was a talented mender and maker with any kind of material, but that the red-faced, squat Irish woman with the voluminous pockets would have anything else to offer was unthinkable. But she would ask, rather than risk offending the countess.

Cook was the servants' everyday provider of poultices and other simple medicines, usually made from things she kept in the kitchen. Moira was unfamiliar with herbalism, but inclined to think of it as a primitive practice. But the past six months of nursing her husband through his illness, decline and death, the death of both of her parents from influenza, and her sister's recent horrific death, gave her pause for thought. If the doctor could do nothing, she would do anything she had to do to save Esme.

Chapter 39

Within an hour of the countess's departure the doctor arrived in his carriage, wrapped up in his greatcoat against the wind and rain, looking rather put out.

"I said I would return in the morning, Mrs Davies. Why have I been summoned?"

"My niece is worsening, Doctor. Your remedy is not working. And her breathing is becoming more laboured. Her Ladyship asked that you be called immediately."

At the mention of the countess he raised his eyebrows. "Take me to the child immediately."

"Of course, Doctor."

As they walked towards the patient's room, Mrs Davies saw Honora in the doorway of the kitchen, so she beckoned to her.

"Mrs Fitzgerald, I need to speak to you as soon as the doctor is gone. Will you wait"

"Of course, ma'am. I'm ready."

"*Ready for what?*" Moira thought, but the doctor was already in the bedroom, so she nodded and followed him. As she shut the door she noticed that Honora was fingering something in her pocket.

As soon as he looked at Alice, the doctor shook his head. He carefully removed the bandage covering the wound and as he did so, the foul smell of pus oozing from the gash hit Moira. More than half of the little girl's face was obliterated by the swelling and was black.

"As I feared, Mrs Davies. The illness is too far advanced. I believe the poison has spread into the blood. I can do no more. You must be prepared."

Moira sank heavily into the chair next to the bed. "Nothing?"

"The infection is spreading. If you wish I could take her to the hospital, but I don't believe that their nursing would be any better than that which she is receiving here. Until the new hospital is built, the current building is not very… satisfactory, on any account."

"No, thank you, Doctor. If the worst is to happen, I want my Esme here with me." Moira knew the reputation of the hospital at Newport for killing more of its poorer patients than it cured. Indeed, it was one of the reasons why the earl had set up a board of subscriptions to build a modern institution which was nearing completion. But not in time for her niece.

"Very well. Keep her warm and clean, ma'am. Try to get her to take nourishment of some kind. And hope and pray." He smiled compassionately at her, but was momentarily taken back by the look of fury she cast at him. He put it down to grief. "I shall return in the morning." He went to shake her hand but she turned away from him and returned to the bedside, her stiff back making it clear that she wanted him to leave.

Moira sat, unmoving, by the bed, holding Alice's hand and listening to the sounds of the doctor's departure. She stood and turned to the door, where Honora Fitzgerald was standing, silently staring at Alice in the bed. The bandage hadn't been replaced and the candlelight cast dancing shadows over her blackened face, making it appear to pulsate and seep. Honora moved to the bed, never taking her eyes off the girl, signalling to Moira to move away.

She sat and leaned over, putting one hand on Alice's forehead and one on her chest.

Moira had her back against the wall to steady herself. She was momentarily distracted by an idea that, as they touched the child, Honora's hands gave off tiny green flashes, but it must have been a trick of the candlelight. The only sound in the room was Alice's laboured breathing. The seamstress nodded decisively.

"This is very bad indeed… but maybe not fatal."

Moira let out the breath that she didn't know she had been holding as Honora turned to her.

"The thing is, Mrs Davies, I'm not a medical. I have knowledge, as Her Ladyship has told you. My remedies are old, but you must decide if you want me to try."

"I have nowhere else to turn. Do whatever you can."

"You have faith, Mrs Davies."

"I don't know what I have, Mrs Fitzgerald. I just know that she will surely die and you are my last hope, whatever the outcome," she added, looking directly at the other woman. "And I think you knew already."

Honora reached into the pocket where Moira had seen her fingers move earlier, and brought out a small tin. As she removed the lid, sweetness filled the room.

"Honey is part of the blend, good for wounds. But there's more in here than that, Mrs Davies. A strong… remedy. You're sure, now?"

"Yes." Moira didn't hesitate. She felt certainty now, making the decision without needing to think.

"Is this water clean?"

"No, I washed her face before the doctor came."

"I need clean water, boiled and cooled. Can you arrange that?"

"Yes, but…" Moira felt reluctant to leave.

"Sure, she'll be safe with me, ma'am. I am going to give her a little of this now." She held up a small vial of brown liquid. "It's for the wet lungs, to dry them out. She'll breathe better for it."

Moira left and ran to the kitchen, as Honora poured a few drops of the liquid into Alice's mouth.

When Moira returned, Honora hadn't seemed to have changed position, and was still intently watching Alice, while swaying gently backwards and forwards, muttering under her breath. It also seemed to Moira that the child's breathing was easier.

"I think the breathing is a little relieved. But it's early yet. Sure now, we'll start on her poor face. Put the water here, ma'am." Moira did as she was told, gratefully.

Honora carefully washed Alice's face in the clean water, then took a wooden stick, dipped it in the tin, and applied the thick paste from within to the wound and its surrounding flesh. All the time she gently swayed back and forth, eyes closed, chanting incomprehensibly. The paste seemed to ripple and flutter around Alice's face. Moira told herself it must be the candlelight causing the apparition.

"Are you going to need a fresh bandage?"

"No, ma'am. This will work best without covering. It must stay on for four hours, then be removed. Very gently, mind, peeled away, and re-applied. We'll do this for twenty-four hours. Only then we'll know what will be." She looked at Moira.

"I would like to suggest, ma'am, that I'll stay with the child for the night." She saw a protest coming and put up her hand. "I'm versed in this. Begging your pardon, ma'am, but you are not. You look like you haven't slept for days. If you care to go next door you

214

can refresh yourself and sleep a little while. I can call you if there's a change."

"You were about to go home, weren't you, Mrs Fitzgerald. What about your family?"

"If you please, ma'am, send a message to my husband to say I'm detained overnight. Please don't tell him why." She smiled a thin, grim smile.

Despite her reluctance to leave the bedroom, Moira knew that she was at the point of collapse and would likely fall asleep during the night anyway, so she consented to Honora's instructions.

Her first visit was to the butler. Mr Hughes immediately arranged for one of the junior footmen to visit Mrs Fitzgerald's house to give the brief message. Hughes asked no questions, although his disapproving expression suggested that he knew more about the seamstress' strange expertise than he was prepared to admit. But he was pleased to hear that Moira intended to get some rest.

"A good idea, Mrs Davies. If the child survives the night, there's still going to be a job to bring her back to her strength."

The kitchen was dark and silent as she walked past back to her sitting room. Someone had lit the fire and she was grateful for the thought. In her bedroom, she washed and changed into clean clothes, then went back to her armchair in front of the fire, intending not to sleep but to rest. On the table next to her were photographs of her husband and herself taken at the servants' holiday the previous year in Porthcawl, just weeks before the discovery of his illness.

"How happy we look," she thought, closing her eyes to recall the moment when the photograph was taken on the esplanade, on a warm summer's day. The wind had blown her hat off, she remembered, and Arthur had jumped to catch it. Then someone was shaking her arm.

"It's dawn, ma'am. I thought you should know."

Honora was gently shaking her arm, her expression blank. For a few seconds Moira struggled to understand where she was and why Honora Fitzgerald was there. Then it came back with a wave of gut-wrenching panic and she jumped up out of her seat.

"She's still with us, ma'am. I think, a little better. Come and see," said Honora encouragingly.

As soon as she entered the bedroom, Moira could sense the change. Alice's breathing had lost its rattle. The rancid smell was gone, although it wasn't possible to see if there was any lessening of the swelling, because the thick paste blanketed the blackness.

"I'm about to clean her face, ma'am. Shall we see if there is any improvement?"

Moira nodded and watched as Honora peeled back the slick brown paste, once again muttering an incantation. It came off the child's face with a slurping sound and Moira gasped when she saw what was underneath. The blackness and swelling had receded to leave the skin looking bruised, but certainly more recognisable as a girl's face. Honora nodded approvingly, then began to clean off the remainder of the paste with a cloth and steaming water. Moira watched, transfixed, as the little face was made completely clean. The smell of sweet honey filled the room as fresh paste was applied.

"The wound is still dangerous and will take some care. But I think another twenty-four hours will do it." She looked quizzically at Moira. "What are you going to tell the doctor?"

"The truth, Mrs Fitzgerald. I owe you nothing less."

"I would prefer you said nothing, ma'am."

"Whatever you wish, Mrs Fitzgerald. But knowledge such as this is extraordinary! Can't it be put to good use elsewhere?"

"No, ma'am." Honora said adamantly. "It goes no further than me. It's the old ways. I haven't taught my children and it'll die with me. There's more to it than just mixing herbs. It's old ways. People don't like it. My husband doesn't like it."

"I see. Well, we'll have time to consider this when Esme is fully recovered. What, are you still concerned?" She had seen a wary look in the seamstress's eyes.

"Sure, it isn't over yet, ma'am. Another twenty-four hours. Then she'll still need much more care. She hasn't woken at all, and that's not good. It may be some time, and there's no knowing what has happened to a brain struck by such a grievance."

Moira's sense of relief at the girl's apparent improvement was tempered now with fear.

"Are you saying she might not wake up?"

"No, ma'am. I believe she will wake, in her own time. But I don't know if she will be... sensible, when she does wake, if you understand my meaning."

"That would be a great blow. But, she is my only flesh and blood now, and I'll do whatever is necessary. Now, you need some rest, Mrs Fitzgerald. Tell me what I must do and I'll take over."

"Something very wicked has troubled this child, ma'am. Very wicked. I felt it when I spoke to her. She escaped it, and my labour will help, but it will find her if it can. You must protect her."

"I don't understand. Her mother was murdered. Is that what you mean?"

"No, ma'am. Worse. Much worse."

Honora left. Moira waited for the doctor. She now understood the implication of Mrs Fitzgerald's "knowledge" and she was concerned about the real extent of what she had exposed her niece to. But what was done, was done; she should concentrate on Esme's physical well-being.

Cook brought her a cup of tea and three slices of bread and butter. She realised that she hadn't eaten in two days.

A few hours later the doctor arrived. His surprise that Alice was still alive was followed by anger at the sight of the brown paste across her face.

"What is this… this… mess?"

Moira carefully peeled it away, exposing the now normal-shaped, but bruised-looking face. Without speaking, she carefully washed the remainder of the paste away. The head wound was still ugly, but the redness around it had reduced and the smell had gone. Moira watched the changes of expression spread over his face as he stared, open-mouthed at the transformation.

"You will also note, Doctor, that her breathing is easier. Not entirely normal, but improving. I believe the lungs are drying out. However, I will not be satisfied that she's entirely out of danger for another day."

"Whose work is this?"

"I would prefer not to say. I can understand that you're not happy that I took alternative advice," she was trying to placate his angry countenance, "but you can see that there's a notable improvement."

He nodded, reluctantly. He was not an unreasonable man and besides, professional interest moved him to hope for more information.

Moira went on. "I would be very grateful if you would continue to watch over Esme. Once she is indeed out of danger I will need your help and advice to manage her further recovery." She looked at him with an expression that she hoped conveyed contrition.

The doctor looked from Moira to the child and back. He mused for a moment. "Very well, Mrs Davies. Of course, I'm delighted that the child *seems* to be improving. But as you say, it's still early days. I shall visit again tomorrow."

"Thank you, Doctor."

As soon as he departed she went to the kitchen, where Cook informed her that Mr Hughes had taken advantage of a ride with the doctor into Newport and that Mrs Fitzgerald was waiting in the servants' dining hall to speak to her, before going home.

Moira crossed the open courtyard from the kitchen and went down the steps into the large dining hall, where Honora sat at the end of one of the long benches. The hall was cold as always, due to its sunken floor and its thick walls. It was the original and oldest part of the house, the medieval hall, with a high ceiling and the remains of a minstrels' gallery. Although it had a row of tall, wide windows facing the courtyard, the sun never shone in here. After eating with the servants, Moira was always glad to retire alone to her comfortable sitting room to take her pudding and coffee. She shivered.

"Thank you for waiting, Mrs Fitzgerald. The doctor has gone, but will come back tomorrow. I think more from fear of offending the countess if he refused. But he will return and continue to care for Esme."

"Sure, it's right that he should, ma'am."

"Indeed. But I will never be able to thank you."

The Irish woman shook her head, put her hands onto her knees and pushed herself to her feet. "Please, ma'am, I don't want thanking and I would prefer it that we don't discuss it. I've looked at your girl. I think she'll live, but I can't answer for her mind. The doctor must do that. Now, I would like to go home if I may be excused?"

"Of course. I've asked Cook to make up a basket of food for you to take with you. A small thanks. Please don't refuse. I shall respect your wishes and not speak of Esme with you again, but you must take this small token of my thanks. I've arranged for a carriage to take you home. Alfred is waiting in the back yard now, as soon as you're ready."

Honora thought for a moment then nodded. Moira guessed that she was thinking about how to explain to her husband where she had been. They walked together up the steps and out of the hall, then separated as the seamstress waddled down the hallway to the back entrance and Moira returned to the sick room.

Chapter 40
May 2015

As she had anticipated, shortly after she arrived home with Alice, Jack, and Alice's two friends, Fiona arrived. The girls ran upstairs into Maggie's room and began to examine the clothes from the trunk. Maggie had reluctantly agreed that Alice could try them on if she wanted, but she had to do so very carefully. Maggie wasn't convinced that Alice, despite her promises, could remember to be careful if she got over-excited.

Maggie and Fiona went into the kitchen, Maggie listening out with one ear to the shouts and exclamations coming from upstairs as she made two mugs of tea.

"Well?" Fiona asked. "Did you get a reply?"

"Yes."

"And was it a positive one?"

"Yes."

"So, are they going to interview you?"

"Yes. Next week, Monday."

"So soon! They must be keen. Aren't you excited?"

"No. You're excited enough for both of us, Fee. That'll have to do."

"For goodness sake, Maggie! You've got two children and very little money. How are you going to keep them and this house? You have to be practical. It may not be exactly what you want, but responsibility to your family comes first."

Maggie's exasperation turned to anger. "Do you think I don't know that?" she snapped. "Do you think I don't spend nights worrying about how I'm going to manage? You think I haven't learned anything after what we've been through? You've had it easy, Fee. You have no idea what it's been like for me." She paused, leaned against the dresser and folded her arms. "Look, I know you mean well, but I don't need a lecture. I have an interview on Monday. I'll put on my best suit and my best smile. I may even get the job. I'll be miserable but solvent. OK?"

She knew that she had hurt her sister, knew that Fiona meant well. But she also knew that she was still holding out hope that something would turn up that would solve her money worries. It was like trying to win the lottery, an impossible madness, but still one hoped. But she couldn't admit this to her sister.

Fiona lowered her voice. "I'm only thinking about your welfare. I worry about you. You know that Graeme and I will help…" she put up a hand to halt Maggie's protest, "…which I know you don't want, but you know that the offer is there. You have to help yourself and be practical, Mags."

Maggie sighed. "Thanks, Fee. I'll let you know how the interview goes. There's something else I want to ask you. Did Mum or Dad leave any papers that you know of, anything about the family?"

She was expecting the usual brush off from her sister, but Fiona's response surprised her. "Yes, Mum left some stuff. Some of it was hers but mainly it was dad's. How about coming over later, for supper? We can get it down and see what's there."

"That would be great, thanks. I'm taking Alice's friends back at six. Shall we come straight after?"

Maggie knew that Fee had no interest in old papers and was indulging her, but that was fine. She hadn't expected there to be anything, assuming she would have thrown out anything that held no obvious value. This was a huge bonus and there might be some information that would help her to find out what had happened to Alice and Ruth. Fiona left, and Maggie went upstairs to see how Alice was getting on.

Just before six they delivered Alice's friends home and were driving towards Fiona's village up the valley. As they drove, Maggie told Alice and Jack that she had an interview for a job on Monday and would likely be returning to full-time work. She was surprised that both were disappointed. Alice immediately worried about how she would get to school.

"That will be a condition of taking the job," Maggie reassured her. "I'll be able to take you, but I'll have to find someone to pick you up and stay with you 'til I get home."

"Ugh, another childminder. Why can't we look after ourselves? We're old enough." Jack complained.

"You don't want to be looked after like small children, I get that. I promise I'll find someone you like. In fact, you can interview them with me. I'll only hire someone you choose. How about drawing up a spec for me of the person you'd like? Not too Mary Poppins, please!"

"Cool! Thanks, Mum. It might not be so bad. Not as good as having you at home, though."

Maggie was touched. Jack rarely said anything spontaneously nice to her since becoming a teenager.

"What about you, Alice? Can we find someone you'll get on with?"

"I guess I'll have to try, won't I?" The tone was resigned. "I wanted you to pick me up right to the end of term."

"If I'm offered this job, and it's not a certainty, I don't know when I'll start. I told them I was available immediately and I can't put it off for a couple of months. But I will tell them I need time to find someone to pick you up." *It will give me more time to finish off the research*, she thought. "Next term, you and Jack will be in school together so one pick up will be easier than two."

"Please try to keep picking me up to the end of this term, Mum."

"I'll try. Is there a problem, Alice? Are those girls bothering you again?" When they had first arrived, Alice had been picked on by a group of girls. This included teasing her at the school gate and, although it had been sorted out, Alice was still nervous whenever she couldn't see her mother waiting.

"No, it's not them."

Maggie heard Jack's whisper: "Tell her."

"Tell me," she said to Alice in the rear-view mirror.

"I keep getting DTs." This was detention, which Alice hated. Maggie was surprised, not just because Alice hadn't told her, but because she had always been well-behaved in school. Parents' evenings had consistently confirmed that Alice was a model pupil.

"What's been happening"?

Jack replied. "They've got a new teaching assistant, who doesn't like kids… or teaching."

"I can see that that would be difficult," Maggie joked, "but it doesn't explain the DTs."

"She picks on *everything* we do. If we whisper or laugh, or drop a book, she gives out a DT."

"What does Mr Rees have to say about that?" Maggie found Alice's class teacher pleasant enough. Alice liked him, too.

"He's away on a course for a couple of weeks and we have a supply plus *her*."

"I know you don't like DTs. But is it fair, what she's doing?" Maggie asked.

Again Jack replied. "No, Mum. She picks on them too. This week, it's been Alice's turn."

Maggie could see in the mirror that Alice was close to tears. "Right, I'll go in and…"

She was interrupted by Alice's nervous reply. "No! I'll deal with it. Speaking to her will just make things worse. Believe me, other mothers have tried."

Maggie felt guilty that she hadn't known what was going on. She'd been so caught up in what she was doing that she hadn't noticed that Alice was anxious at school.

"If you don't want me to, I won't. But you mustn't allow a teacher to make your life miserable. They can, I know. When is Mr Rees back?"

"In a week, I think," Alice replied. "We all know it'll be better when he's back. That's why I can manage for now. Anyway, we've got a nickname for her." She checked her mother's profile in the mirror, a naughty grin on her face.

"Do you want to hear this? She's a funny shape and she's got a big bum so we call her Miss Bigbutt," she laughed.

"Well, make sure she doesn't hear you, or she'll have the last laugh."

They arrived at Fiona's house. As they got out of the car, Maggie whispered to Jack to keep an eye on Alice. Maggie wouldn't hesitate to go into the school if Alice wasn't coping, but she'd leave it for now.

Fiona greeted them enthusiastically and they sat together on the decking in the evening sunshine. A question that Maggie had been pondering for some days now came back to her and it occurred to her that Fiona or Graeme might be able to help.

"Fee, do you know of a place up the mountain near us, where children play sometimes, called The Pond?"

"I know it," Graeme grinned. "I used to go up there with my gang. We used to make boats from bits of old pram and corrugated iron and see if we could sail them. It was great!" His face was flushed with excitement, until Fiona pointed out how dangerous it must have been. "You'd never allow our children to go there!" she finished accusingly.

"No, I don't suppose I would. No-one got hurt, though!" he replied cheekily.

Maggie jumped in before the argument escalated. "No, we all did things when we were kids that would horrify us if we found ours doing them now. Remember the rope swing over the river, Fee?" Fiona blushed. "Where exactly is it, Graeme?"

He described the road leading to it from Maggie's house. There was now a car park that allowed visitors to enjoy the view, and a path that led to The Pond.

"It's about five minutes from the car park. Used to take us at least an hour with all of our bits of boat."

Maggie grinned at him, then changed the subject.

Over supper, Maggie replied reluctantly to Graeme's questions about her prospective job. He was surprised by her lack of enthusiasm, saying that she needed to show commitment to get it. Maggie agreed, although she knew that she wasn't committed and was hoping that she could find some enthusiasm on the day.

Fiona had been in the loft and found the documents. At supper Maggie saw them on the coffee table. By the time they finished and Jack went off to join his cousins to play computer games upstairs, she couldn't wait to see them. Alice elected to stay with her to see them too.

"Have you looked at them?" Alice whispered to Maggie. "No, I have no idea what's in there," Maggie replied. "It's so exciting!"

"She's getting as bad as you about this stuff." Fiona commented from behind them, holding a coffee tray.

"So much for being interested in mum and dad's papers," Maggie thought wryly.

She and Alice sat on the settee in front of the box, with Graeme sitting opposite. Fiona wandered off upstairs to check that Jack was getting a chance to use the computer. Maggie noticed that Graeme had seemed interested over dinner when she spoke about the papers, but a stern glance from her sister had shut him up. Now she wasn't around, he leaned forwards, eager to see what the documents were going to reveal.

They were in a brown envelope, which Maggie picked up and turned upside down, spilling the contents out onto the table. Old bills, receipts and letters appeared, some inside fading envelopes, others loose. She and Graeme went through them, checking for anything significant, which there wasn't.

"Most of these can be thrown away," Graeme murmured, putting aside a bill for a three-piece-suite that had cost seventy-five guineas in 1955. "Unless you think there's a reason to keep something like this."

"There's no reason, other than sentimental value. That was the only suite mum and dad ever owned."

As they sorted through the pile, Alice had taken and opened two sealed envelopes, and was examining the contents. "Wow! Look at these, Mum." She handed Maggie a pile of certificates of births, marriages and deaths.

Maggie's heart missed a beat, this was the sort of thing she had hoped for. Her mother and father's certificates were there. The remainder were certificates of the births, marriages and deaths of her father's parents, of which she already had copies. The opportunity to handle these documents was a source of wonder. The oldest of them was her grandfather George's birth certificate, from 1883. The paper had worn thin with age and Maggie handled it carefully, showing it to Alice and Graeme.

"Look at the handwriting, isn't it fantastic?" she said, pointing to the beautiful nineteenth-century copperplate of the registrar, a Mr Henry Shillingsworth. For a quarter of an hour they admired and studied the certificates. It was very interesting, but they revealed nothing that Maggie didn't already know.

She reached across to the second envelope, carefully pulling it open and upending the contents onto the table in front of them. It was a pile of monochrome photographs. There were holiday snaps, pictures of group outings taken in front of cars, buses, horses and carts. There was a wedding with many of the male guests in army uniform, which they guessed was of the World War One era, gathered around a solemn bride and groom. There was a series of portraits, classic Victorian posed shots of well-dressed individuals, and family groups staring disdainfully at the camera.

"Who are these people, Mum?"

"I have no idea," Maggie replied. A few were dated and labelled only with first names, none of which Maggie recognised. The majority gave no indication of who the people were, or when they had been taken.

"It's like looking at another world," said Graeme. "It *is* another world," said Maggie, "but, whose?"

"Does it matter?" They were so absorbed that they hadn't seen Fiona come back into the room. She stood by the door, frowning at the top of Graeme's head.

"What do you know about these pictures?" Maggie demanded. "You knew they were here, didn't you, Fee?"

"I'd forgotten." Fiona shrugged. "I think they're mostly dad's family. They belonged to Nana."

"But you knew what I've been doing all this time, looking for our family's history, and you've been sitting on this lot. It would have saved me hours!"

Graeme shuffled on the sofa, opened his mouth, then closed it again. The room was silent. Fiona balled her fists and drew in a deep breath but Alice screamed.

"Oh my God, look at this!" Alice was holding up one of the Victorian portraits from the bottom of the pile. She thrust the stiff card at Maggie.

"Look at it, Mum! It's you!" Maggie took the portrait and stared at herself, in a Victorian floor-length dress with her hair dressed high off her forehead. She flipped the card over. The back was decorated with a floral pattern in each corner and the photographer's stamp and the words: "Jones 1899." Maggie looked up at Alice. "It's not me. I think we're looking at great-grandmother Ruth."

Chapter 41

May to June 1883

Alice remained unconscious and still, but by the evening she was breathing quietly. Moira left her side for short periods and only to speak to Miss Eskwith about household arrangements, as the countess would be leaving the following morning to join the earl in London. Moira ate alone again that evening, and had just finished her meal when there was a knock at her door, preceding the entrance of the countess.

"Please sit, Mrs Davies." She sat opposite Moira. "Thank you for the message earlier. I'm relieved to hear that your niece is improving. I am also delighted that my advice was of some help. Sometimes, Mrs Fitzgerald's knowledge is wondrous indeed." The countess briefly stared into space. "I shall be leaving in the morning. Is there any other help you need? I believe that Nurse is relieving you so that you can sleep?"

"Yes, Your Ladyship, Nurse has been very attentive. I need nothing further, thank you. I must wait now to find out Esme's state of mind when she awakes, and we can't tell when that will be."

"May I look at her again?"

"Of course, Your Ladyship."

Moira followed the countess into her bedroom. Nurse stood as they entered and moved away from the bed. The countess walked to the bedside and looked down. Then she put her hand out and gently touched Alice's hand and held it for a few seconds, and Moira Davies thought that she saw a moistening of tears.

"Well, Mrs Davies. You have some hope now." She walked back into the sitting room, followed by Moira. She returned to her usual, business-like manner. "When the Earl and I return from London we will have a party of friends. I hope that you will be able to prepare?"

"Of course, Your Ladyship. Miss Eskwith and I will not let you down."

"I know. Thank you. I shall write when we are to return."

Almost immediately after the countess had left, Mr Hughes appeared in the doorway with a tea tray. "I thought you might be in need of refreshment, Mrs Davies."

She beckoned him in, to the seat vacated by the countess. They sat drinking tea in silence. Hughes regarded her with a look she knew well.

"You have something on your mind, Mr Hughes?"

He put the porcelain cup carefully back onto its saucer, set it down on the occasional table, and folded his hands in his lap.

"I'm pleased the child is improving. Have you considered the manner of her arrival, Mrs Davies?"

"I haven't given it much thought, Mr Hughes. Except that I suppose she received my letter and came to find me. How else would she have known where to go?"

"Indeed, that would seem to be common sense, Mrs Davies. Except, you don't yet know if she can read."

"Someone else may have read it to her."

He nodded his head slowly. "And she managed to find her way here, alone and sick. That's quite a feat, don't you think?"

"A miracle. How else can I think of it?" She turned to look into the fire.

"I shan't need this in the evenings any longer, Mr Hughes. It's a little too warm in here now. I'm feeling rather sleepy."

"Your niece is much… smaller than I expected her to be. I had understood that she was a rather large girl. 'A big lump of a girl' was how you described her."

"The shock of losing her mother, being put in the workhouse, then travelling so far to get to me, has worn her away to a skeleton, Mr Hughes. When she's well she'll have a healthier look."

He sat back in his chair looking at Moira as she gazed at the cup in her trembling hand, the only sound the gentle crackling of the wood on the fire. He shuffled forwards, hesitated, then sat up.

"I was in Newport earlier. There was a great to-do a few days ago. Some people thought they had seen a leper. Can you believe that? And the leper was looking for a girl who had been trying to get onto the paddle steamer. The constables and the crowd gave chase, but both disappeared. There's now a great deal of concern to contain the leper."

"But not the child?"

"No. The child had no sign of the disease."

"Then we must hope they are discovered quickly."

"Indeed. Of course, the child may not have been connected with the leper. There was also a farmer in town, searching for his missing daughter. He thought she might have crossed the Channel on the paddle steamer. He was going there to view a body that had been washed up just off the pier."

"And did he find his child, Mr Hughes?"

"I don't know, Mrs Davies. I didn't hear the end of the story."

"Poor man." She looked up from the cup.

"Although Esme is not my own child, I feel as much for her as if she were. I was in despair when she went missing. And the relief

232

at finding her is great indeed, but I won't be happy in my mind until I find out her condition."

"You've endured a good deal this past twelve-month, Mrs Davies."

"When my parents went I was very much saddened, but one loses parents. Arthur's passing was different. When I heard that my sister had died in such horrible circumstances…" she stopped and put her cup down, knocking it so that some tea spilled out. She stared at her hands as she twisted and rubbed her long fingers, before continuing I thought I would go mad. Now I have Esme. And whatever her condition, I will be her mother and father. I will be everything to her. We will be everything to each other." She put her hands out to the fire as if to warm them, but quickly pulled back from the heat.

Mr Hughes stood up, shaking his head imperceptibly. "I'm going into Newport again in a few days. Shall I enquire about the end of the story?"

"As you wish, Mr Hughes. Now, if you will excuse me, I must go to my niece."

"Of course, Mrs Davies. Good night."

After he had left, the housekeeper didn't go to the sick room, but sat down in her armchair, in front of her fire and stared into the flames.

Chapter 42

Three days later, Moira received a letter from the countess saying that she had been delayed in London and wouldn't be returning for a further two weeks, which gave her and Hughes some time to themselves. The doctor had called twice, and found improvement in the head wound. Alice was still barely conscious, although able to swallow the liquid broth made up by Cook. Honora had recommended that the poultices and the drops could stop after five days, provided there was no relapse. By now Mrs Davies could see her face clearly. There was no resemblance to her sister or herself.

"She undoubtedly resembles her father's line," she remarked to Cook, who was helping her to raise Alice by the shoulders to pour a few spoonfuls of broth into her mouth.

On the fifth day, Alice was restless and sweating profusely and Moira had to change the sheets twice, which she thought might be a good sign. But now the child was still again, so she decided to rest in her chair for a few hours.

At daybreak, she awoke suddenly, startled by a noise. Seeing that light was coming into the room she assumed that one of the servants had called out. But then she heard the noise again, a low moan, like that of a wounded animal. Jumping from her chair, she ran to the bed and found a pair of unblinking eyes staring up at her, mouth opening and closing.

"Esme! My dear! You're awake. Don't worry about anything. Here, try some water." Very gently she lifted the child's head, put a glass to the lips and felt a thrill of relief as the girl swallowed a few sips.

"Carefully, my dear, carefully. You've been very ill." She rested the head back on the pillow.

"Can you hear me?"

The small head nodded very slightly. "You came to find me. I am your Aunt Moira. Do you remember?"

Her head shook once and she winced.

"Oh no! Don't try to move your head. You have a bad wound on your temple that will hurt if you move."

Her eyes closed again.

"That's my lovely girl," Moira whispered, bending down to kiss her brow. "Go back to sleep. I am going to be here when you wake again."

One more, tiny nod of her head. Then stillness. Her breathing was measured and rhythmic.

Moira sat perfectly still, watching the sleeping child, tears tracking down her face unchecked. She didn't look up when Cook came into the room half an hour later with a cup of tea. Seeing her tears, Cook opened her mouth to say something, but Moira looked up and put her finger to her lips, whispering, "She woke, Mrs Collins. She saw me and nodded and understood when I spoke to her. Her brain has survived."

Cook put the tea onto the table, squeezed Mrs Davies's hands, then ran to tell the rest of the servants.

For the next few days, although Alice didn't fully regain consciousness, they were able to sit her up to swallow broth, which she did uncomplainingly. The doctor attended daily, and professed himself delighted with the improvement and confident that full health would be regained with proper nursing. He prescribed a tonic, which Honora approved of when secretly consulted by Moira.

On the tenth day, after increasing periods of semi-consciousness, Moira found the girl awake, lying still, but watching her move around the room. She sat on the edge of the bed and took hold of Alice's hand.

"Can you hear me, my dear?"

"Does it still hurt to move your head?" A nod and a wince.

Moira smiled and said, "Don't move, now. I'm going to wash your head – very carefully, I promise. Squeeze my hand if I hurt you."

Smiling reassuringly at her, Moira took up a flannel from the dish of hot water on the bedside table and carefully smoothed it over Alice's face. She hesitated a few times as she neared the wound and little fingers squeezed hers tightly. Eventually, she moved the flannel down to the neck and arms, and then the hands.

"There, that's that over with. Would you like to try to sit up and drink some tea?"

"Yes, please." It was the tiniest whisper, but to Moira, it was like the trumpeting of angels. Supporting Alice's back, she quickly pulled up the cushions behind her, gently moving her up the bed. She could see that this caused some pain, and she realised that Alice had no strength in her arms and legs, to help her to move. She put her arm around Alice's shoulders and put the cup to her lips.

"Thank you."

"You enjoy tea."

"Yes."

"Did your mother make tea for you?"

The girl looked puzzled, then scared. "I don't know."

Moira could see that her simple question had caused distress. The child's eyes were moving around quickly, trying to make sense of the room, and failing, Mrs Davies could tell.

"You don't know this room, Esme, so don't be worried. I am your Aunt Moira and you are in my house. Don't concern yourself now about how you got here or what has happened to you. You had an accident and have hurt your head. This is why you can't remember. I'm taking care of you, and you are safe." A sigh of relief at the word "safe" told Moira that she had chosen her words well. No point taxing the child to try to remember yet. She saw the girl's eyelids droop.

"That's enough exertion for now. Time to sleep. Let's slide you back down."

Once Alice lay flat, she sighed and opened her eyes with a struggle, but her expression was again one of fear.

"You're frightened. There's no need. You are safe and recovering. If you don't remember now what happened to you, it will come back as you get better. Now, sleep, my dear."

Her words and expression seemed to calm the girl. She closed her eyes again and slept.

Chapter 43

Moira had spoken as she truly believed, that memory and understanding would return with improving health. But this didn't turn out to be the case. As Alice's health slowly improved and her strength returned over the following weeks, her memory showed no sign of improvement.

Increasingly, Moira found her awake and wide-eyed in panic. She understood that the girl was trying to remember, but telling her about her life in Weston-super-Mare seemed to make things worse rather than better. Instead, Moira talked to her about the house, explaining her position, detailing her day-to-day life as housekeeper and telling her stories about the earl and countess. She told of parties, balls, and the famous people who had stayed there. She saw the child soak it all in, although she rarely spoke.

Because she liked stories so much, Moira read to her, and this became a regular and happy time for them both. Alice was particularly fond of stories by Mr Dickens, so every night, before supper, Moira read to her from *Little Dorrit*, *Oliver Twist*, or *Great Expectations*.

"One day soon, I will teach you to read these yourself," Moira told her as she closed the latest book. "Would you like to learn your letters, Esme?"

Instead of nodding, the girl held out her hand for the book. Puzzled, Moira handed it to her and watched in amazement as the girl began to read slowly, mouthing the words silently to herself as she read them. Moira sat watching as the girl read through a few pages and put the book down and closed her eyes.

"Does that make your eyes hurt, Esme?"

"Yes."

"But you are able to read well enough?"

"Yes, Aunt."

Moira bit her lip. She asked no questions for weeks, fearing the return of the panic attacks and the nightmares that had started when she had begun to question. But this was not what she had expected and it was troubling.

"Esme, I must now join the servants for supper. I shall call in afterwards to bid you goodnight." She kissed her and received a contented smile in return. The relationship between them was growing in confidence and trust. But Moira went to supper with a frown.

She returned to find the girl awake.

"Esme, you have done so well lately, that I have a treat for you." The girl's eyes opened wide, in surprise and expectation. "How would you like to leave this room, and go outside to look around the gardens?"

The excitement in her look spoke volumes. "How?"

"The best surprise of all. The doctor has brought us a chair on wheels. Tomorrow morning, as soon as it's warm enough, we shall put you in the chair and take you outside."

The smile widened across the girl's face and gave Moira a feeling of warmth and pleasure that she hadn't experienced since her husband's death.

In truth, the doctor hadn't been at all keen on letting Alice outside. He believed in bed rest. The urging had been Honora's.

"Sure, the girl needs to breathe fresh air now, ma'am, and see something new. Her limbs must move more. Get her into a wheeled chair and take her around a little. Talk to her about the flowers and the gardens."

Moira saw the reason in this, but with as much fear as anticipation by the girl's memory returning.

The two women had continued to speak about the girl's progress. Honora had reluctantly provided a remedy for the terrible headaches that Alice had been experiencing since she had regained consciousness. The doctor's remedy had produced no relief and he had recommended laudanum, but Moira was averse to the use of the drug, having had experience of the state to which her husband had been reduced, and his eventual dependence on it.

Honora had produced a liquid that she instructed should be used only when the headache occurred. It was an exceptionally bitter-tasting and cloudy liquid. Alice hated the taste of it at first and struggled to keep it down, but it relieved the headache within minutes and the feeling of relief was so great that she learned to bear the taste.

The following morning Alice woke an hour before Moira brought her now regular breakfast of tea, and bread and honey. "Well, look at you! Would you like to sit by yourself?" She encouraged every effort by Alice to take control of her recovery, against the doctor's wishes.

Taking Alice's head and shoulders in both arms she slowly sat the girl on the side of the bed. Her small spindly legs hung down to the ground and the feeling of pressure on the soles of her feet caused her to squirm and almost fall sideways, but Moira caught her.

"Not too much, Esme. Your ankle was damaged and is still weak. Does your head hurt? Do you feel faint?"

"No."

"Good. Then we shall sit here for a few minutes more. I have work to do this morning. No, don't worry, we're still going outside, at about eleven o'clock. His Lordship and Her Ladyship are returning tomorrow, with several guests, so we're in for a busy time. So, I thought…" she looked down at the girl and smiled in anticipation of the pleasure she was about to bring, "that this afternoon I would take you around the ground floor, to look at some of the special rooms."

A beam of delight in return was her reward.

"Back into bed, now. Finish your breakfast and sleep a little more. Cook will be looking in and I'll return for you with your chair at eleven."

"Thank you."

Up to this point, Alice had been wearing nightdresses, but Moira had paid Honora generously to make a day dress and pinafore. Just before eleven she brought these with her and some fresh undergarments. It took a while to get Alice dressed and manoeuvre her into the wheelchair. Once in, Moira strapped her in around the chest to keep her upright, and placed a light blanket over her legs.

Watched by the smiling and gently applauding Cook and junior kitchen maids, they made their way down the long corridor that led from Moira's sitting room out of the back entrance, outside and to the formal garden.

As they passed through the archway, Moira heard a gasp of surprise and an "Oohh!"

This part of the garden was enclosed by high red-brick walls, with a central lawn divided in four by pathways, an enormous ancient oak at the centre, and in one quarter, a monument to a horse ridden by a previous earl at the Battle of Waterloo. Around the edges of the walls were deep flowerbeds, filled with exquisite shrubs and scented blooming flowers. The mixture of colours, shapes, and smells caused Alice to turn her head and reach out as they passed each new part.

"It's beautiful, isn't it, Esme? Your Uncle was head gardener here for ten years, and a junior gardener before that. He loved plants, especially the early summer flowers."

"Beautiful."

"Now, let's go to look at the monument."

Moira wheeled the chair to the shade of the great oak. The morning was warm, with a light breeze. The only sound was the buzzing of bees and the chirping of birds. She went to sit on the grass next to the chair, but the child held out her arm and, taking the blanket from her legs, she gave it to Moira.

"Don't get your dress dirty, Aunt."

"Thank you, Esme." This was the longest phrase that Moira had heard from her niece and she was thrilled. She sat and told the story of the bravery of a horse and its rider at the Battle of Waterloo. As she spoke she could see that Alice had relaxed into the chair and was twisting her legs from side to side.

"You know, Esme, if you keep moving your legs like that, you may like to try standing on them."

Another beam.

"Now, let's go a little further. Shall we go to the side of the lake?"

"No! No! No!" The outburst caused Moira to run to the front of the chair, where she Alice was holding her head in her hands and shaking violently.

"Hush now, child, hush." She took the girl in her arms and hugged her as tightly as she could. "We won't go. We won't. You don't want to go near the water, I understand."

The suggestion to go the lakeside had been thoughtless. Alice had been having nightmares for weeks in which the words "drowning her!" and "help me!" were frequently shouted, suggesting to Moira that they were not mere dreams, but memories of some terrible event.

"You're safe here, Esme. Nothing can hurt you. Do you understand?"

"Not safe, not safe."

"Esme, look at me. Look at me!" She waited until the girl's gaze met hers, and was horrified by the wild look she saw.

"You are safe with me and you always will be. Whatever happened to you has gone. I won't ask you to try to remember, but if you ever need to talk to me, you know that you can."

She nodded slowly. Then she leaned forwards onto Moira's shoulder. "I don't remember. Anything."

"You don't need to remember. Whatever happened is gone," she repeated, holding the girl's hands. "This is your life now, with me. A safe life, here at Knyghton." Alice sighed with relief.

Chapter 44

May to December 1883

It took John a further two hours to find Ruth and another hour to carry her back down the mountain. The doctor's advice was that, because the baby was still alive, she should be nursed at home, but that they should expect recovery to take some time. Ruthie sent John back over the mountain to let her husband, William, know she would be staying for some time, then set herself to nursing Ruth.

Ruth had rare moments of consciousness, but was never lucid and she developed a fever. For the next month, she lay close to death. She became pale and skeletal and fought attempts to feed her.

In the first week of her unconsciousness, Richard Robinson returned to the chapel; Robert Pugh, true to his word, departed within a day of his announcement. But the most surprising news came at the end of the following week when William returned home from school.

"Dada, Miss Probert has gone."

John was deep in thought in the parlour and didn't take in what William had said.

"Dada, don't you want to know?"

"I'm sorry, William. Was that something about your teacher?"

"She's gone, Dada. Mr Robinson taught us today. He told us that Miss Probert has gone to Herefordshire. Mr Pugh invited her to work in the school." William was grinning. "That's better, isn't it?"

John smiled back at him. "Yes, William, I think so."

"Oh, and Mr Robinson said to tell you he'll be round this evening, as usual."

Richard Robinson had visited daily since his return to Garth Hill. He had also spoken to everyone about John and Ruth and had prayed for Alice at chapel on Sunday, and at every other opportunity. With the support of the Ellises and other friends, he had made sure that there would be no more stories about Esme Ellis's death.

"That teacher was a nasty piece of work, so good riddance as far as I'm concerned. But, there was something familiar about her. I wish I could remember what," said Ruthie. John had heard this several times since his mother-in-law had arrived, so took no notice.

"I've been wondering how I might recall. I think it might have something to do with my sister in Carmarthen. Do you think we could write to her, John?"

"Yes, Mrs Evans, if you wish. What would you like to say?"

"Describe the woman and ask my sister if she sounds familiar to her. There's something about a teacher and a child, but I can't remember the story." She shook her head. "Margaret might remember. Did you write to the school board?"

"No. The community is better without her, and Richard will find a good replacement. We should let it lie." Ruthie wasn't sure that her daughter would agree.

Richard Robinson's visits had proved to be of benefit to all the family. Unlike Pugh, he played with the children, sat with Ruth, and spent hours discussing matters with John. However, even he was unable to move John on the matter of re-starting the search for Alice.

After two months, Ruth's fever was gone and she regained consciousness but without much memory of what had happened. She was well into her pregnancy and the swelling and dizziness were increasing. She was conscious each day, and whenever she opened her eyes her first question was for news of Alice.

One afternoon in mid-September, she awoke to find her mother sitting in the rocking chair beside the bed, holding a letter.

"What's that, Mam? Is it about Alice?"

"Yes and no, girl. It's from my sister Margaret in Carmarthen. You remember your grandmother Ruth who lived there?"

Ruth nodded.

"Well, her mother was also called Ruth, that's my grandmother. I told you, you should not have used the name Alice!"

"She's called 'Alice Ruth', Mam. It's good enough. And you know I don't hold with family tales and bad luck."

Her mother grimaced slightly. "Ever since I met Eira Probert something in my mind has been telling me that there was a story in the family, but I couldn't remember what it was."

Ruth rolled her eyes to the ceiling and turned away. Not only was her mother not of the Baptist faith, but she clung to the traditional ways. She treasured old folklore and superstitions which Ruth had abandoned as soon as she attended chapel and met John. Ruthie caught the exasperated expression.

"Well, just so you know, my sister has replied to tell me that one of our grandmother's first-born children, twin girls, drowned one day after school when she was ten years old."

"Why do I need to know this, Mam?"

"Their names were Ruth and Alice. And suspicion fell on a schoolteacher in their village, who disappeared shortly after the accident."

Ruth turned slowly towards her mother. "When was that?"

"It would have been about seventy years back."

Ruth had begun to sit up, but shrugged and lay back. "How can that matter to us? I see that the names are the same, but all children go to school."

"Not then, girl. Our family, the Gwyllims, were well-to-do farmers. They paid for their children's schooling. They chose it."

"Do you know any more details?"

"No, Margaret doesn't remember any more."

"Does she remember anything about the teacher? Or why he was suspected?"

"No, that's it, really. Just coincidence."

"Yes." Ruth looked away.

"Just a couple of things that Margaret says, too. The teacher disliked our family, for no reason they could understand. That's why he was suspected. And no child in our family since has been called Alice. It's bad luck."

Ruth sat up so quickly that she swayed with dizziness. "Are you saying that this happened because I chose the wrong name!"

"No, of course not! I was just telling you what Margaret said. Lie down, now."

"No, I think I'll walk a while. It seems sunny. Perhaps it will do me good to sit in the warmth." She saw her mother's frown. "Don't worry, I'll sit under the tree in the shade. John moved the bench to make sure there's no sunlight on it. The baby isn't due for at least another six weeks, so I'm fine to move around a little."

With huge effort, she reached the bench an hour later and sat under the shade of the oak tree at the corner of the garden. This was the furthest she had been for some time. The weight of the baby, her massively swollen extremities, and the pain of being upright had made it impossible to leave the bedroom. As a result, she had existed in isolation, connected only by visitors.

The journey to the far corner of the garden had made Ruth feel light-headed. She sat as still as she could, breathing deeply and listening to her mother and Gwen chiding the children, trying to make sense of her life.

She accepted that, for now, there was nothing she could do to search for Alice. John was implacable. She knew that he'd received a couple of reports from the detectives at Newport telling him that the trail was cold. She'd remonstrated with him until he'd left the room in exasperation. And when he'd returned she'd told him that she hated him and would never forgive him for abandoning their daughter. That was three weeks ago. Their relationship since then had been polite, but frosty. John enquired about her health, but made no further comment. His former habit of discussing all matters of the farm management with her ceased. He said from concern of tiring her, but she knew that he wouldn't speak to her openly again until he was sure that she wouldn't bring up the subject of Alice.

Sitting under the tree, thinking of John's behaviour – his refusal to speak and his pushing her away – Ruth finally understood that she was being asked to choose between her husband and her child. She was in no doubt what choice she would make. Ruth closed her eyes as a wave of dizziness overcame her. She decided to walk back to the farm. Although she'd promised her mother that she wouldn't attempt this without assistance, she was in no mood to call for help.

Holding firmly onto the arm of the bench, she pulled herself to her feet. Immediately she felt a rush of heat throughout her body, and looked down to find a pool of blood at her feet. She screamed for her mother. The world spun as she felt a spasm in her stomach, then everything went dark.

George was born two hours later. The massive loss of blood again caused Ruth to hover close to death for weeks after his birth, unable to nurse him. Her mother, who had delivered the baby, was never far from her side.

Insensate to happenings in the world around her, Ruth didn't know that John had told the detectives to stop searching for Alice, at the end of October. Not a trace had been found. It was as if she had disappeared from the world. November saw Ruth's recovery, and at the beginning of December she felt well enough to leave the bedroom.

She ventured downstairs, where she was greeted with delight by the children and by Gwen, who had managed the family's domestic affairs in her absence. There was a fire in the range and food on the table.

"Gwen, I cannot thank you enough, there are no words," but she stopped when she saw tears run down her cheeks.

"I'm so pleased you are recovering, Mrs Jones. Arthur and I have prayed every day." Ruth smiled, then turning to her mother, who was sitting with a bottle of milk in George's mouth, "I'll do that, Mam. A few more days and I should be well enough to take up the reins again."

"Weeks, I think, girl. You're still unsteady on your feet. Here," she stood, motioning Ruth to sit, and handed over the baby. "He's a hungry one. No harm done to him for appearing so early. Three fine, great boys, eh!"

Ruth bent over her new-born baby as pain stabbed at her like a stake. "But no fine girls," she muttered to herself. She felt guilty that she had reacted without considering Maud but Alice's loss was catastrophic.

When John came home at the end of the day, he warmly acknowledged her presence with the family again, and spoke movingly of how much they had all missed her. Then, to her surprise, he began to talk about Christmas. He had decided to invite his family to share Christmas dinner with them, plus Ruth's parents.

"We shall be a crowd indeed!" He beamed at the excited children. "I shall be going to Shirenewton to visit my family next week. It's a pity you can't travel yet, Ruth. But perhaps I shall take William and Walter with me." The boys smiled politely. "You'd like to see Great-grandma Eliza, wouldn't you?"

"Of course, Dada." William replied for both of them. He and Walter had visited before and didn't like the small, dark cottage with its open hearth that choked them with smoke, nor the old woman who muttered and swore at them.

When the evening meal was ready and Gwen had gone home, they sat around the table.

"So, let's look forward and give thanks for what we have." He glanced at Ruth as he began their prayers. "It's good to have you here again, my dear. The children have missed you so much."

Then he began, and spoke of everyone in the family, except Alice. Ruth knew that this was his final sign to her. Alice's name would rarely, if ever, be spoken again between them. She was never to enquire. Alice had gone from their lives.

When the children were asleep and John was reading in the parlour, Ruth excused herself and went into Alice's room, for the first time in months. Maud was sleeping there and all of Alice's few possessions were gone. She searched around and found them in a small trunk under the tallboy. Ruth went to her bedroom, took a small package from the bottom of a drawer and crept back along the landing. In the trunk she placed the set of new handkerchiefs that she had been embroidering with Alice's initials as a Christmas present.

"Happy Christmas, my beautiful girl, wherever you are. I know you are not dead and one day I will know what happened to you." She kissed the soft linen, closed the trunk, and went to bed.

Chapter 45
June to October 1883

After they had lunched quietly and Alice had slept for a while, Moira returned with the wheelchair. She began the ground-floor tour with the five rooms that made up the kitchens, just around the corner and along the corridor from her sitting room. The servants' hall and the kitchen rooms formed two sides of the square house around an open courtyard, which was paved and had a central well that dated from the original medieval building. From the kitchen, they turned again. The third corridor ended in a short flight of steps that led down to the cellars.

Mrs Davies explained that the cellars at Knyghton ran below two sides of the house and had an ancient spring and stream running through them, the latter having had a conduit built to conduct its passage through the various underground rooms. The cellars housed the earl's extensive wine collection, as well as acting as a cold room for the storage of meat, poultry, and dairy products from the home farm.

Before the cellar stairs, there was a short, wide flight of three steps going up to the main part of the house. One of the footmen came to carry the chair and Alice.

Then they began the tour of the most magnificent rooms. Alice saw with wonder the two dining rooms, the smaller one panelled in oak, the larger in cedar. They passed through the ballroom where Knyghton held its famous Yule Ball, on Christmas Eve. Finally, the countess's favourite sitting room, exquisitely gilded from floor to ceiling, with inlaid paintings of gods and goddesses from ancient times. The little girl's face had shone throughout the hour or so that it had taken to go around the building.

"So, this is to be your home, Esme. With me. We don't often visit these rooms unless summoned when His Lordship and Her Ladyship are here. Most of the servants never come here at all, except to clean. But I can wander as I please." She paused for a moment, before asking what she had been leading up to all day. "Shall you be happy here, Esme?"

"Oh yes. Safe. Can't find me here." Her expression changed for a moment. "No water?"

"No, Esme. You need not go near the lake."

The girl nodded happily. Moira quashed her desire to probe for what could be so terrifying about water.

"Now, to finish our tour, we're going to visit Mr Hughes, in his pantry. That's what we call his rooms."

Mr Hughes had been waiting in his room, occupied with bringing out the silver plate for the coming weeks' entertaining, and supervising the two junior footmen who were diligently polishing.

"Welcome, Miss Esme. Have you enjoyed your tour?"

"Yes. Thank you, Mr Hughes."

"We visited the gardens earlier, as you know, Mr Hughes. Esme thinks she will be very happy here." He heard the warning note in her voice.

"Let me show you my treasures here." He raised his eyebrows and Moira nodded.

For five minutes he showed Alice silver treasures from the Knyghton collection.

"We're very proud of this one, Miss Esme," he said, holding up a salt and pepper shaker. "It's believed to be over three hundred years old, bought in Ghent by an earl who served King Henry the Eighth."

"Six wives."

"Why, yes." He paused and looked speculatively at Alice. "Do you know where Ghent is?"

"Belgium."

"You are a bright one, Miss Esme. Well now, I need to get on with our preparations here, so I must bid you farewell," He turned to one of the junior footmen and wiped a finger critically on the silver plate he'd been polishing. "More effort, Edward."

* * *

Dinner that evening was a rushed affair, the servants hurried back and forth with each new instruction from Hughes and Moira, but once the meal was finished, the two retired to her room for a discussion of the state of their preparations.

Knyghton is ready, I think, Mrs Davies?"

"Just the flowers tomorrow morning, Mr Hughes, and we shall be ready to welcome His Lordship and Her Ladyship back."

"And your niece is well enough to cope alone when you are occupied in the coming weeks?"

"She's almost ready to walk, I believe. Thank you for asking." She smiled at him and to speak again, but he interrupted her.

"I have some family news of my own."

"My nephew, Alan, has just turned fourteen and is ready to begin his service. His Lordship has agreed that he may join me here as a junior footman, under my care. As you know, Edward is leaving us."

"How wonderful for you, Mr Hughes! It's good to have family nearby, especially young ones." She spoke so genuinely and with such feeling that he hesitated to say what he had been planning.

"Esme is a great comfort to you, Mrs Davies."

"She has saved me, Mr Hughes."

"I understand how much you care for her. She hasn't turned out to be the 'big stupid lump of a girl', has she? The girl is intelligent."

"I've thought a great deal about that, Mr Hughes. I have to face the galling fact that my sister was not a good person and was a poor mother."

She pointed to a small pile of papers on the table under the window.

"The poorhouse and the constabulary have both written to me with details of my sister's death. The information is distressing."

"I'm sorry to hear that."

"I value your friendship, Mr Hughes, and I know that I can trust your confidence. The truth is, my sister was… a woman of the streets… a prostitute. Little wonder that she cared so little for her child!" A sob caught her breath.

"She lied to me, you know. She told us that her husband, Absolom Peach, was a sailor who drowned at sea shortly after Esme was born. Sailor, my foot! At our parents' funeral, she'd been drinking. She admitted to me, laughing, would you believe, that she'd found the name in a church graveyard. She had no idea of who Esme's father was!" Tears ran down her cheeks. "That poor little child must have had a terrible life. It might have been her mother who gave her that terrible wound, or the man who killed Margaret. Her head was held down in a drinking trough, you know. Perhaps Esme was there when it happened. That thought keeps me awake at night. And I could have done something. But I didn't know, Mr Hughes. I didn't know!"

Hughes watched her, uncertain how to proceed. He had intended to tell her what he had found out about the farmer's daughter who had gone missing, but this felt cruel in the face of her obvious anguish.

"You must be quite devastated, Mrs Davies."

"More than I shall ever be able to admit, apart from to you, Mr Hughes. But I trust you to keep this secret for me. Especially from Esme, who must never know what her mother was."

"Did you receive your sister's belongings?" He knew that a parcel had arrived for Moira.

"Yes. The poorhouse sent me hers and Esme's clothes. I burned them." She didn't tell him that the clothes that she had received that had belonged to her niece were several sizes too large for Alice.

"So, is the subject closed? You were expecting to go to Weston-super-Mare, were you not?"

"The murderer has been apprehended. A drunken regular. There was no service and the burial was undertaken by the poorhouse, for which I paid."

He sensed that there was more, and waited in silence for her to make the decision to continue, or not.

"They wrote to me about the body of a girl found in the sea at Weston-super-Mare, in case it was Esme. But I wrote back to explain that she had come to find me and is now living with me. They expressed themselves satisfied, so there's nothing further to do."

"I wonder who the girl in the sea was, then?"

"It must have been the poor farmer's daughter."

"Yet when I was in Newport I heard that the constables are still searching."

"Then it must have been some other poor child," she replied impatiently. "Please excuse me now, Mr Hughes. I must check on Esme again before I meet with Her Ladyship's personal maid and the head gardener."

She stood, but he remained seated, his fingers knitted under his chin. Moira watched him intently, neither spoke. At last she could no longer contain herself.

"Is there something you want to say to me, Mr Hughes?" Her tone made it clear that he should speak now, if he was ever going to do so.

"No, Mrs Davies."

With a faint sigh of relief, she walked to, and opened, the door to her sitting room. "I shall look forward to meeting Alan. When does he arrive?"

"In September."

"Perhaps he and Esme can become acquainted? It will be good for her to have a friend who's also new to the house."

"Indeed. So, a busy month for us both, Mrs Davies."

"Yes, Mr Hughes." He left the room, defeated.

* * *

Over the next four weeks Moira and Hughes met frequently, but briefly, to speak of domestic issues. Alice's condition improved daily and the doctor pronounced himself satisfied to limit his visits to once a week. Moira felt that she no longer required intervention of any kind from Honora.

By the end of the earl and countess's visit to the house Alice still only spoke rarely, but had been enthralled by stories Moira had told her at bedtime, about the guests, the dinners, the clothes, and the jewels. Her appetite had improved but she was still unable to stand unaided. The earl and countess left Knyghton House at the beginning of September to visit their villa in the south of France, and Mr Hughes' nephew, Alan, arrived to take up his new position.

Alan turned out to be a shy boy, tall, bespectacled, blond-haired and gangly. He was also quietly spoken and reticent with his opinions, rather like his uncle, and he possessed his uncle's quiet firmness. He learned his duties quickly, taking the ribbing of the older junior footmen without complaint, and without telling Mr Hughes, which the other boys respected.

Alice had been introduced to Alan almost immediately and it was clear to Hughes and Moira that within two weeks the two had become firm friends. They seemed to have recognised in each other an ability to keep confidence and absolute trust. Alice spoke to Alan more than any other member of the servant household and while this sometimes gave Moira a pang of jealousy, she knew it was important that the girl should speak more. And she noticed that the nightmares had diminished since Alan had arrived.

Alan liked to push Alice in her chair into the gardens, to sit with her under the oak tree and talk about their day. He had many stories to tell and she was a willing listener.

By mid-October the weather had deteriorated and the warm evenings that they had enjoyed throughout September came to an end. On a Sunday afternoon at the end of the month, Alan pushed the chair into the garden for the last time.

"Is there anything special you'd like to see this afternoon? How about the orangery? It'll be warmer for you in there."

"Yes, I'd like to see how the lemon tree is growing."

The sun had been just warm enough to heat up the orangery to maintain the wealth of exotic plants that grew there. It allowed Alice to take the blanket off her legs once they were ensconced in the long glasshouse.

"I don't suppose I'll be able to get here in the winter. I shall miss the lovely smells."

"Are your legs getting any stronger, Esme?"

"I think so. I tried standing by holding onto the bedpost, like you said. It hurt and I wobbled a lot, but I did stand for a minute."

"That's good. Keep trying."

"Yes, I will. But Aunt Moira mustn't know!"

"She doesn't want to keep you an invalid, Essy!"

"Don't call me that!" she protested.

"I'm sorry. Why not?"

"I... I..." she seemed to be searching for something. "I don't know. But I don't like it." Her hands were gripping the sides of her chair, her eyes screwed shut.

Alan tentatively placed his hand on hers. "I'm sorry. I didn't mean to upset you. You are my friend, Esme."

She opened her eyes. "My friend Esme." She slowly repeated the phrase as if savouring it like a new dish.

She began to sob, "I see a face in my dreams. A girl. Like me but not me. She's trying to call for help, but she can't speak. She's underwater and I'm looking at her as she opens and closes her mouth." She had confided before that she had nightmares, but never their content.

"Perhaps it's a memory of something that happened to you on your way here. You know that no-one knows how you got here, or how you got your wound."

She put her hand to her head. The swelling had gone, but a thick scar remained.

"I see faces, Alan. But I don't know who they are."

He was uncertain whether to let her keep talking or distract her from what was clearly a distressing subject. He was very fond of her but his uncle had communicated doubt about this strange little girl, albeit vaguely.

"Do any of them mean anything to you, Esme?"

"No. There's one that's very horrible and I wake up crying under my covers. It's a face that's falling apart, the skin melting and dripping off, with a terrible smell."

Alan pulled a sympathetically disgusted face. "Do you ever have nice ones?"

"Yes, sometimes a man with a moustache. He's shouting at me, but not in a bad way, like when something's just missed you, and your family is relieved. And a little boy with blond hair. He's crying. And children playing."

"Do you recognise anything about them?"

"Nothing at all. I don't know who they are. And I don't know who I am!" At this, she began to cry.

"You are Esme Peach." He spoke assertively but gently, then added. "Mrs Davies's niece, her beloved niece. And I'm your friend Alan." His reassurance helped her.

"My aunt is wonderful, I know. And this house is like a fairy tale. But none of it seems right. I just wish I could remember something, anything about my old life. Make sense of the faces, at least."

He had heard snatches of her mother's fate. "Perhaps it isn't worth remembering, Esme. From what my uncle has told me, you would not have been as happy as you are here."

She nodded uncertainly.

"I think that one day more of it may come back to you. If it does, you can talk to me. I'll always be here for you."

"Thank you. I'm so glad you came to work here."

As he handed her the blanket, she looked at him, a lost look on her face, and whispered, "I just don't remember."

Chapter 46
May 2015

As soon as she was clear of the main doors of the glass-fronted building, Maggie picked up her pace. Back straight, chin up, and looking ahead in case anyone was watching, she reached her car at a smart trot. Checking right and left, she unlocked the car, threw in her briefcase and coat, plonked herself down in the driving seat, and let out a lengthy shriek, banging the palms of her hands on the steering wheel. When there was no more sound left, she let her head rest on the wheel until she felt back in control. She fished her mobile phone out of her bag and turned it on. It rang immediately.

"Maggie? It's Zelah. Do you have time to talk? Hello, Maggie? Are you there? Have I got the right number?"

"Sorry, Zelah. Yes, it's me. I'm just a bit… never mind. I was about to call you. How about coming out to my house this afternoon?"

There was a moment of hesitation. "What's the matter?"

"Nothing, really. I'll tell you later. Can you come?"

"Yes. But you've never given me your address."

"Haven't I? Oh. I've talked so much about the house I assumed you knew. Well, it's about time you came to see it." She rattled off the address and directions. "What about some lunch, say in an hour?"

"Yep." Zelah finished the call.

Maggie stared across the car park to the two storey corporate headquarters, pulled a face, then started the car and drove too fast out of the car park.

Once home she had changed out of her corporate black suit and into shorts and t-shirt, and prepared lunch. She set it out in the garden down by the canal and waited for Zelah. While she was waiting, she turned on her laptop. After speaking to Zelah at the library the previous week she had checked out a couple of websites and posted her story on two. There hadn't been any replies and there were none now.

The sound of a roaring car engine caught her attention and she walked to the front window. There, in front of her house, peering up at the house name carved above her front door, was Zelah at the wheel of a snazzy red sports car. Grinning, Maggie opened the front door.

"What is this?" She walked around the car as Zelah hauled herself out from the low-slung seat.

"It's an Audi R8 Spyder."

"I don't know why now, but I saw you in a Mini or an estate."

"Who the hell drives one of those?"

"Me?" Maggie led the way into the kitchen.

"Oh." Zelah shrugged her shoulders. "Well, you need room for passengers; I don't."

"How fast does that thing go?"

"Very," Zelah replied.

"My son will go wild if he sees it. He's going to have his provisional licence ready and waiting on the morning of his seventeenth, and expect me to pay for his lessons and insurance. That's boys for you."

"I wouldn't know."

"Sorry, you don't have children."

"Don't apologise. You'll know when I'm offended, and I'm not. If I'm here when your son gets home, I'll take him out for a spin."

"Fantastic! He'll be thrilled. Now, would you like to see the house, or eat first?"

"Let's eat. I've got more information for you."

Maggie led Zelah down the garden to the edge of the canal. Lunch was set on a table under a newly erected rose pergola.

"It's warm in the sun today. Eventually the roses will make a canopy over the top, but this year it's not going to give much shade. Are you OK being in the open? Sorry about the smell. I think there may be a problem with the drainage in the canal."

"It's fine. I can't smell anything. This is lovely." Zelah had been looking around the garden as they walked down. Seating herself in view of the canal, she breathed in a waft of lilac.

"Did you do all of this?" she asked, sweeping her arm around, when Maggie came back with a tray of drinks.

"Most of it was here, hidden under a mass of weeds and five-foot-high grass. It'll need a bit of TLC, but it's got potential. I love gardening."

"So, what's up?" Zelah asked as they began to eat. "You were grumpy this morning. And now."

"I had a job interview this morning."

"Oh. Do you have to work?"

"Yes, I'm afraid I do. I don't particularly like what I do, never have done much, but I'm good at it. I prefer the people I work with to the work itself."

"So why can't you work with good people now?"

"I can't afford to pick and choose. And the team I worked with before were special, somehow." She expected Zelah to pooh-pooh this but she didn't.

"You're right. People are much more important. There's no pleasure in doing a job just for money."

Maggie looked at Zelah. "Glad you agree. But I have to work. I spent more than I should have on this house. I was supposed to buy a small ex-council house and have enough money to last me a few years," she went on, "We're so happy here, but it's come at a price. This morning the guy would have offered me the job then and there, but he has to confirm it with his boss, who's abroad at the moment, thank God. So I've got a reprieve. You know, I felt such a sense of relief when he told me that there'd be a delay."

"I can tell."

There was silence as they ate.

"There's no sound from any roads at all, is there?" Zelah said, sitting back in her chair. "It's amazing."

"It must have been just the same when my great-grandfather built it. I can imagine them out here, too. There would have been a few barges on the canal in those days."

"Yes, but not many. Trains had taken over. Anyway," Zelah bent down and took some papers out of her bag. "I've managed to do a bit of digging into the paddle ship. It was a new venture in 1883. It rarely got up the river to Newport, because of the high tidal range. Nowadays, it's just once or twice a summer. Usually, it goes from Penarth."

"What! You mean, it's still going? The same ship?"

"No, but it's an exact replica. And it's still the PS *Waverley*. Here's the timetable for this summer." She handed Maggie a leaflet. On the front cover was a picture of the paddle steamer in the Channel.

"I'll have to take the kids over in the holidays." She looked up. "Would you like to come with us?"

"Love to."

"Have you found anything else?"

"No. I haven't had time. Had to be in the blasted museum all weekend."

"Not really your thing, Zelah. Meeting and greeting people."

"Quite right."

"I posted my story on two websites over the weekend. No replies yet. So we have a bit of a lull. Any ideas what we can do next?"

"Well, there's a million things you can still do," Zelah snorted. "For a start, what about the farm? You've got the address, but not the location or history. We can find out from the county architect and planning department. So that's worth a visit. Then there's the history of your great-grandfather. You've come to a halt, but there's plenty we can do there to find out who his parents were. And," she sat up, "there's a story there, I can smell it." Zelah tapped her nose. "May not be much, but worth finding out. We'll check more parish records. I'll find out if they're at the county or at the church."

"Sounds good. I might as well use the time I've got left to do as much as we can. How about coming to look around the house now? There's just enough time before the kids come home from school. They've been looking forward to meeting you." As they stood up, she added, "and Jack will look forward to meeting your car."

They finished their lunch, and cleared it up, taking everything back to the house. The crashing of doors and dropping of bags in the hall told them that Jack and Alice were home. "Mum? Mum! Have you seen that car outside! It's an Audi…" Jack stopped abruptly when he saw Zelah with his mother.

"Hello, you must be Jack." She held out her hand and he shook it tentatively. "It's my car. It's an R8 Spyder, as you obviously know. You mother says you can have a ride, if you're up for it."

"Sick!" Jack's eyes shone.

"Come on then. Let's go." She marched out of the house to the car. Jack shrugged his shoulders and pulled a surprised face at Maggie, who signalled him to follow.

While they were out, Maggie fetched the school photograph, the portrait and the clothes downstairs. Alice, who had brought two friends home with her, was in the garden, playing in the summerhouse that they had put up over the weekend. She laid out the clothes in the living room and waited for the returning roar of Zelah's car.

Ten minutes later Jack and Zelah walked back through the front door, Jack grinning happily.

"That was… the best ever." He went back outside to sit in the car as Zelah came back in.

"Thanks, Zelah. You've made his day."

Zelah shrugged. "Let's have a look at those clothes and photos."

They were in the sitting room examining the photos when Alice shouted from the kitchen that she was getting drinks.

"Al, come in here a moment, please. There's someone I'd like you to meet."

Alice popped her head around the door, saw Zelah and grinned. "Hello, I'm Alice."

"I can see that," Zelah replied, smiling back and holding up the photograph. "This is certainly your double, isn't it?"

Alice shouted something over her shoulder in the direction of the kitchen, then walked into the room and stood next to Zelah, looking at the photograph.

"Do you have any idea what happened to her? I'd kind of like to know."

"Not yet, Alice. But your mother and I will find out, I promise."

"Thank you. It's nice for Mum to have a friend. Specially one she doesn't have to argue with all the time, like Aunty Fee. I'm going back out. The summerhouse is great. Thanks, Mum. My friends love it."

When she was gone Zelah turned to Maggie. "What a self-possessed little girl."

"She's certainly her own person," Maggie looked outside pensively as Alice and her friends ran back down to the summerhouse with their drinks and biscuits.

"Time for me to go, I think. Shall we try the architects' department this week? I can ring and make an appointment."

"That would be great, thanks. I won't be able to do much next week. It's half term."

"I'll call you. Now, I need to prise your son out of my car."

On the doorstep, Zelah paused and looked up again at the carving of the name and date.

"I envy you this link to your history," she said, and without waiting for a reply, got into her car and roared off.

Maggie put her arm around Jack and they went back into the house.

"She's a funny little woman, but I think she's really nice," Jack said to her as they walked into the garden. "She doesn't judge people. And she doesn't pretend to be nice and be interested when she isn't."

"She just dislikes everyone," Maggie replied.

"But I think she sees you as a friend," Jack said.

Maggie squeezed his shoulder.

Chapter 47
December 1883

It snowed in earnest, covering the gardens with a harsh whiteness that obliterated all signs of flowerbeds. The great oak stood forlornly in the middle of the walled garden, snow smothering every branch.

The wheelchair trips outside had stopped weeks before, due to the winds and prolonged November rains that had turned many of the pathways into muddy traps for Alice's wheels. She had started to walk since her last outing with Alan, just a few steps from her room to Moira's sitting room to start with. Eventually, she made it along the corridor to the kitchen, where she met the junior cooks and kitchen maids. They spoke to her about their duties, showed her around the rooms that made up the kitchen complex, and told her how privileged they felt to work in such an establishment. Positions were hard to come by, and appreciated by their families. Servants mostly lived in the rooms above the main house, off two long corridors. Although their days were long, they made little complaint. Their rooms were pleasant enough and they were permitted a fire in winter.

The kitchen maid, Mary Evans, invited her to visit.

"You can come and see my room, if you like, Miss Esme. I have a nice bed and a chair, and we keep our fire going. It's just at the top of the back stairs."

Alice hadn't yet been to see the upstairs rooms, and wasn't sure that her aunt would approve. So she thanked the girl and said that she would see, with a genuinely appreciative smile. It was her smile and good manners that had drawn the servants to Alice. She always seemed interested in them, whoever she spoke to. Even the starchy Miss Eskwith, who never spoke to anyone from the kitchen other than to give an order, took to bringing books for her. She even offered to read to her, on days she was confined to bed because of the pains in her legs. On Christmas Eve morning the house was the busiest that Alice had ever seen. The earl and countess had returned a few days before with a party that included the earl's heir, his nephew, Viscount Cadwallader, the viscount's Lady and their three small children. Nurse had spent a week preparing the nursery and the servants had decorated the house with holly and mistletoe, and a recent innovation from London: a Christmas tree.

The tree, as tall as the ceiling of the morning room in which it stood, was decorated with red and green bows, and candles, and was a triumph. All of the servants had been allowed to see it and each stood in awe when they did so. When the candles were lit in the evening, two footmen had to be allocated to keep a watch on the flames. Miss Eskwith lived in a permanent state of terror that the house would burn down, which Moira eventually lost patience with.

"Miss Eskwith, a Christmas tree stands in Windsor Castle, sanctioned by the Queen herself, and in honour of Prince Albert, in whose family it had been a tradition for many years. I hardly think he intended to set light to the entire royal family, do you?"

The thought of the royal family burning was too much for Miss Eskwith, who scuttled off sobbing.

"Really, she's a wonderful organiser and I wouldn't be without her, but sometimes…" Moira raised her eyes to the ceiling, then back to Alice who was sitting with her in front of the roaring fire in her sitting room. They were putting the final touches to the wrapping of presents from the countess to the servants.

Alice smiled back, but it was perfunctory. Beside her on the chair was a present from Alan, which she knew was a book by Charles Dickens. He had found five minutes just before lunch to give it to her, and had found her in the same, pensive mood.

"What's the matter, Esme?"

"I don't know, Alan. Something about Christmas gifts. I think I once had handkerchiefs. But I don't know why I think that." She sighed.

"Are you remembering something, do you think?"

"Maybe. It's more feeling than memory."

"What do you feel?"

"I feel a quietness. I feel children around me. Small children. That's all."

He had to leave, but promised to return soon.

Now, in the sitting room with Moira, the feeling came back again, a feeling of closeness and children. Moira saw Alice's wistful look and felt the need to distract her. "I have a surprise for you, Esme."

She succeeded in getting the girl's attention.

"The family will be gathering in the morning room after dinner this evening, to enjoy Christmas carols with their guests. I and Mr Hughes and Cook and Nurse have been invited to join them. Her Ladyship has invited you, too. Will you enjoy that?"

"Oh, yes, Aunt. That would be very nice."

Moira sensed hesitation. "Are you not pleased, Esme? This is a great honour you know."

"What shall I wear, Aunt?"

"Well, I had intended to keep this until tomorrow, but under the circumstances, you shall have it now."

She went to her store cupboard and brought out a package, which she gave to Alice, then sat down in front of her as she untied the strings. It was a dress, made of green silk, floor-length, with embroidered sleeves. Alice gasped as the material ran like water through her fingers.

"I had Mrs Fitzgerald make it up for you, my dear. Happy Christmas!"

"Oh, Aunt, it's the most wonderful thing I ever saw!" Alice held the dress up and pressed it to her face. "Better than all the handkerchiefs!"

"Handkerchiefs? What do you mean, Esme?" Her voice was sharp and caused Alice to look away.

"I don't know, Aunt. It's just that lately I've been thinking about handkerchiefs as Christmas presents. I don't know why. Is there something wrong?"

"No, of course not. Why should there be? Now, go and try on the dress. We must make time to dress your hair, now that it's growing back so well."

She smiled her usual smile and Alice took her new dress to her bedroom, leaving Moira sitting rigidly in her seat. Once the girl had gone, she got up and walked to her store cupboard. In the drawer marked "Spices" she dug deep and brought out a grubby piece of material. It was a small dirty square of what had once been white cotton. In one corner were the initials A.R.J.

273

She returned to her seat, balling the material in her hands, rocking back and fore. She stared at the fire and raised her arm to throw the scrap onto the flames, but paused, looked at the piece of material, and put it back into the deepest drawer of her cupboard.

At eight-thirty, Moira pushed Alice, in her chair, to join the group of servants around the fire in the morning room, as the assembly watched the countess at the piano.

Outside it was snowing again. In the morning room, all of the candles had been lit on the tree and the fire had been banked up with logs that crackled as they burned. Hughes had thrown orange peel onto the fire so that the smell of burnt orange filled the room. Alan was on candle duty next to the tree. He saw Alice as she came in and managed to wink at her. Alice gazed around the room and felt a rush of peace, so profound that she pulled on her aunt's sleeve, to make her look down.

"Thank you for letting me stay, Aunt. I'm so glad this is my home now."

Moira couldn't speak, the violent thumping of her heart like a pealing bell of joy.

The countess finished her last carol, announced a short break, then walked over to the group of servants, who curtsied before her.

"Miss Peach, how are you enjoying your first Christmas at Knyghton?"

"Very much, thank you, Your Ladyship. It's magical," replied Alice.

The countess smiled. "Are you fond of music?"

"Yes, Your Ladyship. I like the piano. I like to play." She stopped, appalled by the audacity of her own words, as the servants stared at her.

The countess raised an eyebrow. "Come over with me." She indicated to a pale Moira to push Alice to the piano. Mr Hughes pushed the piano stool to one side. Alice placed her hands on the keys and, without thinking, began to play a simple version of "Silent Night".

Moira leaned against the door frame, afraid her trembling legs would not hold steady. Hughes watched her, but didn't move to help. Alan watched Alice in amazement.

"You are a talented pianist, my dear," the countess said when she stopped after the first verse. "I think your aunt must arrange for you to take lessons." She looked up at Moira, who smiled thinly and tried to nod in a way that she hoped would convey gracious acceptance.

"Miss Peach is very welcome to practise here, Mrs Davies. Talent should always be encouraged." She turned back to Alice. "So, what of your future, my dear? What would you like to do now?" Moira held her breath.

Alice replied without hesitation. "I would like to stay here, Your Ladyship, if that can be allowed. And work with my aunt." She smiled at Moira, whose cheeks had coloured

"I'm sure something can be arranged. But you must continue your education a little longer, I think."

Moira saw the girl hold her breath at the mention of school, a subject that had previously caused her to have a panic that took a lot to calm down. She stepped in.

"I have arranged a local tutor for the time being, Your Ladyship, as Esme still can't walk far."

"Good. Now, back to our carols, I think. My nieces and nephews are becoming rather restless."

This was dismissal and Moira wheeled Alice's chair back to the group of servants. She saw Mr Hughes step over to speak to Alan, who nodded and smiled at them.

At bedtime, Moira helped Alice into bed and sat on the chair next to her. "So, niece. You are content to spend your life here at Knyghton, with me?"

"Yes, Aunt."

"I'm thrilled, Esme. We shall be family and friend to each other." She took a deep breath. "Are you still trying to remember what went before? Would you like me to do more?"

"No, Aunt. I'm happy here. I didn't truly know that until tonight."

"Good. Sleep now. Tomorrow will be busy, then on Boxing Day, we'll both attend the servant's ball. You'll enjoy that."

Esme Peach nodded sleepily. Outside thick snow fell. As she watched the flakes settle on the window pane a glimpse of a face, a dark-haired woman, crossed her mind, but she pushed it aside. There was no more thinking to do. No more faces rushing at her out of the dark. No more children crying. She was at peace. She was home.

Chapter 48
May 2015

Alice and her friends played in the garden for an hour until they were collected.

"See you tomorrow. Don't let Buttster give you nightmares!"

"More DT?" Maggie asked as they walked back to the kitchen.

"'Fraid so. Sorry, Mum."

"Did you deserve it?"

"Well, I don't think so, but Buttster says I'm a bad character."

"I told you, Al, I'll go to see the woman. If she's picking on you, it's my place to speak to her. Anyway, you're not bad, and it's not right for her to say so."

"Don't worry about it, Mum. Mr Rees is back after half term. I'll be OK."

Maggie wanted to protest. She didn't think she should let this go on, but just at that moment a blip from the computer told her that there was an incoming message. The moment's hesitation as she turned her head in the direction of the computer was just enough to allow Alice to escape up to her room. Deciding she'd just have time to check the message before starting their evening meal, Maggie opened the email.

As they sat down to eat, Maggie waited for an opportune moment to tell the children what had happened, trying to contain her excitement. They began their ritual of talking about their day, first Jack, then Alice, then Maggie, who noticed that Alice didn't mention the detention. If Alice had escaped earlier from talking about it, to bring the subject up again would only upset her.

"OK, my turn. Two things to report. One, I had the job interview today." She screwed up her face. "Ugh."

Alice brightened. "You didn't get it?"

"Not so lucky. The man wanted to offer it to me but he has to wait until his boss comes back from holiday, which isn't until after half term. So I'm OK for a couple of weeks. And talking of half term, we should make plans."

"What's the second thing?" Jack asked. "And before you make any plans to go away, I've made some with my friends, so check with me first, OK?"

Maggie looked at him wryly. She'd always known this would come, but being the chief organiser and planner, even when David was alive, being instructed to consult someone else was a bitter pill to swallow.

"I'd like to invite the girls back again, next week, if that's OK, Mum. We've made plans to decorate the summerhouse."

"Looks like everyone has plans." She smiled. "That's fine with me. I have just one thing to do next week. I had an email this evening, in reply to my post about the family history."

Alice looked expectantly, but Jack showed no interest. "It's from a nurse in a nursing home, in Newport. She thinks she recognised some of the story, particularly about this house. It's not her, it's one of her patients, a very old lady, ninety-seven, apparently. Her name is Louisa Jenkins."

"Can we go and meet her?" Alice was enraptured.

"Yes. The nurse said that we'd be very welcome to visit. I emailed back, said that I would, probably early next week."

"How's she related to the story, Mum?"

"I don't know, yet. We'll have to speak to her to find out. In the meantime, Zelah and I are going to find out more about this house, and the farm that the family had, too."

"It's such fun, this detectiving, isn't it?" Alice put her elbows on the table and leaned forwards on them.

"Yes, it is."

Jack rolled his eyes heavenwards at them both.

* * *

On Thursday morning, after depositing the children at school, Maggie headed up to County Hall to meet Zelah. She was waiting for her in the foyer. They were expected on the fifth floor, and were taken by a young clerical officer to a conference room where several maps were spread out ready for them on a large table in the centre of the room.

"Here you are, Mrs Fitzgerald, all the maps and papers we hold about the two properties you mentioned."

"Thank you." Zelah nodded dismissively to the boy. "We'll let you know when we're finished." He left.

Maggie raised an eyebrow at Zelah. "Mrs Fitzgerald?"

"Need to use it sometimes. You don't think they do this for everyone, do you?" She looked quizzically at Maggie. "Are you feeling uncomfortable?"

"No. Not at all. Well, yes. A bit. I'm not used to special treatment."

"I don't do it often. Don't get used to it."

Maggie looked at the documents spread out on the table. Her house was instantly recognisable on a map dated 1910, with the canal running past the end of the garden. She could see that the

279

parcel of land it stood on had been bigger then, stretching down to what was now a main road on one side, and almost as far as the canal lock in the hamlet of Henllys, a few hundred yards on the other side.

"They must have sold off the land over time. It was on its own then, look."

"You can see why they chose it." Zelah pointed to the chapel half a mile or so away, on a direct line along the canal path. "It would have been an easy enough walk. Aha!" She pointed to a building a short walk from the chapel. "Here's the farm. It has a lot of land, too. Bigger than usual for this part of Wales." She looked at Maggie. "Most farmers were tenants. Your great-grandfather owned his and it looks like the farm was more than thirty acres. That's quite a feat, you know."

"I think he must have been a remarkable man," Maggie replied, tracing the line of the canal with her finger from house to chapel to farm. "I wonder when the farm disappeared. It's definitely not there now."

They checked through the other documents on the table. "Here!" Zelah picked up a packet of papers. "The farm buildings and land were sold off in 1948. They knocked them down and built houses in their place."

"Who was the beneficiary?"

"It was…" Zelah leafed through several pages. "It was a Mr William Jones. Sold for the grand sum of £40,000. Must have been a fortune then. Probably worth over a million today. Is there any other information about the farm?" Maggie was still examining papers relating to the house.

"Uh, no. That's it. According to this, the council bought it lock, stock and barrel. Could even have been derelict. You'd have to find William Jones's will to know what happened to the money.

Probably left it to his children, unless he was settling a debt. You don't know who the children are?"

"Not yet. Anyway, they'd be elderly or dead now. It's gone. That's the end of it. But there's some interesting stuff here about the house. Look." Zelah took the paper Maggie was holding out, a long piece of old, thick paper, covered in old-fashioned typing.

"It cost two thousand pounds to build the house. Amazing, considering what I paid for it!"

"You know, you've probably got copies of this and other documents that will give you the history of the ownership of your house."

"Yes, I know. I lodged them all with the solicitor who organised the purchase for me. I've been meaning to get them back to have a look. But I don't think I'll find much more, do you?"

"Probably not, but every new bit of information adds to the completeness of your story."

Maggie nodded and went back to the map.

After a further half hour they decided that there was nothing else to be learned from the papers and maps. Maggie had made copious notes and was putting her notebook away when a thought occurred to her. "Zelah, would you like to come and see John and Ruth's graves?"

"Love to."

They let the clerk know that they had finished. Maggie was amused by his deferential attitude towards Zelah, who barely acknowledged him, even though he accompanied them out of the building, waving as they got into their cars and drove away.

They were the only people in the cemetery. Approaching the grave, Maggie suddenly felt reluctant to get closer and she stopped a few yards away.

"That's it. Have a look at the inscriptions."

Zelah walked up to the stone and bent over to peer at it. "Beautiful, and just like you said. Why are you standing over there?"

"I'm not sure."

"Explain?"

Maggie thought for a moment. "I feel… like there's something else going on."

"Then there probably is."

"You don't find any of this odd, do you?"

"No. What do you think is happening?"

"I have no idea. I just know. I have an odd feeling, that's all. Is this weird?"

"No. It's your history and your memories. They are connecting you to your past and this was – is – a significant place," Zelah replied.

"I can feel a strange atmosphere now, as if… as if, if I just reached out, I could touch something that I can't see, but that I know is there." Maggie sighed. "Let's go and get a coffee, shall we? My place?"

I woke up and expected to find one of the kids standing next to my bed. But there was no-one there." She paused. Zelah said nothing.

"Lying awake last night, I thought over everything that's happened since I moved here, all the strange things, you know. The picture of the arm, the girl in the graveyard, the face at the window, the family likenesses. On their own they're all fascinating and interesting, exciting even. I thought of it as telepathic experience, or your theory of the inherited memory, but this is different. It's threatening. I've thought since the beginning that I was being impelled, like something was *making* me discover the story of my family. But now I think there's something else, something behind the events that happened back then." She looked at Zelah wryly. "Am I reading too much into this stuff?"

"Why are you asking me? If you want reassurance, I'm not going to give it to you." Zelah considered for a moment. "Most family history research is just a trawl through records to find something that's only meaningful to whoever's looking. But sometimes a story stands out. You've seen it in those celebrity programmes. But some of us find more than that. And I think you've gone further still. I've said from the start that it's up to you. You can stop whenever you like, but if something's there now, looking for you, I don't know that you stopping will prevent it."

"What do you mean?"

"You set out to look for something. Now, maybe something is looking for you."

Maggie cradled her hands around her cup.

"I've almost stopped a couple of times. It's getting weirder, not clearer."

"Your choice, Maggie"

Chapter 49

Zelah went straight to the kitchen and sat, arms folded, at the table, waiting while Maggie pottered around, talking of trivialities. When the pot of coffee was ready she indicated the sitting room and led the way, where they sat in the chairs at the back window.

"I was sitting here when I saw the face – my face – looking back at me the evening I found the grave. I think she sat here a lot too, and thought about what had happened to her. I've wondered if, when I sit here, I might be recalling her thoughts."

"I get the sense that you're still troubled," Zelah said. "But you told me Alice is fine, and not having nightmares any more. What's wrong now?"

Maggie didn't look at Zelah but stared out of the window, her cup at her bottom lip, but not drinking.

"Lately, I feel… I feel like I'm being watched." Zelah raised an eyebrow, but waited for more.

Maggie spoke slowly. "I feel, and it isn't a nice feeling, like whatever it is, it's coming closer. At first it was just an uncomfortab sensation, nothing connected with anything in particular. It ju came on me suddenly, like a shiver, but went away at once. The it started to feel a bit more solid, like when I'm in the garden I look up suddenly as if I expect to find someone standing on t towpath. Or in the supermarket the other day I thought someo was looking at me from the car park. But there's no-one. Last nig

I woke up and expected to find one of the kids standing next to my bed. But there was no-one there." She paused. Zelah said nothing.

"Lying awake last night, I thought over everything that's happened since I moved here, all the strange things, you know. The picture of the arm, the girl in the graveyard, the face at the window, the family likenesses. On their own they're all fascinating and interesting, exciting even. I thought of it as telepathic experience, or your theory of the inherited memory, but this is different. It's threatening. I've thought since the beginning that I was being impelled, like something was *making* me discover the story of my family. But now I think there's something else, something behind the events that happened back then." She looked at Zelah wryly. "Am I reading too much into this stuff?"

"Why are you asking me? If you want reassurance, I'm not going to give it to you." Zelah considered for a moment. "Most family history research is just a trawl through records to find something that's only meaningful to whoever's looking. But sometimes a story stands out. You've seen it in those celebrity programmes. But some of us find more than that. And I think you've gone further still. I've said from the start that it's up to you. You can stop whenever you like, but if something's there now, looking for you, I don't know that you stopping will prevent it."

"What do you mean?"

"You set out to look for something. Now, maybe something is looking for you."

Maggie cradled her hands around her cup.

"I've almost stopped a couple of times. It's getting weirder, not clearer."

"Your choice, Maggie"

Chapter 49

Zelah went straight to the kitchen and sat, arms folded, at the table, waiting while Maggie pottered around, talking of trivialities. When the pot of coffee was ready she indicated the sitting room and led the way, where they sat in the chairs at the back window.

"I was sitting here when I saw the face – my face – looking back at me the evening I found the grave. I think she sat here a lot too, and thought about what had happened to her. I've wondered if, when I sit here, I might be recalling her thoughts."

"I get the sense that you're still troubled," Zelah said. "But you told me Alice is fine, and not having nightmares any more. What's wrong now?"

Maggie didn't look at Zelah but stared out of the window, her cup at her bottom lip, but not drinking.

"Lately, I feel… I feel like I'm being watched." Zelah raised an eyebrow, but waited for more.

Maggie spoke slowly. "I feel, and it isn't a nice feeling, like whatever it is, it's coming closer. At first it was just an uncomfortable sensation, nothing connected with anything in particular. It just came on me suddenly, like a shiver, but went away at once. Then it started to feel a bit more solid, like when I'm in the garden I'll look up suddenly as if I expect to find someone standing on the towpath. Or in the supermarket the other day I thought someone was looking at me from the car park. But there's no-one. Last night,

"I know. I've arranged to go to the nursing home to meet a Louisa Jenkins on Tuesday next week. I'll see how that goes, then decide whether or not to pack it all in. Anyway, I'll be hearing more about that job soon. The decision may make itself."

"Let me know what you decide. I need to go. My turn on the desk in the library this afternoon." Zelah picked up her bag. "For what it's worth, whatever decision you take, it's OK with me. And tomorrow, back to county to look at some parish records?"

"Yes, great. Same time. I'll drop Alice at school, then meet you in the lobby. Jack will be on holiday, but he'll be OK on his own."

Zelah nodded, started to smile, changed her mind, then was gone.

For the rest of the day, Maggie couldn't settle to anything. Fiona phoned to find out about the interview and enthused down the phone, oblivious to Maggie's lack of interest. When Fiona began to plan Maggie's future, starting with how she could arrange their summer holidays and childcare, Maggie made an excuse and put the phone down. Her sister meant to help, she knew that, but speaking to her made Maggie more depressed than hopeful, and less certain about what to do next.

Having nothing much else to do, she set out early for school and found herself with ten minutes to spare before the children came out. Remembering that Jack had said that he would meet her there she looked around, but there was no sign of him.

She got out of the car and walked down the path towards Alice's classroom. The side door to the classroom was open, letting out a low hum of chatter that attracted her attention. Looking in, Maggie spotted a couple of Alice's friends. They saw her, but quickly looked down at the books in front of them. This puzzled her, knowing that Mr Rees wouldn't have taken umbrage at a quick smile to a passing parent, so she slowed down and looked more closely at the faces of the children as they worked. They were all frowning with concentration, as a teacher walked among them. As the teacher approached, each head went further down. Maggie could sense the tension. Then she spotted Alice, working alone, and she appeared to be crying.

Turning away from the door she walked briskly round to the back entrance, as the bell rang for the end of the day. Jack was waiting, hovering at the door and looking anxiously inside. She walked past him, straight into the school.

"Stay there!" she barked at him without stopping. She marched to Alice's classroom, just in time to spot the teacher she had just seen, walking out of the side door. Another teacher was talking to the class now and they were putting their papers away. As the children filed out of the classroom, Maggie pushed past them to the teacher's desk. Alice was still in the corner, not moving, but Maggie ignored her.

"Excuse me, are you the supply teacher or the assistant?" The young woman looked blankly at her. "I'm Alice Gilbert's mother. Why is she sitting alone and crying?"

"I don't know, Mrs Gilbert. I was out until a few minutes ago. My assistant told me that she caught Alice cheating in a test."

Maggie looked slowly from the teacher to Alice, stared at her daughter's forlorn expression then turned back.

"No, she didn't."

"I beg your pardon?" The teacher was unsettled by Maggie's challenge.

"Alice, come here," Maggie called her. Alice stood and walked slowly to the teacher's desk.

"Did you cheat?"

"No, I didn't."

"Has anyone asked you what happened?"

"No. She just said I cheated and put me in a corner, then said I had to do a detention."

"By 'her' I assume you mean the teaching assistant?"

"Yes."

"Did she have any proof?" Maggie asked the teacher.

"She just said that Alice had cheated. I had no reason to assume that it wasn't true." The teacher was rattled, but wasn't backing down.

"But you were given no proof?" The hesitation, the glance that didn't quite meet Maggie's, was enough. Looking down at the pile of papers in front of her she muttered, "No, I assumed she had seen something."

Maggie put her arm around Alice's shoulders.

"Alice has always been a model student and she doesn't cheat. There will be no detention and I'm taking her home now. She won't be in school tomorrow. I'll arrange to see Mr Rees after half term. Good day."

She put a hand on Alice's shoulder and steered her out of the classroom, leaving the teacher gaping. At the door she signalled to Jack to follow her. They walked to the car in silence and got in.

"Enough is enough," she barked at Alice and Jack. They both nodded and she drove home.

As soon as she could, Maggie called Zelah to tell her that she couldn't keep the appointment at the archive the following morning, relating the story of what had happened at the school. "Quite right, too. Of course you should keep her away. I'll wait for you before I do anything else."

"Yes, of course. Zelah, since we spoke, I've been thinking about whether or not to carry on, but I'm still shaking after the school thing and I can't reflect on anything in a meaningful way right now. So, I've decided to go away with the kids for a couple of days. It'll give me chance to think and give Alice some breathing space. I'll be back Monday night."

"Sounds like a good decision. Call me when you get back." Zelah put the phone down abruptly, as usual.

Maggie drew in a deep breath, and went to her computer. Half an hour later she called Alice and Jack and told them that she had just booked four nights away, starting immediately, and sent them to pack.

"Where are we going?" Alice asked, dancing happily. "Down to Cornwall," Maggie replied, pulling rucksacks from under the stairs. "I'm going to get the camping stuff ready. We're leaving in an hour. The weather's looking good. Let's get going!"

Alice loved travelling of any kind so she bounded up the stairs two at a time, but Jack stood his ground.

"What happened at the school, Mum? Why are we going away?"

"Alice is having a bad time there, so I want to give her some room. I'd like a break before I start work. The weather's looking good from tomorrow, so let's not waste it. OK?"

"I thought you were going to ask me first."

Maggie handed him a rucksack. "Yes. I'm sorry. Are you OK with this? It's only until Monday. You can have the rest of next week with your friends."

"Suppose so. I was going to look after her, you know."

Maggie had been trying so hard to keep the children from realising how angry and upset she'd been, that she hadn't considered why Jack had met her at Alice's school. The realisation dawned that she had practically knocked him out of her way, and with it how much she had hurt his feelings. She reached out and put her hand on his cheek, stroking it gently.

"Jack, I'm so sorry. I know you were there for her. But I sensed something when I saw her in the classroom that made me rush to get her out of there. I didn't mean to ignore you, really, I didn't."

The anxious look went. "Fair enough. Is she all right?"

"I think so. I'll talk to her about it while we're away. Let's just go away together and have a good time, eh? Get the barbeque out, and your surfboard. OK?"

"I suppose." As he turned away and dragged his feet slowly up the stairs it occurred to Maggie that maybe she was being impetuous, acting from panic as well as anger and that she would regret this sudden decision.

Chapter 50
June 1909

Accompanied by Richard Robinson, Ruth arrived at the cemetery just before noon. Despite the bravado she displayed in front of Cerys, she was aware of how she would be watched and her every move judged. So in the end she had decided to ask Richard to go with her to visit John's grave.

She had thrown off concerns about the strange feeling she had had in the graveyard during the burial, and arrived with anticipation. But as soon as she began to walk towards the grave, it seemed that this had suddenly become a strange, airless, overcast day and she walked with dragging steps.

Richard accompanied her to the chapel, but she stopped him there.

"I would prefer to be alone, if you don't mind, Richard."

"Of course. I shall wait here. Take as long as you need."

Ruth didn't look back as she walked off the path and across the short stretch of grass, but she felt the minister's eyes on her. When she came close to the grave itself there was an atmosphere, a warmth that wasn't in the air. Slowly she put her hand towards the granite and marble.

"Just a few weeks, John. But it seems a lifetime."

Her outstretched hand hesitated, then touched his name on the headstone. As her fingers made contact, the stone felt surprisingly warm and Ruth thought she felt again the touch of his hand on hers. Then she realised that she was touching something that felt like flesh. Her first instinct was to withdraw her hand but, although it was a strange sensation, it wasn't unpleasant and, after the shock, felt benign. She deliberately didn't look around, in case her face betrayed her and brought Richard over. Instead, Ruth leaned over the headstone.

"John, I am going to search for her. You will think I am letting you down. But I must go."

She bowed her head and waited, for what she wasn't sure, but convinced that she would sense something emanating from the grave. But there was nothing, which was frustrating. She had come to believe, after recent events, that she was still somehow connected to him. Uncertain what to do, she decided to try again.

"John, you must not deny me this, not after all this time! I have always needed to know."

The sound of the voice next to her ear, just as it had been on the day of his funeral, froze her to the spot.

"It's not John, Ruth. You don't know who I am, but I know you. I'm your friend. I'm more than your friend, I'm family and I'm trying to help, please believe me. We will find out what happened to your Alice."

It was a woman's voice, again. Ruth's head swam and she let out a long sigh. Fear clutched her stomach and quickly rose to her head as she turned and walked as quickly as she could, without running, back to where Richard was waiting. Any hope of keeping the panic to herself was dashed as she approached him.

"Ruth, whatever's the matter. Your face is white!"

She stumbled and half collapsed against him, shaking. "I heard a voice at the graveside. What is it, Richard? Who is it? Is this just grief? It spoke of Alice!"

He took her shaking hands and helped her back into the cart. As they drove back to Garthwood House she said nothing and Richard, watching the turmoil pass over her face, kept silent until they arrived at the door and he called to Cerys.

"Mrs Jones is unwell. Please make her some tea and bring it into the parlour. I'm going to send for the doctor."

"No!" Her firm exclamation stopped them. "I'm in no need of his attention, thank you. Just a cup of tea and I shall feel well again." She put up a hand to stop him saying more.

Maud came running down the stairs. She took Ruth's arm and led her into the sitting room, to her chair in the window. Richard followed. Ruth sat, breathing deeply, then she smiled calmly at Maud.

"Just a little overwrought, I fear. Nothing to worry about. Do go back to whatever you were doing, my dear. I really don't need you." Her voice was dismissive enough to make Maud stand, hover uncomfortably, then disappear back upstairs, but not without giving Richard a stern look of disapproval. He sat opposite her and waited until she finished her tea.

"Would you like to explain to me? That dismissal of Maud is quite unlike you. You hurt her feelings."

She looked directly at him. "Richard, we've known each other for a long time. Am I a woman given to hysteria? Am I likely to be unable to cope with my husband's death? Tell me, honestly, what you believe."

"Ruth, I have always judged you to be a most sensible woman. I saw how you coped with John's illness. You knew his death was coming and you were prepared. Why are we having this conversation?" He leaned closer to her. "What is happening here,

Ruth? What did you mean when you said that you heard a voice at the graveside?"

"Actually more than one voice. It started at the burial, Richard. I actually saw Alice, as a child, standing looking at me. And a woman's voice said, 'Say hello to Ruth, Alice.'" She said this so matter-of-factly that Richard was nonplussed.

"Then, later, I saw a face in the window, that window, there, staring back at me. It was my face, but not my face. I was crying. She wasn't."

Richard was still stunned. "What do you think is happening, Ruth?"

"I don't know, Richard. I've thought over it at length and I've been considering the past. I do believe that it's connected to Alice; that's the only certainty I have." Her emphatic expression told him not to argue with her certainty. "I dismissed Maud because I don't want any of them to know what I'm about to do. Which I will need your help to do."

"You know that I'll always be pleased to help you, Ruth. But this worries me deeply. I would hear everything from you. What is this plan of yours?"

Slowly and carefully, she told him everything from the day of John's funeral onwards, plus her memories of the events during and after Alice's disappearance. Finally, she told him her theory of what had really happened, and her plan. He sat for a long time, considering his response.

"What do you want me to do?"

She looked determinedly back at him. "I want you to accompany me to Hereford, to visit Robert Pugh. I have written to him to request a meeting at his convenience."

He looked shocked at the proposal. The idea of a widow undertaking such a journey so soon after her husband's death was unnerving, as she had known it would be.

"This is not the time, Ruth. You should wait at least six months. It's not possible now."

"I've waited over twenty-five years, Richard!"

"Then another six months won't matter."

"Every day that passes without knowing matters. You are my only hope. But I'll understand if you don't want to be tainted by such shocking behaviour. I had thought that your attendance would afford me some respectability, but I am determined to go and I shall go alone if you feel that you can't accompany me."

"I don't think I can, Ruth." He shook his head. "Not because of what you've told me, but for your sake and your reputation. You cannot do this."

"I'll not force you, Richard. I had hoped to convince you, but I see that I haven't succeeded. So, let me tell you some more of what I believe."

Chapter 51
June 2015

The moment they arrived back in the house after their break in Cornwall, the phone rang. Maggie dropped one of the rucksacks and ran to answer it.

"Hello, Mrs Gilbert? It's Nurse Crowley at the nursing home. About tomorrow?"

"Yes. What, is there a problem? Sorry, we've just got in from a weekend away."

"No, no problem. I was just checking that you're still coming, actually. Mrs Jenkins has perked up in the past few days and she's looking forward to seeing you."

"Oh, good. Is it still OK for us to come at eleven?"

"That's fine. See you tomorrow. 'Bye."

Maggie and Alice left Jack in bed the following morning. The nursing home turned out to be a large, converted house on the edge of Newport, on a hill with views over the Bristol Channel, with wide, manicured flower beds, and benches under the trees on which a number of the residents were braving the heat, sitting with nurses.

Nurse Crowley met them in the foyer and led them to Mrs Jenkins's room.

"Likes her privacy, but she can still get outside now and then. Not today, though. Too hot. You won't be able to stay long. She can't concentrate."

They entered a large room on the ground floor that immediately reminded Maggie of the inter-war era. The room was furnished with Mrs Jenkins's own furniture, masses of it, so much so that it was difficult to find floor space. It was all lace and chintz with mementos and photographs everywhere. A set of double doors opened onto a walled garden at the side of the main house. One of the doors was open, allowing a gentle breeze and a waft of lavender into the room.

In a large upright chair, with a blanket over her knees and another around her shoulders, Louisa Jenkins sat with her head forwards, snoozing in front of a large unlit fireplace. Maggie felt Alice take a step behind her at the sight of the old lady, and Maggie put her hand back to reassure her.

"Is she alive?" Alice whispered.

Maggie grinned and turned away from the nurse, who was now gently shaking the old lady's arm. Louisa Jenkins grunted a few times, and opened her eyes. Through opaque slits she looked slowly at the nurse, who was shouting at her that she had visitors. She looked up at Maggie. Her old eyes widened in surprise.

"I'm your visitor, Mrs Jenkins. Margaret Gilbert," Maggie said loudly. "Before I married I was Margaret Jones. Are you OK? Is she all right?" she asked Nurse Crowley, as the old lady continued to stare at her.

"Are you the one? She said you'd come."

"I'm Margaret Jones. I believe we're related."

"Looks like she's seen a ghost," the nurse said, tucking in the blanket that had slipped, exposing the old lady's reed-thin ankles

"Ah," Maggie understood. She moved closer to the old lady, "I believe your grandmother was Ruth Jones and I look like your grandmother, is that it? I look like Ruth. But I'm not

Ruth. I'm her great-granddaughter. Do you understand that? I'm not Ruth."

Louisa Jenkins seemed to struggle with some fleeting memory, turned her eyes away, then back directly at Maggie.

"You look like her. Just like her. I knew you were coming." Her voice was shrill. She put a skeletal hand on Maggie's arm. "Who did you say you are?"

"I'm Margaret Gilbert. My father was John Jones, but I believe you knew him as 'Cyril' and he was George and Agnes's son. They would have been your aunt and uncle. My dad was your cousin."

"Aunt Aggie? She's gone now. Like my Sidney."

"Yes, she died thirty years ago." Maggie was beginning to wonder if this was going anywhere.

"You're family! I haven't seen anyone. I've been waiting for years. Lovely to meet you, Margaret." Louisa smiled at Maggie, who pulled over a chair in front of her and signalled to Alice to do the same.

"This is my daughter, Alice."

Alice leaned forwards and smiled uncertainly. "Hello."

"You're pretty, aren't you? Got a boyfriend yet?"

"No. I'm a bit young. I'm ten." Alice pulled a face at her mother.

"Met my Sidney when I was fourteen. Married at sixteen. Just children, both of us, my mother said." The old lady closed her eyes and Maggie pitched in.

"Your mother, that would be Maud? And your father was James?"

"That's right. How do you know? Who are you?"

Maggie told her again and added, "I've been doing some research about the family. I bought your grandparents' house, Garthwood House. Do you remember it?"

297

"Garthwood House? I was born there. So were my brother and sister. I thought it was long gone."

"No. It was in a state, but I've made it look good. I've brought pictures. Would you like to see them?"

Louisa nodded and held out her hand to the nurse, who produced a hefty magnifying glass.

"Cataracts," she whispered to Maggie. "Don't know how much she'll be able to see."

Maggie and Alice handed the photos one by one to Louisa, who hunched over close to each one, peering through the outsize glass.

"Hasn't changed much, has it? Just like when I was a girl. Who lives there now?"

Alice stifled a giggle.

"I live there now, Louisa. I'd like to know about your grandmother Ruth. Do you remember her?"

"Of course I remember her. She chose my name. Mother wanted to call me Eliza, but Nana said I had to be Louisa. I was her favourite. She talked a lot to me, 'specially when I was growing up, before I met my Sidney. She didn't mind when we got married. I knew my own mind, but she liked that." As she spoke the old lady gazed around the room, smiling to herself.

"What sort of person was your grandmother, Louisa?"

"Nana? She was a lovely woman, fair, kind. Could be angry, though, when we were naughty." She leaned forwards conspiratorially. "Never let us in the attic. Got angry with Elwyn when he tried to open those trunks. Thought she was going to beat him."

Maggie sat up. "What trunks, Louisa?"

"Like I said, in the attic. Forbidden, it was. Never tried again. Too scared."

"Were they brown trunks? Two of them?"

"That's right. How do you know?"

"Because they were still there when I moved in. They've never been moved. Did you know that they were left there?"

"Hid them, she did. Told me one day. At the back of the attic. Wanted me to go back for them when she died. But Sidney said best left alone. 'Family secrets, don't disturb them,' he said." Louisa nodded with a conspirator's smile, pulling at her thin, short, white hair.

Maggie was breathing quickly. "Do you know what was there, Louisa?"

"No, never found out."

"They were full of the clothes of a child."

"Ah," Louisa paused and nodded again. "That would be the one they didn't talk about."

"What do you know about that child?"

"Went missing, Nana told me. After her best friend got drowned."

"Do you know how old the child was when she went missing, Louisa?"

"About ten or eleven, I believe. Mustn't talk about it, my mother said. Stir up old bad things. But Nana told me. Said we all had to be careful. She found out…" she stopped suddenly. "I've been expecting you." She nodded at the nurse. "She said you'd come."

"Careful of what… of who? Do you remember anything about the story?"

"What story?" The old lady turned her attention back to Maggie.

"Who are you? Why are you here?" She looked up at the nurse with a fearful expression.

"I think that's as much as Mrs Jenkins can manage today." Nurse Crowley moved to stand next to her patient.

"Thank you so much for speaking to us, Louisa. It's been wonderful to meet you." She reached into her bag. "I found some old family photos for you to look at." She handed the package to the nurse. "Perhaps I can come again soon." Then to Louisa, "If you'd like to take a look through the photos, perhaps you can tell me who some of these people are."

"That would be lovely," the nurse enthused, "but time to go now." She lowered her voice. "She's asleep again. Sleeps a lot now," she added, nodding meaningfully.

"Does she have any other visitors?" Maggie asked.

"No. Her lawyer calls every couple of months, when she decides to make some adjustment to her will. And the vicar of St Cadoc's calls in occasionally. That's where she used to live. But no family. She'll be talking about this for weeks, if she remembers."

She led Maggie and Alice out of the room, back to the entrance hall.

"Do come again. She'd like it."

"Thank you. We will. How about Thursday?"

The nurse nodded dismissively and trotted back in the direction of the bedrooms. Maggie and Alice walked outside and across the lawn to where they had left the car. There were still a few people around, but most were making their way back to the main house.

"Must be nearly lunchtime, I guess," Maggie said to Alice as they walked.

"Probably takes them all morning to get out here and back. Hope I can still walk when I'm old. Will I look like that one day?"

"If you get to be ninety-seven, probably, yes."

"I'm glad I came. She was a bit scary, though. Don't you think?"

They reached the car and Maggie opened the doors to let out some of the heat. "Wow, it's really hot today. No, I don't think she was scary. She knows something about our girl, that's clear. Some kind of family scandal, maybe."

"I thought it was a bit scary. Why did she know you'd come?"

"Well, she probably remembered what the nurse told her. Old people can have problems with their memory, you know. They can remember loads about the past, as if it were yesterday, but often forget things that happened a couple of days ago, or even minutes. But, doesn't it just confirm how much I must look like my great-grandmother? It feels strange to meet someone who can remember the people that I've been researching. It really brings them to life."

"I didn't think that was what she meant," Alice said as they drove off.

Chapter 52

When she got home Maggie phoned Zelah to give her an account of the visit.

"So, I was right about the missing child! They never found her," Zelah exclaimed.

"Yes," Maggie replied. "And it looks like there was definitely something not right about it. I mean, why else would Louisa have been told not to talk about it, that it would stir up 'bad old things'. And what was she supposed to be careful about? How on earth do I find out more about this?"

"Do you want to?"

"Yes, I do. I've calmed down. I thought it over when we were away. We all talked about what to do and the kids think I should carry on. I've promised Alice that I'll be around more to help with her school problem, but I can't stop this now. Not until I find out the whole story."

"Good. What's next, then?"

"Well, I'm going back on Thursday to see Louisa again. See if she can remember any more details. Zelah, can you take a look at the papers again, see if there was anything reported at the time? Surely if a child went missing, even then, there must have been a search."

"I'll give it a go. Call me after your visit on Thursday. 'Bye."

By Thursday midday, when she set off for the nursing home, Maggie hadn't heard anything from Zelah. She was alone this time as Alice had opted for a visit to the coast with her friends.

Nurse Crowley met her again at the reception desk and told her that Louisa had expressed a wish to go out into the walled garden.

"She doesn't get outside often these days, so it'll be nice for her to sit out for a while. Not long, mind. She can't concentrate for very long, you saw that on Tuesday."

"That's fine, I don't want to upset her."

"Quite the opposite!" the nurse responded as they reached the room. "She really enjoyed seeing you. She's remembered a lot since. Oh, and we looked through the photographs, too. And put names to some of them."

"That's wonderful!"

Louisa was waiting in a wheelchair, a shawl over her shoulders. As Maggie approached she reached out and grabbed her arm with a surprisingly strong grasp, smiling up at her.

"Hello again, Margaret."

Maggie bent over and kissed her wrinkled cheek. "How lovely to see you, Louisa. You look well today. Nurse Crowley tells me we're going to the garden."

"Bit of fresh air. Do me good. Keep me awake, she says!" She cackled a throaty "ha-ha" at the nurse.

Together they went out to the walled garden. It was a pretty space with beds of bright flowers, a neatly cut lawn and a small tree at the centre sheltering a wooden bench. The high red-brick wall separated them from the main garden, accessible through a wooden door. Maggie could see that two other bedrooms also led into the garden.

"How long have you lived here, Louisa?" Maggie asked as they settled her under the tree and she and the nurse sat on the bench.

"About five years. When Sidney died I managed on my own for a while. Then I fell and broke my hip. Couldn't manage after that. Sold up and came here."

"It's a lovely place."

"I like to have my own things around me. They allow it here. Lots don't."

"You and Sidney must have been married a long time?"

"Seventy-five years nearly," Louisa replied. Maggie saw a tear in the corner of one eye. "Not a day goes by I don't miss him. Heart attack. Here one day, gone the next."

Maggie put her hand on Louisa's trembling hand. "It's wonderful to hear about people so happily married, especially these days."

"Do you have a husband, Margaret?"

"He died. In a motorbike accident."

"That's sad, my dear. Sad for that little girl, too."

"And my son," Maggie added. "I have a boy of fourteen. He misses his dad. But they're both good kids."

"We had a boy. Died when he was five. Diphtheria. Our Christopher. Didn't think Sidney would get over it. Near grieved himself to death. Nana helped us. She understood." Louisa was gazing down at her hands.

Nurse Crowley leaned across to Maggie. "She's never mentioned this before," she whispered.

"You must have been devastated," Maggie spoke gently to Louisa. "But it was good that you had someone there to help you."

"She told me she lost her first baby, born dead, ahead of his due time. Then her next one went missing when she was ten.

Then Uncle Evan went off to the war and got his arms blown off. Nana thought he was going to die. But she saved him. Her babies made her sick, she told me. Nearly died herself a couple of times."

"I believe she was a remarkable woman," Maggie said, smiling at her.

"But strong, she was. Lived till she was eighty-two. She was waiting, too, she told me. But I never knew what for. Right after that visitor, it was. That woman who turned up on the day she died." Louisa was staring into space again, "Never said who it was. Probably didn't matter. Died later that day. They sold the house after that, my parents. Your house now." She grinned approvingly at Maggie.

"I found her grave," Maggie said. "She's buried with her husband, John, in the cemetery in Garth Hill."

"That's right! I'd forgotten that."

"It was a bit overgrown, so I've cleaned it up. It's a beautiful monument."

"I'm going to be with my Sidney and Christopher. I've told that solicitor, and Nurse." She reached out for Maggie's hand. "Make sure I'm with them, won't you?"

"Of course," Maggie replied. "Louisa, is there anything else you can tell me about Ruth's child who went missing? Did she die?"

Louisa sighed. "She went after her friend died. Something very wrong about it, Nana said. Nana never believed that her girl was dead. All the others did, though. My mother and Uncle William and Uncle Walter. She told me."

She leaned forwards and whispered in Maggie's ear: "When Granddad died, she went to find out what happened. She believed something had frightened her girl away. And she was right! They

305

didn't like it, mind, her going about like that. Wasn't seemly. Said she was imagining things. But they were wrong and she was right."

"What?" Maggie exclaimed. "You mean, she found out something?"

"Oh yes. She found out what it was. Told us to be careful… for our children. She was frightened, was Nana. Scared it might come back, again. She told me things." She began to breathe heavily.

"Quietly now, Mrs Jenkins. Don't upset yourself," said the nurse, concerned.

"Needs to be told. Have to tell her. I can't remember… but she said important not to be afraid. It needs your fear. Waiting for you. Ninety-seven now! I'm so tired." Louisa was sobbing now and the nurse looked alarmed.

"Time to go back in, I think." It was a rebuke to Maggie. She pushed the wheelchair back into the room and the nurse got Louisa into her bed. "Time for a sleep."

"No!" The nurse's head shot up in surprise at the emphatic shout from the old lady. "She needs to know. Nana said. It'll come back. Mind out for Alice," she whispered to Maggie.

Maggie hovered uncertainly, desperate for Louisa to keep talking but not wanting to cause distress. Caution won out.

"Louisa, I'm going to sit in the foyer until you feel better. I'd like to talk to you about the photographs, too. I'll come back shortly."

In the foyer, Maggie got herself a glass of water and wondered how she was going to get Louisa to talk without causing more upset. Clearly, there was much more to this and Louisa had vital information. But the old woman's frail condition made it risky. She could find out slowly, over a series of visits. After ten or so minutes Nurse Crowley appeared again.

"I can't have you upsetting her, Mrs Gilbert," she began sternly, "but she's determined to speak to you again, so you'd better come back in. But please be careful."

Louisa was sitting up in bed.

"Are you feeling better now?" Maggie asked tentatively.

"I'm very well. Just a bit tired. About those photographs. Told Nurse who they were, the ones I knew, and she wrote the names on them."

Maggie sat down next to the bed, took the envelope and checked the back of the photos. Louisa had confirmed what she suspected, the photograph that looked like herself was Ruth. Louisa had identified her own parents, her sister and one of her brothers.

"Went in the war, did Elwyn." She softly stroked the photograph. "Blown up by a shell in France. Only recognised him because he's the image of my father."

Maggie looked at the photo of a young man, taken at a beach outing in 1915, when he would have been around fourteen, with a group of laughing boys and girls.

"Would you like to keep this, Louisa?"

The old woman looked up through misty eyes. "Yes, I would." She took the photograph from Maggie and gazed at it.

"So much I can't remember now. It was important. She said you'd come," she muttered quietly to herself. Within a few minutes she had fallen asleep, the photo still in her hands.

"Take the rest of them," the nurse whispered. "I've put names on the back where she knew them. Time to go, now."

Maggie took Louisa's hand. "Look at her smiling in her sleep! She looks so peaceful."

She gently placed her hand on the bedcover and walked to the door, whispering to the nurse. "I'm so pleased I've found her. I'll come back next week. In fact, I'll come every week."

"That would be lovely," beamed the nurse, closing the bedroom door.

Later that evening, after she had collected Alice and they'd had a barbeque in the garden, Maggie sat at the window watching the sunset over the mountain, piecing together the information from Louisa.

"Something bad happened to your girl, Ruth," she murmured to the window. "Your granddaughter Louisa told me. I went to see her. She's ninety-seven now. I'll find out, somehow. I got your warning. She's so very frail but she waited. For me. Someone told her I was coming. I don't understand how but I think – somehow – it was you."

Chapter 53

Alice had been particularly difficult on Sunday, whining that she didn't feel well and being unusually rude. She had refused to eat all day, blaming an upset stomach and then, at bedtime, had burst into tears. Maggie sent Alice to bed but sat with her for a while, talking to the uncommunicative lump under the duvet.

"I'll be coming in with you, like we agreed. I'm going to speak to Mr Rees. He's a nice man and he's always been very positive about your behaviour and your work. He knows you don't cheat." After another long silence, she said, "unless you don't want me to, of course. I could just not come and leave it up to you, if you'd prefer."

The bedclothes shuffled slightly. "But they'll believe the teacher."

"Why do you think so?"

"Because she's a grown-up and I'm just a kid and no-one takes a kid's word against a teacher."

Maggie considered. There was truth in this. "Well, maybe so. But they should hear the truth, then it's up to them to believe it or not. Maybe that's the best we can do, but I think it's better than doing nothing."

A short pause, then, "OK."

The following morning Alice had dark circles under her eyes and got ready in moody silence. Throughout the ride to school she only grunted in response to questions and remarks by Maggie and

Jack, and by the time they arrived and Jack took himself off for the short walk to his school, Maggie was exasperated.

She walked beside a foot-scraping Alice to the classroom door. Mr Rees was already at his desk and welcomed Alice with a smile. He looked surprised when she put her head down and went to her desk without speaking. Maggie went through what had happened at the end of the half term.

"I can understand why you're unhappy, Mrs Gilbert. And I agree that Alice has always been a pleasure to have in the classroom. I say it and I mean it. There should be a report on the incident, so I'll check it out and get back to you."

She nodded thanks to him and was going to leave, but he spoke again. "The teaching assistant was a little harsh, maybe. But discipline *is* important. Some children can take advantage when their regular teacher isn't here. Anyway, she can't be with us this week. Family problems, I believe." He lowered his voice and nodded imperceptibly in Alice's direction. "Leave it to me. She'll be fine by the end of the day."

Feeling relieved, Maggie thanked him, smiled briefly at Alice, and left the school. On the way out she bumped into the mother of one of Alice's friends and explained why she was there, curious to find out if there had been any similar experience. She was surprised by the vehemence of the reply.

"So, that woman's gone, eh? Good riddance, I say. My Janine hated her." She put a hand on Maggie's arm. "Nothing changes much, does it? There's always one!"

Maggie smiled at her and went back to the car.

Over the weekend, she had finally got around to buying the family history software that Zelah had recommended, and spent the day entering in everyone that she had discovered, distracted occasionally by the pouring rain. By the time she was ready to collect the children, she had a complete family tree printed out.

As Mr Rees had promised, Alice was in much better spirits. Maggie could see her and Jack chatting animatedly at the gate under their shared umbrella as she drove up, and they jumped into the car still talking.

"Good day?"

"Fine thanks!" they both replied and she was satisfied with that.

Later that evening Zelah rang to say that she had found "interesting" information, but wouldn't elaborate, saying that she was going out and had to hurry.

"Don't ask me now. I'll come round tomorrow morning, if that's OK. 'Bye then," and rang off without waiting for Maggie to agree.

But the next morning brought no sign of her. At eleven o'clock Maggie was about to call, when the phone rang.

"Mrs Gilbert? It's Nurse Crowley, from Goldendays."

"Oh, hello. Sorry, I was expecting a friend to call. I was planning to come on Thursday, is that OK?"

"No, I'm afraid not, Mrs Gilbert." The nurse had lowered her voice and Maggie's heart pounded.

"Is anything the matter?" she asked, trying to sound hopeful, but sickly anticipating what was coming.

"Mrs Jenkins died yesterday morning, I'm so very sorry to have to tell you. In her sleep, quite peacefully."

Maggie shoulders sagged. "I see. Thank you for letting me know." She sat down on the chair next to the telephone.

"The funeral will be on Friday. At St Cadoc's Church, followed by the interment. You know her wishes on that. Might you be able to attend?"

"Of course, I'll be there," Maggie replied immediately. "What time?"

"Ten thirty. Thank you, Mrs Gilbert. I'm so sorry."

'

Chapter 54
June 1909

"These are only my thoughts for now, you understand."

Richard Robinson slowly nodded agreement and, with a sense of relief, Ruth gathered her thoughts.

"I have spent so much time thinking, considering. All the time John was ill, I thought. Ever since he died, I have thought. At last, I believe I'm close to the truth."

"Now, I know that you remember Alice, and you know that she was a good girl, not given to truly bad acts. Well, from the time the new schoolteacher, Miss Probert, arrived she seemed to pick out Alice for her disapproval."

"On the day that Esme Ellis died, we were told that Alice had been kept behind at school, which she was angry about because she had arranged to meet Esme at The Pond. She was supposed to have been insolent to Miss Probert. But I don't think that was the case. I don't think she was kept behind at all. I think she and Esme went to The Pond together, at the invitation of Miss Probert. It is my belief that another child, probably one of the Morris girls, probably Elsie, told Alice that Miss Probert wanted to meet with Alice in a quiet place. Something that Bessie Morris said made me think that the Morrises were more involved and knew more than they admitted to. But Alice and Esme formed a plan to fool Miss Probert by having Esme put on Alice's hat and coat and wait by The Pond, out on the platform, whilst Alice stood watching from the wood."

She saw his eyes widen in surprise but she couldn't be interrupted now. "You're going to ask how I know this. I don't know for sure. But I do know that Alice's description of how she was supposed to have found Esme didn't make sense. I went there myself. It couldn't have happened like she said. And at one point, our dear Lord forgive me, I thought Alice might have accidentally pushed Esme into the water herself!

"But then there was the question of the wound on Essy's head. I knew that Alice would not have done that. They were great friends, as you know."

She paused and he nodded, silent while she concentrated. "Alice wasn't just frightened after Esme died. She was terrified. But of what, or who? There had been plenty of trouble with the Morris girls, but I think it had to be more than that. William told me that Alice truly believed that if she told the truth, no-one, including John and me, would believe her. She even thought I would not believe her. I remember she tried to tell me the night before she went." Her voice trembled.

"I went to see Gwen Ellis. She grasped my hand and repeated over and over what Cerys had told me, 'She wasn't there.' And she looked so frightened. Why would that make her so frightened? I believe she was trying to let me know who wasn't there, when she should have been and said she was. There were only supposed to be two people in the school that afternoon – Alice and Eira Probert. I know that Gwen never once suspected Alice. But Eira Probert – now she insisted that she had been at the school, then at the minister's house. Pugh never contradicted that story.

"Then, quite suddenly, Eira Probert disappeared, saying that she was going to teach at a school in Herefordshire, invited by Mr Pugh. Yet, I'd seen once before that he looked puzzled when she said that she had been invited by him to come here to Garth Hill, although, again, he didn't contradict her.

"You know how ill I was before and after George was born. By the time I recovered, Alice had been gone six months and both Miss Probert and Mr Pugh were gone, too. John had stopped searching. Eventually, I accepted his decision, I felt I had no other choice. But in my heart I knew that Alice was still alive. I have never given up hope of at least finding out *why* she went."

She stood up and walked to the bureau, returning with a letter, which she handed to Richard. "I received this from Charles and Bessie Morris."

He read through it then looked at her. "What have you deduced from this?"

"Why, that Miss Probert lied when she said why she was leaving and where she was going."

"That's a strong word, Ruth. She may have changed her mind, or had to attend to some family issue."

"Yes, Richard, I know. That's why I've written to Mr Pugh to ask to speak with him."

"Pugh might refuse. Have you considered that?"

She sighed. "Of course. He wasn't at all friendly towards us. But I hope that the passage of time has mellowed those feelings, and, as John is dead, he will agree to speak to me. I think he'll want to, you know."

"I'm not so sure, from what I know of Pugh. He's an unpleasant man. So, are these your conclusions?"

"Not all. I believe…" her voice began to shake, "I have come to believe that it was Eira Probert who hit Esme on the head, and drowned her, thinking that she was Alice. And she——"

The ringing doorbell interrupted her. Ruth waited, listening to Cerys go to the door, speak to someone, then close the door. She walked into the sitting room.

"I'm sorry to bother, Mrs Jones, but there's a letter for you." Ruth took it from the girl with a smile, which disappeared when she saw the postmark.

"It's from Hereford. We'll find out what Mr Pugh has to say."

Richard sat attentively in his armchair while Ruth read the letter. The arching of an eyebrow, followed by a frown, then a look of satisfaction caused him to shuffle in his seat.

"Robert Pugh is dead. This is from his widow. He died six months ago. She is surprised to hear from me after such a long time and offers condolences on John's death. She is willing to meet me, as she has information that she can offer me. She suggests that I call on Monday next." She looked directly at the minister. "Well, Richard? What do you say now?"

Chapter 55

June 2015

The revving of Zelah's car brought Maggie out of her reverie. She walked to open the front door, but stood at the porch, leaning against the door frame, hugging her arms tightly around herself. Zelah had hopped out of the car and started up the path, but stopped when she saw the expression on Maggie's face.

"What? Not the children!"

"No. I just got a call from the nursing home. Louisa Jenkins is dead."

Zelah hesitated. "Was it a natural death?"

Maggie frowned at her. "Yes, of course. She died in her sleep. She was ninety-seven."

"Well, shouldn't really come as a big shock, I suppose, at that age. But, bound to make you sad, having just met her." She was about to add something else, but thought better of it and followed Maggie to the kitchen.

"I've been invited to the funeral, on Friday." Maggie said over her shoulder.

"Are you going to go?"

"Of course! She was family and I think I'm the only one likely to be there, apart from the nurse." They had reached the kitchen.

"Would you like me to come with you?"

"Yes, thanks, Zelah. That would be nice. It's at ten thirty at St Cadoc's. Do you know the church?"

"Yes. Now, how about looking at the information I found out about your family?" A look of unaccustomed sympathy passed across her face. "This is quite a roller coaster, isn't it?"

Maggie nodded miserably and sat at the table. "I hate funerals."

"It's going to be tough for you. I had an idea, but I'm not sure if this is the time to mention it."

"What idea?"

"Do you remember I said the paddle steamer, the *Waverley*, sometimes goes out from Newport, when the tide on the river is high enough to allow it up to the town and back again? You said you'd like to take the kids?" Maggie nodded.

"Well, it's going out from Newport on Saturday, at nine thirty, down the river and across the Channel, and cruising for the afternoon, then coming back early evening. How about taking the trip?"

Maggie smiled. "That would be excellent, Zelah. I think we'd all enjoy that. Do we have to book?"

Zelah shook her head. "Leave it to me. My treat," and she put up her hand as Maggie started to protest. "I want to. Don't argue. I can more than afford it. Now, how about this news of mine?"

"Yes, OK. What have you found?"

"Well, nothing about your great-grandfather yet, but I've got further back on his male relatives. It came from a clue on the census. Do you remember that his father or grandfather, whichever he was, said he was born in Shirenewton?"

"He listed more than one birth place on the census returns he appeared in, didn't he?" Maggie compared the records that Zelah had laid out on the table, tracing each one with her finger. "Look, this one in 1851 says Shirenewton, but 1861 says Pen-something and 1841 just says he was born 'in the County of Monmouthshire'."

"That's all they had to confirm in 1841. I checked the records, such as they are, in parishes that start p-e-n, but there are no birth records for a man of his age. He was illiterate but he does seem to be consistent about his age and the year he was born."

She fished into her bag again and brought out a photocopy of the old-fashioned writing that Maggie had seen at the county records office.

"Look, this is a set of entries for the parish of Shirenewton for 1780 to 1810." She had highlighted several entries and now pointed to one of them. "John, in the year 1781, also born to John, and to Anne. I'm as sure as I can be that this is your John's ancestry. The dates and place match and there aren't any others by this name thereabouts." She looked pleased with herself. "And you can see that he had a brother called William, a name that was used in all of the following generations."

"It may not have been his father, you know. It could be his grandfather and great-grandfather. Is this definitive?" Maggie asked.

"Not a hundred per cent. I'd like to do some more ferreting to be certain. If I can find the marriage of John and Eliza, I might get something more certain."

"Zelah, this is great. I took your advice and got a proper computer program. Come and see." She led Zelah into the office at the front of the house.

"This is handy," Zelah remarked as she looked around. "You could run a business from here."

"I suppose I could."

"Hmm. Let's see what you've got."

Together, they went through Maggie's ancestry records adding Zelah's findings.

"So, what next?" Maggie asked, when they had printed out a new tree. "Back to the county records?"

"Yes. I think there's more to find in the parish records before we go further afield. But first, let's get the funeral and the *Waverley* trip out of the way. OK?" She checked her watch. "Damn, I'm late. I'll see you at the church on Friday morning. 'Bye." Zelah let herself out, leaving Maggie looking over the family tree. She had entered her John as the son of Old John and Eliza, but still didn't feel that this was right.

"It'll have to do for now, until I find out the truth. And there is definitely more to find out about you, Farmer Jones."

Chapter 56

On Friday morning, just before ten thirty Maggie waited in the sunshine outside the medieval porch of St Cadoc's Church. She had arrived early, in time to look around the graveyard and had found that both Sidney, Louisa's husband, and Christopher, their son, were buried there. The grave had been opened, ready for Louisa. The vicar arrived as she was waiting and joined her in the porch.

"Good morning, are you a relative? Are you all right?" he added. Maggie had wrinkled up her nose.

"Yes, I'm fine, sorry, it's the smell. I'm Mrs Jenkins's great-niece. I don't think there's going to be anyone else." They shook hands and Maggie added, "A friend of mine is coming, too, and the nurse who looked after her at Goldendays. Did you know Mrs Jenkins?"

"Oh, yes!" he replied, beaming. "Louisa and Sidney lived here in the village for many years. A great stalwart of the parish, she was. It was sad when she left and went to the nursing home, but best for her. She was frail after her fall. I visited her there many times."

"Is it unusual for anyone to be buried in this church graveyard these days?"

"Indeed," replied the vicar. "But Louisa was a long-time resident and the rest of her family is here, so we make an exception.

Otherwise you're right, it's closed." He glanced around, sniffing surreptitiously. "Ah, here they are."

Around the corner came the hearse, followed by one black car. Both drew up outside the church gate, followed by a taxi from which a black-suited Zelah emerged. From the funeral car came Nurse Crowley accompanied by an elderly man, tall, thin and with sparse grey hair, dressed in a dark grey suit and mourning tie. As the vicar walked down the path to meet them at the church gate, Zelah joined Maggie and they went together into the church to await the coffin.

The service was brief. The vicar had decided that with such a small congregation there was no reason to speak from the pulpit, so he stood in front of them to speak more intimately about Louisa's life and family.

Maggie learned that Louisa and Sidney had lived in the village almost all of their married life; Sidney had worked in Cardiff as a surveyor and Louisa had been a doyen of village life and a great supporter of the church. The vicar briefly mentioned the death of Christopher and offered up his hopeful prayer that they would all be re-united for eternity.

When the service ended they followed the coffin out of the church, an organ playing softly in the background, and to the open grave. Emerging into the sunlight after the cool dark shade of the church, Maggie blinked several times, then stopped suddenly and whispered to Zelah as they turned the corner.

"Did you see that?"

"See what? I can't see anything with this damn light shining in my eyes."

"Someone hiding behind that tree, over behind the graves."

Zelah glanced up. "I can't see anyone. Where did you say?"

"See the tall cypress behind the grave? Someone was standing just behind it, watching. I could see a head and part of the body"

"Probably someone from the village. Didn't you notice that there were a few old people at the back of the church? Maybe people who remembered her when she lived here." Zelah glanced back. "Look, there are some of them."

A small group of men and women in their seventies and eighties stood at the entrance to the church.

"No, this wasn't someone that old, they were more middle-aged." Maggie looked puzzled. "I've seen that face before."

They followed the procession to the edge of the grave where the vicar stood at the head of the gravestone and said the final prayer before the undertaker's men lowered the coffin out of sight.

As they turned away, Maggie started again. "There, there she is again, by the gate!"

Zelah turned quickly. "I don't see anyone."

"She was only there for a second. It's the same feeling I've had recently. It makes me shudder."

"Well, whoever she was, she's gone now." Zelah said briskly and was about to lead Maggie away when Nurse Crowley and the elderly man approached them.

"Mrs Gilbert, thank you for coming. Can I introduce you to Mr Robyn?"

Maggie put out her hand, which the man took and shook firmly, but with a sour look.

"Mrs Gilbert, I'm Marcus Robyn, of Robyn, Hanley and Hicks. We are Mrs Jenkins's solicitors."

"Nice to meet you," Maggie replied, still glancing around to see if she could spot the mysterious figure.

"We need to meet, Mrs Gilbert." His expression became even more sour. "I understand you only recently met Mrs Jenkins."

"That's right, just last week. Er, why do we need to meet?"

"After she spoke with you, Mrs Jenkins summoned me and altered her will, to your benefit. I shall need proof of your identity, of course. Would you be so kind as to visit my office next Tuesday at nine?" He held out a business card with the tips of his fingers.

"I suppose so, but I only met her last Tuesday! This is a shock," Maggie replied, looking at the card.

"Really?" He looked disdainfully down his aquiline nose. "Well, well. I must go. Good day." Marcus Robyn walked off, one arm swinging regimentally, the other supporting a black umbrella.

Nurse Crowley looked uncomfortably from Maggie to Zelah. "This is my friend, Zelah Trevear," Maggie said. "She's the person who's been helping me with my family history. It was Zelah's idea to put my story on the website that you saw."

The nurse smiled at Zelah. "I've spent years tracing my own. Fun, isn't it?"

Maggie nudged Zelah, who smiled back and said "Yes, isn't it?" through gritted teeth. "Time to go."

The three women walked through the graves to the church gate, where the nurse got into the waiting limo.

"Didn't ask if we wanted a lift," Zelah muttered.

"Doesn't matter," Maggie responded. "I'll give you a lift back to Newport."

"So, who do you think was watching?" Zelah asked as Maggie drove away.

"I really don't know, but it made the hairs stand up on the back of my neck. At first, it was just a feeling. Now it's actually a person. What next?"

"Something will happen. Anyway, is everything OK for tomorrow? Are Jack and Alice OK with coming?"

"They're delighted, thanks, Zelah. But what about…" Maggie was unceremoniously cut off.

"Don't you dare mention money! Right, here we are. Drop me off here. I'll see you on the wharf at nine tomorrow. 'Bye!"

Chapter 57

Maggie stood on the wharf looking dubiously at the paddle steamer, with Jack and Alice chatting excitedly beside her. They had been delighted when she had mentioned the trip, assuming that she had chosen this for her "special occasion".

"Stop worrying, Mum. It's a really calm day. You'll be fine!" Jack put his arm around her.

"I know, and I am excited, really. I'd just like to get going, now."

"Are we really going to fit under that bridge?" Alice asked for the umpteenth time, looking down-river at the gigantic iron transporter bridge that ferried passengers across the river in a hanging carriage.

"Duh, no. We're going to get stuck under it – that's if we don't run aground in the mud before we get there," Jack retorted, realising too late that his mother wasn't laughing. Fortunately, Maggie was distracted by Zelah's arrival in a taxi, today dressed in dark slacks and a bright blue twinset, and the inevitable high heels. The children ran across to meet her, whispering to her as she got out of the car. Maggie watched as she threw her hands in the air, then scowled at her.

"You kept that well hidden!" she exclaimed as she strode across the wharf.

"I don't like fuss," Maggie replied. "Each year I like it less and less."

"And the seasickness? I thought this was meant to be a treat!"

"It is, thanks. It looks calm enough so I should be OK and I do, honestly, love boats. I'm nearly always fine." She smiled confidently at Zelah as one of the ship's funnels trumpeted a great bass blast to the waiting passengers to get ready to board. "Too late now, anyway," Maggie muttered under her breath, as they made their way to the gangplank.

They settled themselves on the top viewing deck of the two-funnelled steamer. The paddle wheel began to turn with great thudding noises. The ship pulled away, into the river, under the bridge, and slowly out into the Channel. It was a calm day, with a light breeze and no swell. Maggie breathed a sigh of relief and settled down.

"It's been a dream of mine to go down the river, Zelah. When I was a child I sometimes used to watch the ocean-going ships come into the dry dock, and imagine where they might be going, but I never got to see round the river bend, until now. And on my birthday!" She smiled happily.

"I didn't know you came from the docks area."

"I don't. My mother did, though, and all of her family, the Irish side. My grandmother lived within smelling distance of the river and I used to play on the mud banks. It was exciting for us kids. Nowadays, there'd be too much health and safety and anyway, it's been cut in half by that new dual carriageway." Maggie gazed wistfully at the passing shoreline. "I need some cheering up. I've got the final job confirmation on Monday. I'll probably be starting work in a couple of weeks."

The ride across the Bristol Channel was uneventful. Jack spent a lot of time below deck, watching the pistons working the gigantic engines that powered the paddle wheel. Alice sunned herself on the deck.

After a visit to Ilfracombe, where they spent a couple of hours having lunch overlooking the small harbour, and then briefly exploring the town, the steamer returned across the Channel and up the river at sunset. As the wharf came into sight they all stood on the lower deck admiring the sunset over the mountains behind Newport.

"I don't suppose much has changed since the Victorians first took this trip," Maggie said to Zelah. "I wonder if whoever owned that newspaper clipping got to take the trip to Weston-super-Mare?"

"I don't suppose we'll ever know. Right, we need to move along to the gangplank."

As they reached the edge the crowd pushed together and Maggie felt herself being pulled away from the children and Zelah. She had one foot on the gangplank when she heard Alice call her and gesture that they would meet her at the car. As she turned back she felt a jolt, lost her footing, and fell. Unable to hold onto the rope, she struggled for something to cling on to and for a few terrified seconds thought she was going to fall into the water between the ship and the wharf. But then a strong arm grabbed her and pulled her back.

"That was close, madam!" A member of the crew had reached her just in time to stop her going over. She had lost one of her shoes in the scramble and bent down to find it. She could hear the children shouting somewhere behind. Suddenly, she was overwhelmed by a terrible, putrid smell.

The children and Zelah reached her. Alice was in tears. "Mummy! I thought you'd fallen in! Are you alright?"

"I'm fine. Really," she added, seeing Jack's frightened face. "Must have been that last glass of wine!" She smiled confidently at them, retrieved her shoe and ushered them along the gangplank. "I'm glad to get away from that pong! Did you smell it? Just like the canal the other day, and the cemetery," she said to Zelah.

They shook their heads. Clear of the departing passengers, she chatted cheerfully until the children seemed calm. They thanked Zelah, then took the key and headed off to get into the car.

"Are you OK?" Zelah asked once they were out of earshot. "What happened?"

"A hand in the small of my back happened. I was pushed. Don't let on to the kids, keep smiling."

"Of course," Zelah replied, nodding her head. "Was it deliberate?"

"Yes, I think so. It was too hard to be an accident. Did you see anything?"

"No, I was trapped in the crowd. Maggie, I think we might be getting close to something, but I have no idea what it is. Whatever it is, it doesn't look good. Or smell good. Take care. Of all of you."

"I will." Maggie gave Zelah a quick hug. "I'll call you Monday. It's been a wonderful day. Other than that. Thank you." Zelah waved her away and got into her waiting taxi.

Chapter 58

On Monday morning, with a heavy heart, Maggie entered the corporate headquarters of FutureLife Computing plc, signed in and sat in a rather scruffy armchair to wait for her interviewer. The Operations Director was almost twenty minutes late and took her into a windowless room without apologising.

Despite trying, Maggie didn't warm to him. The more the interview went on, the more she sat back and let him talk, which he seemed happy to do. She had tuned out during his speech about how busy he was with staff issues and how much he needed the support of someone like herself, when he suddenly stopped. He asked her when she could start.

"Oh, um, when would you like me to start?" Maggie was caught off guard and cursed inwardly.

"Well, we could do with you starting next Monday, but I understand you have some domestic issues, Mrs Gilbert, or can I call you Maggie, now you're almost one of us?" he leaned forwards and flashed his teeth. "We have a lot for you to get started on!"

"Well, I have to find someone to look after my children. How about the beginning of July? That's just a couple of weeks. And, of course, I did say that I have a holiday in August."

"Oh, is it already booked?"

"Unfortunately, and there's a big cancellation charge," Maggie lied.

"Well, we'll honour that, unpaid, of course. But next year, you'll have to check with me first and I'm afraid you won't be top of the list for August. But anyway," he went on, "the beginning of July will be fine. Glad to have you on board." He began to punch numbers into his Blackberry. "I'll have HR send out your contract. I'll see you out."

Maggie followed him along corridors past offices full of grim-faced people scowling at computer screens, until they reached the foyer.

"Goodbye, Maggie, see you soon!" They shook hands and he turned away.

As Maggie thanked the receptionist and headed for the door, she could hear him shouting into his mobile.

"I need this job. I need this job!" Maggie muttered through clamped teeth as she walked across the car park.

Back at home she phoned her sister. Fiona was thrilled at the news and offered at once to pick the children up from school for the remainder of the term until Maggie could find a sitter.

"You must be so relieved, Mags. And it sounds like a wonderful opportunity. Plenty of chances for promotion! And what's the boss like? Tell all!"

Maggie replied despondently, "Uninspiring, but you're right, it's a job."

There was silence on the phone for a few seconds. "Mags, please try. For the children if not for yourself."

Maggie said her goodbyes and put the phone down.

Later, in the car, she told Jack and Alice in a predictable silence. When she explained that Aunty Fee would be picking them up, Maggie thought she heard a groan from the back, but ignored it.

"Will she bring us home, or back to her house?" Alice asked.

331

"She can bring you home, I think. I'd like to be able to trust you both to be at home for an hour or so until I get back. You *can* manage that without arguing?"

"Suppose so," Jack replied, although Alice didn't.

As they got out of the car, he put an arm around her shoulder. "Sorry, Mum."

"I know," she sighed, "but I'm going to have to grit my teeth and get on with it. They'll be paying me a good salary, which we need."

In the hall she tried to hug Alice, but was pushed away. "Don't worry, Mum. She'll get used to it."

I'm not sure I will, Maggie thought.

Chapter 59

The office of Robyn, Hanley & Hicks was on one of the roads leading into Newport from the east, a red-brick Victorian conversion on three floors. The reception area was silent, the clattering of the receptionist's fingers on a keyboard the only sign of activity. The hollow tick of a big clock echoed from the hall.

"More like a funeral parlour," Zelah remarked in a voice loud enough for the receptionist to frown.

Maggie was about to say something placating when a dignified secretary entered and announced that Mr Robyn was ready to receive them. Zelah flashed a wicked grin, as the secretary led them out of the reception office and up the wide staircase, through a set of double doors, and into a conference room, in the middle of which sat an ornate, highly polished, dark wood conference table with twelve chairs. Zelah went straight for the chair at the head of the table. When Maggie suggested that they sit at the side, she raised her eyebrows.

"Give the old boy a chance to feel even more superior? I don't think so!"

Mr Robyn entered, the secretary walking in step behind him carrying a stack of papers. He shook hands briefly with Maggie, frowned at Zelah, and walked to the opposite side of the table. The secretary sat next to him.

"I requested proof of your identity, Mrs Gilbert."

Maggie handed over her passport and birth certificate, which Mr Robyn handed on to the secretary with a perfunctory wave.

"I have the last will and testament of Mrs Louisa Jenkins, Mrs Gilbert. She summoned me a few days before her death, indeed the day after your second meeting with her, to make an addition to her disbursements. A portion of her funds has been left to the Goldendays Nursing Home, in gratitude for the care they gave her. Another goes to St Cadoc's Church restoration fund. There is a modest sum for Nurse Crowley. The remainder," he paused and coughed as if trying to expel something unpalatable from his throat, "…the remainder is left to yourself. A sum of ten thousand pounds."

Maggie's eyes widened in amazement and Zelah bared her teeth at him in a polite smile. "So that's what you were so annoyed about," she remarked.

"I beg your pardon, Mrs…" he turned to look with disgusted at Zelah, then frowned. "Have we met?"

"Yes, we have. And been introduced. Zelah Fitzgerald. I'm a friend of Mrs Gilbert, but you would have found that out if you had bothered to ask, wouldn't you?" The words were spoken politely enough, but Maggie shuffled in her seat awkwardly. The expression that came over Mr Robyn's face stopped her and she understood at once that he remembered who Zelah was and when he had met her. His face widened into a fawning smile.

"Mrs Fitzgerald! How lovely to meet you again. Wonderful exhibition! Can I offer you ladies some refreshments?" He turned to his secretary, but Zelah stopped him.

"No, you can't."

Maggie cut in firmly to keep the conversation on track. "Thank you, Zelah. Now, Mr Robyn, please continue. We don't need tea, but thanks for the offer."

"Very well, Mrs Gilbert." Another wave of the hand at the secretary, this time to remain in the room.

"As I was saying, Mrs Jenkins has left you ten thousand pounds, and her few pieces of jewellery, for the kindness you showed her and your determination to do your duty as a relative." He smiled unctuously, any sign of the previous disapproval gone.

"In addition, she has left you these papers. They had been kept here and were due to be destroyed under her previous will. How delightful they will now go to a member of her family!"

From the secretary he took a large envelope and handed it to Maggie. "I shall arrange for the cheque to be sent to you following the usual probate which will take some months."

Maggie stood up. "Thank you, Mr Robyn. I left my address with your receptionist."

"Let me see you out," he replied, still smiling, and led the way downstairs, chatting amiably, but primarily to Zelah. At the entrance, he opened the door for them.

"If there is anything else I can do for you, Mrs Gilbert, do let me know." He shook her hand quickly then turned to Zelah. "And if I can be of service in any way, Mrs Fitzgerald, my firm would be delighted."

"I'll let you know," Zelah smiled at him, pulling away from his two-handed grasp.

As they walked around the building to the car park, Maggie waited for the explosion, but Zelah remained quiet. When they reached their cars, she said, "How about coming back to my flat to have a look at those papers? It's only five minutes' away."

"Great," Maggie replied. "And well contained." Zelah grimaced and got into her car. "Follow me."

They drove along the main road until they were almost out of the town. Zelah turned off and up a steep, winding hill. Sitting on the flat ground at the top of the hill was a small hamlet, an old church at its centre and a group of houses of varying ages surrounding it. Although she had passed near to this place many times Maggie had never driven up here before. The view was stunning, across the Channel on one side and mountains on the other. Zelah stopped outside an elegant block of flats and walked back to Maggie.

"There's a garage underneath, but the cars are safe enough here. Follow me."

Using an electronic passkey to open the front door, she went to the lift in the foyer and pressed the button for the third floor. The carpeted lift rose silently. Outside the lift there were two doors. Zelah opened the door on the left. Maggie followed her in, and stopped immediately.

"Wow!" she gasped, gazing around, then followed Zelah, who had swept open the double living room doors and stood back.

The room ran half the length of the building. One wall comprised three full height windows, each framing a view of the mountains. The décor was pure white: walls, curtains, furniture and luxurious deep carpet. On the remaining walls were three of Martin Fitzgerald's paintings.

"This is…" Maggie paused to find the right word, "…this is stunning. It's beautiful. It's like something you see in one of those designer magazines. Zelah, what fantastic taste!"

"Thank you. Not many people get in here. I like my privacy. Nice view, isn't it? Come see the view from the kitchen side." She led Maggie across the hallway to the kitchen on the opposite side of the corridor.

The kitchen was small and functional, again exquisitely designed and decorated, but instead of a window, it had double-width sliding doors that led out onto a wide balcony. Zelah pulled back the door. "Let's sit on the balcony. This is where I have breakfast, when it's warm enough."

The balcony ran the width of the building, with another door opening onto it further along. Around the black glass table and chairs there were a number of pots full of delicate, pale-coloured plants, and an extending white shade spread out overhead.

"Wait here. I'll get us some tea." Zelah disappeared into the kitchen and Maggie admired the view. The balcony had a thick smoked glass barrier, about four feet high. Maggie had never thought about where Zelah might live; although she'd been initially shocked, it fitted with her style.

While she waited, Maggie opened up Mr Robyn's foolscap envelope and peered in. She could see envelopes and papers tied up with ribbon.

"I think this is old correspondence," she said to Zelah who had returned with a loaded tea tray.

"Don't open it yet. In case the wind catches it. We'll go back in, in a minute. I just want you to see the view."

At the foot of the hill, and across a flat plain, the Severn Estuary wound like a silver ribbon towards the sea. In mid-Channel, the air was misty, but Maggie guessed that on a clear day the hills and coastline of Somerset would be in clear view.

"How long have you lived here, Zelah?"

"Since Martin died. We used to live in Caerleon. Nice house, near the Roman ruins. But I couldn't stay there after he died. Too big. Too empty." She gazed at the Channel as she spoke. "Then I found this place. Nice and quiet. No children. Sorry, no offence!"

"None taken," Maggie grinned. "Did you ever think when you were a child that you'd end up somewhere as luxurious as this?"

337

"When I was a child I didn't expect to live long enough to grow up," Zelah replied, still staring out across the water. Maggie sat back, startled.

After a few seconds Zelah continued, "I don't talk much about Cornwall. It's hard. Anyway, let's go and look at those papers."

Chapter 60

Maggie spoke first. "This is Louisa's birth certificate. And this looks like, yes, it's John's death certificate. I've already got a copy."

She opened another envelope. The first letter was addressed to Ruthie Evans from a Mrs Margaret Robertson at an address in Carmarthen. There were four in all, and the last, a letter from Ruth to a Mrs Picton in Carmarthen, was written but not sent. The first four were dated 1883 and 1884, the final one 1909. Maggie opened the first letter.

Zelah had done the same with the package of documents she was looking through. "These are condolence letters to your great-grandmother, when her husband died, all from 1909, I think."

"I'm not sure yet who wrote mine," Maggie replied, "except this last one from my Ruth to Mary Anne Picton, which never got posted. I think we're onto something here. Listen." Maggie read the letter, dated September 1883:

My Dear Sister,
 May God keep you well. I am indeed most sorry to hear of your daughter Ruth's sore trouble.

Maggie broke off. "This sounds like it was written to my Ruth's mother, Ruthie Evans, my great-great-grandmother." She continued:

We pray daily for the safe return of your Ruth's little daughter and for her own return to health.

I can give you a little of the knowledge you have asked of me, but not, I fear, a great deal, for my memory fails to recall much of my youth. Our great-grandmother's life was blighted by the loss of a child, a girl, ten years of age. She drowned in a strange accident, her friend with her. Our grandmother told me a little of the events that she had from her own mother. That no-one could understand how it happened from the accounts given and the evidence present. Of course she was herself much overcome at the death of her twin sister. But the rest of our family did not speak of the events. You know that they lived at that time in Carmarthenshire, being farmers. They felt unable to stay after the loss of their child and moved to Monmouthshire. You are right in remembering that there was a story about a teacher. My grandmother told me that he was not popular, that he showed great resentment towards her mother and sister. And he could not account for his whereabouts when her sister and friend died. But nothing was proved and he left soon after.

Our grandmother told me that her mother was frightened of the teacher and warned her to take care. They thought he might be some kind of madman. But the family was in Monmouthshire, so why be concerned?

Our grandmother remembered her sister, of course. But the family never spoke her name again, nor used it for the naming of another child.

That is all I can tell you of these events, my dear sister. Please write to me with news of your unfortunate granddaughter.

Your sister in God's mercy,

Margaret.

"Well," said Maggie, looking at Zelah. "Two children accidentally drowning in my family. Coincidence?"

"Keep reading," Zelah replied committedly.

"OK. The next one's also from Margaret, again to Ruthie. It's dated six months later, March 1884."

My Dear Sister,

I thank God for your excellent news of the birth of your grandson, George, and of course we thank Our Lord that he has seen fit to bring your dear daughter, Ruth, to a good recovery from near death once again. We continue to pray for the return of little Alice, but I agree that there can be little hope now. I too believe that Ruth's husband knows best. She must come to accept it.

I regret I can give you no more information about the drowning of our great-grandmother's child. I do not believe she ever told me the schoolmaster's name. I do recall our grandmother telling me of her fear of teachers! Strange that your daughter has found such a one also. But if the woman is gone, best for all, I say.

May Christ keep you in His Grace.
Your sister,
Margaret."

Maggie looked up from the letter at Zelah. "Your thoughts?"

"Let's read them all through before we decide what to think."

"Well, there are two more, addressed to Mr J Jones, Esq, and one from my Ruth, that she must have written but not sent."

"Who wrote the letters to her husband?"

Maggie opened the envelopes and scanned the contents. Each contained a single sheet.

"This is from a detective. And this one's from a police inspector in Weston-super-Mare. Shall I read them out?" Zelah nodded. She had been making notes in a pad as Maggie had read out the first two letters.

To Mr. J. Jones, Esq.

Sir, I write to acknowledge your instruction that I and my colleague should cease in the search of your daughter, Alice Jones. Having traced her to Newport, we can find no further sighting. As the cadaver you viewed in Weston-super-Mare was not that of your daughter, we cannot at this time make any further recommendations for action, but will be available to assist you, should you wish to re-commence your search in the light of any new information you receive..
J. R. Williams. Williams & Andover

Detective Agency.
November 4, 1883.

Zelah carried on making notes and told Maggie to read the final letter. "Right, this one is dated September 1883."

Mr. J. Jones, Esq.
Dear Sir,

I respond to your kind enquiry of 5th of this month but can give you no news of the identity of the young girl found in the sea at Weston-super-Mare. We had report of a missing girl, the daughter of a murdered prostitute, Margaret Peach, of this town, by the name of Miss Esme Peach. The girl had run away from the Poor House in which she had been placed and following your confirmation that the body in the sea was not that of your daughter, we considered that the remains might be those of the girl. But I have recently received news from the girl's maternal aunt that she went to her home where she is now residing, alive and well, in south Wales. I wish you success in finding your missing daughter.

Yours truly, Edward Mathers,
Inspector of Police,
Weston-super-Mare.

"I'm struggling to take this all in," Maggie said.

Zelah stopped writing and looked up from the table. "OK. Here's what we've got. There've been two drownings close to your family in four generations. Interesting, but not significant. An unpleasant teacher seems to have been close to both. Again, interesting, but difficult to see if they're connected, as the events must be about eighty years apart. The bit about the names could be something, though. We'll need to look at Ruth's family to find out what the first drowned child was called." She paused and nodded at Maggie. "I think we know, but I want to check. Now, when it comes to your great-grandmother, Ruth, we knew that she was ill when she was pregnant. Louisa told you, and this confirms it. So, if she was pregnant when Alice disappeared, she would have had to leave the search to her husband, John. Her mother's sister's letter hints that Ruth wasn't happy with his efforts. But, he did quite a lot actually, employing private detectives. But now, let's look at this story of Miss Esme Peach."

"Why so?"

"If you want a coincidence, here's one. Alice Jones goes missing and her parents believe that she might have washed up in Weston-super-Mare. Enough for John to go there to check. An article about the *Waverley* which goes to Weston was found in one of your trunks. But the body isn't Alice. Then, another missing girl, with the same name as Alice's drowned friend, Esme, turns up in south Wales, having supposedly run away from Weston." She saw Maggie's puzzled expression. "Surely you can see there's something odd in that?"

"But the letter from the inspector says Esme is with her aunt. The aunt would have known her own niece, surely?"

"That's for us to find out, isn't it?" Zelah replied, eyes gleaming.

"Well, I'm not convinced, but I suppose there's no harm in checking it out. One more to go."

She teased the last letter out of its envelope and unfolded it. The writing was small, neat and even, the ink still clear after more than a hundred years.

My Dear Sister,

Thank you for your kind and thoughtful sentiments. I am feeling much better now, thank you, and can look forwards a little more to each day. The house still seems strangely quiet. I have told Maud and James that they must not keep the children quiet for my sake. But they shake their heads and say it is not seemly. Poor things.

I wanted to tell you how grateful I was for your attention following John's funeral, and for listening to me. I still cannot reconcile the strange events of those days. James and Maud, and indeed, William and Sara, believe that I was not in my right mind to think that I saw and heard such strange things. But I know that I did and that it was not just brought on by grief. But how to explain it? I cannot, by any means sensible and acceptable to God-fearing people. That only leaves – but I need not tell you what that leaves us to imagine. It is too shocking.

Richard Robinson has been exceptionally kind and thoughtful, as always. He is very concerned that I am planning to visit Hereford, and counsels against it. And I know that it may cause much scandal in the village that I am going about, albeit it in my widow's weeds. But I must know. You alone seemed to understand my need to find out the truth. I hope that Richard can be persuaded to accompany me, however reluctantly.

I did indeed pay my visit to Gwen Ellis. She is so much troubled and wandering in her mind now and is failing fast. But when her Cerys introduced me I thought that she seemed to know me. When I talked to her about Alice

344

*and her Esme and showed her the school photograph she grabbed at my hand.
She kept saying, she wasn't there.' I explained to her that they were both gone a
long time, but she shook her head and said, 'I looked through the window and
she wasn't there.' I asked who she meant because we always knew that Alice
and Esme weren't there, but she looked frightened. It has taken me some time to
realise what she could mean, but I believe I have it now. I do believe the visit
to Hereford will confirm my fears.*

*You may wonder why I want to know, after all this time. But this, I now
understand, is not just about what happened to Alice. It was there before and
will be there again. We must all be watchful.*

*I confided in William that I had seen the teacher, Probert, at John's
funeral. Of course, he remains doubtful and thinks I need to rest. He refused to
believe that she was unchanged after all this time, but I know the truth. I tried
to put him on his guard, as I have all of them, but I am sad to say that they
look at me with troubled eyes. I must find a way to tell their children. It must
not happen again!*

*I do believe that my Alice is still alive, somewhere in this world, although
I may not be united with her until the glory of the next. I opened the trunk in
the attic again and found her clothes and possessions. I remembered how little
she took with her, just a clean dress and apron and one of the handkerchiefs that
John and I gave her for her birthday last year that I sewed with her initials.
I still believe that she did not intend to be long away from us. I will visit John's
resting place again tomorrow. I will write again soon, my dear Mary Anne.*

*Your sister,
Ruth."*

Maggie put the letter down and looked up at Zelah. "When
was that letter written?"

"June 14th, 1909."

"So tomorrow to the day, a hundred and six years ago, she'll be going to visit the grave. How about you do the same?"

"Do you think…" Maggie's voice trailed off as she realised the implications of what Zelah was saying. "No way, that would be too much of a coincidence! Anyway," she added after a moment's thought, "she doesn't say what time she'll be there."

"You'll have to take a guess. Worth a try?"

"I don't know. But I want to think through all of this other stuff. Is the teacher thing a coincidence?"

"I don't know. The first was a man, now a woman. But there was something strange, yes. If she's talking about Alice's teacher, there was a gap of over twenty-five years, but she seems to be suggesting that the woman hadn't changed at all. And something has scared her, the same as her great-grandmother, making her believe she has to warn her grandchildren. Which makes me think…" she trailed off and frowned.

"Is there anything significant in your letters?" Maggie asked.

"I didn't think so at first, but now I'm not so sure. Just one, from a Mr Charles Morris, on behalf of himself and his wife, Bessie." She rummaged through the papers. "Ah, here it is."

Dear Mrs. Jones,

I write to express the most sincere condolences of my wife, Bessie, and myself on the death of your esteemed and respected husband, our dear friend, John. Such a great, God-fearing man will be much missed within our community, as well as by his family. The other elders will, I am sure, write to you, but I wish to condole with you on behalf of those of us at chapel who knew him best.

Bessie sends her wish that you will call upon her for any service at any time and asks that you be assured of her sincere friendship. She has also asked

me to relate to you that she did not herself see Miss Eira Probert at the funeral
service. She agrees that it was unexpected that Miss Probert would attend after
such a long time, but is sure that you will take solace from her presence. In regard
to your questions, Bessie also asks me to advise you that when Miss Probert
departed to join our dear Mr. Pugh at his congregation in Hereford, Bessie wrote
to her on more than one occasion, but did not receive any reply.

Please be assured of our kindest wishes and our desire to do whatever we
can to help you bear your loss.

Charles Morris.

"They sound nice," Maggie commented. "It seems Ruth was making enquiries shortly after John's death about the schoolteacher that she thought she saw. I wonder what she found out? She told her sister she was going to Hereford, where this man Pugh went. Zelah. Zelah?"

For a moment Maggie thought that something bad had happened. Zelah was staring into space over Maggie's head, with an expression of amazement.

"What's the matter?"

"I… I remembered a story, Martin's dreadful mother used to tell tales from what she called 'the old country'. Something just rang a bell."

"What?"

"Not now. Let me think."

Maggie got up and walked back into the kitchen to pour herself another cup of tea. Returning to the living room sipping tea, she found Zelah packing up the letters.

"No time for that," she said briskly, taking the cup from Maggie's hand. "Plan of action, I think. First, you go to the cemetery tomorrow. See what happens. Then, we need to spend

347

time on census and parish records, looking for Ruth's ancestry. That's going to be a challenge because of the female name changes, but we can do it. Can you get to Carmarthen this week, if we need to go there?"

"I suppose so," Maggie replied. "I'll ask Fee to look after the kids after school. But just this week," she added. "I've only got two weeks after this week and I want to spend as much time with them as I can."

"Understood. How about tomorrow I start on census records, and you go to the cemetery?"

Maggie's looked reluctant.

"Come on, Maggie, it's quite safe. They're all dead!"

"Someone has been watching me and tried to push me over the side of the boat. It doesn't feel safe."

Zelah hesitated for a moment. "OK, I understand. If you don't want to do it…"

"Of course I want to do it. I'll call you when I get back tomorrow."

Chapter 61

Maggie dropped the children at school, but instead of going home she followed a compulsion that had grown since her conversation with Graeme. She headed up the mountain towards The Pond. The higher she went, the narrower the track became. At first there were high hedges on each side and the remains of old cottages, but then she came to open land. Across the cattle grid, the landscape opened up into a mountain vista. She reached the empty car park, as Graeme had described.

As she got out of the car Maggie's hair was whipped around her face by a succession of small, chilly breezes that whisked around her body, like tiny whirlwinds, each enveloping her for seconds. The view was magnificent, to the sea and across the Channel to her right, down to the town in front of her and more mountains to her left. Behind her, a stony path led off in the direction of The Pond, signposted by a wooden marker.

The path rose steeply at first and followed a bend to the left. Maggie caught sight in the distance of the medieval mound at the far end of the range and a thought came to her suddenly, out of the past.

We never went there, after all! She remembered, recalling an aborted Good Friday family trip to walk to the summit. *And I never went there, ever. But I know exactly what the view is like from the top.*

There was a large stone at the side of the path and Maggie sat and closed her eyes, recalling the view she had never seen. It was clear, but there was something not right about it. She saw in her mind across the Channel to the Exmoor hills, the Brecon Beacons behind, and an uninterrupted view inland up towards Gloucester where the Channel narrowed to the river, with a startlingly blue sky, much more piercing than today. The scene gave her an uncomfortable, panicky feeling.

Within minutes she was at The Pond. The Pond itself was elliptical and the path approached it from one end. To the right and at the far end the slopes of the mountain came down to the shoreline. Maggie saw immediately that it would be impossible to walk all the way round. The path ended at a small, broken wooden jetty.

As she approached she could see that the jetty was rotten, several of the wooden slats were missing. One or two were sticking into the air. She was amazed that there was no barrier to the water's edge, no warning signs. *Perhaps not enough people come here. Or they just forgot it was here. This is not a pretty place.* The Pond was certainly well hidden, and unadvertised in local guides.

It was cold, although the slopes kept the wind out. Maggie reached the water's edge and bent down to look in. There were a few large boulders under the water next to the end of the jetty. The newspaper report from 1883 had said that Esme Ellis had hit her head as she fell.

Possible. The girl must have been unable to reach the shore and had drowned, unconscious. She dipped her hand in, scooped up some water and let it run through her fingers. *How terrible it must have been for Alice, seeing her friend like that. Hang on, how do I know that?*

Something clicked in her brain and Maggie saw the story running through the dreams that her Alice had been shouting out for weeks. Ruth's Alice had seen Esme dead in the water. But would that have made her run away from home? Alice seemed to have seen more than just a floating body. She had been shouting out "No!" and "Stop!" So, what had Ruth's Alice actually seen, that Maggie's Alice was dreaming about?

Instinctively, she turned to walk to the copse of trees behind her. But there were no trees, just flat barren land a few metres wide, leading to the slope. But she had seen them as she walked up the path! She walked rapidly into the centre of the patch of ground. There were a few patches of grass and trampled remains of bluebells. Maggie turned and ran back down the path to the car.

Now, she had to face the graveside.

* * *

Despite feeling some trepidation as she approached the plot, Maggie walked determinedly to it. She had decided to try the same time as before, half past eleven. As she reached the tombstone she felt none of the atmosphere she'd experienced on previous occasions.

In case other people were there, Maggie had brought her secateurs, a bunch of flowers, and a jam jar, and she set about clearing the weeds that had grown back. Working under a cloudless sky she dug up grass and dandelions, humming to herself. This was the most peaceful the cemetery had ever felt to her. After twenty minutes the grave was tidy and she had placed her flowers in their jar in front of the headstone.

Glancing around, she was still alone. There was nothing left to do now and no reason to remain. In the distance a clock chimed twelve. She collected up her things and turned to leave. At that moment, a slight breeze fanned her arms, and the hairs on the back of her neck stood up. The cloudless day had instantly become overcast, but she knew this wasn't real. Then a voice whispered next to her.

"John. I am going to search for her. You will think I am letting you down. But I must go."

Something brushed Maggie's arm with the tenderest of strokes and goose pimples reared all over, yet the sensation was warm. Maggie put out her own hand in the direction of the headstone, rested her fingers for a second on the carved name and was met with a warmth that felt as if she was putting her hand into sultry liquid.

"John, you must not deny me this, not after all this time! I have always needed to know." She was pleading, yet firm.

"It's not John," Maggie whispered and felt the warmth withdraw. "Ruth. You don't know who I am, but I know you. I'm your friend. I'm more than your friend, I'm family and I'm trying to help, please believe me. We will find out what happened to your Alice." She sensed a sigh, then footsteps retreating from the graveside.

As soon as she got home she called Zelah to let her know what had happened.

"So you were right about someone being there, and she can hear you. But she's probably terrified, poor woman."

"That's why I didn't really want to do it. Voices in her head when she's grieving could make her think she's going mad."

"No, you've always thought she was a sensible woman. She'll sit in your chair and rationalise it. Anyway, I've got to go. Got

352

some important personal business for the next two days, no time to research."

Maggie was crestfallen. "What about getting back into Ruth's family? I thought we were going to concentrate on that?"

"Why don't you do it? You've got the internet census records. There's plenty there. See what you can come up with. Sorry, Maggie, got to go. If you need any quick help with checking birth, marriage, or death details, leave me a message and I'll get someone to check it out." She hung up.

Maggie sat for a moment, feeling abandoned. So little time left and Zelah was suddenly going off doing her own thing! She hadn't even had a chance to tell her about her experience at The Pond. But Zelah had a life of her own and it wasn't fair to expect her to take all of her time researching Maggie's family, no matter how absorbing it had become.

Over the next couple of days, she heard nothing from Zelah. She had left one message asking for certificate details to give her female names before marriage. This allowed her to jump back generations. Replies came by email.

By Sunday evening, Maggie had gone back a further three generations of Ruth's family on the female side. She had steadfastly ignored the urge to follow up some of the more fascinating information she found en route and kept to her task. The most important thing she had confirmed was that the first drowned child was called Alice, almost a hundred years before Esme.

By the time she called Zelah on Monday morning, she knew that her four-times-great-grandmother, Ruth Gwyllim, the twin sister of the Alice who died, had been born in 1786 in Llanybri, in Carmarthen, had married a James Evans in 1805, and had died in 1861 in Monmouthshire. She also discovered that the county records office in Carmarthen held details of school records for the eighteenth and nineteenth centuries. So, there was a chance that they could find out more about the schoolmaster at the time of Alice Gwyllim's death.

"Excellent! I've just picked up the new family tree you emailed me." She paused, checking it.

"How sure are you that these are the right people?"

"As much as I can be from just looking at internet records. What else can I do to be absolutely certain?"

Zelah thought for a moment. "I'm sure this is right. It fits in with everything Louisa told you and what we found out from the letters. The names are all there. I'd like to be sure of the Carmarthen births and marriages, though. Shall we go there tomorrow? We'll have to stay overnight, to be sure of having enough time to check the facts and search school records."

"I'll have to check with Fee, make sure she can have Jack and Alice, but otherwise, yes, we might as well."

"You don't sound very enthusiastic?"

"I just got my contract. I start two weeks today."

"Oh. Are you going to sign it?"

"Well, of course I'm going to sign it! It's not like there's a choice for me." Maggie knew that she had raised her voice.

"If there was a choice, would you take it?"

"I don't know. I suppose that would depend on what it was." She interrupted again as Zelah began to speak. "Why? Is there one? Do you know about another job?"

"No," Zelah said quietly, after a brief hesitation. "Now then, how about you speak to your sister and I pick you up at ten tomorrow? I'll book a couple of rooms at a B&B, OK?"

Maggie sighed. "OK. By the way, I went to visit the lake up on the mountain, the one that used to be called The Pond. Where Esme Ellis drowned. I felt I had to know where it is. It's important, but I don't know why."

"Anything interesting?" Zelah asked.

"No, not really. Just that it was *very* familiar. I had a strange feeling of having been there before, although I know I never have been."

"Maybe your great-grandmother went there. She wanted to see where it happened, too. It's another one of her memories."

"Hmm. See you tomorrow."

Chapter 62
June 1909

Richard Robinson called for Ruth at ten as agreed. She had informed Maud and James that she would be away for the day in the company of Mr Robinson, but no more than that, and she steadfastly avoided further discussion about where she was going or what she intended to do.

They travelled to Garth Hill station in a hired cab and at ten twenty they took their seats in the private first-class compartment of the train. Richard deemed this to be the only possible way of travelling to protect her reputation and identity. Fortunately, they knew no-one waiting on the platform.

"Just as well not to say anything, I think," Ruth remarked as they settled themselves amidst the whistling, shunting and bellowing of the steam train that marked the start of the journey. "No point in causing unwanted gossip. I am very grateful, you know, Richard. I know how difficult this is for you, and you know how much this means to me."

"Well, Ruth, we have an hour or more to pass before we reach Hereford station. The views along the route are delightful."

"I have never travelled by train before," she remarked.

When the train had passed through Pontypool and out into the country, Richard spoke.

"Ruth, you shocked me to my very core last week when you told me that you believe that Eira Probert killed Esme Ellis. I've thought about almost nothing else since. But your evidence is tenuous. What else can you tell me about those times? What else allows you to believe that a schoolteacher might be a murderer?"

"I know now that Eira lied about her whereabouts on the day that Esme died. As I told you last week, I finally understood what Gwen Ellis tried to tell me at the time, that Eira wasn't at the school, as she had told the constables. That is a big lie for a woman who was supposed to be respected in our community."

He reluctantly nodded.

Ruth went on: "Gwen went to the school, looking for Esme. When she said 'she wasn't there' she meant the teacher, not Esme. Eira Probert wasn't at the school. But she claimed later that she went to visit Pugh once Alice was released from her detention. I don't believe that either. I'm hoping that his widow will confirm this."

He spent a few minutes looking out of the window, at the river next to the track, frowning at his own silver-haired reflection.

"It does seem as though Miss Probert was not entirely truthful, but that doesn't lead to her killing a child. Why on earth would she do so? I know that she wasn't popular with them, and that she singled out Alice. I know that Mr Pugh caused a rift in the community. But the murder of a child is a serious accusation to make, Ruth." He shook his head.

"There's a history in my family, that may be connected," she replied. My mother's great-grandmother lost a child through drowning. I don't know much about the story, but I know that suspicion fell on a schoolmaster."

This was too much for him. "But there must be a hundred years between the two incidents, Ruth!" he exclaimed. "You can't believe that they're connected."

357

She was disconcerted by the force of his indignation, not sure of how to respond, for only now she realised how much she had relied on his belief as well as his support.

"Can you say with certainty that they aren't connected Richard? What if Eira Probert was a descendant of the schoolmaster in Carmarthen?"

"What if she were, Ruth?"

"And how do you explain her appearance at John's funeral service? She looked as if no time had passed since I last saw her."

He looked away, shaking his head and Ruth knew that he was succumbing to her children's belief that she was so overwrought at John's death that her imagination was leading her into strange places.

"I know what I saw," she said firmly, "and will not be told that I didn't see her."

"Perhaps you saw someone who looked like her."

There was no point in continuing to debate with him. She didn't want to fall out with this man who had been her and John's greatest friend and supporter. For the remainder of the journey they watched the scenery, Richard pointing out landmarks of interest, keeping their conversation to less contentious matters.

One and a half hours later, the train arrived at Hereford. Outside the station, Richard located the hansom cab that he had written to reserve for the drive to the Pugh's house in Gwynne Street.

This was also the first time that Ruth had been to England. She was captivated by the old cathedral, staring at the grand edifice as the cab skirted around it, passing the market, through the main streets, and to their destination.

"This is a pretty town, Richard. In better times, I should like to visit the cathedral."

"It has a very beautiful interior. Well worth a visit. Ah, we have arrived."

The cab had descended into a sloping and curving street of medium-sized terraced houses, bounded from the roadway by a high wall. They found Mrs Pugh's house and, instructing the cab to pick them up again in one hour, went to the door.

Their ring was answered by a maid, who took them into a dark, musty, heavily furnished parlour, where Mrs Pugh was waiting for them. Ruth's nose told her this room was used only for receiving occasional visitors. Mrs Pugh instructed the maid to bring in tea, and sat herself regally in a high-backed chair.

Ruth could barely remember the small, stout woman, dressed in black crêpe, as was Ruth. Her face was impassive as Ruth and Richard sat.

"Thank you for seeing us, Mrs Pugh. This must be a very difficult time for you."

"As for yourself," the woman inclined her head in acknowledgement, speaking with a broad West Country accent. "You feel able to travel now."

"Yes, thank you," Ruth replied and went on before Mrs Pugh could ask more detailed questions. "This is my first visit to Hereford. It seems to be a pretty town."

"My husband was content in his time here. It was a respectful chapel."

Ruth knew that this was as much directed at her as at Richard, but she smiled as the maid brought in the tea tray. Ruth had already decided to be direct. When they were all served, she spoke.

"Mrs Pugh, when I wrote to your husband I asked him about the schoolteacher who taught at Garth Hill during his time there, Miss Eira Probert."

Mrs Pugh nodded, her face remaining expressionless.

"At my husband's funeral, I believe I saw Miss Probert in the crowd at chapel. She didn't approach me."

The teacup in Mrs Pugh's hand rattled against its saucer and she put it quickly to her lips.

"Miss Probert's appearance was strange. She seemed not to have aged since I'd last seen her, thirty years ago."

Mrs Pugh looked up. The redness of her lips was distinct against the whiteness of her face. "At my dear husband's service, I believe I saw her, too."

"And her appearance?" Ruth sat forwards eagerly.

"Unchanged, as you say."

Richard, who had been content to sit back and allow Ruth to lead the conversation, now put his cup and saucer on the table at his side and spoke directly to Mrs Pugh.

"My dear Mrs Pugh, can you be certain that it was the same woman?"

"Yes, Mr Robinson, I can. She smiled at me. If you have seen that smile but once, Mr Robinson, it's not easily forgotten."

Ruth nodded. "That's what I saw." She drew a deep breath. "Mrs Pugh, may I ask, when you and Mr Pugh left Garth Hill for Hereford, did your husband invite Miss Probert to join him?"

The woman's reply was firm. "No, he did not. He did not wish to see her ever again. Nor did he invite her to teach at Garth Hill at the beginning. He had never met her or heard of her when we arrived at… that place."

She spoke the last few words with a grim expression and a look of distaste.

"Thank you, Mrs Pugh. I believed that to be the case, but I wanted your confirmation. I have one more question." She hesitated, trying to decide how to ask and conscious of Richard shifting in his seat.

"You know that my daughter Alice disappeared during your time at Garth Hill."

She nodded.

"We have never been able to find her," Ruth's voice shook, "but since the death of my husband there have been several instances, including the appearance of Miss Probert at his funeral service, that have led me to think again about her disappearance. On the day that she disappeared, Miss Probert said that she was in the schoolhouse with Mr Pugh and that she walked with him from there to your house, where she stayed." She paused, watching Mrs Pugh closely. "Can you tell me if that was what happened?"

The colour had returned to Mrs Pugh's cheeks in the form of two bright red spots and Ruth guessed that Mrs Pugh was fighting an inner battle between truthfulness and the urge to protect her dead husband. She waited, keeping her eyes fixed firmly on Mrs Pugh.

"It was a long time ago, Mrs Jones. My memory is not so clear."

"I think, Mrs Pugh, that you would not have invited me here if you intended to lie to me."

She ignored the small gasp from Richard.

"I lost my child, Mrs Pugh. Please, help me to understand anything I can about why that might have been. I just want to know."

Ruth looked up at the mantelpiece, at the photograph of Robert Pugh standing haughtily behind his seated wife and their three children. Mrs Pugh saw her looking. It must have been the pleading in her voice that decided Mrs Pugh to speak. "It was not the truth. Miss Probert did not see my husband at all that afternoon." Now the words came out in a rush. "The next Sunday, she didn't appear at chapel, nor at Sunday school. When my husband went later to enquire, she told him to mind his own business. She was… strange in her behaviour. She seemed panicked. He couldn't understand it. And… she smelled, quite horribly. There seemed to be something wrong with her face. My husband returned that evening to see her, fearing she might be ill. What he saw affected him for the rest of his life." Mrs Pugh was now trembling so much she had to put down her cup. Richard was alarmed and offered to send for the maid, but Mrs Pugh refused.

"Allow me to finish, then I shall never speak of this again." She took a moment to compose herself, put her hands together in her lap, then continued.

"When my husband arrived at the schoolhouse cottage, Miss Probert had wrapped up her face. She was taking the wrapping off as he entered. He saw… he saw that her skin seemed to be dripping off her face. She opened her mouth and howled at him. The inside of her mouth was completely black." Mrs Pugh put her hand up to her mouth, as if to hold in the horror of what she was saying. Richard moved to help, but she put up her hand.

"My husband left immediately. When he returned home he was violently ill. The next day she seemed normal. Mr Pugh resigned his position immediately and we left as soon as we were able. We never saw Miss Probert again."

There was so much that Ruth wanted to ask, torn between sympathy for the woman's distress and her own anger at what they had concealed, information that might have helped in the search for Alice.

"Did Mr Pugh have an opinion on what it was that he saw?"

"He never spoke of it. Ever! And now I have related this to you, I shall never speak of it again."

"One final question, Mrs Pugh. I am right in surmising that you are the person who told Mrs Ellis not to speak of what she discovered, or her children would be taken away?" Her face instantly reddened. She said nothing, but after a moment, nodded, then looked defiantly at them.

"I have nothing further to say." She stood.

Both Ruth and Richard understood the dismissal.

"Thank you for speaking to us, Mrs Pugh. I understand that this was hard for you," Richard said, anxious to leave before Ruth said anything she might come to regret.

As the door closed behind them, Ruth turned to him, her face blazing. "Well, Richard, do you still think me overwrought with grief?"

Chapter 63
June 2015

As they drove down the motorway, Maggie told Zelah that she had posted her job contract.

"So that gives me only ten days. And I think this will be the last major chunk of time I can devote to research. Next week, I want to spend time with the kids, help them with homework and projects, just be there for them. They don't like the idea of having to depend on their aunt for a lift home, but I've explained that they'll be there for just a couple of hours without me. And I've agreed that if they can manage themselves without fighting, I'll review the sitter. But I need someone for the summer holidays, so I need to get on with that next week."

Zelah grinned, "As you say. Let's get the most out of this then. By the way," she pointed to a page of a newspaper on the floor, "I found that at the weekend."

Maggie picked it up and saw an advertisement for a tour of a stately home.

"It's Knyghton!" she exclaimed, reading through the small print under the photo. "A tour for old girls. I'll definitely book myself to go on that. I've been promising myself that I'd go and look at it again, ever since I got back." She read on. "Next Saturday. I can take Alice with me. I've told her so many times about where I went to school. It'll be fun and it'll get me away from the graveside stuff."

"Are you still bothered about that?"

"Much less than a couple of weeks ago." Maggie paused, considering. "I never thought I'd reach a point where I'd know that I've been communing with a ghost," she gave Zelah a "don't interrupt" look and continued, "and talk about it as if it's like an everyday happening. Like putting out the bins, or hanging out the washing."

"We all get there, in the end." Zelah kept her eyes on the road.

It took a couple of hours to reach Carmarthen. They found the hotel Zelah had chosen on the main street and checked in, then walked to the records office. It was market day.

"This is a nice place," Maggie remarked as they walked down from the hotel to the small central square at the base of the hill, dominated by the eighteenth-century colonnaded magistrates' court. They paused for a moment to look at the war memorial around which shoppers and sightseers relaxed in the sunshine. Then they continued out, past the market stalls, and on to the road to the records office.

An old school building now housed the county records: a group of small rooms and offices, much less imposing than Newport library. They were the only people researching, which Maggie remarked on.

"Weather's too nice today," the curator replied. "Just fifteen minutes from the coast here. On a busy day, now, you'd have to book in advance to get a seat at the table." He showed them into the research room, explained everything, and offered as much help as they might need.

"Welcoming, aren't they?" Maggie looked sideways at Zelah and grinned as they settled themselves down.

With their papers spread out on the table, and using copies of Maggie's family chart and notes, they began to search records for the parish that contained the hamlet of Llanybri. Zelah had insisted that they verify all the information they had. It didn't take long to find the Gwyllim family. The register in which they were recorded had survived in excellent condition.

Zelah found the first entry. "Here's a marriage, of Ruth Jones to Robert Gwyllim, in 1785, in the chapel at Llansteffan." Maggie looked up at the curator, who was working nearby. "Do you know Llansteffan and Llanybri?"

"Oh, yes. Llanybri is just a small village. Llansteffan is about three miles away, on the coast. It's a pretty place, quite popular with holiday visitors. There's a castle on the hill above the sea, just a ruin, you know, but a big one. And some cottages. The village is just back aways."

Maggie smiled at him. "It sounds lovely."

"Oh, yes. Very pretty. Worth a visit, if you have time —"

"We don't," Zelah interrupted, not looking up from the register.

The man stood awkwardly for a moment, then walked away.

"Leave the people stuff to me, Zelah," Maggie whispered. "We'll probably need his help and he was just being friendly."

Maggie shook her head at the mumbled retort. She had been tracing her finger above the rows of records of births, searching for the Gwyllim family.

"Here!" she exclaimed, "this must be the first child. It's a girl, Margaret, born in 1785. What next? Ah, here they are, twin girls, Ruth and Alice, born 1786." She felt a moment of sadness, reflecting on how the birth of the girls would have been celebrated, knowing the tragedy that would overtake them ten years later, overshadowing the family's lives. This was a strange, powerful part of research, knowing the ultimate fate of the newly born.

Going on down through the list, she found another two Gwyllim children, both boys: Robert and Evan.

"So, Zel, what I found on the internet was correct. These are my ancestors and Ruth's family?"

"Yes. It's them. Now try the death records. Find Alice's death."

Maggie went off to find the curator, to fetch the death records for the parish.

"Interesting that they kept separate records," Zelah remarked as they waited for the book to arrive. "Some small parishes recorded everything in the same book."

"So, if it was lost, then everything went." Maggie replied. "No more records of those people."

"You'd be surprised how little care was taken of records until quite recently," Zelah said indignantly. "A couple of months ago I went up to north Wales to look for a parish register and found it in the old rectory next to the church." She paused, frowning at the memory. "The place wasn't lived in, the roof leaked and everything was damp. When I finally found the books in a heap in a corner, the pages practically disintegrated in my hands!" She had raised her voice as she spoke and was now glaring at Maggie. "The vicar called it 'that old stuff'. They'd just let it all rot!"

"I never used to be interested. Not until it became personal."

The curator returned with a small, black book bound with black ribbon. "Book of the dead," he remarked with a grin. "Can I ask what you are searching for?"

He looked at Maggie, who could see a flicker of trepidation as he avoided looking at Zelah.

"Of course," she replied, as Zelah snatched the book and started to go through the records.

Maggie summarised her story, leaving out the more difficult to explain parts, but giving him enough of a flavour to preserve his interest.

"So you need to find out where these children went to school, then?"

"Yes, if you think you have that information."

"Well, I'm not sure. But it's too late today, we close in ten minutes. I was just coming in to tell you. But I'll be happy to go through what we have first thing tomorrow."

"That would be great, thanks," Maggie replied quickly, noticing that Zelah was about to protest. "Can we just finish checking the death records, though? It shouldn't take long."

"I've found it," Zelah interrupted. "Alice Gwyllim. Aged 10 years. Died by accidental drowning. Now look at the next entry. Esme Davy. Aged 10 years. Died by accidental drowning."

She looked up at Maggie, saw the sick look. The curator looked from one to the other.

"Is something the matter?"

"No, it's fine," Maggie replied quickly. "Thanks very much for your help. We'll be back again in the morning to look at your school records."

"How about a trip down to Llansteffan?" Zelah asked as they walked back to the hotel. "Sounds like a nice place."

"That would be good."

* * *

They drove across the river on which Carmarthen sat and followed its estuary to the sea. This was a place where three rivers from the vales of south-west Wales widened out at the end of their

368

journey and joined together in one broad estuary that led to the Channel. They caught glimpses of green water on the far side of the hedgerows. The countryside was rolling and luscious, gentle green hills on both sides, with fields of grazing dairy herds.

In the village of Llansteffan, a sign directed them to the beach and the castle. A narrow lane dissected low sand dunes with the estuary on one side and a row of small traditional cottages on the other. Maggie could see that they were nearing the end of the land and in a few more minutes they reached a small car park that sat in the middle of an open square with more cottages along one side, a cliff, and the mouth of the estuary.

Leaving Zelah to lock the car, Maggie walked across and up onto the sand dunes, kicked off her shoes and walked down onto the beach. The sand was hot on her feet. She walked to the water's edge and stood in the small rippling wavelets, contemplating the expansive view.

"I don't like walking on sand. Gets in my toes and rubs." Zelah had walked up behind her, but was keeping her distance from the water. "Hell of a view, though. I never knew this place was here. Walk up to the castle?"

"You aren't seriously contemplating it in those shoes, are you?" Maggie pointed to Zelah's six-inch-high shoes that she was holding in her hand.

"What? No problem! Climbed Snowdon in these." Maggie raised her eyebrows.

"Well, I got out of the train at the top and walked to the café in them." Zelah smirked. "Let's go."

They walked back across the car park to the footpath in the far corner of the square that signposted them towards the castle. Fifteen minutes later, panting and puffing, they reached

369

the entrance. The castle turned out to be a vast, rambling ruin covering the top of the hillside. They were the only visitors.

"God, it's warm!" Zelah had taken off her shoes again, plus her jacket, to walk across the grassy interior. "Wonderful view, though. Martin would have loved it."

The last mackerel clouds had disappeared as they climbed up, leaving an azure sky over the hills and water. They sat on the low ramparts at the edge of the cliff, overlooking the sea.

"No more coincidences," Maggie said.

"I agree," Zelah replied. "The incidents in your family are connected. We need to find out how. And why. The school records will be critical, but we'll be lucky to find them."

"How so?"

"In the late eighteenth century, education in this part of Wales was given by what was called the circulating schools. The school would be set up in a convenient building – a farmhouse, or a barn, or whatever – and the teachers moved from school to school for up to three months at a time. Then there were night schools, again in any old building, because the children worked with their parents on the land in daylight hours. These were all supported by charity. And, it was dominated by religion. But not too many records."

"Then we might never find out?"

"Maybe not. But there's plenty of places to look and we won't give up until we've tried everything. Will we, Maggie?"

"I need to find out why Alice had her dreams and her visions. And I know that this is part of the story." Maggie jumped down onto the grass. "So, no, we won't give up."

She gazed out to sea. "Wonderful view. Nothing spoiling it for miles." She was about to add something, but stopped in her tracks. "Damn!" She spun around and looked again. "That's it! An uninterrupted view."

"Yes, it is. What are you talking about? What's the matter?"

Maggie's face was pale. "I believed what you said about inherited memory. I really did, but I think there was always a bit of me that stayed sceptical."

"Understandable. But now there's another 'but'?"

"Yes," Maggie replied. "You remember when I said that I was thinking about the view from the top of the mountain at home that I could see so clearly, although I was almost certain that I'd never been there? Well, I'd convinced myself that my parents must have taken me at some time, I just couldn't remember."

"But?"

"An uninterrupted view. Up the estuary. No bridges. No suspension bridge and no second Severn Crossing!"

"The first bridge was opened around 1966," Zelah nodded. "It took over three years to build."

"Exactly," Maggie replied, "I could never have seen that view *without* a bridge there. So it must have been Ruth's memory. She stood on top of that mountain at a significant time. I can see it so clearly! And the towns below were much smaller. If I was small they should have looked huge. But they didn't."

"So now you really believe me?"

"Yes," Maggie shuddered, then jumped down from the wall.

"Right, then," Zelah said, jumping down beside her. "Back to Carmarthen, dinner, then back to the archives tomorrow morning."

* * *

They were the only visitors waiting to go into the archive office again. The curator opened the doors and smiled.

"I've been seeing what I could find this morning," he said as he let them into the research room. "I've put out some books for you to look through. But there's not much from that period. Education wasn't that well organised back then."

They sat in front of a collection of old records and logbooks.

"But," he smiled in anticipation. "I found something that I think might refer to the story you're looking for. Wait there."

He returned five minutes later, as they were looking through the records of school rolls from the early nineteenth century. He wore protective white gloves and was carrying a small box.

"One of our treasures," he said, putting the package on the table in front of Maggie. "You'll have to wear gloves."

She noted that he had only brought one pair, which she put on as Zelah sat stiff-backed. Above her, the curator was hovering, hands clasped, fingers working restlessly together. She opened up the box, leaning across to show Zelah, and began to examine the contents.

"I can see there are records, from what looks like an estate, judging by these land records. Is that right?"

"Yes," replied the curator. "We only got it last month. Turned up in a box from a house sale. That's why I remembered the story. It's from an estate near Llansteffan, mid to late eighteenth century. They owned huge tracts of land in the area and employed most of the local community, one way or another."

"What am I looking for?" Maggie asked. There were several papers in the set. The curator leaned forwards and carefully picked out two small, stiff, yellowed pages between his thumb and forefinger.

"These are a couple of pages from a diary. We don't know who wrote it and we've pinned down the year to 1796." He turned to the second page and pointed to an entry for the twenty-eighth of June. Maggie read: "*I must record a sad event this day, being the burial of the children of two of our tenant farmers, drowned together in a pool which forms in a branch of the river at the high tide. It is reported that they were dearest friends.* Yes," Maggie confirmed in a quiet voice. "I think this is our story. The deaths were recorded a couple of days before, wasn't it, Zelah?"

"Twenty-fifth of June."

Maggie turned to the curator. "Thank you so much. This has been very valuable." She handed back the box of papers and took off the gloves.

"I'm going to write down the exact wording, plus anything you can tell me about the estate and the people who owned it, then we'll carry on looking through the school records."

Two hours later, as the research room was about to close for lunch, Maggie sighed, sat back in her chair and rubbed her shoulders. Zelah was still looking through rolls of paper.

"I think we have to admit defeat on this one, Zel. What do you think?"

The table in front of them was covered with books, and papers, none of which had revealed any details from the time period they were looking for, nor a school in the area of the estate.

"Yep, 'fraid so. Nothing more for us here."

"We'll need to go soon. I promised to be back for the end of school."

They packed up, letting the curator know that they had finished with the research material.

"Didn't find what you were looking for?"

"No, unfortunately not."

"If you really need the information, you might think about the National Library of Wales."

"I have thought about it," Zelah replied. "Come on Maggie, let's get going."

Maggie thanked the curator as Zelah went ahead to the car. As she ran to catch up, waving goodbye behind her, Zelah started the engine.

"We're not in that much of a hurry," Maggie panted, dropping her bags onto the back seat.

"Yes, we are. After I've dropped you home I'm going to go up to Aberystwyth. Spend tomorrow looking for this school information."

"You want to know, don't you? The National Library has more records. If it's not in Carmarthen, then that's the only chance of finding it."

Chapter 64

Jack and Alice were delighted to see her waiting for them. As soon as they set off they let her know just how much they hadn't enjoyed having to go to their aunt's. Over dinner, they returned to the subject, despite Maggie's attempts to talk about something else.

"She means well, Mum," Jack began. "But she's so formal, you know what I mean?"

"I assume you're going to tell me, whether I want to know, or not."

"Last night she made us change our clothes and do our homework before dinner. Then she made us eat everything on the plate. I thought Alice was going to be sick."

As they were currently eating Chinese takeaway from cartons, Maggie felt reluctant admiration for her sister.

Alice pulled a face and Maggie could see the glistening of tears. "I just don't like meat. I told her." Maggie handed her a tissue, not sure how much was genuine, and how much a last-ditch attempt to make her feel too guilty to start working again. "Why do we have to go there?"

"We've been through this, so don't ask again. It's just for the summer and I'll review it in September when you're both at the same school. Now, if you don't want to get me worked up, go and do any homework you have now, then we'll go and get a film to watch."

They both stood up and took their cutlery to the dishwasher, another positive outcome of her sister's much tougher regime.

As she reached the doorway, Alice turned back. "It's good to have you back again, Mum. I feel much better with you around."

The next day Maggie resigned herself to sitting in her office, reading up on the files and information that she had received for her new job. Not having worked for ten months, she knew that she was probably rusty on the latest developments in the world of business. They would expect her to hit the ground running, as had been spelled out at the interview. For a couple of hours she read diligently, made notes, and tried to summon up enthusiasm for the projects that she had begun to map out. But the thought of what they had found in Carmarthen and what Zelah would be finding in the archive material in Aberystwyth constantly pushed its way in. After lunch, despite trying again to get back to work, she gave up and turned to her family chart to organise her new material.

She was so engrossed that the sudden noise in the hall of the children arriving home with a couple of friends took her completely by surprise. Going out to greet them, she remembered that she had agreed to cook a barbeque later. This was one of the concessions for the week. She was going to be up to her neck in visiting children. The family tree would have to wait.

* * *

The last of the children were waved off at seven, not a moment too soon for Maggie.

"That was great! Thanks, Mum. You're the best!" Jack hugged her as they turned away.

376

"Wish we could do that every day," Alice said as they went back out to the garden to clear up.

"You'd get bored if you did that every day."

"No, I wouldn't."

The phone ringing in the hall gave Maggie the opportunity to escape the argument. It was Zelah.

"Well, have I got some news for you!"

"It was a worthwhile trip, then?"

"It most certainly was. Do you want to meet up, or shall I give it to you now?"

Maggie sensed tension in Zelah's voice. "Tell me now. I can't meet you until Monday and I don't think I can wait."

"Well, it took some searching, but I found a list of teachers who visited the Llansteffan area as circulating teachers at the time of the drownings."

"Great!" Maggie exclaimed. "And you found something that'll help us? Zelah?" There was an uncharacteristic silence at the other end of the phone.

"I'm not sure about help. But I think your great-great-grandmother made an assumption when she spoke about the teacher who was suspected at the time as a "he". They may just have assumed that it was a man."

"Why?"

"Because one of the teachers was a name we've seen before. A woman, by the name of Eira Probert."

"The same name in Charles Morris's letter to Ruth!"

"Maggie, I think it was the same woman."

Chapter 65
June 1909

Once they were seated in their carriage and the train pulled out of the station, they faced each other and spoke at last.

"Well, Richard?" Ruth was pale, outwardly calm but beneath her skirt her legs were shaking.

"I don't know what to say, Ruth. This is the strangest set of events I have ever come across. It defies explanation."

"I think," she began slowly, "that we should not spend our time looking for an explanation. I agree that there is none that God-fearing people can understand. I believe that we have stumbled across something evil." She stopped, waiting to see if he would disagree, but he slowly nodded his head.

"Loath though I am to admit such thoughts, I have it in my mind that you may be right." He clasped his hands together and twisted them around. Ruth realised the dreadful upset she had forced on him. Then, suddenly, he slapped his hands onto his knees.

"But we must do something. Now that we know, we must do something."

"When we left Mrs Pugh I felt the same, my mind was in turmoil. I had expected much of our meeting and I wasn't disappointed." She smiled a thin grimace.

"When I heard what that dreadful woman had to say I wanted to take action, any action. To find out at last that there *was* something to know, and that it had been kept secret for so long! But now I know what I must do."

"What, Ruth?" Richard asked hopefully. "Nothing, Richard. I must do nothing."

The shock of her response froze him in his seat and he stared at her, open-mouthed, searching for words.

"I wanted to believe that the Pughs knew something that would help me to find Alice, although I knew that was unlikely. We know now that Alice ran away from Eira Probert, that much is definite, you agree?" Richard nodded. "But what are we to do with this information? Probert – whatever she is – disappeared thirty years ago. She has made two appearances, both at funerals. It's in my mind that she is still watching my family. And the more we fear her, the closer she comes."

Richard sank into his seat, his shoulders hunched. Ruth saw a small shudder run through his body.

A blast of the steam whistle signalled their arrival at Abergavenny station. The train slowed to a halt, where they sat in silence, listening to the banging of doors, the slow puffing of steam, and the calling to and fro of porters and passengers. Then, at last, they heard the station master's whistle, a slight bumping of carriages, and a billowing of smoke, as the train pulled away again and out into the countryside.

"I am going to write to the school board, Ruth. At least we can find out how Eira Probert came to teach at Garth Hill."

"Will they be able to tell you, after all this time? John was going to write at the time, you know. But he never did. If only he had."

"I would expect there to be some records."

"And I shall write again to my sister in Carmarthen. Perhaps there will be records there, too. But I can't tell her why I want to know. She'll be suspicious, but she's a good woman and will do what I ask." She had already written to Mary Anne but had not yet posted the letter. Now she would write a new letter instead.

"But, Richard, we must be careful. Nothing to arouse…"

"I understand, Ruth. I really do."

* * *

Arriving home, Ruth said nothing to her family. She took off her hat and coat as quietly as possible and went to sit at the back of the sitting room. Maud brought her a cup of tea an hour later. She still hadn't spoken.

"You had an interesting day, mother?" Ruth didn't miss the disapproval.

"Thank you, Maud. Yes, I did. It was very… illuminating." She smiled at her daughter as she lowered her teacup. "You know, Maud, I never thought of you as second best."

Maud stiffened. She made as if to say something, then changed her mind. She gave her mother a brief, half smile, then walked away.

Too late, I should have told her a long time ago, Ruth thought. She turned back to the window.

The following day Ruth wrote to her sister. She took her time over the letter, trying to make sure that she appeared more interested in the story than in the outcome. She knew that Mary Anne wouldn't be fooled, but hoped that she would agree to follow up the request.

At chapel on Sunday, Richard told her that he had written to the former clerk of the school board, an old man now, living in Cardiff. So, there was nothing for them to do but wait. They had, by unspoken agreement, not discussed the visit to Mrs Pugh, keeping private their ominous, fearful thoughts.

His reply arrived quicker than either of them expected. On Thursday morning, Richard arrived unannounced. Maud let him in and showed him to the parlour. He had news.

"Ruth, I have to tell you that Gwen Ellis died last night." She sighed and ran her hands along the arms of the chair.

"I know it was expected, but still it's a shock. Gwen was one of the first people I met when John and I arrived here. And she was kind. A lovely, caring woman. And our lives became so bound together," Richard looked as if he had more to say.

"Is there something else, Richard?"

"I received a letter from Thomas Jenkins in Cardiff this morning, the retired clerk to whom I wrote. I've come straight here."

Ruth put her hands on her knees to stop their trembling, and composed her face.

"Shall I read out the letter?"

"Yes, Richard."

Dear Mr. Robinson,

So wonderful to hear from you after such a long time and my thanks for your kind enquiries after my health. I am a little weaker than when we last met, but still I manage to walk out each day. My daughter and her family are very good and look after me well.

Your enquiry surprised me, I must say. Despite my no longer retaining the actual correspondence, I remember the case well. Your mother had suddenly become ill, causing you to leave the district unexpectedly, at the same time as the then incumbent schoolmaster, Mr. Parsons, who had also lost his mother.

was required to leave to attend his family. It was this coincidence that caused me to remember the particulars.

I must assume that you have forgotten that it was you who wrote to me, Richard, to ask the Board to take Miss Probert. You gave excellent references and assured the Board of her good faith. The letter was written in your own hand, in December 1882.

Six months later you wrote again to say that Miss Probert would be leaving unexpectedly and that Mr. Parsons was able to return.

Assuring you of my best wishes and willingness to serve your interests at all times.

Thos. Jenkins."

As he read the letter his voice had reduced to a whisper. He looked up at Ruth, anguished.

Chapter 66
June 2015

The ornately carved double doors at the entrance to Knyghton House drew back and Maggie, Alice, and the rest of the waiting group filed into the reception hall for the Old Girls Tour. Including Maggie and Alice, there were only twelve, which was disappointing, and when they introduced themselves there was no-one that Maggie knew. Most were a couple of years older or younger. Still, she decided, it wouldn't detract from the tour. And she needed a distraction, following a restless night after Zelah's news.

During the guide's welcome, Maggie craned her neck to see beyond the reception hall. The glimpse that she got of the rooms on either side, told her that much had changed since she was last there.

The guide was well informed about the time that the house had been a school. Now, by way of introduction, he gave a history of the building from its beginnings in the late fourteenth century, through to the 1950s when the house had been handed over to the religious order, that had turned it into a boarding school.

Maggie was fascinated and whispered to Alice, "I never knew any of this stuff. We never learned the history when we were here."

"That's really stupid," Alice whispered back.

"That's just how it was," Maggie replied.

As they moved from room to magnificent room, each now restored to how it would have looked before the turn of the nineteenth century, Maggie and her companions marvelled at the beauty of it all and chit-chatted amiably about their memories of what they had done in each room when they'd been there. They passed through what had been the assembly hall, now the music room, and Maggie's third-year form room, now covered from ceiling to floor in gilt and decorated with paintings.

"I remember this was done when it became our form room. It was restored back to how it had been in the nineteenth century. We never put a finger on the gilt," she remarked to Alice. "Amazing control for thirteen-year-olds. But the head would have expelled us without a second thought if anything had been damaged."

Alice was fascinated, asking Maggie what else she remembered and laughing at her mother's memories of rigid lessons, a strict uniform that included a straw boater in summer, and absolutely no running anywhere, anytime.

"We weren't allowed to put so much as a finger on this panelling either," Maggie explained as they walked along the dark oak panelled corridor on the first floor, "on pain of death and lots of detention."

"What sort of detention did you get in those days?"

"No idea, I never got one."

Alice stared at her in amazement. "Never? Not a single one?" Maggie responded with a quizzical look.

On the first floor they reached a door that led to the servants' stairs, which Maggie identified as the original entrance to the house for the schoolgirls, up from the cloakroom at ground floor level.

"But I only ever got to this level," she explained. "We came up from the cloakrooms then we went off to classrooms on this level. But the boarders lived upstairs." She pointed to where the uncarpeted wooden staircase wound up to a higher floor and laughed. "I never got up there, not once in seven years. So, this is the highlight of the tour for me, to find out what's at the top of those stairs!"

The group followed the guide up the rickety, uneven staircase, which turned a corner for the last three steps into a corridor with a low sloping ceiling. Maggie could see many doors leading off the corridor.

"These are the rooms used by the boarders at the school," the guide informed them. "Did any of you board here?" No-one had. "Of course, before that, they were the servants' quarters. They shared rooms and you'll see that they didn't have much space. We've arranged two of them as they would have been around 1900 and kept a few as the boarders would have known them. Follow me."

He led them into a sparsely furnished servants' bedroom, explaining who would have lived there, then along the corridor to a ninety-degree turn into a further corridor, mirroring the family bedrooms below. At the end of the corridor he stopped. The rooms that hugged the corner were barred by iron grille gates, one of which was open.

"We usually keep this area closed, but this morning our archivists are here. Perhaps you'd like to meet them. They're always interested in finding out anything about the history of the house."

They filed through the prison-like gates into a large corner room that was filled with desks, hundreds of files and random piles of paper. The walls were covered with documents and newspaper cuttings. Two men stood at desks in the room. One looked up and smiled as they came in. The other, a tall, thin man with short, wavy dark hair, remained bent over a pile of papers next to the window that he picked through with white cotton gloves.

385

"Let me introduce our archivists, Ted Morgan," smiling Ted nodded to them again, "and Nick Howell." The tall man glanced up, blushed, attempted a smile, thought better of it, and returned to his pile of papers.

"So, you're our first group of old girls, not that you are old, of course… you know what I mean!" Ted beamed. "Downstairs, when you're done touring, we've got some plans of the house for you. We'd like you to tell us everything you can about how it was back then."

Members of the group began to chat again about schooldays but Maggie noticed that, pinned to a noticeboard on the wall next to Nick Howell, there was a photocopy of an old newspaper headline, with a picture of the PS *Waverley* and an announcement of its voyages across the Channel. And there was a family history chart. She walked straight across to it.

"I went on that recently," she said. The man grunted, but didn't look up. Maggie could see that he was drafting a notice for a forthcoming tour, part of the headline of which was "Family History".

"Are you organising something with a family history theme?" she asked. Another grunt. "If so, I'd be very interested. I see that you're researching. Is that a local family?"

"Yes."

Maggie walked forwards and checked the chart close up. "There's something familiar here, but I can't think what it is."

"Anything would be helpful." His tone had taken on an interest and at last he looked directly at her. Maggie saw that his eyes were very blue.

"I'm not sure. Let me think. I see you have the name 'Fitzgerald' pencilled in next to the head of the line. Is that an Irish family?"

"Yes," he replied. "A family that came over from Ireland in the 1860s. Do you know them?"

"One of my friends is a Fitzgerald, by marriage. I know that her husband's family came over from Ireland."

"Perhaps we can talk," he said with a smile that made Maggie think he was probably younger than he had first looked. "Are you staying on downstairs to fill in the maps?"

"Yes," she smiled back. "I thought I would."

"I'll meet you there, then." He turned back to his copywriting.

The tour reached its finale in the housekeeper's sitting room, then followed the guide into the oldest part of the building, down three steps into the original medieval banqueting hall. Tea and cakes had been laid out for them on a long trestle table next to the tall, small-paned windows that faced out to the enclosed courtyard.

"It's cold in here," Alice whispered to Maggie. "How can it be so shivery in summer?"

"It's below the level of the rest of the house because it's so old," Maggie replied. "The walls are several feet thick. I don't think it was ever warm in here."

"This was the servants' dining hall and I understand that the tradition was kept up at the school, and this was your lunch room," the guide said. "Now, please help yourself to refreshments and take a clipboard and pen. We need your help!"

Maggie and Alice helped themselves to a cup of tea and a cake each and had just sat down at the long table when Nick Howell, still wearing his white gloves, arrived in the doorway. He glanced furtively around, and walked down the length of the hall, shoulders hunched, staring at the floor. Maggie thought she ought to call his attention, but he came straight to them, sat down next to them and launched into a story, without preamble, in a low voice.

"A couple of months ago I was contacted by a local man, name of Alan Kerr, who'd been doing some research around his family. He'd found out that his great-grandmother was housekeeper here. Her name was Esme Hughes. But there are some parts of her story that he thinks don't quite add up." He looked at Maggie. "She appeared here in May 1883, aged twelve, to live with her aunt, who was housekeeper at the time, a Mrs Moira Davies."

"What's this got to do with me?" Maggie asked.

"Well, when the girl arrived she was very ill, almost dead. A woman called Honora Fitzgerald saved her life."

"Ah. That's interesting. So, who was this Honora Fitzgerald?"

"She was a seamstress."

"Yes, she was. So how did she come to save someone's life?"

He glanced quizzically at her, but didn't probe into her comment. "According to the diary of Mrs Davies, which we have in our archives, Honora Fitzgerald was an excellent herbalist healer and provided remedies that saved the child."

"That's a great story," Maggie responded, with no expression in her voice and a very straight face. "But by herbalist healer, I think you mean 'witch'?"

He looked at her, perplexed. "The Kerrs have been looking for any link to their ancestor. Maybe your friend is related?"

"No, I don't think so. Do you know any more about the girl, and why she almost died?"

"Her name was Esme Peach, before she married one of the footmen, Alan Hughes. How do you know your friend isn't related?"

Maggie had gone very still. She ignored his question. "So, Esme Peach is your mystery. I've got one of those in my family. I'm trying to find a girl who disappeared in or around May 1883. She was ten. That's a coincidence, isn't it?" She paused. "But I'm coming across those thick and fast. So much so, that nothing surprises me any more. Not even this. Which it should. But doesn't."

"What happened to your girl?" Nick looked slightly alarmed now. ´

"That's what we're trying to find out," Maggie replied. "There was a suggestion that she went to Weston-super-Mare, and her father went to view a body that was found there, but it wasn't her." She paused. "You're giving me a funny look."

"That's because Esme Peach was supposed to have made her way *from* Weston-super-Mare, in 1883."

"Yes. As soon as you said it I recognised the name, Peach. It's in my letters. A prostitute named Margaret Peach. She had a daughter, called Esme."

They stared at each other, silently, until Alice broke the silence.

"I don't understand all of this. Mum!"

"Nor do I," Maggie replied. She looked directly at Nick. "But, as I said, this is happening so fast that I can't even try to understand. This story is running away with itself."

"I'm sorry, but I really don't understand what you're talking about." He got up and shuffled as if about to walk away. Maggie shook her head. "Sit down, Mr Howell, please. I've got something else to tell you. Something that will help the Kerr family."

He lingered uncertainly. Maggie guessed that the look of alarm was probably just the reaction of a shy man who was being babbled at by a strange woman. Her own voice had begun to tremble a little, although she was making a great effort at control and she needed him to listen.

"As I said, I'm in the middle of a mystery, and you've just helped me to add what I think will be some particularly crucial pieces. But let me begin by telling you why I know that my friend wasn't related to your Honora Fitzgerald. I know that her husband's family arrived much later. But *my* Irish ancestors arrived in the eighteen-sixties. My mother told me, when I was at school here, that her own great-grandmother worked here as a servant."

"What kind of servant?"

She smiled at him. "A seamstress. Honora Fitzgerald was *my* great-great-grandmother. We still have the shawl that was presented to her when she retired."

"Do we?" Alice asked, leaning across into their conversation. "Which one?"

"The red and blue one in your dressing up box."

"Wow. I've been playing with history."

"I did a bit of research when I got involved in my family history, but she was more of a distraction than anything. I remember that she came from Ireland, from Cork."

He nodded and she continued.

"My mother was Kate O'Connor, her mother was a Dillon, Mary Dillon by marriage. Her mother was Margaret Collins and Margaret's mother was Honora Fitzgerald, but sometimes she called herself Norah. It changes in the census records. Are you alright?" A wide smile had spread across his face, lighting up his eyes and, Maggie thought, making him look quite handsome.

"But the story of Esme Peach. Now, that's something else," Maggie continued. "I need to think this through. If I'm right, we may just have the crucial clue."

Alice had been scribbling on the paper on the clipboard as Maggie was speaking. Now she held it up. "I wrote down the chain as you spoke, Mum. And I put you and me on the end. Is this right?"

Maggie examined the line of names. "Yes, Al, that's it exactly. Now if we put next to it my other chain, taking me back to Ruth and John, what can you see?" She reached into her handbag and took out a copy of her family tree and put it on the table next to the clipboard. Ruth's Alice had been highlighted as missing, with the relevant dates and some scribbled notes.

"I'm not sure," Alice said. "What am I supposed to be looking for?"

"Don't worry. It's in the story." She looked up into Nick's face. "But if I'm right…"

"If you're right," he interrupted, pointing to the paper, "this Alice and that Esme Peach could be the same person?"

"Yes," Maggie said. She put her hand on her knees to stop her feet tapping rapidly on the stone floor.

"That will be difficult to prove."

"I know, but we can give it a go. Could you arrange a meeting with the Kerr family?"

"Of course," he responded. "I'll call Alan this afternoon. How can I get hold of you?"

Maggie wrote her number on the clipboard and tore it off for him. "I'm going home now. I need to speak to my friend Zelah. I'll wait for your call." She stood up, then hesitated.

"Do you know why Esme Peach was almost dead when she arrived here?"

"No, but Alan has some information. May I tell him your story?"

"Of course, And tell him I look forward to meeting him."

391

Chapter 67
June 1909

Several times during the week following Richard's visit, Ruth had seen Maud and James talking quietly in the parlour, occasionally glancing in her direction. William must have been party to the discussions, for when he and his wife had come to visit after chapel, he embarked on a discussion of the past. But Ruth politely refused to be drawn. She did, however, hint to him that she would have something to say to the family soon. William tried to encourage her, to cajole, and to fool her into explaining, but to no avail; he and Sara remained perplexed.

Ruth thought she would burst if she had to keep her thoughts to herself any longer. So she decided to visit John's grave alone. This time she had no qualms about approaching it. Standing beside his headstone, Ruth felt peaceful. There was the instant of sadness when she first looked on his carved name, but as she ran her hand over one of the marble columns, the sensation was serenity.

"I miss you so much, my dear, but I think you know that." She bent down to place the flowers she had brought in the vase at the foot of the stone, speaking in a low voice.

"Our girl was hunted, John. She didn't run from us. And I believe my family is hunted, by something I cannot understand but that wishes us only harm and misery. You would have been shocked; you would have been horrified at such ungodly ideas.

I would myself never have thought I could believe such things. But I must, because I cannot deny them."

"My duty now is to protect our grandchildren and their children. I don't know how yet. But I will know. It shan't win over us."

Hands against the headstone, she pushed herself upright, staring intently as if the power of her need might move the granite.

"Ruth, I hope you're there." The voice again! Inside her head and outside at the same time.

"Ruth, I met Louisa, your granddaughter. She told me what you told her, how much you loved her, and how much you tried to protect her and the others. How you wanted to protect us all."

Ruth looked around but saw only darkness, as if her eyes were closed, although she knew they were open. She didn't have a granddaughter called Louisa!

"You succeeded, Ruth. If you hadn't told Louisa, we would never have known. You saved us all."

Ruth took a step backwards, catching her foot and stumbling. A man and woman standing at a memorial across the path saw her and got to her as she fell to her hands and knees.

"Why, Mrs Jones! Let me assist you!"

But she pushed away the helping arm and struggled to her feet, turning back to the grave, moving her head wildly from side to side, straining to hear. The man and his wife gaped at her wide-eyed. After a few seconds, as if acknowledging defeat, she put her head down and hunched her shoulders.

"I apologise, Mr Llewelyn. I was overcome. I shall go home now." She turned her back on their protests and walked down the path towards the house, pressing her hands to her head to try to bring back the words that she thought she had heard as she fell.

"You will see her again, Ruth. Just wait."

Chapter 68
June 2015

As it turned out, Alan Kerr was very keen to meet Maggie. The phone rang as soon as Maggie got home. Nick told her that Alan was delighted to hear about Maggie and her research and had suggested that they meet for a pub lunch at a place on the road past Knyghton House, the following day.

"I know where that is," Maggie said. "I'll see you there, then."

"Me?" He sounded surprised.

"Of course. You brought this about. Don't you want to be there?"

"Do you want me to come?"

"I just said so. I'll see you there tomorrow." She put the phone down. "Strange man," she muttered as she walked into the kitchen on her way to the garden for lunch. She had left a message for Zelah but by the end of lunch had received no reply, which was strange as they had agreed to meet up to discuss Zelah's news. Maggie hadn't wanted to discuss it on the telephone.

By early evening there was still nothing, so she rang again and left a longer message, giving Zelah the time and date of the rendezvous in the pub.

To her surprise, the following morning both children wanted to go with her to meet the Kerrs. The phone rang as they were about to leave the house.

"Sorry, been away. To do with Martin. See you there."

"Hang on," Maggie shouted. "Don't you want to hear any more?"

"No time. Don't want to be late. See you there." The phone went dead.

The pub was a pink-washed, low, square building at the end of a long country lane, behind a high retaining wall that held back the high tides of the Bristol Channel. As they got out of the car, the wind blew them sideways.

"This is not good," Alice shouted as she fought her way towards the pub door, hanging onto Jack's arm. "What's the matter with the weather?"

"It's often like this here," Maggie yelled back. "It's because of the Channel, I think. We'll go up the steps and take a look after lunch."

Alice yelled back something that sounded like "you must be joking", as Zelah roared into the car park. Maggie signalled to the pub entrance and followed Jack.

The entrance led straight into a carpeted lounge bar with groups of armchairs and settees. At the far side, seated against a picture window, Nick Howell was sitting with a small group around a low coffee table. He acknowledged Maggie's wave with a quickly raised, leather-gloved hand. The Kerr family looked up in her direction. There were three of them, mother, father, and a girl about Alice's age who had her back to Maggie. She turned round with a prompt from her mother. The result was startling. Glancing from Alice at her side to the Kerr's daughter, Maggie knew that she was looking at related children.

Alan stood up as they approached. He was about her height and Maggie guessed that he was fortyish, his blonde wife probably younger. He held out his hand, smiling openly.

"Mrs Gilbert, this is very exciting. We're thrilled to meet you. This is my wife, Lucy, and our daughter, Esme."

Lucy stood and prompted her daughter to stand at her side. The two young girls stared at each other. "Are you my cousin?" Alice asked.

"I don't think so," Esme replied, with a grin as wide as Alice's. "But my dad says we may be related, from ages back. Come and sit with us."

Lucy and Esme moved along the settee. Alice sat next to Esme and they began to chat.

Maggie waited as Zelah came through the door, both hands clutching her head. Her appearance – today she was in a bright red suit with black accessories – had the usual effect. Maggie watched Alan and Nick stare as she approached them at her usual brusque pace.

"This is my friend, Zelah Trevear. She's the person who's helped me with my research. I wouldn't be here today without Zelah's help." Zelah nodded curtly and shook the hands held out towards her.

When they had got over the fuss of buying drinks and settling themselves, a silence descended, except for the two girls who were sitting back in the settee and keeping up a non-stop conversation, oblivious to the adults.

"Well, where should we begin?" Maggie waded in.

"How about you tell your story?" Alan suggested. "Nick's told us the basic details, but I'd appreciate hearing it again from you."

"OK," Maggie replied. "Then I'd like to understand how you came to be searching. Let's see if we can establish that my Alice Jones and your Esme Peach are the same person."

Alan nodded and Maggie began her story. She put in as much detail as she could, checking with Zelah who nodded occasionally but didn't add anything. She left out any reference to her less explainable connection to Ruth.

Alan and his wife listened intently throughout, asking no questions. But Lucy's pursed lips and cocked head told Maggie that the woman was sceptical. When Maggie had finished, Alan sat thoughtfully, nodding to himself for a few seconds before he began to speak.

"My great-grandmother, Esme, was housekeeper at Knyghton House, but you know that already." He nodded in Nick's direction. "She married the nephew of the butler who was at the house when Esme appeared. He was called Alan, too. Alan Hughes. They had three children, Esme, Alan, and Joyce."

"It's a tradition in my family that the first girl is always called Esme. Lucy wanted to name our little girl after her mother, but I insisted. It's tradition." He smiled ruefully at his wife and Maggie got the impression that if Lucy had deferred to her husband in this matter, she hadn't in much else.

"Do you know why?" she interrupted.

"No, just that my great-grandmother insisted. She never said why." He paused, looking hopefully at the expression on Maggie's face. "Do you know?"

"I have a theory. But, please, go on."

"Well, when I began to trace my family history, I got back to Esme. I found out by talking to my grandmother about how Esme appeared quite suddenly one day. She told me the story of Esme's mother dying in Weston-super-Mare and Esme somehow making her way to Wales to find her aunt, Moira Davies. Moira was housekeeper at Knyghton at the time and she was apparently thrilled to find her niece. The story was that she was just about to set off to look for her, when the girl just turned up on the doorstep, but in a terrible state. She had a cut on her head that had turned septic, a twisted ankle and a dangerous fever, possibly pneumonia. She would have died if it hadn't been for the ministrations of Honora Fitzgerald."

"What else to you know about Esme?" Zelah chipped in.

"I'm not sure what you mean." He looked quizzically at her.

"Yes, you do. Ignore what your wife thinks, just tell us."

Alan blushed and gave his wife the same look that Maggie had seen earlier.

Lucy spoke for the first time. "It's all conjecture. Stuff and nonsense about what might have happened in the past. They're all dead and gone. Why disturb everything?"

Maggie caught hold of Zelah's elbow in time to stop her rising out of her chair.

"Lucy isn't interested in family history." Alan paused. "But I am, in mine." There was a determination in his voice, which seemed to surprise his wife, who bit back a further comment. "The past affects the present and the future. We are who we are because of people who went before us and sometimes what happened to them can affect us."

"Yes, I know what you mean," Maggie replied. She ignored the derisive sniff from Lucy as Alan carried on.

"It's just… Look, I know this sounds strange, but I feel that there's things about Esme's story that I need to know, because it's strange and, and… unfinished. Maybe I'm wrong, but it's a gut feeling." He rested his hands on his knees and sat upright. "From what I learned about Esme, she didn't seem to fit with what you'd expect from the daughter of a prostitute deliberately drowned in a horse trough in Weston."

"What kind of things?" Maggie asked.

"Well, she played the piano, for a start. And she was educated, she could already read and write, but she hated school and wouldn't go, not even when she recovered. Moira Davies paid for private tutors, with help from Lady Mary Knyghton, the Countess of Monmouth, who had apparently taken a shine to her."

"And?" Zelah asked with even more emphasis.

"I believe that Moira Davies came to doubt Esme's identity."

"What led you to think that?" Maggie asked.

He paused to gather his thoughts, then began slowly. "I said that Esme married Alan Hughes, the nephew of the butler at the time of her arrival. Well, it seems that Alan's uncle, Mervyn Hughes, always had doubts, but kept them to himself until he died. Just before he died, he spoke to Alan and Moira, who was retired by that time, and told them both. Moira didn't contradict him, just said that it had all worked out for the best.

"Alan was upset, but didn't share his uncle's information with Esme until years later. My grandmother told me that Alan told her all this before he died, and that Esme had been reconciled with her *mother*. I couldn't understand that at all. Moira was her aunt, not her mother, and if her mother was murdered, how could she have been reconciled with her? I wondered if my grandmother was embellishing the story, but I don't think she was. She didn't understand it either."

"Can I talk to your grandmother?" Maggie asked quickly.

"She died six months ago," Alan replied. "When I asked her what her mother's reaction to hearing the news had been, Nana said Esme just went quiet, for weeks apparently. Then she told Alan that she had been having flashbacks for years. None of them made sense to her and she still didn't understand why she was afraid of water, but that perhaps the time had come to find out."

"Do you know when all this happened?"

"Yes, it was around 1936. Nana remembered that. But that was all she could tell me. Whatever Esme found out, never got passed on."

"But your grandmother did say that Esme had been reconciled with her mother?"

"Yes," he replied eagerly. "Can you make anything from it?"

The atmosphere around the table was hushed now, all eyes on Maggie. "Not directly, not as proof, but again, there's a coincidence in the dates. Ruth died in November 1936. She was eighty-two and had been very ill for some time. Louisa Jenkins told me that Ruth hung on at the point of death – none of them understood how or why. At the very end, she had a visitor, unknown to any of them except the local minister, a man called Richard Robinson. Later that day, she died. I think now, from what you've just said, that her visitor may have been Alice."

"But it's just surmise," Nick broke in.

"Yes," Maggie replied with a sigh. "And maybe that's all it will ever be." She turned to Alan. "It's frustrating, isn't it, that we almost know, but we can't prove it definitively."

"Well, if you can't, you can't." Zelah's voice broke the hush. "Isn't there anything else you know about her, Mr Kerr? About her personality? Likes and dislikes? Didn't you ask your grandmother anything about Esme as a person?" The question carried a rebuke, and Alan blushed.

"No, I'm afraid I didn't. At the time I didn't think of it. It didn't matter much to me. Now, of course…" He let the sentence hang in the air.

"But is there anything else?" Zelah was even sharper and Alan turned and frowned at her.

"No, there isn't. Why do you keep asking?"

"She's trying not to prompt you." It was Jack who spoke.

"What do you mean, Jack?" asked Maggie.

But he shook his head. "I think I understand where Zelah's coming from," he said, hesitantly. "Everything's just a guess. To really get to the truth, Mum and Mr Kerr have to have the same part of the story and unless they get to it independently, each one may be unknowingly influenced by the other."

"Clever boy!" Zelah exclaimed. "There is another common part to this story, but until you both tell it, I'm not going to say anything." She waved away Maggie's protest. "If a fourteen-year-old boy can figure it out, then you should be able to, too." Lucy scowled at Zelah and she pulled at Alan's arm to whisper in his ear. Zelah took the chance to speak in a low voice to Maggie. "I told you I've got some more information for you, but I don't want to tell it here and now. We need to talk about Eira Probert."

Maggie nodded, as Alan turned from his wife and addressed the group. "Lucy thinks we've gone as far as we can go today. And we have another engagement this afternoon. There's just one more thing, though. You said you might know about our family naming tradition."

"Again, just a guess." Maggie said hesitantly. "It's based on something I found in the library. I know from my letters that our Alice was upset by the death of a friend. I found a small newspaper article talking about the accidental death of the daughter of a girl who worked for her father, a girl called Esme Ellis. Alice ran away from home within days of Esme's funeral. Esme died in a drowning accident, by the way. I think *she* may have been Alice's best friend.

I also think they looked a lot like each other. I have a photo I can show you. I'm sure it's of Alice, and standing next to her is Esme Ellis. If your Esme was actually Alice, and if she somehow turned up at Knyghton in a poorly state, she may have been confused enough to think that she was called Esme, especially if Moira Davies kept calling her that. And if, as you say, she had flashbacks later in life, it may be possible that she remembered who Esme really was and kept her memory alive by remembering her name. Or, she liked her new life better than the old one, and decided to keep up the pretence." She paused and smiled ruefully. "But it's all just guesswork without any actual proof, I'm sorry to say."

"Yes, I'm afraid it is." He stood up.

Maggie stood to face him. "Here's my telephone number, Alan. I'm going back to work next week, so I'm spending this week doing as much as I can, but my time for research effectively comes to an end by Friday. If I find anything new, I'll let you know at once."

He nodded and shook her hand. They all stood, as Lucy called sharply to Esme. The girls, who had part listened and part chatted, were exchanging online chatroom details. Lucy took Esme's arm and led her away.

Chapter 69

Nick Howell hadn't followed the Kerrs out, and was hovering uncertainly.

"You might as well sit down with us," Zelah said to him. "Anyone want another drink?"

The children nodded enthusiastically and went to the bar with Zelah, leaving Maggie and Nick together.

"So close," Maggie murmured.

Without speaking, he jumped up and ran across the pub lounge with a great lolloping stride, and straight out of the door, leaving Maggie sitting with her mouth open. Zelah had seen him and turned to give Maggie a quizzical look, to which she replied with an open-handed shrug.

"What do you think?" she asked Zelah as they came back to the table with their drinks.

"It's very close, but not enough. Margaret Peach's daughter was called Esme, which could also account for the naming tradition. But I agree with your interpretation. Something terrible happened to Alice when she ran away. She was heading for Weston, but never got there and somehow ended up at Knyghton, more than half dead. If Moira Davies was about to set out to find her niece, she's likely to have called the child 'Esme' and that's why Alice thought it was her name. If she was close to death, she wouldn't have been able to explain or understand. She turned into Esme Peach. 'Flashbacks' suggest she had amnesia. It all fits."

Before Maggie could reply, Nick came running back in and sat down beside them, breathing heavily.

"Something I wanted to ask Alan about. Sorry. Had to catch him before he left."

"Anything useful for us?"

"Yes, I think so. I'll see him tomorrow. I'll let you know."

"What's your take on what we all heard today, Nick?" asked Maggie.

He looked at her, picked up his glass and finished his drink, then looked at a space a few feet above her head. Zelah began to fidget.

"What happened to make Alice run away from home, from her mum and dad? It would have taken her days to walk from that farm to the port. She was only ten."

"Do you think that's important?" Maggie asked.

"Yes. I think it's at the heart of your mystery. Did she fall out with her parents? Or did something else happen that made her run? Was it to do with her friend's death? Is that strange schoolteacher anything to do with it?" He was muttering inner thoughts out loud rather than actually asking her for answers to the questions.

"I think you can solve this by sitting down and putting together everything you know, in a list, point by point," he continued into his glass.

Maggie looked at Zelah, but found only a blank face. "What do you think, Zel? You and I need to talk anyway."

"Why not now?"

As Zelah spoke the wind blew the pub door open, distracting them all. Jack got up and walked across the room to close it. He came back holding his nose. "We aren't thinking of eating here, are we, Mum?"

"I hadn't really thought about it, but why not? It'll save me having to do it at home and it'll make a break in your entertaining schedule."

"Because there's a terrible smell outside, like something's going off." He pulled a disgusted face. "If it's yesterday's food, I'm not going to try today's."

Without a word, Maggie stood up and walked out of the bar, leaving them all staring at her back, except for Zelah. After a few minutes she came back in, hair ruffled into a bird's nest by the wind.

"Same?" Zelah asked.

Maggie nodded, smoothing her hair back into shape with one hand as she picked up her bag with the other.

"Time to go home, I think." She paused for a moment, then turned to Nick.

"Would you like to come with us, have some lunch and hear the rest of this story?"

He looked surprised at being included. "Thank you, but I'm not sure why you're asking me," he mumbled.

"Because you see significant, objective detail in the story and that's what we need, now. But it's up to you."

"Then I will, thank you." He shuffled to his feet. "Follow you in my van, shall I?"

Maggie nodded. "Come on, kids. Let's go and take a look at the Channel before we go."

"I think I'll pass," Alice replied as they walked out. "Too windy."

Maggie gave Alice the car key and she went with Zelah to sit in the car. Maggie and Jack climbed the steps to the top of the high breakwater. Nick walked to his white van. The lettering on the side said, "Howell Window Cleaning". Maggie hadn't thought about what he did for a living.

At the top of the breakwater they had to fight to stand up in the wind blowing straight at them off the Bristol Channel. It was a clear day, with the rising blue-grey coastline of Somerset visible across the expanse of muddy water. Maggie stood for a moment staring at the choppy waves that were rising up the embankment. Lost in her thoughts, she suddenly noticed that Jack was mouthing something at her, but his words were lost in the wind.

"Say that again, I can't hear you."

"I said, I'll keep a close eye out."

"Oh, OK." she responded, not really giving any thought to what he was talking about.

Seeing that he wasn't going to get any more of a reply, he shrugged his shoulders and went back down the steps, leaving Maggie alone. Halfway down he stopped, sniffed and screwed up his nose.

"Mum!"

She turned to look down at him, held her forefinger to her lip, and ran down the steps to join him. He opened his mouth to try to engage her in conversation, but she hushed him again and pointed to the car, where Alice was sitting with Zelah.

"We have to get home. It's safer there. Then we'll talk."

Chapter 70

Maggie organised a makeshift lunch. The force of the wind had increased and rainclouds loomed heavy. It was too blustery to eat in the garden, so they sat around the kitchen table, chatting a little, but mostly pondering what they had heard. After lunch Maggie led the way into the sitting room. Nick stood hesitantly in the door until Maggie nodded him to the settee. Jack and Alice decided to go to the computer, to see if they could resume Alice's conversation with Esme Kerr.

Once they were safely out of earshot, Maggie turned to Nick. "Before we start," she began, "I want to tell you the parts I missed out at the pub. There's another… dimension to this story."

For the next few minutes she spoke about her connection with Ruth, the events Alice claimed to have witnessed, the troubled dreams, the likeness in the photographs, and the events at the graveside. As she finished, she looked at him, waiting for a comment, but none came.

"Well, what do you think?"

He looked puzzled. "I think there's another dimension to this story."

"Aren't you at all sceptical?"

He thought for a moment. "At Knyghton," he said slowly to the carpet, "I've heard strange stories. Some are nonsense, just imagination and nerves. But others aren't. There's seven hundred

407

years of history there. I've had strange experiences. There's another dimension. That's all, really."

"But," he went on, to Maggie's surprise, "what about that smell? It bothered you."

"I've smelled it before, when I was almost pushed off the boat. It's vile."

"Like something dying?"

"I imagine it's what gangrene must smell like. And the boat wasn't the first time, either."

Zelah looked up at this. "You never said!"

"I didn't connect it until today. There was a very slight whiff, the day I found the gravestone. But nothing like as strong as it is now. Like a distant echo, not the sound itself. You know what I mean?"

"How much stronger has it got?"

"Today, for me, it was overpowering, Nick. I don't think Jack got the half of it."

"Hmmm."

Maggie could see Zelah frowning. "Anyway, Zelah, we've come to the point. Eira Probert."

Zelah sat forwards, clenching her fists. "I told you that something rang a bell, something Martin's dreadful old Irish mother used to talk about?"

"Vaguely. I don't remember you telling me what it was, though."

"I wanted to be sure of the story first."

Looking at Zelah's face, Maggie felt anxious. She hadn't known Zelah long, but had never seen her display pity, or anxiety. Of course, she knew it was there, but she kept it well hidden. Now, her friend was looking at her with tense eyes.

408

"You're worrying me."

Nick suddenly sat bolt upright on the settee and slapped his hands on his knees. For the first time he looked directly at Maggie's face.

"It's a hunter!"

Zelah's exasperation burst directly at him. "Let me finish, damn it!"

He looked over at her in amazement. "But it is, isn't it. It's stalking her family." It was an affirmation, not a question.

For a moment they stared at each other. To Maggie's amazement, it was Zelah who gave way. "Yes, I believe it is. It's stalking her."

"What are you two talking about? I'm not being stalked." Maggie looked from one to the other and back again, puzzling to understand their horrified expressions.

"Not the kind of stalker you mean," Nick replied. "Not some pervert following you around, peeping through your windows."

"What then?" She looked to Zelah for an explanation.

"It's a legend. Martin's mother used to talk about it as 'the old bad luck'. And when people talk about being *haunted*, what they sometimes are is *hunted*." As Maggie put out her hand to remonstrate, Zelah ignored her and went on.

"You know how some families just seem to have problem after problem, tragedy after tragedy?" Maggie nodded guardedly. "Well, sometimes it's more than just coincidence. It's something that hunts one particular family. I think Ruth's family was a victim."

Zelah's voice had sunk lower as she spoke and she had leaned further forwards at the final sentence.

"Think about what you've learned about your past," Zelah added. "Tragedies, disappearances, drowning. All with the same

409

pattern. With one common link. A school teacher called Eira Probert. Think about what Ruth's letter said. She saw the teacher at her husband's funeral, unchanged after over thirty-odd years."

"The photograph!" Maggie jumped up and ran out of the room.

"She found a photograph of Ruth's Alice and another girl we think is probably Esme Ellis. A school photograph," Zelah explained.

"This is strong," Nick spoke to Zelah. "Some of those shapes at the house are just shadows, unfinished parts of a human body. They can't get themselves out of one place, or find the people they're looking for. If they're glimpsed they can scare people, but that's all they can manage. But not this one."

"No," Zelah replied quietly. "Not this one. Maggie inherited Ruth's memory, and once she actively remembered, she created the way for it to come back again."

"They shouldn't be here, of course." He paused for a moment, then looked directly at Zelah. They seemed to be finishing each other's thoughts.

"I've been researching for years. I don't really know what they are. They can reform themselves from pure energy when the conditions are right until they look like us and talk like us. They don't die, like us. They disintegrate and re-form. Over and over." He paused for a moment. Zelah didn't comment. "And it can't be stopped. They are malicious and evil. And the worst thing for Maggie and her family is…"

The sound of Maggie's footsteps made them turn their heads towards the door. She ran back in and threw herself into the armchair.

"Here it is!" She held out the photo towards Zelah. Nick moved off the settee and the three of them gathered around it, staring at the picture of the class of 1883. None of them noticed Jack entering the room behind Maggie. He stood just inside the doorway, watching their heads bend together over the picture.

"It's her, isn't it?" Although he had spoken quietly, all three adults turned to look at him.

"You've seen it already. You know the likeness to Alice," Maggie replied, frowning.

He looked as if he was about to speak, but Zelah got in first. "What's the connection, Jack? You talked about it in the pub. What do you know?"

He walked into the room and sat on the floor in front of Maggie, looking up at her.

"They were talking about it in the pub. You weren't listening, but I was. They thought it was a coincidence, but when I heard your conversation just now, I knew it wasn't. They're chatting about it now on the internet."

He looked at Zelah with an agonised expression. "It is her, isn't it? What's she going to do?"

"What are you talking about, Jack? I don't understand what you are talking about?" Maggie raised her voice, angry with him. "You're not making sense!"

"Yes, he is," Zelah snapped at her. "He's put it all together quicker than you have. Alice has been having trouble at school with a teacher, hasn't she? Did you ever ask the teacher's name?"

"It was a teaching assistant, not a teacher, and she's gone now." Maggie looked from Zelah to Jack. "I don't remember the name. It was a nickname, wasn't it, that the kids used to call her."

411

"Bigbutt," he replied. "They called her Iva Bigbutt."

As she stared at him, realisation began to dawn, with a feeling in her stomach like slithering snakes. "What was her actual name, Jack?"

They hadn't heard Alice come running down the stairs. She burst into the living room finger pointing at Jack. "Where did you go?" she accused her brother. "You'll never guess what, now!"

Maggie stood up and took both of Alice's hands. "What was your nasty teaching assistant's name, Alice?"

"You prick, you told before I got a chance!" Alice struggled to get her hands out of Maggie's grip and take a swipe at Jack.

"What was the name, Alice?"

The little girl paused and looked fully at her mother. She never normally got away without punishment for using bad language.

"Why are you looking at me like that?" When Maggie didn't answer, she looked at Jack, then at Zelah and Nick. "Why are you all looking at me like that?"

"What was the name, Alice?"

"Her real name was Miss Probert, but we called her…"

"We know what you called her. Did you talk about her to Esme Kerr?"

"Yes, isn't it amazing, she was at Esme's school, on Friday." She smirked in satisfaction. "What's the matter with you all? You look like someone's just died or something!" When nobody answered, she tutted at them and walked out of the room, calling back, "I'm going back to speak to Esme. At least she answers me."

Maggie turned back to Jack. "You've seen her. Look at the photo. Is it her?"

"Yes." He looked as if he was about to be sick. Maggie bent down and put her arms around him. He was shaking.

"She's gone, Jack. She left the school. Alice is safe." He nodded. "Are you going to tell Alice, Mum?"

"No!" Her reply was emphatic and Zelah protested immediately.

"You have to tell her, Maggie. It's only fair!"

"She's ten!" Maggie shouted back. "If the thing's gone, she doesn't need to know! She's just a child." Maggie slumped back in her chair. "When she first saw this photo she knew she'd seen someone else in it, before. I didn't question it at the time. But it must have been the teacher. The face is faded. I didn't think."

"For God's sake, don't start beating yourself up." Zelah turned to Nick. "She does this, blames herself for something that isn't remotely her fault."

"We all do," he replied. "Just natural, when it's one of your kids. Thing is, what are you going to do now? If you don't want to tell her, that is." He went back to the settee and settled himself back, staring at the ceiling.

"I can't say," Maggie replied, feeling dejected. "I can't just react to stuff like this. I need time to think it all over." She turned to Zelah and Nick. "Would you mind going now? I need some quiet time."

Nick jumped up immediately and made for the door. "I'll call you tomorrow. I've still got to sort out that thing with Alan, that I think will help you." And he was gone, banging the front door behind him.

Zelah hadn't moved. "If you're going to try to rationalise this, don't bother. Don't question it, just accept it as truth. Think about everything you've learned, think about what Louisa told you and what's in the letters. It all fits." She stood up.

"It wasn't supposed to be like this," Maggie suddenly broke into a sob. "It was supposed to be fun, exciting, researching history. Not this!"

"If you want sympathy, I'm not the person. If you want support, I'm not going anywhere, apart from home." Zelah paused at the door. "I'll let myself out. I'll call you in the morning. Tell Alice!"

Her heels echoed on the tiles in the hall, as Maggie and Jack sat on the floor with their arms around each other.

"Should we tell her, Mum?" he whispered. "No," Maggie replied, more firmly than she felt. "Tell her what?" Alice asked, from the doorway.

Chapter 71

The wind had worked itself up into a gale and lashing rain slammed into the windows and rattled the frames. As the evening drew in, Maggie found logs in the shed and lit a fire in the grate. Although it was still light, they closed the curtains and toasted bread and crumpets, sitting on the hearthrug in front of the flames.

"Apparently, it's the tail end of a hurricane," Maggie explained. "I just saw it on the news."

"This has been a great day," Alice murmured to Maggie, leaning against her shoulder and staring at the flickering lights. "I found a new friend."

"A whole family of them," Maggie replied.

"Can I invite Esme over sometime, to see my summerhouse?"

"Of course. If it's still standing tomorrow," she joked, as the entire back window rattled alarmingly. Alice clapped her hands to her mouth. "Don't worry, Alice. The summerhouse will be fine. I'll be speaking to Nick tomorrow. He thinks he's onto some more information for us. I'll get Alan's number."

"Do you like him?" Jack, lying full length on the settee, looked up from his car magazine.

"He seems OK. Not sure about his wife, but I liked Esme."

"No, I mean Nick."

"Yes, he seems OK, too. He likes history."

"That's not what I meant, Mum."

Maggie turned her face to the fire. "It's the only question I'm answering."

"Why does he wear gloves all of the time?" Alice asked. "I have no idea," Maggie replied. "Perhaps he has something wrong with his hands, that embarrasses him. I'm not going to ask, either. Right! Time for bed."

Ignoring the protests, she ushered them out of the room. Once they were both in their rooms and ready to sleep, she went back down to the sitting room, dragged her chair from the back window to the fire, and settled herself down, knowing that she wouldn't sleep for many hours that night, if at all.

Maggie finally fell asleep just before dawn, with the result that she was sluggish and bad tempered when it was time to get up a couple of hours later. They were, predictably, late. After snapping at Jack and shouting at Alice, she returned home from the school run feeling edgy.

The storm had finally abated, the garden forlorn in its aftermath. The roses had borne the brunt of the wind's ferocious battering, petals strewn like confetti across the lawn.

Angry, billowing clouds still rushed across the sky as violent gusts of wind whipped the bushes to the ground. But patches of blue were visible here and there and at least the rain had stopped.

This time next week, I'll be facing another kind of storm, she thought as she wandered around the garden in her wellingtons, cup of tea and ball of twine in hand, surveying the damage. "Battering me down, just like you, you poor little things." She bent to tie up some delphiniums that were lying on the earth.

"Pathetic!" she muttered. "Get over yourself, Maggie Gilbert. Don't be such a whinger." The wind swirled around her suddenly, making her check over her shoulder.

The phone rang. It was Fiona, and Maggie spent a futile half hour rebuffing her sister's enthusiasm and offers of help. She was too tired not to let Fiona collect the kids for the first week of her new job. That could change when she was more up to arguing with her sister.

The phone rang again. Gritting her teeth for a continuation of the conversation with Fee, she picked it up. It was Nick.

"I spoke to Alan this morning. He's got what I told you about. You need to come and see."

For a few minutes, Maggie struggled to focus. Her mind had been so full of thoughts of the monster that was Eira Probert she had forgotten about whatever it was that Nick believed would help.

"OK, when? Today, please? It has to be this week and for me, the sooner the better."

"Lunchtime? At Knyghton?"

"Yes, if it's early. I must be back by three."

"How about half twelve?"

"That's fine. Can I invite Zelah?"

"Of course. See you later."

Maggie rang Zelah, and arranged to meet her at the entrance to Knyghton at twelve thirty, then went upstairs to shower and wash her hair.

* * *

Maggie arrived early. Zelah wasn't due for another quarter of an hour, so she headed to the formal gardens. The gardeners were busy repairing the storm damage. She stopped for quick pleasantries, then wandered around the paths and the beautiful flower borders. When she was at school the beds weren't tended

417

and nurtured as they now were. The mixture of colours, textures and sweet smells was relaxing and she wished that she could develop just a small scrap of the talent that produced such beauty. She was leaning over a gate, craning her neck to see around to where the greenhouses stood, when she heard her name called.

"Nick's wandering round looking for you! I thought you'd be here." Zelah shouted across.

"Why?"

"Peaceful place to think. That's what you've been doing non-stop since yesterday, I presume."

Maggie smiled in response. "Let's go and find him, before he gets agitated."

As she and Zelah walked under the stone arch and around to the back entrance of the house, they met Nick coming towards them, waving.

"Alan's here. He's up in the archive room." He looked excited, like a child with a secret.

Nick took them through the housekeeper's room, up the back stairs to the top of the house, and into the archive area where Alan stood chatting to Ted Morgan.

As soon as he saw her, Alan held out his hand to Maggie. "Esme had a smashing time yesterday. She'd love to meet up with Alice again."

Maggie noticed that he hadn't mentioned his wife and was deliberately avoiding Zelah.

"Alice said the same. I gather they were chatting on their computers last night."

"Yes," Alan replied. "Esme tells me they've had the same teaching assistant, which is a bit of a coincidence, isn't it? And

Esme didn't like her either." He beamed at Maggie, who tried to smile back.

"Thank goodness it was only for a day." She glanced at Zelah who was frowning, and Nick, who had stuck out his bottom lip, like a pouting schoolboy.

"Anyway, what do you have to show me?" She went on quickly, before Zelah could cut in. Maggie suspected that Zelah would want to reveal what they knew to Alan for his daughter's sake. But Maggie still wasn't ready to tell Alice, and wanted to tell her before confiding in Alan.

"Well, it's something that Nana left behind. We found it in amongst her stuff, wrapped up in tissue paper and tied with a silk ribbon. It's such a grubby old thing, we couldn't understand why she had treated it with such care."

In his left hand he had been holding a small carrier bag, from which he now took a paper bag. From inside the bag he carefully slid out a small package, so small that it fitted into the palm of his hand. Maggie, Zelah and Nick gathered closely around. Maggie could see that the tissue paper was faded to a dirty off-white, but the ribbon retained its rich blood-red colour.

"We know from the diary this was the only thing that great-grandmother Esme had when she arrived at Knyghton. Her aunt said that it was clasped so tight in her hand that they almost had to break her fingers to get it out. Moira almost burned it, but decided to keep it and gave it back to Esme. Esme wanted it kept in the family, so she gave it to Nana and she passed it down."

A gentle tug on the ribbon caused it to fall away. Alan unwrapped the tissue paper with the tip of his thumb and forefinger, holding it as if he expected it to melt like a snowflake in a warm hand.

419

On the palm of his hand lay a square of cloth, small and thinner than the tissue paper. Once it would have been white, but time had faded it to grey. The edges were frayed on three of the four sides.

"It's a rag," Zelah muttered.

Maggie leaned in so closely that her nose almost touched the material.

"I think it was linen," she said. "May I?" She gently rubbed the material. "It's very fine. I think this was a handkerchief. And," she paused to steady her nerves, "perhaps it could be 'the' handkerchief. Do you remember, Zelah?"

Zelah looked puzzled, but then she snapped her fingers. "The little thing that she took with her. It could be."

Maggie looked at the two men, who were frowning at her and Zelah. "One of the letters I inherited from Louisa Jenkins. It was written by my great-grandmother Ruth to her sister Mary Anne Picton, but never posted. For some reason she left it among her possessions. In the letter she says that Alice took with her a handkerchief that Ruth had embroidered with her initials. It was a gift," she added, a lump in her throat. Quickly she turned to the piece of material. "Look, in the corner. Have you noticed this, Alan?"

With her index figure she traced over what looked like a thin dirty line. "It looks like two sides of a triangle. Could it be the shape of an A? What do you all think?"

They all bent in to look, then Nick's head shot up. "Machine," he said and pointed to what looked like a small photocopier in the corner of the room. "Got it just recently. Might show us."

Alan nodded slowly. "I can make out something now you've pointed to it. I never saw it before, thought it was just a stain in the material."

"You didn't know that you were looking for it," she replied, following Nick to the corner.

He carefully placed the piece of material underneath the cover of what looked like a photocopier, then told them all to stand back. "New kind of X-ray scanner. No danger, very low level, but best be sure. Not supposed to get too close."

They all moved to join him on the other side of the room, where he picked up a small remote control. He pressed a button on the hand-held pad. "It'll go straight to the computer." He gestured towards his desk.

"That's impressive!" Zelah whispered, "Must be worth a bit!"

"Gift from a former pupil. Did quite well for herself and likes the house. She wanted to help us with our research." A ping from the computer told them that the result was ready. They moved quickly across the room and crowded around the screen. "Moment of truth," he whispered.

The screen filled with shades of grey and white, a light square in the middle of a dark grey background. Nick focused on the corner where the marks were and enlarged the section.

Maggie gasped. There, as clear as it would have been when they had first been sewn in, were the initials A.R.J. Alice Ruth Jones. She felt a tear well up and run down her cheek.

"I found you," she murmured. "You were lost, but I found you."

Nick looked curiously at her. "You feel like you know her?"

"Yes," replied Maggie. "It's become close, almost like I was looking for my own daughter in a maze of truths and half-truths. I can't imagine what Ruth must have gone through, never knowing if she was alive or not. But at least she knew at the end. That's what we think, isn't it, Alan? Now that we know for sure that Alice and Esme were the same person, and your great-grandmother was reconciled with her mother, somehow. They found each other."

He half smiled, half grimaced. "Yes, I suppose so. Until I met you I don't think I really thought of them as living, breathing people. They were just interesting names from my past. But the last couple of days have brought them to life."

"Can you print that out for me, Nick?" Maggie asked.

"No problem," he replied.

Maggie spoke to Alan again. "I brought this to show you." She rifled in her handbag and brought out the school picture of Alice and Esme. Alan peered at it and whistled. "It's the spitting image of your daughter, isn't it? And I can see a resemblance to my Esme. Oh my goodness! That woman at the back looks just like the teaching assistant that Esme disliked so much."

He looked puzzled.

"You met her?" Maggie asked quickly.

"Just last Friday," he replied, surprised at the anxiety in her voice. "I had to pick Esme up as she wasn't well. She was with this woman," he pointed to the picture, then grinned. "Well, she was with someone who looks rather like this woman. Strange, isn't it?"

Zelah and Nick glanced rapidly at each other. Zelah asked Alan, "Do you have any photographs of your great-grandmother?"

"I'm not sure. I have some old photos, somewhere in the attic. After yesterday, I plan to go and look for them. I'll see if I can find them tonight." He paused, then said enthusiastically, "This is like an adventure, isn't it?"

No-one replied.

Chapter 72

They made their way in silence back to the car park. Maggie spoke first. "Time to go. I have to be back to fetch Jack and Alice from school. Zelah are you coming with me?"

"No, something I need to do."

Maggie waited but she didn't elucidate.

"Oh well, speak to you later then. Alan, let me know if you find any photos."

She started to walk towards her car, when Nick called out to her. "Be careful, Maggie."

She frowned, thought about speaking but changed her mind, half waved an acknowledgement, and left the grounds.

Driving home, Maggie thought over Nick's parting remark. She understood his concern but as far as she was aware, there was no imminent danger. But she rang his mobile anyway.

"What did you mean?" she began without preamble.

"Eira will be waiting, somewhere," he replied immediately. "Just be prepared, that's all I'm saying. Anywhere, any time." He paused, then, "Stand firm, Maggie. Don't feed her with your fear. You know what I mean."

"Yes. No. OK. Thanks." She was too tired to think.

"No problem."

Back at home she had almost an hour before setting out again for school. Alice was going to be late today. Her class had been to visit the comprehensive school at the top of the hill where they would be starting in September and they were going to walk back to the primary school afterwards. Parents had been told to be at the school at three thirty. Jack had agreed to walk down and wait at the gate.

After the revelations of the day, Maggie was restless. She sat down to study the X-ray of the handkerchief. The letters were symmetrical and exact, although she knew that they would have been sewn by hand, with no pattern to follow. She imagined Ruth sewing under lamplight in the dark evenings leading up to Alice's birthday. A heavy weariness came into her eyes and she found herself fighting to keep them open.

"Just for a moment," a seductive voice whispered. "Just a few minutes rest, eyelids closed, not sleep." This was a familiar voice, an old deceiver which Maggie knew would lull her into a treacherous doze if she wasn't careful. But, she was in control, she could just close them for a moment…

She came to with the image of a half-formed face coming closer to her and the hint of a very bad smell. In panic, she looked around for the time, as the clock in the hall told her it was half past the hour. She had slept for almost thirty minutes and Jack and Alice would be waiting at the gate.

In alarm, Maggie grabbed her keys, ran out of the house and jumped into the car. She made the journey in record time, despite the rain and wind having started again. She hoped to disguise her tardiness among other stragglers and their parents. But there was only one mother there, anxiously peering down the drive from under a small umbrella. There were also plenty of parking spaces. Ominous.

She vaguely knew the woman, the mother of a girl in Alice's class. "What's happened? Have they been delayed?" she asked breathlessly, locking the car with a backwards jerk of the key.

"No," the woman replied, hesitatingly. "I think they were early. Something wrong with the teacher today, so the assistant took them. Beverley's just gone back for her homework."

"Assistant? What assistant?"

"Didn't you know? Mr Rees's mother had a fall at the weekend, so they got a supply teacher and a supply assistant in for a couple of days. But…" she broke off as Beverley came running back up the drive and stopped, panting, in front of them.

"I can't get in. The classroom door's already locked." The girl put her hands on her knees, trying to catch her breath, and looked up at Maggie. "Alice left a few minutes ago, Mrs Gilbert, with Miss Probert. I think she was giving Alice a lift home, because you were going to be late."

As the words came out of the girl's mouth, Maggie began to run. Rain lashed into her eyes, making her peer half-blind to keep to the path.

"We were told to wait here!" the mother called out behind her.

Half way down the drive she saw Jack, entering at the far gate. He stopped, stared at her and waved. She flung her arm up, but didn't hesitate. At full pelt, Maggie rounded the corner. Jack followed her at a run.

The front door to the school was locked. She slammed her fingers on the bell and intercom buttons. No-one responded, but a cleaner passed in the corridor that led from the assembly hall to the classrooms. Maggie banged on the glass, her heart hammering faster than her fists. The woman looked at her, a puzzled expression on her previously vacant face. Maggie wanted to scream at her, but knew that she had to keep herself looking as calm as possible so that she'd open the door. The cleaner watched her for a few agonising seconds. Then she walked to the door and opened it.

"Yes?"

"My daughter – Alice Gilbert – she left with Miss Probert. Where did they go?" She was shouting now and the cleaner was stepping back from her. "Where did they go?" she yelled again, aware of doors opening close by.

The cleaner gripped her mop and shook her head. She had her back to the wall and Maggie was in her face.

"Mrs Gilbert, what on earth are you shouting about?" The voice came from behind her, and she turned to see Mr Philips, the small, bald-headed headmaster standing at her shoulder. His voice was stern, but his face showed concern.

"Alice! Miss Probert! Where did they go?"

"They went home, Mrs Gilbert, as you requested. Although," he paused, nervously, "I didn't understand why you specifically asked for Miss Probert."

Maggie looked at him with a confused expression. "I didn't ask anything. I didn't call."

"Now just a minute," he spoke firmly. "You rang us not twenty minutes ago to say you'd been delayed, and you asked that Miss Probert take Alice home. You said you'd already agreed it with both of them, and that it might happen because of your work."

Maggie's expression of horror sent him a couple of paces back.

"That wasn't me! I didn't call you!"

"Mrs Gilbert, please, I know your voice!"

Maggie's tone changed to cold anger. "That wasn't me and she isn't who you think she is. Now, where did they go!"

The headmaster's voice reduced to a whisper. "She said she was taking Alice home."

Maggie stepped back, running a hand violently through her hair. "Oh my God! Oh my God! Where could she have taken her? Where?"

Jack was standing with his back to the front door, staring at his mother. Maggie felt herself suddenly weak at the knees. Panic set in. She put her head in her hands and was about to scream, when Jack's voice penetrated through the fog of fear. He took her elbow and shook it, and she looked at him.

"Think, Mum. You know what's she's going to do. Just calm yourself down and think! Think!"

Maggie looked around at the teachers who had gathered in the hallway, all staring at her, no-one speaking. It seemed like an age as she went from face to face. The supply teacher. The man who coached the football team whose name she could never remember. Mrs Frost who had taken them pond-dipping.

Taking Alice home. It came to her.

She shook herself free from Jack's grasp. "I know where she is. Call Zelah, and stay here where it's safe." she shouted to Jack as she ran out of the main door. "And you," she said, pointing at the bewildered head teacher, "call the police! Tell them to look in The Pond. Alice didn't go willingly. Probert isn't who you think she is!"

Chapter 73

Maggie calculated that Eira had about a ten-minute start on her. It was enough time to drown Alice, but first she had to get an unwilling and feisty little girl to the water. She didn't know how Eira Probert had done it, but she was certain that Alice hadn't gone willingly. She must have been overpowered somehow. She was just a small, slight girl, but nevertheless, the hunter wouldn't be able to hurry along a rough path carrying Alice's weight. Which gave Maggie a chance. She knew the route. And she had not a moment's doubt of where she would find them. Less than ten minutes after leaving the school, Maggie reached the car park that led to The Pond.

Her shoes weren't ideal and as she tripped and stumbled through the ruts and over the bigger stones Maggie cursed that she hadn't had time to change into trainers. As she rounded the final bend thick clouds dropped down in a fog, cutting her off from the world below the mountain. Fine drizzle clouded her eyes. There was nothing now, except Maggie and the path and, at last, The Pond.

The only sound in her ears was her own breathy wheezing and her pounding heart, as she stopped abruptly, seeing Eira Probert trying to force Alice's head under the water.

"Alice!" Maggie's scream caused Eira to look up. It was just a second, but it was enough. With the pressure off her head Alice was able to push her head out of the water, and now she was struggling madly. But Eira was too strong and she'd turned her back on Maggie to resume her monstrous task. Maggie saw the panic in Alice's eyes, as her daughter tried to reach out for her mother.

There was a small rock in Maggie's hand. She had no idea how it had got there, but with all of her might, she threw it at Eira. It landed in the water a foot or so away, next to her. The sound of it turned the hunter's head for just a moment. Maggie had covered the distance between them and grabbed Alice's arm.

They tussled, and Maggie was able to pull her daughter a few feet from the water's edge. Pulling at Alice, Maggie feared she was going to rip her daughter's arm off. She could see Alice's eyes rolling in her head. She swore and shouted Alice's name and, for a moment, she seemed to respond, but Maggie realised that she was too weak. The hunter was incredibly strong, and they were both being pulled back towards The Pond.

Maggie screamed her daughter's name long and slowly one more time. It was enough. Alice's head sprang up. She looked at her mother, then at Eira. Taking aim, she landed a kick on Eira's shin. The force of it took her by surprise and she loosened her grip just enough for Maggie to wrench Alice away. As she pulled her daughter behind her, Maggie hurled out her arm, catching Eira on the shoulder, sending her stumbling into the water, where she sat, neck-deep, staring back at them.

The smell hit Maggie. She knew it, the foul, gangrenous, overpowering stench. The smell of rotten, decomposing flesh, that made her gag. She had smelled it for weeks without knowing what it was, until now.

Maggie backed away, shielding Alice and pushing her back towards the path. "My phone's in the car. Run and call the police! I'll handle Eira," she whispered to Alice. Alice looked startled, but for once did as she was told without questioning her mother.

Eira Probert stood up. As she walked out of The Pond, Maggie could see that the water had made no impact, she was completely dry. It seemed to Maggie that the monster had grown. Her skin was the colour of putty, her enormous hands reached out for Maggie's face. Eira was smiling, but with a trace of uncertainty. It was the smile that finally made Maggie remember what Louisa had tried to tell her about Eira needing the fear. Then she was calm. She would not give up her child. She stood firm, raised herself up, and spoke.

"I know everything about you, Eira Probert" she said, dodging the swiping hands. "I know how you drowned the children in Carmarthen. I know you drowned Esme Ellis. And I know now you tried to kill Alice. But you failed then, and you've failed now."

"I don't think so, Maggie Gilbert." Eira whispered softly, in a menacing child-like voice.

"I am not afraid, Eira Probert. I know what you are and I do not fear you."

"I see you are going to get in my way. So I must take you first."

"Good. So, it's you and me now."

For what seemed like an age, the only sounds were the pattering of rain on the water and a low hiss coming from Eira Probert's mouth, which was opening wide Maggie breathed unhurriedly, not thinking, knowing somehow that the actions she would take would come instinctively. With slow steps, she walked forwards, looking directly into Eira's eyes. When they were no more than an arm's length apart, she stopped. The hiss ended. Eira opened her mouth and roared. Maggie saw inside was like a pool of blood. A red mist developed over the hunter's eyes.

"If this is meant to frighten me, you're going to be disappointed. I know all about you. I know what you are. And I am not afraid of you," said Maggie in as dispassionate a tone as she could manage, shaking her head and smiling.

A great gust of wind hit the water and rattled the struts of the jetty, momentarily distracting Maggie.

When she turned her eyes back, Eira had edged backwards. "Ha! Got you going!" Maggie felt a flare of excitement.

"What do we do now, Miss Probert? You won't have my Alice. You didn't get Ruth's Alice either, did you?"

She saw a flash of red eyes, like an explosion.

"I got what I wanted. They never saw her again. I always get what I want." Maggie was surprised by her petulant, childish snivel.

"No," she said adamantly. "She got away from you; she hid, and she lived out a full life. A very happy life. She had children. And she met her mother again. You failed completely!"

"I did not fail! I never fail!" The voice was intense, but her shoulders fell slightly.

"You failed, Eira. I tracked her down, and her family. You may be strong, and a little bit scary, but you aren't clever. You've made some simple mistakes."

Maggie walked towards Eira, one hand raised, shaking her forefinger back and fore, and tutting, backing Eira towards the water. An overpowering dose of stench shot across at Maggie, carried on trails of yellow phosphorescent-like string. Maggie simply held her nose. She knew now that she had rattled Eira. Her bluff had worked. She hadn't known how Ruth and Alice's story had ended, but she did now. She didn't need to find any documents to confirm the story, Eira's reaction was enough evidence.

"God, you stink. But that's the essence of what you are, Eira. Big mistake, to have your photograph taken. I can warn my family now. They'll be able to see what you look like, forever."

"I will wait. I can wait. There are others."

"Yes, you found Esme Kerr, didn't you? You went to her school and then you saw her at the pub, and she and Alice do resemble each other. I'm betting you don't quite know who she is, though, do you?"

The hunter growled in puzzlement and thwarted anger.

"She is related. She'll make a good consolation prize."

"You won't get anything there. You wanted to hurt Ruth and her family, but you got it wrong."

"I am never wrong." A leer appeared on the thin lips, but the rapid movement of her red eyes told of mounting uncertainty.

I'm winning, Maggie thought excitedly. *She needs me to grovel and be terrified of her, she feeds on it. She needs the knowledge of success that comes with it. She can't keep herself together when she knows she's failed!*

She pressed her advantage. The hunter's feet were in the water by now, and she glanced down with a puzzled expression as she felt the cold, staring at something she didn't seem to understand. Maggie followed the stare and her eyes widened in amazement as she saw that the feet were wet. Maggie had broken through!

"I don't know why you p icked my family. I don't know how to finally stop you. Yet. But I'll find out. Somehow I'll find out how to stop you ever coming back. I am not afraid of you, now or ever. I am stronger than you will ever be. And you will never understand why." She pointed to the floor. "Look, Eira. Your feet are wet. You are starting to merge with this world. The end of you is starting." She smiled triumphantly.

She glared at Maggie. She twitched, raised a hand, then lowered it. Eira seemed bewildered. Then a look of horror came over the hunter's face and she put one hand to her brow. A yellow teardrop rolled down Eira's cheek. Maggie watched the slow rolling progress. It dropped onto the grass with a squishing

sound, followed by another, then another. She wasn't crying…
Eira was disintegrating. Robert Pugh had seen a hint of it after
Eira had failed to find Alice at Newport dock. In slow motion the
woman's face began to distort as it gradually collapsed in front of
Maggie's eyes. Maggie was transfixed, rooted to the spot, watching
the dissolution until the smell and the running slime became so
horrific that Maggie was forced to turn her head away, choking

"If you think you're escaping, think again, Eira. I will always
be in your way!" She was shouting now.

In the background, she could hear Alice shouting too, pulling
at her arm.

Summoning a huge effort against the stench and the miasma,
she raised her voice again. "You won't be able to come back near
my family. I'll make sure of that!" Now she was yelling at the top
of her voice, arms flung out, fingers pointing. "You will never hunt
another member of my family! I am greater than you are, and
I have beaten you!"

The yellow slime ran faster to the grass, with putrid, nauseating
squishes and thumps.

Maggie and Alice were becoming enveloped in a yellow fog
and Maggie fell to her knees, clasping her daughter close to her.
As she hit the ground, with her hands to her nose and mouth, she
heard the sound of a gargled snarl that faded away. Then silence.

The darker clouds had gone and the rain had stopped. The
sky was clearing. At the edge of The Pond there was a flat yellow
stain. Maggie and Alice stood and walked slowly towards it. As
they approached, the stain sank into the grass, and was gone.

Maggie lowered herself down slowly, staring into the water.
She pulled Alice down into her lap and they sat for what seemed
like a long time, wordlessly, hearts thumping, bodies trembling.

"Mum! Let go of my arm!" The voice seemed to be a long way away. Maggie was staring into the distance, and had to shake her head to bring herself back.

"What?"

Alice was trying to pull away. "You're hurting me. Please let go of my arm."

Maggie was gripping Alice's forearm so tightly that her fingers had bruised her. She pulled her hand away, as if it had been struck by lightning.

Her daughter was looking at her strangely, and Maggie opened her mouth to speak, but nothing came out.

Alice shook her gently. "I'm OK, Mum. She's gone. Let's get out of here."

Maggie watched as Alice pulled herself to her feet, then took Maggie gently by the elbow and helped her to stand. She managed to raise herself, but her legs couldn't take her weight and she began to wobble, reaching out for something with which to steady herself and save herself from falling. Alice moved in and put her arms around her mother, holding her determinedly.

"It's OK, really, Mum. We're fine. Let's go now. We'll walk slowly. You've got to get strong. You're going to have to drive home."

Maggie nodded. She began to move her legs, tripping, holding onto Alice for balance. Nothing more was said until they reached the car.

"Did you call the police?" Maggie remembered that she'd told her daughter to run.

"I didn't come down here. It was too scary in the fog, so I hid. I saw what you did to Miss Probert, Mum. You were amazing. Are you going to be OK?"

"I'll be alright now. Just a few minutes, then I'll drive us back."

* * *

As they pulled up at the school, they could see the group Maggie had left standing outside the school entrance. She parked the car and walked slowly past them, into the entrance hall.

"Mrs Gilbert! What the hell is going on?" The headmaster stared belligerently at Maggie. "Where's Miss Probert?"

"She's gone. Don't let her back again, Mr Philips. She's not who she says she is." She began to laugh shakily, hysterically, then slumped down onto the nearest small chair, as her legs gave way. Alice sat on the floor beside her.

"Mum! Mum!" Jack was screaming from the doorway. "Are you OK? Where've you been?"

Maggie drew a long deep breath, and then exhaled slowly. "Yes, I'm fine. I'll explain later."

"The police are here, in my office." Mr Philips had recovered his authority. He turned to the cleaner. "Open the door and windows. Let that dreadful smell out."

The cleaner crossed to the door in front of Maggie, glancing at her with a mixture of curiosity and fear.

Maggie shrugged. "Sorry, I think we may have brought some of that back with us."

Jack walked up to his mother and hugged her.

"Zelah's on her way," he whispered. "She rang my mobile just as I got into the school. I told her and she screamed." He paused. "I think… I think she thought you and Alice were going to die."

435

"There was never any chance of that. Really," Maggie said firmly. "Never any chance. As soon as I got Alice out of her grasp and into mine, she knew that she'd lost, this time."

"I don't understand what you're talking about. I don't understand anything," said Alice. It was no more than a whisper, but it pierced Maggie's heart like a needle.

"I'm so sorry, Alice. You've been so patient. I'm going to tell you all about it when we get home. But there's some explaining to do here, first."

The three Gilberts stood together. As Maggie went towards the headmaster's office she found that her legs were still like jelly, each ankle and knee wavering as she applied weight. In the middle of the corridor she stopped to rest against the wall, and as she did so, she saw the gallery of pictures, portraits of the staff painted by one of the younger classes in thick, vibrant colours. Real people, important in their everyday lives. Eira Probert wasn't there.

She tried to assemble a story for the headmaster and the police, who she could see waiting in the office. Any explanation she could think of seemed preposterous. As soon as they saw her, two police officers hurried towards her to support her. They were halted by something, or someone, behind Maggie and her children. With a wave of relief, Maggie knew that Zelah had arrived.

Chapter 74

"Let me speak to her!" Zelah pushed her way past the headmaster and marched up to Maggie. "Did you see her?"

Maggie nodded. She tried to talk but found that her tongue was sticking to the roof of her mouth, so she licked her lips.

"Get some water!" Zelah barked at Mr Philips over her shoulder. "This woman has had a shock, can't you see that?"

"Yes, but…" He was drawing himself up to his full height and bristling, when Zelah turned around to face him. "I'll get it now," He said, running away down the corridor.

She turned to Maggie. "Do you want to sit down? You'll have to speak to them," she lowered her voice, flicking her head at the policemen hovering behind.

Maggie nodded. "What am I going to tell them?" she whispered, her voice beginning to quaver with alarm, now that her adrenaline was subsiding.

"As you know, I always go with the truth," Zelah spoke softly. "A lot of people think I'm crazy, but of course I don't care what people think."

"Not helpful," Maggie muttered.

"I agree, Mum, tell the truth. Ask how Big Butt got to teach here. She's not even a real teacher!"

"I'm not sure. She's not as clever as she thinks but she is devious. We have a lot more security and protection for her to get past these days, but she seems to have succeeded."

Jack had taken one arm, and Zelah had the other, as they helped Maggie into the office. As she leaned on his shoulder Maggie became conscious for the first time that her son was now as tall as she was.

Mr Philips rushed into his office with a glass of water. As soon as Maggie was seated, with Zelah, Jack and Alice around her like a human shield, she began to talk.

When she explained that Eira Probert was an imposter, the senior of the two officers stopped the interview and made a call to the county schools administrator.

"They say it won't be difficult to check. The references seemed to be acceptable and her criminal records check came back OK. But they're calling the schools, and a children's home now." He turned to Mr Philips. "Do you have a photograph, sir? That will help with the ID."

The man thought for a moment, a series of conflicting expressions passing over his face. "No, we don't. She was never around for any of our school photographs." The last part was said questioningly, as much to himself as to them.

"You'll also find," Maggie interjected, "that her portrait isn't among the staff portraits that the children painted in the corridor."

"I have a picture." She took her car keys from her pocket and gave them to Jack, with a nod. "Go and get the photo, please."

"So, what's happened? Why have we been called exactly?" one of the officers asked Maggie.

No-one else spoke as Maggie recounted the story. Part way through, Jack returned, but didn't interrupt. After the story

438

had been told, both police officers appeared incredulous. Their increasingly impatient and aggressive questioning made Maggie uncomfortable, but she stuck to her story. As she finished, she turned to Jack and held out her hand. Instead of giving the photograph to either of the police officers, she handed it to Mr Philips, who studied it carefully.

"Yes, that's Miss Probert," he confirmed. "But I don't remember the children being dressed up for this photo." He scanned it again. "I can see Alice, of course," indicating her face on the photo to the younger officer, who looked at Alice and nodded back. "But I don't remember the occasion. The rest aren't our children."

"You won't recognise them." Maggie replied. "It was taken in 1883."

She watched the expressions of Mr Philips and both police officers, as they looked from Maggie to Alice, to the photo, and back again.

"Is it definitely your supply assistant, Mr Philips?" He hesitated, unsure of what was going on.

"Yes."

Zelah spoke to the police officers. "Can I make a suggestion?" They both nodded.

"I suggest you let us all go home now. There's nothing more we can do here. Maggie needs to speak to her daughter. I also suggest a couple of days off for Alice?" She raised an eyebrow at Mr Philips, who nodded. "And let me tell you a few more things, in case you aren't sceptical enough already."

She told them about the family at Carmarthen and the Eira Probert at the circulating school, where two children in Maggie's line of ancestors had also been killed. They all listened attentively.

439

The silence was shattered by a mobile phone ringing. The older officer answered it. He listened, nodding and grunting for a minute or so, while everyone else remained politely quiet.

"That was the county schools administrator. According to her C.V., your supply teacher is supposed to have taught in two other authorities. But they've never heard of her. One of the references was handwritten. But the person who was supposed to have written it says he didn't."

"And whatever else it was they said before you hung up?" Zelah demanded.

He looked curiously at her. "We sent a patrol car to the home address she gave to the school. It's derelict. Hasn't been lived in for years, and there's no evidence of anyone even squatting there."

"I'd like to go home now," Maggie said, then turned to the headmaster. "I'm very sorry, really. This has been a terrible shock. But Zelah's right. There's nothing more anyone can do. My suggestion is that you keep this as quiet as you can, don't upset parents and children needlessly. Eira Probert won't be coming back and I don't think the children will mind." She smiled ironically at him. "They all hated her, you know. Not just Alice."

"Yes, you can go, but I'll want to speak to you tomorrow," the older officer said tersely, shaking his head.

She nodded and stood up. She was exhausted. But as they turned to go, he called her again.

"Mrs Gilbert, I'll need to speak to your daughter tomorrow as well, to understand why she went with Miss Probert. This is kidnapping. I don't think you appreciate how serious this is. It's a criminal matter. I'm going to need statements. There will have to be an investigation."

Maggie smiled and shrugged. "She has no idea how she came to leave with Miss Probert, and I'm not pressing charges." Maggie looked at Alice, who nodded in agreement.

He waited a moment, shook his head again, then signalled her away and turned back to Mr Philips, as Zelah closed the door behind them.

"Jack, you come with me," said Zelah. "We can put the roof down, and Alice should go with Maggie."

* * *

An excited Alan Kerr was on the other end of Maggie's landline. "Maggie, hi! It's Alan. Fantastic news! I found the photograph in the loft! It was taken in the 1920s, at an outing in a charabanc! Esme is part of a group of ladies standing in front of it." Maggie pictured the long open-topped motor, the forerunner to the bus, with genteel ladies posing in front of it. It would have been an exceptional day out for them.

Alan continued excitedly "And – I went to the cemetery and spoke to the superintendent and, guess what? I've found Esme's grave! She's buried with her husband, Alan." As he paused for breath, he noticed the silence on the other end of the phone. "Hello, are you still there?"

"Yes, Alan. Sorry. That's wonderful news." Maggie hoped that she was conveying some enthusiasm. At any other time, she would have been excited, but for now, she just felt numb.

"Can you come and see it and visit the grave with me?"

"How about tomorrow?" Maggie asked.

"I finish work tomorrow at four. How about four thirty at the cemetery entrance? It's on Western Avenue, going out of Newport."

Maggie knew it. The cemetery there was bigger, older and better known than the one at Garth Hill. As soon as she had put the phone down, Maggie picked it up again and dialled another number. When she returned to the sitting room, they all looked up at her.

"That was a long call, Mum." Jack remarked.

"Two calls," Maggie replied. "The first was Alan. He's found the real Alice's photograph and her grave. He's very excited." She smiled. "I've agreed to meet him tomorrow to see them both. Anyone want to come with me?"

All three nodded. "I'd like to see where she's buried, Mum," Alice said. "So I can say goodbye."

"I think it will be goodbye for all of us. It feels like we've reached the end." She paused for a moment, then asked, "Zelah, would you like to stay to dinner? We can talk some more?"

"Thanks, but no," Zelah replied. "Things to do."

Maggie was taken aback. She'd assumed that Zelah would want to stay and support her through the discussion with Alice. But before she could say anything, Zelah jumped up, took her bag and left, calling back that she would see Maggie the following day. Neither of the children took any notice. They were getting used to Zelah's sudden, unexplained departures.

"Who was the second call, Mum? Was it Nick?"

"Yes," Maggie replied. "He'd warned me earlier in the day to be careful. I wanted to let him know what had happened."

"What did he say?"

"Something rather surprising, actually. He wasn't surprised. He said that I had fulfilled my duty. Sounded rather Victorian!"

"What does that mean?" Jack asked curiously.

"No idea. I invited him to the cemetery tomorrow and he said he'd explain to me then. I suppose I'll just have to wait. Anyway, I need to explain to both of you about this whole story, without leaving anything out," she added. "It's *our* family history now."

Chapter 75

Just before leaving for the cemetery, Maggie received a call from a police inspector Pugh. He was curt, clearly embarrassed at what he was having to discuss. Paranormal events were not in the normal line of policing. He'd clearly been briefed by the two officers that had attended the day before, and was, to put it mildly, sceptical. Nevertheless, enquiries had elicited that whoever Eira Probert was, she had invented her persona. There was no record of her birth, and both her National Insurance and passport numbers were inventions, even though she had passed all security checks.

"So we're ensuring she won't get onto a teaching register or be able to work with children anywhere in the country, Mrs Gilbert. We don't know what her motive is, but she has committed a number of criminal acts and she's officially wanted for questioning."

Maggie thanked him, but asked no questions, and gave no more details.

Despite his urging, Maggie steadfastly refused to allow Alice to be interviewed. She knew that he was only trying to do his job. She told him that if he wanted to go through the motions, he could do so, but she wouldn't help. They had been through enough, and she just wanted things to get back to normal. Although unsatisfied, there was little that the inspector could do. He asked that if she did have any information pertaining to the whereabouts of Eira Probert, that she should let him know. She agreed, and the call finished.

Zelah was waiting inside the cemetery's main entrance. As soon as she saw Maggie and the two children, she rushed over to them, looking uncharacteristically untidy.

"Maggie, I need to talk to you and Nick. It's urgent," she whispered.

"Is something wrong, Zelah?" Maggie was concerned by Zelah's demeanour.

"Yes! No! Oh, I can't tell you now. Can we meet at your house, this evening?" She was out of breath and she held onto Maggie's arm.

Maggie looked at her, with concern, just as Nick's van pulled in and parked next to Zelah's car, immediately followed by Alan and his daughter. Lucy wasn't with them. Esme and Alice hugged each other and began to whisper together, as if they'd known each other for years.

"I asked her not to talk about Eira Probert" Maggie whispered to Zelah. "I don't think anyone else is ready for it, yet."

"She respects you," Zelah replied. "She'll ask if she feels the need. How are things with the school?"

"Well, the decision to keep Alice off for a few days is probably the best one. They can sort out the mess at their end, and hopefully we can all get back to normal. When she does go back, it doesn't need to be mentioned. She agreed to that, too. The class will simply be told that Miss Probert has left."

"She was sent away, by you."

"Shhh, not in front of them." The Kerrs and Nick were approaching rapidly. Alan was holding a piece of paper that Maggie could see was a map of the cemetery.

"Here we all are then, well, apart from Lucy. She couldn't make it," said Alan.

"What a shame," said Zelah, looking directly at him.

Maggie noticed a slight flushing of his cheeks and she said quickly, "Yes, but never mind. We've got two cemeteries to visit, then I thought that you and Esme might like to come back to our house, perhaps have some supper? Do you think Lucy might like to join us later?"

Alan's blush became more intense. "Um, no, I'm afraid she's busy and we promised to pick her up as soon as we've left Garth Hill cemetery. Sorry." He didn't quite look Maggie in the eye as he spoke.

Zelah was going to say something, but Maggie shot her a look and, for once, Zelah bit her lip.

"No problem," Maggie smiled at Alan. "Perhaps we could see the grave first, then we can look at your photograph. I see you've got a map." As she spoke she began to walk up the low rise leading to the inner gates of the cemetery. Nick and Alan fell in beside her, with Alice and Esme, arms linked behind them, and Jack and Zelah at the rear.

"Lucy's trying to avoid us, isn't she?" Jack asked Zelah when they were out of earshot of the others.

"Looks like it. But your mother's got enough on her mind, so I didn't say anything." She looked at him. "Some people find this unnatural, this interest in dead people."

Alice's ears pricked up at Zelah's last remark and she stopped and turned around, making Jack and Zelah stop abruptly to avoid walking into her.

"I see dead people; they don't know they're dead," she said, eyes popping and arms out like a zombie.

For a moment Zelah was flummoxed, until Jack laughed and Alice turned back around and started to walk on again.

446

"It's a line from a film," he explained to Zelah. "She's just joking. It's cemetery humour, that's all."

"Oh. But she *has* seen dead people. Anyway, how did Alice take her talk last night?"

"She seemed to take it all in her stride," he replied, considering. "When Mum went through it all, she just listened and nodded. Then she said, 'I knew I was right. I saw Miss Probert at the funeral, with Alice. She saw me, too.' It was more about being right than anything else. She seems to accept that being a bit…" he paused, feeling for the right word, "being a bit… psychic is perfectly natural."

"Good. For some people it is. It doesn't disturb them. They just are, and that's it. If Alice can think like that, then good. But what about Eira Probert?"

"We talked for a long time. Didn't really decide anything. Mum said that we'll have to find a way to keep the story alive, but we don't need to rush to figure out how, now that she's gone."

"Sensible," Zelah nodded. They reached the gates and looked out over the vast sea of gravestones that stretched across three small knolls to the horizon. "This is one of the biggest graveyards in Wales," she explained, amused by Jack's expression of wonder.

They caught up with the others and stood surveying the headstones. Alan looked at his map. "They're in organised rows," he explained. "Esme is in block five, row seventeen, plot number two hundred and thirty-eight. The warden said the rows are marked with signposts and the plot numbers are on metal plates in the ground, at the start of each row." He held up the map and Nick and Maggie began to walk with him, checking the signposts.

At block five they turned left and walked downhill counting the rows off.

447

"Here it is," Nick pointed, row seventeen, plots two hundred to two fifty. She must be somewhere beyond the middle of the row."

Now, they had to walk across the grass. Alice took her mother's hand, squeezing it tightly. Maggie, looking down at her, saw that Alice was suddenly pale. She gave a reassuring squeeze. Nick let the way across the bottom end of the plots, carefully counting, followed by Alan. The ground was uneven and they were careful not to tread on a grave. Above, gulls wheeled and cried and the sudden screech of a crow caused Nick to look up, before moving on, checking each headstone. Then he stopped.

"Here it is. Alan, Maggie, come and see."

Maggie moved to the edge of an overgrown grave. The headstone inscription hadn't faded, the words stood out in clear relief in contrast to the dark grey background. It was a simple grey stone, about four feet high, shaped to a pointed top.

Maggie read out the inscription: *Alan Edward Hughes. Departed this life Tenth January 1937.* Below, slightly larger: *Esme Alice Hughes. Beloved wife of Alan, mother of Esme, Alan and Joyce. Died thirty first October 1950.*

Maggie's voice broke as she bent down and read the last line, in smaller letters, at the bottom of the stone, *Daughter of John and Ruth.*

Maggie knelt down on both knees and put her hands on the gravestone, tracing the words. "She knew. And she wanted it to be remembered."

Alice knelt beside her, saying nothing, and Jack came up behind her and put his hands on her shoulders. Alan was the first to break the silence.

"There we are then," he whispered. "There we are, Maggie. That's it, isn't it?"

Maggie stood up. She momentarily looked as if she was going to burst into tears, but then she shook herself, and smiled. "Yes, here she is. Lost for so long, and now found."

Activity began at once, as if a spell had been broken. Alan got out his camera and photographed the grave, then arranged them all in various groups next to the headstone. As the children stood together to have their photo taken, Nick sidled up to Maggie.

"Are you alright, Maggie?"

"Yes, of course. Why wouldn't I be?" It came out abruptly, but she didn't want to share how she was feeling at that moment. She felt apart from them all.

"You look distant."

"What did you mean, about my duty?"

He sucked in his cheeks for a moment, staring intently at the ground. "I think you're a very unique person. You didn't know it, but you've always had a specific purpose, to be fulfilled at a moment in time. That time came when you confronted Eira Probert. You've stood in the path of something moving through time. Time moves around us. You've prevented something moving ahead. Whatever you said to the thing that's Eira Probert, it must have been significant. It stopped her."

"I just said what came instinctively to me, but I also remembered what Louisa had said to me, that it was important not to be afraid of her. So that's what I told her. I meant that she would never take something that I love so absolutely. But how could that stop her?"

"That thing has hunted your family for a long time. We know for hundreds, but maybe even thousands of years. You didn't know you had that ability in you until it needed to come out, amazing energy, much stronger than Eira Probert's. The strength to keep calm and show no fear in the face of something absolutely

449

terrifying. I know something about this. Perhaps we can take some time together for me to explain more?"

Maggie nodded her head. "Yes please."

"And you know that Alice is special, don't you?"

"What do you mean, Nick?"

"Think about it, Maggie. Of course Alice is connected to you and to Ruth, but she has no direct linear connection to the girl she saw at the funeral. Yet she is identical and they could both see each other. Esme Kerr is actually the direct descendant, but Eira Probert chose your Alice. Because she is special."

Maggie was aghast. "I hadn't seen that, but yes, it should have been Esme. What does it mean?"

"There will be other things in Alice's life, strange things. But let's talk about it later."

Maggie grimaced, then responded. "I don't understand. But when I don't understand something, I don't waste my time trying. I'm going to live a normal life and make sure that Alice does too," she added, forcefully.

"Pragmatic," he nodded. "But you are, aren't you? Will you be OK?"

"She'll be fine!" Zelah intervened. "It's been a long journey. Now it's over, is all."

"Not quite," Maggie replied. "One more visit to go." Zelah nodded and began to chivvy Alan and the children to get back to the cars, to drive to Garth Hill.

On the way back Maggie walked next to Zelah, as Nick chatted to Alan, and the three children talked together.

"Jack says Alice is OK," Zelah said as soon as they were out of earshot of the others.

"Yes," Maggie replied, "I think she'll be fine. But I'll keep talking to her about it, even after I get back to work next week, and hopefully back to normal. They've asked me to go in tomorrow, by the way, to attend a couple of meetings."

Zelah didn't reply at first, then said, "I have something important I need to discuss with you and Nick. Something significant."

Maggie was worried by the frown on Zelah's face and she wondered if something was wrong. Zelah had been absent so much recently and preoccupied. It was unlikely to be a financial problem. Maybe it was her health, although she looked well enough.

"What about you, Zelah? Are you well?"

"What kind of question is that, for goodness sake? Of course I'm well!" Zelah prickled.

"You haven't been around lately and you seem anxious."

"I said I'll speak to you later. We need to get this next visit over with first. I'm guessing you may want some time alone, this time?"

They had reached the cars. Jack made a beeline for Zelah's car, while Maggie explained the directions to Alan. Alice accepted an invitation to ride with her new best friend, so Maggie drove alone with just her thoughts as company to Garth Hill cemetery.

* * *

She wasn't really sure how she felt. Seeing Alice's grave had been an emotional experience, both sad and happy. Now, it all seemed like an anti-climax. The job was almost done.

Until now, Maggie hadn't appreciated that she was going to miss the excitement of the whole mystery after today, despite the horrifying experience with Eira Probert.

What was it Jack had said recently when she had helped him with his homework, "This is what you should have done, Mum?" A bad decision when she was younger had meant a working lifetime of unfulfilled boredom.

But what was worse? To have never had it, or to have had the enjoyment at least once. She was going to miss the drama of the past couple of months, despite the near disaster. Back to spreadsheets, graphs, strategies and meetings. God, she was dreading it!

She snapped out of her reverie. She'd arrived at the cemetery. The others were all waiting for her, standing in front of the chapel.

"Have you been waiting long? Sorry, I was thinking. It's this way." She led the way to the grave. Then she stood back as Alan and Esme read John and Ruth's inscriptions.

Alan looked pleased. "So, this is my great-great-grandmother, and Esme's great-great-great-grandmother. Both of ours, in fact." He looked as if he'd just had a revelation. "We really are connected, aren't we?"

"Yes," Maggie replied, "we really are." Then she turned to Alice. "Why don't you take Esme and her dad to see Esme Ellis's grave, Al? Why don't you all go?"

Alice nodded and led them all away. Maggie gave Zelah a significant look, which she understood, taking Jack and Nick by the arm, and pulling them towards the chapel.

"Thanks," Maggie mouthed. Then she turned back to John and Ruth's grave. Checking over her shoulder that no-one could see her, she put her hand on a marble column and felt a warmth go through it.

"Ruth, I hope you're there."

She felt the slightest of shudders, like air running through her mind and a sensation of panic in her stomach, or was it Ruth's?

452

"Ruth, I met Louisa, your granddaughter. She told me what you told her, how much you loved her, and how much you tried to protect her and the others. How you wanted to protect us all. You succeeded, Ruth. If you hadn't told Louisa, we would never have known. You saved us all."

There was only one thing left to say. Her hand had started to go cold.

"You will see her again, Ruth. Just wait."

"Mum, Mum! Esme wants to know the story!" An urgent voice whispered in her ear. Alice had run across the path from Esme Ellis's grave. "Can I tell her some of it? Please? It's her name, too!"

Alice was pulling painfully at her shoulder. Maggie took her hand away from the gravestone.

She drew in a deep breath. "Yes, we can tell her the history, but at the moment I don't think we can give her the full details. Is that OK?"

"Yes, thanks, Mum. Can I arrange to meet her at the weekend?"

"If her dad says it's OK."

Alice ran back across the path. The jumping up and down and flapping of hands told her that Alan Kerr had agreed. Maggie walked away from John and Ruth's grave, knowing that in the future it would no longer connect her to her past.

Chapter 76

Alice and Esme insisted on returning to Maggie's house; Alice wanted to show off the summerhouse and Maggie was glad of the opportunity to show Alan the ancestral home. But she didn't press them to stay. As he waited to take Esme home, Alan hovered nervously, shifting from foot to foot and checking his watch when he thought Maggie wasn't watching. Alan and Esme finally left at dusk, no doubt with an angry encounter with Lucy in store.

"Why was Alan so desperate to get away from us?" Alice asked over dinner.

"Because he's scared of his wife!" It was Zelah's first comment in some time.

"Zelah! He isn't scared of her! He'd just made a promise he had to keep. That's all, Alice."

"Actually, he is," Nick interjected, causing all of them to turn towards him. "But not because she isn't nice," he added, inclining his head at Alice. "It's because she's scared, for Esme." He turned back to Maggie. "Lucy understands, you know, she gets it, much more than Alan does and much more than Zelah gives her credit for. He's very nice, but he's a history tourist."

"What's that?" Alice raised an eyebrow enquiringly hoping for gossip.

"Someone who follows a hobby, but not very seriously, and wouldn't really mind too much if there's no outcome. Disappointed, but not touched. Lucy's very conventional. And this isn't. She wants everything normal and ordinary."

"Does she think we're not normal then?"

Nick grinned. "She knows these are very not-ordinary events, and she doesn't want any more to do with it than she can help. She's not brave, Alice, not like your mother."

Maggie looked at Zelah and grimaced, but Zelah was miles away.

A funny remark and a comment slightly off the subject drew Alice away from asking more questions about Lucy and Alan.

As she poured some coffee, Maggie could see that Zelah was still drifting in and out of her own thoughts, barely acknowledging anything said to her.

Enough was enough. Holding on to her cup so she had to look at Maggie, she asked her, "Zelah, what's the matter? You've hardly been with us since we got here and you said earlier that you urgently needed to speak to me. So, what is it?"

But Zelah just sat, looking despondent. Her eyes flicked between Maggie and Nick, but not with the usual flash, rather, a hang-dog look. Maggie felt alarmed. "Is something wrong? You've been away a lot lately." No response. Again, more gently, "Of course, I'll understand if you can't tell us, but we are your friends. Really we are."

"God damn it! Sod it all! I'm trying! Don't be so bloody patronising!"

The response made Maggie jump, and Nick's cup stopped half way to his mouth.

"That's better." Maggie let out a burst of laughter at Nick's expression. "Don't worry, Nick. I think she's going to be OK."

Zelah drew in a deep breath, looked at her watch then back at both of them. Then she folded her arms on the table.

"I have two things to tell you. The first is part of the story. The second isn't, well, not that story, your story. Actually, they're both part of your story."

She held up her hand to stop Maggie speaking. "I need to tell you what I've been doing. I've been trying to decide all evening what to say. Not like me, I know. So I'm just going to get it out. Then we'll be in virgin territory. I've no idea what you'll both say, so here goes."

"First of all, I found Alice Ruth in 1881. She was staying with her aunt, Mary Anne Picton, in Carmarthen. They called her a 'Visitor'. She was eight years old and that explains why she wasn't on the family listing in Garth Hill. And I know who your great-grandfather was, Maggie. He wasn't John and Eliza's son. He was their grandson."

Maggie's mouth formed a silent "Oh", but she closed it in response to Zelah's wagging finger.

"He was the illegitimate son of their eldest daughter, Susan. That was probably Eliza's mother's name. Anyway, he was born when she was about fourteen. She was a promiscuous, illiterate farm peasant. Sorry, rather blunt, even for me." She reached down into her bag, brought out a certificate, and handed it to Maggie.

"See, there," she leaned over and indicated the space where the father's name should be. "Blank. But the birth is recorded by Eliza, who names herself as the grandmother, here." She pointed again. "And if you check the signature, it's just a cross, so she was illiterate."

Nick leaned across to look at the wide certificate.

"So that explains why the description changes from census to census," Maggie said, her eyes still on the paper. "When he was an adult and looking after Eliza, he finally referred to her as his grandmother."

"I expect Old John or Eliza would have given his early information to the census enumerator," Nick added. "If they had brought him up as their son, it's possible that's how they referred to him, or the enumerator misunderstood. I don't expect they questioned the fact that he was a little boy and they were elderly, just accounted for the head, then moved on."

"Not that it made much difference to people, anyway," Zelah continued. "There was a lot of illegitimacy. Custom and practice, especially amongst the uneducated classes. It all changed years later. Became more moral."

"He certainly became very moral," Maggie replied. "I think he would have tried hard to cover it up and keep it a secret."

"Why?" Nick asked. "Like Zelah says, it wasn't unusual. He moved into a different world. Think about it. The son of illiterate agricultural labourers. 'Ag labs', it's a pejorative description. We know that his uncle was probably a clever man, but his aunt also had an illegitimate child and she was illiterate, too. He could have chosen to stay on the farm, but he left, and went to live with his uncle when he was about fifteen. He started at the bottom in the railway company, and worked himself up to become a manager. Then he bought a farm, then a bigger farm. He was a clever, ambitious man, and an avid Baptist, a figure of importance in his local chapel. I just think that the fact that he was the illegitimate son of an illiterate farm girl would not have been something he would have wanted to advertise. And we don't know anything about her, I assume, Zelah?"

"Actually, yes." Zelah nodded her head. "She had another illegitimate child a year or so later. That's Mary Anne. She was his sister. And another child a couple of years later. The other information I have is from a report of the arrest of a drunken woman called Susan Jones, aged twenty, who was then put into the workhouse with her youngest child – no name given. I think this may be Susan, although I can't say for certain. But I found another record of another Susan Jones who died a few years later. Dead in a field, inebriation. She was a well-known vagrant who had been arrested several times. And there's no mention of the last child. Disappeared without a trace. Probably traceable, but I haven't done it."

"Three in four or five years," Maggie mused. "And with a bad reputation. Definitely not something he would have wanted anyone to know about. I wonder if he ever acknowledged her or had anything to do with her"

She was quiet for a few minutes, holding her cup to her lips but not drinking. Nick and Zelah didn't interrupt.

"Well," Maggie said at last. "That's it, then. The end, for now. I can fill in that piece of the puzzle but then the story's over, for a while." She turned to Zelah. "Zelah, thank you. I'm so grateful to you, I can't say. To both of you, for what you've done for me in the past weeks."

Her voice broke for a moment, but she squeezed her fists together and sat up. "I'm afraid," she paused to yawn, "that we'll have to end this evening soon. I have to go to a meeting in the morning and I need to prepare. I haven't done anything professional for a long time!" Her tone was light, but the rueful expression on her face told a different story.

"Well, actually, you don't," said Zelah.

Chapter 77

Maggie turned to look at Zelah who was looking at her with a guilty expression.

"If you're going to say anything about money, don't go there!" Maggie began.

"It's nothing like that!" Zelah raised her voice to the point of shouting and Maggie sat back in her chair. "Just be quiet and let me explain. And don't interrupt. I need to get through this in one go before you say *anything*"

"OK," Maggie agreed, nodding. She was exhausted, but she knew that Zelah did have a sensitive side. She wouldn't be insisting on saying whatever she was going to say in the face of Maggie's obvious wish for them to go, if it wasn't important.

"This whole experience with your family has been fascinating. I've heard about these phenomena before, and you know that I believed you one hundred per cent, right from the start. But I'd never experienced something like this first hand. So I kept detailed notes. And I..." She swallowed. "I put them on a website." She saw Maggie's expression of incredulity and rushed on, her hands moving more quickly now as she spoke.

"Not just any website. I've set a new one up. It's called Maze Investigations. Stupid name, I know, but I couldn't think of anything better. It's not just a website either. I've set up a company under the same name. I've been telling the story in instalments. We've had thousands of hits from all over the world."

Maggie was stunned. "You've been telling my story, to the whole world, without saying a word to me?"

"Yes," Zelah replied. "Hold on a moment." As she had been speaking, her bird-like animation had caused a pin to fall from her hair and a long strand had come down. Nick had the pin in his hand, but held onto it, despite Zelah putting out her hand to take it off him.

"Is this a diamond?" he asked sharply. "Yes. They all are. Give it back, please."

He examined her head. "Then, you're wearing about ten grand's worth of jewellery on your head?"

"Probably."

Maggie bit her lips at his expression.

Zelah snatched the pin and started to talk again as she pinned her loose strand of hair back up. "I'm not apologising for what I've done, Maggie. Well, maybe just a bit," she conceded, seeing Maggie's worried expression. "Genealogy is a real growth area. We've all seen the TV programmes like *Who Do You Think You Are* and we've talked about the shows and fairs around the country. It's a good business to be in. For all of us."

But Maggie was still focused on the revelation of the website. "I'm going to see what you've done." She stood up and marched into her office. Jack was coming down the stairs, but she ignored him. She jabbed so viciously at the computer keys that he walked up behind her, intrigued.

"What's up, Mum?" It was startling to see his mother so angry.

"Ask her," she muttered, not looking up from the screen.

460

She searched for the website and the front page appeared. "Wow, that's a great page!" Jack commented over her shoulder. "Whose is it?"

"Ours," said Zelah. As she and Nick entered the room he flicked on the light switch.

"Yours!" Maggie stated.

"No… ours!" Zelah flung back. "I hadn't finished. It's gone beyond just a website. The interest has been amazing. I've sold the story to a family history journal and arranged talks and interviews. I thought you could do the press and radio interviews, Maggie. Nick can help out with the family history societies. There are twenty booked so far."

"What?" Maggie exploded, spinning round on her chair and jumping to her feet. "You've told the whole world about Eira Probert and what has been happening to me and my children? Without my permission? How bloody dare you?!"

Zelah was taken aback by Maggie's anger. "No, wait," she said. "I haven't told all of it. Just enough to tell the story, but without actual names. What do you think I am?"

"I thought you were my friend!" Maggie yelled.

"I am your friend," Zelah growled. "That's why I did it."

By this time they were an arm's length apart, both breathing heavily, neither prepared to back down, like two lionesses waiting to see who would attack first. The only sound in the room was a rhythmical clicking of four beats, then a pause, then four beats. It was getting louder. Maggie glanced to see what it was.

"Glad to have got your attention," said Nick, lifting his hand from where it had beat out the rhythm on the desktop. "Now, if you'll both take a step back, perhaps we can hear more about what Zelah's done, and why."

The tension broke. Maggie, lips pursed, sat back down at the computer and folded her arms. She indicated another seat to Nick, but left Zelah standing.

Zelah drew herself up to her full, short height, raised her chin and spoke again. "I haven't mentioned Eira Probert by name, but I have put enough detail about what she might have been. It's been left vague, but it's the hook. It's the part that has intrigued people enough for our site to have become a sensation."

There was a sound of footsteps on the stairs. No-one had noticed that Jack had left the room when the shouting began. He returned with Alice in tow. In response to a finger to the lips from their mother, they both stood quietly by the door, all eyes fixed on Zelah.

"I've offered our services as genealogy detectives, to solve strange, unexplained mysteries from people's family history. That's the commercial side. On the marketing side, as well as the website, as I was trying to say, I've sold the story to a journal, set up some interviews with local radio and press, and arranged a series of talks around England and Wales. And one in Dublin. We get a fee for some, expenses for others. For now." Zelah took a breath, seeing that at least everyone was listening now. "Maggie, I truly believe that we can make this work. I'm the expert, Nick is the solid, if dull, researcher, and you're the front."

Nick shuffled in his seat. "Cheers. I think I'm solid. But not dull."

Zelah huffed in his direction. "You don't have the personality to go in front of the press and talk on the radio, is all I mean. But Maggie does." She turned back to Maggie and jabbed her finger. "Look how easily you get on with people. You put up with me, for a start. You managed to get through to me and tell your story and

I was hooked, not just by the story, but by how *you* told it. You can do that. I can't."

"We don't have the expertise," Maggie said. "We're just amateurs. How can we gain any credibility or respect in the genealogy world?"

"Don't call me an amateur! Just because you've only dealt with me on your story doesn't mean I don't know anything else! I'm an accredited genealogist. I have lots of contacts and my name means something," Zelah snorted.

"Sorry. But I still don't see how this can be anything else but a bit of fun."

"But you *are* interested!" Zelah's eyes gleamed. "You've stopped shouting at me and you're asking questions."

Reluctant to admit she was interested and unwilling to let go of her anger, Maggie didn't answer.

"OK," Zelah conceded. "You've every right to be angry and I'm sorry about that. I knew you would be. But if I'd consulted you, you'd have said no. Anyway, you had other things on your mind. Don't deny it! I saw how much you hated the thought of going to that soulless new job. Anyway, if you've got to work why not have fun doing it? Do something you love – and you do love this – and earn your keep at the same time. To me, it makes perfect sense. Same goes for you, Nick. You spend all of your time at Knyghton and almost nothing on your business. Face it, we make a good team. And I don't need the money."

"But I *do* need the money, Zelah. So does Nick. A couple of radio spots and some talks won't pay the mortgage. I'm sorry to rain on your parade, but I can't see how it will work."

Again, Zelah huffed impatiently. "Didn't you listen? Those are just marketing and publicity. The meat comes from selling our services. We've already got commissions, at up to five thousand pounds each, including expenses. All from abroad. I've run through them and they are difficult, very strange in fact. But do-able." She raised an eyebrow with a knowing look. No-one took the bait.

"We need to get started!" Zelah glared at them both, willing them to cave in, desperate for their approval. She looked at Nick, quizzically, then at Maggie with a frown.

"You are an impossible woman," Maggie said. Then her face relaxed. At this, both Jack and Alice bounced off the wall and began talking at the same time.

"Am I going to be famous? Jack said I was going to be famous? Am I?"

"This is fantastic, Mum. You're really good at this stuff. And just think, you won't have to put up with us moaning about Aunty Fee every day!"

"No, you won't be famous," Maggie said to Alice, whose face fell, "and if that's supposed to help persuade me, dear son, you are well short of the mark."

"OK," Jack retorted in what he hoped was his how-to-deal-patiently-with-a-stupid-parent voice. "You don't want to start that job next week. You've said so often enough. You're just doing it for the money, for us. Well," he nodded at Alice, who nodded back, "we'd prefer you to have less money and be more happy. We can cope. We prefer you to the stuff you buy us."

There was nothing she could say to that.

"Take the risk, Mum. Aunty Fee will have a heart attack, but it's worth it."

Unconsciously pushing her chair around with her feet, Maggie moved slowly from face to face. Zelah, belligerent; Nick, hopeful; Jack and Alice, excited. But how did she really feel about this?

Being honest, now that she had got over the shock, both excited and worried. It was a big risk. And she would have to keep Zelah on a leash if this partnership was going to work. Maggie suspected that Zelah had a lot of ideas and plans, but she'd have to get used to working in a team. She'd probably find it frustrating to accept that she couldn't do what her partners didn't approve of. But Zelah had got this far alone and the website was worth a second look. And – the clincher – Nick looked really interested.

She stood up and walked in circles around the room, watching them all stare at her.

"All right, I'm prepared to give it a go, but," she put her hand up like a traffic policeman, "there's a lot of talking to do, about working together and no-one going off on their own." Zelah nodded. "I'm prepared to give it three months. Even if we're a hundred per cent successful with these first cases, it still isn't a lot of money to split between three of us."

"Two of you," Zelah corrected. "It's my company – for now – that's going to change, but I'm not taking a salary. How do you feel about us working out of this office, Maggie? It's bigger than my flat and it is an office, which I don't have. Unless you have a better suggestion," she asked Nick, being deliberately inclusive.

"No," he grinned. "But thank you for checking. I'm in, too. But we have lots to talk about."

"We have lots to do!" Zelah said, waving her hands around. "We can work out the detail as we go along."

Maggie sat back on the chair. "This has been quite a night. But for now, I'm going to ask you all to leave. I have to go into work in the morning and I'm absolutely exhausted."

Their faces fell. "I thought you just agreed to give it up?" Jack asked anxiously.

"Yes, and I'm going to tell them face-to-face. I'd prefer that, I don't want to hide behind the telephone. That's not brave. I'll do it myself, tomorrow."

"Fantastic!" Jack yelled. Zelah and Nick smiled and went back to the kitchen to collect their things, ready to leave.

"What about Aunty Fee?" Alice asked.

Maggie thought for a moment. "I'll phone her in the morning."

Chapter 78
July 2015

Lying exhausted in bed on the night of Zelah's revelations, after Zelah and Nick had gone, it occurred to Maggie that history was repeating itself. She had acted entirely on impulse, rejecting the safe, steady path, choosing the risky one, again.

And she hadn't questioned the role Zelah had set for her, being the front person, the face of Maze Investigations to the public. In fact, she relished the thought, but worried that she might not do a good job. She'd got up in the middle of the night and trawled through Zelah's site. That gave Maggie the reassurance that it wasn't a completely mad idea.

"It's wonderful," she murmured. "No wonder people are flocking to it." She would have done so herself, if she wasn't part of it. And that thought gave her a thrill. "I'm part of it. Wow."

The meeting to quit before she'd started hadn't gone well, but she'd never expected it to. Strong words had been spoken and she had had to bite her tongue and keep apologising.

But that was nothing to the reaction from her sister. Fiona had been incandescent. If they hadn't been sisters Maggie thought that Fee would probably never have spoken to her again. They didn't speak for the whole of the following week. Maggie was content to let it be so. Some of Fiona's comments, although spoken in heat and anger, had been hurtful. Maggie would forgive her, but had decided to let it simmer.

The following days had been made up of meetings and discussions, arguments, on the whole professionally conducted, and decisions made. They now had a plan for the next three months and the amount of work was overwhelming. One of the clients that Zelah had signed up was on the phone twice a day, demanding to know progress, which Nick had already started. But it still stretched all of Maggie's PR skills to keep the man content and off the phone.

Zelah, once she had her plan, kept in the background, using her contacts, helping Nick to do the research and coaching Maggie for the interviews.

"Don't tell them everything at once. Keep some mystery. That's who we are! Get rid of the nuisances as quickly as possible on the phone-in. Why are you looking at me like that?"

Even Zelah had to admit that Maggie had handled the first two radio interviews brilliantly. The audience response had been enthusiastic. Maggie had managed to direct people to their website. Although Zelah knew that Maggie was going to be good at it, she couldn't help pointing out that it had been her idea.

"I told you so. You're a natural. People like you. They don't like me, but they don't need to meet me, do they?"

* * *

Maggie found herself pacing the lounge of the largest local radio station. She was due on in five minutes. This was the important one. The others had been fun and had provoked a good response from the public. But this was the one that would take them to a new level. In discussion with the producer the previous day, he had broached the possibility of a regular spot for Maggie to talk about what they were doing and to offer advice to people searching for their long-lost relatives. This she was nervous about, still feeling like an amateur. But no-one else had been offered this opportunity, it was hers to lose.

Two minutes to go. She was in the studio, headphones on, contorting her face with stretching exercises to limber up. She had been to the hairdresser the night before, and had come home with a drastic new hairstyle, and a manicure. Alice had been very admiring and even Jack had ventured a "You look great, much younger!"

"But it's radio, isn't it, Mum? So it doesn't matter how you look."

"It matters to me," Maggie replied firmly. "And that's something I never thought I'd hear myself say." She wondered if Fee would be proud of her.

One minute to go. The producer was signalling to her.

Counting down: five, four, three, two, the fingers disappeared one by one.

"Now, as we promised you earlier, we have a very special guest this morning. Maggie Gilbert from the exciting new genealogy company, Maze Investigations, is here to tell us about the strange secrets that might be lurking in our past. Maggie, how did this all begin for you?"

"Well, Roy, it all started when I moved back to Garth Hill and found that I had bought my great-grandfather's house! What an amazing coincidence, or so I thought…"

Epilogue
21 November 1936

Three men stood around the bed, staring down at the face and hands above the multi-coloured eiderdown.

One checked a pulse as the other two watched. "Still hanging on. Incredible!" he whispered. "Don't know how she's doing it." He shook his head. "No point my staying. Call me when… well, you know. Any time now." He smiled reluctantly at the youngest man, who smiled back a sad, knowing look, and led the way to the bedroom door.

The woman in the bed groaned, then opened her eyes. "Have they gone, Richard?" The voice was barely audible. "Yes, Ruth. Just you and me now. And before you ask, no visitors yet today."

She closed her eyes again. "I can wait."

Richard Robinson gazed down at his friend of over fifty years, with a contorted smile. Almost ninety and equally frail, barely managing to get up the stairs, yet a regular visitor, he truly wondered at Ruth's constitution.

"I believe you can, Ruth. I believe you can. How much longer you can go on staring at these walls is a mystery to me, though. William tells me you haven't eaten anything for days. The doctor says it would be good for you to try something. I think…" He was interrupted by the sound of the bell jangling in the passage below.

"Aah," sighed the tiny, white-haired figure in the bed. "At last, perhaps."

"Probably the butcher, or the baker or the candlestick maker."

"You're a disrespectful old man, Richard."

Then she heard the sound of footsteps coming up the stairs. William came into the room.

"Richard," he began with a puzzled expression. "There's someone would like to see Mammy. A woman. She says she knew Mammy a long time ago."

Richard turned to Ruth, who opened her eyes wide.

William saw a tear run from the corner of one eye.

"Let her come up," said Richard. "I think your mother would like to see her." He took Ruth's hand, squeezing it and smiling.

"We don't know who she is," protested William but the sound of light footsteps came up the stairs, then hesitated outside the door.

"Come in," Richard called quietly.

A woman of around sixty, grey-haired and petite entered the room. She was dressed in a black coat and carried a small black bag decorated with pearls. In her hand was a grubby piece of cloth, which seemed at odds with her neat appearance. She looked uncertainly at Ruth.

To Ruth, it seemed as if the world had suddenly stopped turning: that the two of them stood frozen in time.

"I knew you would come," her voice rattled. "I knew."

She nodded at Richard, who took William by the arm and led him firmly to the door. As William turned to protest, he saw a tear run from Richard's eye down his cheek and into his beard. Then for a reason he didn't understand, William closed his mouth and walked out of the room. As he turned, he saw the woman sit on the bed and take Ruth's hand. As the door closed, she laid her head down on Ruth's breast as Ruth stroked her head and murmured to her.

471

"My darling girl, you came back. I waited, like she told me. I knew you'd come."

* * *

Downstairs in the sitting room the family sat in silence, watching each other.

"May I get you a cup of tea, Mr Robinson?" a tall, youngish girl asked, jiggling the toddler on her lap.

"No, thank you, Louisa. I think I shall just wait. I should like to see our visitor before she leaves." He sat down in Ruth's chair and the silence returned.

Over the next hour, conversations started up, faltered and died away. William was lost in thought, having to be recalled twice by his wife. Louisa sat with her husband while her mother entertained the baby. The clock in the hall had never sounded so loud.

Then, Richard jumped up and went to the door, his old ears attuned to the footsteps before the others had heard anything. He went out into the hall and stood in front of the woman.

"Were you going to leave without saying goodbye, my dear?"

"I think it best. My husband is waiting for me. And my family," she added.

"Oh, yes, I understand. But don't you want to speak to any of them?"

"No, Mr Robinson." He looked surprised. "Yes, I remember who you are and you're the only one who knows who I am. Best left that way, I think. Don't disturb things. It's been too long."

He sighed and pulled at his whiskers. "As you wish, my dear. She *never* gave up hope, you know." He took her hands. "They

472

searched for you for so long and eventually believed you must be dead. But not your mother. She never, never gave up hope."

"I know," the woman began to sob. "I always felt her with me, even in the years I couldn't remember her." She dried her eyes with the grubby handkerchief. She stared at it for a moment, then showed it to Richard. "She made this for me and I took it with me. She recognised it."

"Will you ever tell anyone what really happened, Alice?"

"My name is Esme. Has been for over fifty years. And no, it's all best left. I was Esme Peach before I married, now I'm Esme Hughes. My husband Alan and I have three children and two grandchildren. The rest is history. I've had a wonderful life as Esme. No need to unsettle anything, or anyone."

"But… William? Maud? They are your family, too. William took a long time to recover from your loss."

"But he did recover, Richard. He looks a contented man. Maud and Walter never really knew me. I never knew George and Evan. There's nothing to be gained by telling them. Let it be, please."

He sighed deeply, a look of sorrow and compassion on his face. "Very well, my dear. Will you come again?"

"No. She has no more time. This was what we've both prayed for. It's done. She doesn't expect me again. I've told her all I can remember, my whole life since I went. And she has told me what she knows. I can go now."

He leaned forwards and kissed her on the cheek. "God bless you, Esme. And your family."

He reached around her and opened the door. She held onto his arm for a moment, pressing deep into his skin, then she was gone. She didn't look back.

As he closed the door, William came into the hall. "Richard, who was that woman? I thought, when I saw her, for a moment…" His voice trailed off and he looked anxiously at the old minister.

"Just an old friend. Back in the farming days. Nothing to concern yourself about. I think we should all go and see Ruth now. I think the end is near and she would want her family around her, don't you think?"

William nodded. He went back into the living room, leaving Richard alone in the hall with the sound of the ticking clock. The old man leaned against the banister, his breath coming in sobs, fighting the emotional tide that was swelling up within him.

The living room door opened and the family trooped out solemnly, led by William. The last was Louisa.

"Are you well, Mr Robinson? You seem…"

He turned a brilliant smile on her, so powerful that she stopped in her tracks. "I have never been so well, Louisa. You grandmother has been very close to you, hasn't she?"

The girl nodded. "She's told me… strange things."

"And they will be important, but not now. Now we must go to say farewell to your grandmother. I believe she's ready, at last." The girl nodded as she tucked her arm in his and together they climbed the staircase.

Thanks and Acknowledgements!

As always, producing a book involves many people without whose help, expert advice and encouragement I would struggle.

My 'first readers', Rose and Maureen, who encouraged me to keep going with this first book when I struggled to believe that I could ever finish it.

This edition has been edited and proof-read by Sue Walton, of 'Sue Proof', North Wales.

Thanks also to Ali Morgan at AliCat Designs for the fabulous cover.

And finally, to Stewart and Alice, my wonderful children, who give me support and inspiration, reassurance and frequent IT assistance. Alice, who was just ten when I began writing this book, now puts together both the ebook and paperback versions of each of my books for Kindle and Amazon print. Both are a constant source of encouragement for my self-belief in my writing when I doubt myself, which is often! Couldn't do it without you, kids.

Thank you for reading this book!

If you have enjoyed it, please leave feedback on Amazon and/or Goodreads. If there's anything I've missed, or if you have any questions about any feature of it, please leave a message on the Maze website:

https://mkjonesauthor.com

and the Maze Investigations Facebook page. I have an author page on Goodreads, where you can read my blog about 'My Writing Life'.

And if you can't wait, you can catch up with the stories of other cases the Maze Investigations team tackle between the books. These are available when you sign up for my newsletter on the website. You will receive two immediately as a thanks for signing up:

"The Missing Air Raid Warden 1941"

And

"Murder in the Family 1840s"

Following these there will be a new story with each newsletter, in the form of a report by one of the Maze Investigators.

Happy reading!

**

Made in the USA
Coppell, TX
20 July 2023

19407379R00281